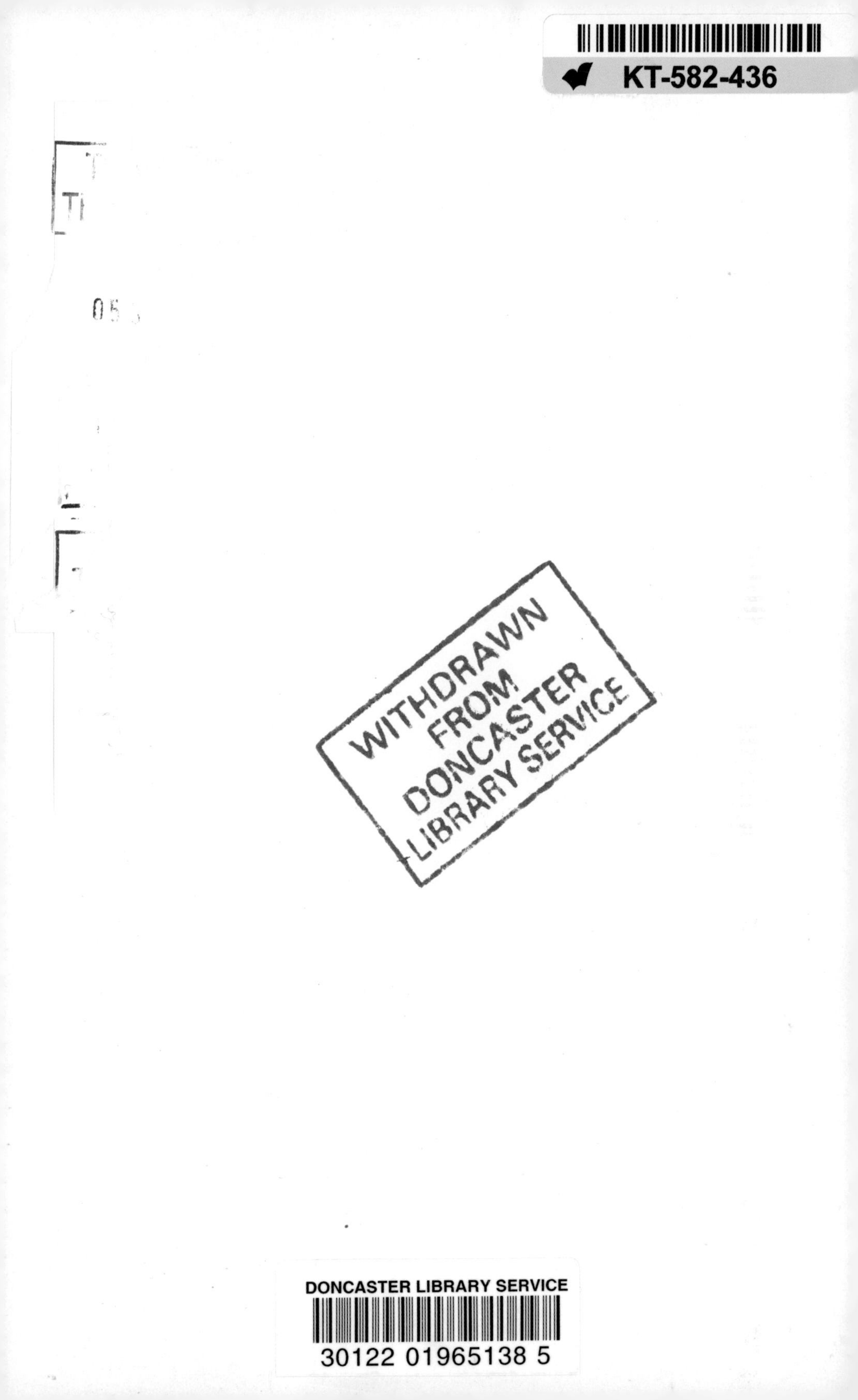

CLEOPATRA KELLY

Pretty and bright, Cleopatra Kelly dreams of a life without the shadow of fear cast by her abusive stepfather, Horace Womack. Her beloved brother, Ant, flees to London and a few weeks later, Cleo makes a daring escape and follows him. However, Cleo is only thirteen and is soon found by the police and sent to a reform school for girls. Undaunted, Cleo escapes again and gets a job at the seaside, where she starts to feel like a normal teenager and has fun with her friend Flo – but Horace Womack is not done with the Kelly family yet...

CLEOPATRA KELLY

Cleopatra Kelly

by

Ken McCoy

Magna Large Print Books
Long Preston, North Yorkshire,
BD23 4ND, England.

British Library Cataloguing in Publication Data.

McCoy, Ken
Cleopatra Kelly.

A catalogue record of this book is available from the British Library

ISBN 0-7505-2104-X

First published in Great Britain in 2003 by Judy Piatkus (Publishers) Ltd.

Published in Large Print 2004 by arrangement with Piatkus Books Ltd.

Magna Large Print is an imprint of Library Magna Books Ltd.

Printed and bound in Great Britain by T.J. (International) Ltd., Cornwall, PL28 8RW

To all those people who, over the years, have listened patiently to my stories, laughed politely at my jokes and yet, despite all this, still remain my friends. And if I have to single one out it has to be my best friend, Val.

Part One

Chapter One

It was cold and dark in the bogey hole. Cleo knew when it was daytime because of the odd splinters of light that sneaked past the badly fitting door, or came down through the joints in the flimsy stairs above her head. In the evening the source of light dimmed to a miserly forty watts from a bare bulb in the passage that struggled to make it through to her pokey prison. Then at night when this was switched off such was the intense darkness it was like being imprisoned inside a tin of black boot polish. Cleo was scared. She would listen to the noises coming from under the floorboards and of course with an imagination like hers it made things so much worse. The noise could have been a draught coming up through the joints in the wood, but in her mind it was rats. Rats as big as cats. Scuttling around. Scuttle, scuttle, scratch, scratch. Maybe they were rats down there, maybe just mice or maybe it was just a draught. If they were live creatures it was to be hoped they had a quick means of escape. They would need one.

At first she'd call out that she was scared and, 'Please can I come out? I'm cold, I'm hungry, I need the lavatory.' But she soon gave up. Horace Womack used to stamp on the stairs above her head and add another day to her punishment. So she just sat there and cried a lot, and Womack would bang on the door and shout, 'Roar more, pee less.'

In a way she was glad Ant wasn't there. If there was one thing Ant couldn't stand it was a cry baby. Although, unknown to Cleo, her brother had done his own share of crying – and with very good reason.

They lived in a mucky old street of mucky bricks, mucky paintwork and only three months rent arrears if you're lucky. Ant reckoned their street aspired to being a slum. Two up, two down; newspapers on whichever windows weren't boarded up, an outside water closet in a mucky old lavatory block four houses away, and thirty feet away from their street door was the biggest, smelliest gasometer in Leeds; but it was all Horace could afford. So he said.

They despised and detested everything about their stepfather, Horace Womack. What they hated most was the physical power he had over them. He knew how Cleo and Ant felt about him and he took the only retribution he could. He hit them.

There was nothing to do in the bogey hole; nothing to look forward to, no hope, no one to comfort her, just the noises. And of course the door opening now and again for the delivery of either a foul mouthful from Horace or a cup of water and the dry crusts off yesterday's loaf from her loving mother. Was there ever such an awful bloody woman? Horace Womack found Cleo's plight amusing.

'Might as well get used to it, yer whinin' little sod ... it's what yer'll be livin' on where you're going.'

‘Can I come out please, Horace? I don’t feel very well.’

‘Don’t feel well? Oh dear I am sorry. I don’t feel too bloody clever with a damn big ’ole in me arm. Yer can come out when I say so an’ not before.’

He had cheap false teeth that clicked when he talked; and clammy skin and stale breath, and a weird haircut that looked like a ten-bob wig reduced in the sale. The children weren’t the only ones who despised him; everyone did. Well, everyone except their mother, Nelly Kelly. He’d been a conscientious objector during the war, which took some living down; especially for a prat like Womack, who had no redeeming features whatsoever. He’d been given the choice between prison and the non-combatant Pioneer Corps. Womack chose the latter and spent five years doing menial tasks and hard physical labour.

They despised their mother, who never once stood up to Horace Womack. Not once. She was too stupid to see through his lies about them being out of control and needing disciplining. And Cleo personally hated her mother for branding her with a stupid name, Cleopatra; to which she refused to answer, preferring ‘Cleo’ – but not by much.

When Nelly went down to register her daughter’s birth she hadn’t decided on a name. In the waiting room there was a poster advertising a play called *Antony and Cleopatra* which was coming to the Grand Theatre; and as she’d already got an Antony she thought her baby’s name had been decided by fate. That was a measure of the woman. Cleo made up her mind to change her name when she was old enough to something modern like Belinda or Lana.

Horace's arm was heavily bandaged and Cleo wished that Ant had stabbed him in his black heart instead. Her brother had talked about that but had decided Horace probably hadn't got a heart anyway, so why bother trying? She'd been locked in there for five days and nights when she realised the house was on fire.

And no one was home but her.

Ant had planned revenge many a time. He was three years older than Cleo and had suffered even more. He had suffered in a way he never mentioned to his sister at the time. It sometimes showed in his eyes which was a shame because normally he had the most cheerful eyes. When Cleo once asked him about it he went into the blackest of moods and sometimes didn't speak to her for a whole hour. Which wasn't like Ant at all.

He never called their stepfather 'Horace', he always called him 'the bugger'. He sometimes called him a lot worse but Cleo didn't like to hear Ant using language like that. Language like Horace used to use.

'First chance I get, Cleo, I'm gonna stab the bugger.'

This was a vow he had made many times. Cleo said she'd help him with the planning but not with the stabbing. Stabbing people was wrong, but not in Horace's case. Ant would have to do it, but Cleo would share the blame if necessary. Ant promised it wouldn't come to that. They'd throw the knife in the canal and vanish off the face of the Earth. He'd read a lot and reckoned he knew how to do this. He reckoned kids stabbed their step-fathers and vanished off the face of the Earth all the time and no one bothered much. Good riddance to bad rubbish, that's what the police would say about the bugger. That's what everyone would say.

Ant had stolen a kitchen knife and hidden it under his bed. Opportunities to stab their step-father had come and gone begging. Cleo once mentioned stabbing their mother as well. Just a quick jab in the arm or leg to punish her. Ant said he'd give her a nice jab in the arse and Cleo scolded him for being so vulgar, but the thought of it made her smile anyway. In the event, Ant left without giving Nelly the promised jab and Cleo wished he had. She vowed if ever she became a mother she would lavish boundless affection on her children and stab anyone who tried to harm them.

Cleo and Ant shared a bedroom, partially divided by a screen which they'd been given by old Mrs Bettison from two doors up, who didn't think it right that a growing boy and girl should share the same bedroom; a fact that had never occurred to their mother or to Horace. Apart from the two beds there was a chest of drawers, two cheap dining chairs for them to hang their clothes on, two nails hammered into the door for their coats, and a mirror which made their faces look longer than they were. In the main it was the only image they had of themselves. Cleo could have mentioned to Ant that he wasn't bad looking and maybe he could have returned the compliment, but it's not something you think about when you're brother and sister. Cleo knew she was very skinny and had fair hair, big feet and big blue eyes, unlike her mother and Ant, who both had brown hair and eyes. If asked what her ambition was, back then she'd have said, 'To grow up in one piece'.

They had been in their respective beds when she heard Horace's drunken, swaggering voice through the floorboards. He stumbled up the stairs and burst into their room. He gave a loud belch and Cleo could smell the stale beer on his breath. She shuddered when he swore at her and she knew that he was coming for her and not Ant. For reasons she didn't understand back then he only went for Ant when he was sober and when there was no one else around. He didn't seem to care who saw him hit Cleo. She pulled the bedclothes over her head and felt him yank them away from her. His breath almost made her puke. She shielded her face with her arms and waited for the hitting to start. Then she heard Ant screaming at him.

'Leave her alone!'

Cleo didn't see her brother stab him in his upraised arm. All she heard was Horace howling like a baby and screaming that he was being murdered. She risked a look at what was going on and saw Horace dancing round in a circle with the knife dangling from his upper arm. It dropped out and blood sprayed all over her bed and her as well, including her face and mouth. With it being *his* blood it was the foulest stuff she had ever tasted. Where her mother was during all this she had no idea, she certainly wasn't volunteering to help her darling husband; in fact she showed no curiosity at all. This would have been strange in a normal person but not in Wet Nelly Kelly.

Womack ran around the house, screaming blue murder and dripping blood everywhere. Then he went down to the Leeds Dispensary to have the wound stitched up. While all this was going on, Ant had grabbed his clothes, stolen some money, and stuck a shilling of it into Cleo's hand. Then he ran away. If Cleo hadn't been so shocked, or covered in blood, or if she'd known what might follow, she'd have gone with him. Definitely.

So Womack wreaked the only vengeance available to him and shoved Cleo in the bogey hole. She knew her brother would never have run away had he known how much she would suffer. Comrades in adversity, that's what Ant said they were.

She nodded off to sleep a lot, which was good. Her dreams were the only bearable part of being under the stairs. Maybe it was her subconscious trying to help her out. Helping her to keep sane. She would dream wonderful dreams of a world Ant had told her about, late at night, in their beds. There was a golden beach and a bright blue sea crashing against the shore, throwing fish on to the sand. And behind the beach was a field full of potatoes and another of tomatoes which would provide them with free fish, chips and tomato sauce every day, and as much swimming as they liked. Ant would shin up trees and throw down coconuts and dates and oranges and bananas and sherbert lemons – because dreams don't have to make sense. Then they'd build a raft and paddle all around the island. It was always an island. There were fierce natives, and horses to ride and wild animals to be hunted with the bows and arrows he would make, and sometimes there was buried treasure to search for. Then she'd wake up; sometimes with a jerk and bang her head against the wall. Then she'd cry. She did a lot of crying under those stairs.

She would listen for evidence of Ant's return. Her feelings about this were ambivalent. Her brother would be severely punished but it would take the heat off her a bit. She knew it was selfish, but she ached for him to come back and share the misery with her. And if Ant wanted to laugh at her tears, that was up to him.

It was an existence of darkness and sounds. Doors opening and closing, voices (never pleasant), pots and pans clattering (but never for her benefit), music from the wireless and footsteps on the bare stairs only inches away from her head. She knew when it was Horace because he was the one who always banged his feet on the fragile steps, no doubt hoping to scare her even more. She often thought the stairs would collapse under his weight and he'd fall in on top of her and blame her for it. His lack of consideration for her toilet requirements was crueller than anything. Fortunately she found a way round this within hours of being locked in there.

A cold-water pipe came in through the wall and went out through the floorboards. She could hear the water rushing every time the tap was turned on. It would have been a help if they'd had hot water in the house, at least the pipe would have warmed the cupboard up a bit. To accommodate the pipe the builder had freed one of the floorboards, cut a notch in it big enough for the pipe, then put it back without bothering to nail it down. Cleo soon found it – and soon made use of it. She lifted it out, pulled her pants down (which wasn't easy under there) and peed through the hole. Her starvation diet ensured that she didn't need to empty her bowels and she was thankful for small mercies.

With it being February it was bitterly cold and she couldn't stop shivering. Splinters from the floorboards had punctured her bottom through her dress, but she didn't notice after a while. The cold had anaesthetised her against any pain – another small mercy. Had it not been for an old coal sack hanging on a nail behind the door she might well have frozen to death. Cleo spent hours picking out a hole in the bottom, then one at each side for her arms to go through. She couldn't see what she was doing and broke every fingernail she had; but she managed it. When she'd finished she pulled it over her head like a jumper and felt a real sense of achievement at making something out of nothing. After that, every time the door opened for her bread and water delivery, or for a cursing from Horace, she'd shrink away from the light in case he saw it and took it off her.

Sometimes she'd sing to herself. The Number One in those days was 'Oh Mein Papa' by Eddie

Calvert – The Man With The Golden Trumpet. Cleo knew all the words and they made her cry, as they reminded her of the father she'd been deprived of. She would then do her trumpet impersonation which she thought was ever so good. If Horace heard her he'd kick on the door and tell her to 'Stop that bloody row or I'll give yer summat ter yell about.'

After five days and five nights she began to think she'd die in there. There weren't too many encouraging signs to indicate she'd be freed soon. What would her teachers say at school? They'd probably think she was playing truant, as she often did; school and Cleo just didn't get on. Ant was the clever one. He'd passed his scholarship to go to Leeds Central High School. Cleo supposed she'd have passed hers if she'd concentrated on her lessons, but she didn't like the teachers. At first they had high expectations of her and caned her when she got things wrong; but they didn't seem to realise that you can't hold a pen with black and blue hands and things got worse. More caning. So Cleo took the easy way out and let herself slip back into the herd and joined the thick kids (Ant's expression). Kids who lived a pressure-free existence. Life was much easier with the thick kids, and she enjoyed their company.

Ant would have still been at Leeds Central if he hadn't been expelled for fiddling the milk money. Acting in his own defence, when taken before the Headmaster, he'd said it was the school's own fault for making him a milk monitor when he was obviously so poor that the temptation would be far too much for him. This was typical Ant Kelly logic. He reckoned the Head had seen the merit of his argument but had been duty bound to expel him all the same. Ant wore his poverty like a badge of honour, always reminding the other kids of how lucky they were not to be him or his sister. Cleo thought this was a bit demeaning and she told him he shouldn't involve her in his daft ideas and he said it was his way of shaming their mother and the bugger.

Despite her sack the cold had seeped into her bones and she constantly rocked herself backwards and forwards to try and generate a bit of warmth. But she still shivered. Then she heard them making going-out-for-the-night noises; being nice to each other; laughing and shouting things such as, 'Hurry up, we're missing valuable drinking time.'

Cleo wouldn't have minded a drink of something other than water. She fantasised about a cup of tea with two spoonfuls of sugar and proper milk – not the sterilised stuff her mother always got them, and freshly baked teacakes from Battye's Bakery. Once, Ant had nicked a shilling from Horace's pocket and spent it on currant teacakes, which he shared with her, fifty-fifty. Horace never found out. Ant reckoned that if Horace's brains were dynamite he wouldn't have enough to blow his cap off. Cleo laughed so much she nearly choked on her teacake.

The very thought of those teacakes made her mouth water. A cup of tea and a currant teacake would have gone down very well right then.

She could picture her mother putting on her home-made make-up. Most women had done away with such stuff back in the late forties, but Womack didn't believe in wasting his beer money on frivolities. Nelly would be rubbing Camp Coffee on her legs and getting Horace to make a false seam with a spent match. Cleo usually did this for her and had a faint hope that she might be released from the bogey hole to help out, but no such luck. Her mother would rub cold cream into her face then dust it with talcum powder. Her eyelashes would be blackened with Cherry Blossom shoe polish and her lips painted with boiled beetroot, and some of the same on her cheeks in place of rouge. And oddly enough she would look okay.

The outside door slammed and Cleo knew things would be worse when they got back; all the laughter would have gone from Horace's voice. He'd be drunk and he'd probably drag her out of the cupboard and hit her again. Cleo wept at the thought of it; and at the thought of other parents who wouldn't have allowed it. She thought of the smile on Brenda Appleyard's mother's face and how Geraldine Mossop's dad always winked and ruffled his daughter's hair. Cleo sometimes ruffled her own hair just to see what it felt like. Other kids had grandparents and aunts and uncles. If Cleo had any of these, no one had mentioned it. She didn't even have a proper father, nor did Ant. The only thing they knew for certain was that they had different dads. This was common knowledge and a great source of embarrassment to them. Ant had been told that he was a posthumous baby, the son of a man who had died four months before his birth. Cleo knew that her father was probably still alive, but anonymous and one of three possibilities. Not even Nelly knew for certain which one he was, although there was a fair chance that she had American blood in her. Ant reckoned it could be Glen Miller because he'd heard the American band leader and his orchestra had been playing at the Prospect Street Temperance Hall around the time in question. But Cleo suspected it was one of her brother's many fairy stories.

There was no room to stand up in the bogey hole, but there was room to kick. She felt as though there might be a bit of strength left in her and it made no sense just to sit about and die like some old gimmer who had nothing better to do. She might as well try to get out. The worst Horace could do was kill her, which was no worse than dying in there. In there was a poor place to die. She knew that if Horace killed her they'd hang him by the neck until dead, which would make it all worthwhile. She pictured the look on her brother's face when they hanged 'the bugger'. He'd find a way of going to watch the execution, no fear of that, knowing Ant.

She braced her back against the wall and kicked with both feet at the cupboard door until what strength she had ran out. Then she rested for a while and kicked again; and so on and so forth. There was nothing else to do. At least it was something. It meant she hadn't just sat there and done nothing – and then shrivelled up and died. She thought if Ant were there he'd be laughing at her efforts and this made her mad. He could make her mad even when he wasn't around. He was like that. She kicked at that door until she hadn't an ounce of strength left in her. He would be teasing her by now. She shouted at him. 'Bugger off, Ant Kelly. I bet you couldn't do any better!'

Before going out, Horace had thrown half a shovel of nutty slack on the front-room fire and turned the damper down. It should be glowing nicely by the time they got back. He would have been wise to put the fireguard up as it would have prevented the spark jumping out on to the hearthrug, which was smouldering by the time Cleo started her kicking.

As she laid back, tearful and exhausted, the flames inched towards a carelessly discarded newspaper which, in turn ignited the hessian underside of the settee, which was blazing within two minutes, setting fire to the curtains. Cleo smelled burning, just a faint whiff at first, which didn't really bother her. Then it got stronger and she began to put two and two together.

Smoke started coming under the cupboard door and not long after that the light from the fire shone through every crack in the bogey hole. She screamed and kicked at the door with every bit of strength she had left in her.

Then the fire began to warm the floorboards beneath her bottom and she could hear flames crackling. The door was burning on the outside and flames were licking underneath so she shuffled backwards as far as she could until her head became jammed against the underside of the stair that creaked the most. She banged at it with the heels of her hands, more in despair than anything else, because she knew she was going to die and she didn't want it to be like this – burned to death, her worst nightmare. She felt the stair tread give slightly. She was screaming and crying as she banged at it with her hands. The door had almost burned through and the heat was getting too much for her. With immense difficulty she managed to position herself on her back and kicked upwards with both feet at the loose stair. By now, smoke was pouring under the door; a few more seconds and it would have been too late. On the second kick she felt the tread give way and she knew the fire wasn't going to get her. No way was she going to lose this chance to live. She pulled herself through the tiny gap she had made and was fleetingly thankful to Horace and Wet Nelly for keeping her nice and skinny for that crucial moment in her life. Another small mercy.

Cleo lay on the stairs, coughing out smoke, with her eyes streaming, but the flames were right behind her; already coming out of the gap she'd just crawled through. She pushed herself upwards and the flames followed her, every step of the way. There wasn't a single bone in her body that didn't ache. Her lungs were burning and she was choking, but somehow she reached the landing and got to her feet. That was when she found that five days sitting in a cramped cupboard had taken a lot of the strength from her legs. She stumbled and fell into her bedroom and shut the flames out by slamming the door on them; then she collapsed on to her bed. Completely exhausted.

But she knew she mustn't fall asleep. It was such a huge temptation just to shut her eyes and forget the fire and give in to it all. She heard Ant yelling, 'Don't be so soft, Cleo!' She could hear him as clearly as if he was standing there beside her. She recited the alphabet backwards to keep her brain alert. Ant did this when he wanted to keep awake for any reason. She had got to D when the bedroom door went up in flames. It was enough to get her back to her feet. When she pushed up the window the cold air hit her and she burst into a fit of coughing. Smoke was pouring through the floorboards which were hot beneath her feet. Outside the window, a couple of feet to the right, was the sloping, scullery roof. Ant had been in and out of the house via that route several times but Cleo was no good at that sort of thing so she'd never tried it. First time for everything. She could hear Ant's voice urging her on. 'Go on Cleo, don't be so soft. It's dead easy.'

'All right!' she screamed. 'Shut up ... I'm going!'

Flames were roaring into the room as she stood on the windowsill, clinging on to the frame. Cleo hurled herself to one side and landed mostly on the roof; then she began to scramble at the slates, next thing she knew she was sliding down and she wasn't a bit scared, just glad to be away from the fire. She came to a halt for a second when she reached the gutter, which she tried to hold on to, but hadn't the strength. The next thing to break her fall was the ground. It was only a six-foot drop so she wasn't hurt. Not by the fall, anyway.

There wasn't a soul there to help her, which was good. In the next street, at the front of the house where the fire had started, a crowd was gathering, but the narrow back street was still deserted, apart from a hissing cat, which arched its back and glared at her.

She lay on the ground for a while, coughing and regaining her breath. Her injuries seemed surprisingly few, considering what she'd just been through; just a few bruises and a mouthful of smoke, which burned the back of her throat and her lungs. The light from the fire was dancing on the walls of the houses opposite and she knew the street wouldn't remain deserted for long. Her options were limited. She could find someone to help her, who would no doubt place her back in the care of Horace and her loving mother, or she could seize the opportunity to run away; just like her brother had. Running away seemed the best option.

Cleo got to her feet and staggered to the communal toilet block where there was a cold-water tap; one of the few things that worked in there. She was thirsty, weak, exhausted, hungry, bruised and shocked at her close brush with death; and yet, despite all that, she had an underlying sense of elation, of liberation. Whatever happened she wasn't going back *there,* because there wasn't a *there* to go back to.

She gulped at the flow of ice-cold water running from the tap past her mouth until she could take no more. It soothed the burning in her throat, but it set her stomach heaving. After washing her face as best she could, she tried to dry herself with the sack she was still wearing then set off up the street. Her legs were collapsing all over the place, like the eccentric dancer she'd laughed at on *Café*

Continental, courtesy of Geraldine Mossop who sometimes invited her in to watch telly on a Saturday night when her parents were out. She moved as fast as she could and it wasn't long before she had used up every ounce of energy, and then some. So she stopped and leaned back against the Co-op wall beneath a big poster that said Bile Beans for Radiant Health and a Lovely Figure. It showed a young woman in an RAF uniform, and judging from her shape and radiance she was a very enthusiastic Bile Bean eater. Unlike Cleo, with her skinny arms braced against her grazed knees, gasping for breath and coughing and spitting, just like Daft Edgar who sat on a wall outside the chip shop and spat on the pavement.

There was a glow in the sky and the strident clang of a fire engine ripped into the otherwise silent night, bringing a smile to her cracked lips – the first for a long time. She felt good about the house burning down. She felt good because she knew *they'd* feel bad; and because she knew Ant would have been howling with laughter had he been there. Maybe they'd think she'd perished in the flames and wouldn't come looking for her – that'd be good. All she had to do was find Ant and everything would be okay.

People walking past looked down at Cleo in her weird outfit and dismissed her distress as normal for a scruffy kid who had probably been up to no good; especially with her being one of Nelly Kelly's brats. A woman tut-tutted as Cleo retched, but there wasn't much inside her worth vomiting. If she'd thrown up every morsel of food she'd eaten in the past five days it would barely have filled a crack in the pavement.

She wiped her mouth with the back of her hand and looked up at the dark, tenement skyline which had warmth and light streaming from its windows. In that light people would be being nice to one another; smiling and laughing and saying, 'Night night and God bless,' to their children. She knew this from what her friends said. Some of the kids had bikes and new shoes every year, and clothes without holes, and skin without bruises. Some of the kids were plump and rosy cheeked and brought sandwiches to school to supplement their school dinners, which was the only decent meal Cleo ever ate. But everything would be all right now. Now that she had escaped. Now there was no bogey hole to go back to.

She stood in the light of a flickering street lamp, looking like a character from a Charlie Chaplin picture, always popular with the kids at the Bughutch Saturday Matinée. Cleo preferred The Bowery Boys. She took a deep breath, set her shoulders straight in defiance of everything in general, and set off at a slow but steady walk.

A week earlier she had learned to ride a bike down that very street. It was an odd-looking gadget with the front wheel slightly bigger than the back one. Ant had made it himself from parts he'd scrounged and it was his pride and joy. He called it The Black Panther and took it with him when he ran away. Once Cleo had learned to ride he promised he'd make her one. As she walked she remembered the tremendous feeling she got when he let go of the saddle and she wobbled off down the street on her own. Scared and elated at the same time. A feeling that told her she'd done it, she was on her own, she didn't need any help any more. A bit like life, really – only in her life there had never been anyone holding on to the saddle. Except Ant.

Cleo thought about throwing away the sack she was still wearing, but decided she was cold enough without making things worse. It wasn't fashionable but it was warm. She kept looking over her shoulder to check that she was in the clear, but only her shadow followed her, flickering in the gas light. She would steal an over-the-shoulder glance and watch it shrink to nothing as she walked under the lamp post, then elongate in front of her, then fade away into darkness until she came within range of the next lamp. This one cast a constant light and her shadow was steady, as if reflecting her returning strength.

Cleo felt at her ribs and wondered if Horace had broken any. If she examined herself she knew she'd find new bruises on top of the fading shades of old ones. Maybe she should go to a hospital to get herself looked at. Maybe she should tell someone what Horace and her mother had done to her, and how she'd nearly died at their hands. Maybe they'd believe her. Pigs might fly, that's what Ant would say. If only she knew where he'd got to.

A genial moon hung like a welcome sign above Battye's Bakery, as if inviting her to call in. The bakers worked all night and her nose had been drawn by the smell of newly baked teacakes. When you're hungry there's no more tempting smell. Her belly was completely empty now and her hunger was physically painful. She reached into her sock and took out the stolen shilling that Ant had given her. During her time under the stairs she had often taken it out and squeezed it in her hand as an act of defiance. Sometimes she bit it like a voodoo doll, in the hope that the pain the coin was suffering might transfer itself on to its evil owner. It wasn't much but it was something.

'Have yer got any currant teacakes, mister?' Her voice was hoarse from the smoke.

A man with a dusting of flour on his face, wearing a white, flat cap and a baker's smock came to the door and gave her a suspicious look.

'No, we haven't... Good God, is that you, Cleo, lass? What's up wi' yer voice? Have yer got a cold or summat?'

He recognised her despite the dirt still streaked on her face and the sack she was wearing. She had an unmistakable face, with expressions ranging from a demonic scowl to a melting smile. Everyone has special qualities to fall back on and Cleo's facial expressions were hers. Unfortunately, they never worked on Horace – or her mother for that matter.

'Yes, mister ... and I'm dead hungry.' She could barely get the words out, her throat was so sore.

He shook his head, determined not to be swayed. 'I'm sorry, lass. Yer'll have ter come back when t' shop's open tomorrow. We don't sell stuff at night. In any case, yer shouldn't be bringing yer germs in here.'

Cleo edged further inside. The aroma was making her mouth water.

'Honest, I'm right hungry, mister.'

The man couldn't help feeling sorry for her. One of Wet Nelly's kids being hungry wasn't beyond the bounds of possibility, such was Nelly's reputation as a parent. She'd arrived in the district with one bastard babe-in-arms and it surprised no one when a second, fatherless baby arrived a couple of years later. Then, right out of the blue she'd married Conshie Womack, who was an even bigger waste of space than Wet Nelly. To everyone in the district she'd always be Wet Nelly Kelly; apparently the kids hadn't taken Womack's name – not much of a loss to them. Horace Womack was a part-time bookie's runner, part-time odd-job man and full-time tosspot. *And he'd been a conshie.* Some conshies were genuine and deserving of some respect (which they never got) for sticking to their beliefs in the face of public humiliation; others were conshies of convenience – basically cowards who hid behind the guise of being conscientious objectors. Womack was one of those.

Most of his money went on the dogs or on beer; none of it went on Nelly's kids, God help 'em. Cleo kept her eyes on him and her smile constant. A winning combination.

'Have yer got any money?' he enquired, defeated. The tone of his voice suggested he thought it was a daft question.

'Yes, mister.'

'Oh!' He was surprised now. 'They're tuppence

each, yer know.'

She held out her shilling. 'Can I have seven for a bob?'

'Go on then,' he said. 'Seeing as it's you.'

'Have you got any butter?' Cleo asked, when he came back with a paper bag full of teacakes.

'No, we flamin' well haven't ... here.' The decent man handed her a half-full bottle of Tizer. 'Finish this off and don't say I don't give yer nowt. And while yer at it, I should have a word wi' yer couturier. I don't think sacks are in this year.'

Cleo mumbled her thanks through a mouthful of teacake, which she was chewing with the table manners of a ravenous dog. Then, swallowing sufficient down to clear her throat, she asked, 'Can I stay here for a bit, mister?'

It was only a brief moment in her life but after what she'd just been through she would remember it as one of the really good times, and she wouldn't have minded the memory lasting a bit longer.

'Sorry, lass,' he said. 'Not in the state you're in. Yer what's known as unhygienic. Haven't yer got no home ter go to?'

'I had, but it's burnin' down.'

'Don't talk so daft, lass.'

'Sorry, Mister.'

She decided not to try and disprove his disbelief of her – it might affect her bid for freedom. She edged, very reluctantly, out of the light and warmth into the cold street, holding the bag of warm teacakes to her skinny chest.

Four hours later she was found asleep under a

tarpaulin in Flanagan's coal depot by a police constable with a moustache and bad breath. The night watchman had seen something moving but hadn't dared go near, so he rang the police. The bag of teacakes was empty, as was the Tizer bottle.

The policeman shook her by the shoulder. His voice started off as part of her dream. She was trapped in a blazing box, kicking at it, trying to get out and she knew there was no escape. Someone was talking to her and shaking her. 'Come on, young 'un, wakey, wakey.'

She was sweating despite the cold night air, then she blinked her eyes and realised, with enormous relief, that it was only a dream – this time. The policeman recognised her.

'Blimey! It's you. We thought yer'd gone up in smoke. What the hell are yer wearin'?'

Cleo stared at him, disorientated for a second. 'I haven't done nowt, mister, honest.'

'Happen not, love. There's a first time for everythin'. They thought yer might o' gone up in t' fire.'

'It were nowt ter do with me, mister, honest.'

'I'm not sayin' it was, lass. But I think my sergeant might want ter ask yer about it.'

The police left the cell door unlocked as Cleo slept. There was nowhere else for her to sleep. At least it was warm and it had a comfy lavatory that flushed first time and they'd brought her a cup of tea with proper milk and two spoonfuls of sugar. A police doctor came and shone a torch down her throat. He said she was suffering from mild smoke inhalation and gave her two aspirins and a Fisherman's Friend.

From somewhere they'd produced a green cardigan. It was a couple of sizes too big but anything was better than the sack. Cleo hadn't explained about the sack, because it would have meant her having to explain about how she came to be locked in the bogey hole because Ant had stabbed Horace – and this could get her brother into a lot of trouble with the police. Ant wouldn't thank her for that. 'Tell the buggers nothing' was his motto.

Her mother and Horace had made their own arrangements that night, which didn't include her. Wet Nelly had squeezed out buckets of tears when she thought her darling daughter had been burned alive. Horace would have been more worried at the thought of Cleo's charred remains being found under the stairs. He'd have had his excuses ready, no doubt: 'She must have gone there to escape the fire, silly lass.'

When Cleo unexpectedly turned up there was no joyous relief at a much-loved daughter's escape from death. Just anger at the trouble she had caused. Cleo saw unspoken questions on their lips but while the police were there they could hardly ask her how she got out of the cupboard, much less question her about the fire. The two of them left without telling the police where they were going or what they intended doing about her, only to say they'd be back first thing. When Cleo woke up she could hear Horace's voice. He was doing his best to disguise his natural nastiness and Cleo hoped the coppers would see through it.

'I hate to say this about the girl, with her bein' me own, so ter speak,' he was saying. 'But I'm not at all surprised ... never out o' trouble ... allus fighting ... yer should see t' bruises on 'er body ... wouldn't know the truth if it jumped up and bit 'er.'

Cleo went to the cell door to listen more clearly. 'I think this is just about the last straw,' she heard him say. 'Her brother stabbed me last week, but I said nowt. When they're yer own yer don't, do yer? Yer try an' make the best o' things. My Nelly agrees wi' me, don't yer, love?'

Cleo didn't need to look at Nelly to know she'd be nodding her head like a demented donkey. Cleo hated her for not sticking up for her, like a proper mother should.

'I think yer'll just have ter throw t' book at 'er, Sergeant,' Horace was saying. 'Teach her a lesson she'll not forget. We can't cope wi' kids what set fire to us 'ouse an' 'ome.

'Were you insured, sir?'

'No, we bloody weren't, as it 'appens. The house were rented but some valuable stuff went up in smoke. D'yer think we're entitled to a bit o' compo?'

'I shouldn't think so, sir. That's what insurance is for.'

'Well, yer never imagine yer own girl's gonna set fire to 'er own 'ome. It shook me, I can tell yer. Standin' there, watchin me 'ouse go up in smoke. Makes yer bloody think.'

'I imagine you were absolutely frantic about the girl being trapped inside.'

Horace missed the irony in the policeman's

voice. 'What? Oh aye, that an' all. Worried to death.'

'And so relieved when she turned up alive.'

'Well, naturally, with 'er bein' me daughter.'

'She's not your daughter though, is she, sir?'

'Not as such, but as good as. I couldn't have tret 'er better if she'd been me own ... an' what thanks do I get? The little sod burns me out of 'ouse an' bloody 'ome an' then runs away. If she 'adn't run away we might 'ave thought it were an accident – but she did run away, so that proves it, dunt it?'

'If you say so, sir.'

This worried Cleo. They thought she'd set fire to the house. How was that? How could she set fire to the house when they'd locked her in a cupboard? Would it do any good to deny it, or would it make things worse? Usually it made things worse – even though she was telling the truth. Cleo considered her options once again. If the police knew about Ant stabbing Horace, she couldn't lose anything by telling them about her being locked in the cupboard and Horace hitting her all the time. On the other hand it would be her word against theirs and grown-ups never believed kids. She went back inside the cell and wondered how long a prison sentence she'd have to serve for burning a crappy old house down. Then someone brought her breakfast and Cleo forgot her troubles for a while. When you've been locked in a blazing cupboard nothing seems all that serious. At least she was warm and safe from that cruel man. She wished Ant was with her.

Chapter Two

On the morning of her appearance in Juvenile Court, Cleo's brother was closely examining the sets of bicycle locks in Morton's Cycle Shop on Harehills Lane, and in particular, the keys. He soon worked out that there were only three or four different keys to fit all the locks. Mrs Morton, the owner's wife, barely spared Ant a glance as she explained the merits of a certain bicycle to a customer. By the time she looked in Ant's direction again he was outside with one of each key in his pocket. From Mrs Morton's viewpoint he was just looking at the bikes displayed on the pavement, all chained together and locked with the locks to which Ant now had a set of keys. He chose the most unlikely machine. Disregarding a flashy racing bike in blue and gold, he unlocked the chain on a JT Rogers Tourer with 'sit up and beg' handlebars and a comfy saddle. It was the one least likely to be missed in a hurry and it suited his purpose.

Up until appearing in court Cleo had been in a local authority remand home, the best home she'd ever had. For a variety of reasons, mostly bureaucratic bungles, she'd been held there for over four months, but she didn't mind. The regime was strict but fair. Her mother, no doubt not wishing to aggravate Horace, hadn't bothered to visit her.

Ant somehow found out what had happened and sent her two postcards, both signed, 'Eccles', his favourite character in *The Goon Show.* The house mother didn't make the connection and failed to notify anyone that her missing brother was now in London and working on a building site. The second card arrived the day before Cleo was due to appear in court. It simply read: 'Tell the buggers nothing, Eccles.'

As this was the only piece of legal advice available to her, Cleo obeyed Ant's instructions to the letter. Even to the extent of refusing to answer when the clerk of the court said, 'State your name.'

She stared at the coat of arms on the wall behind the bench, wondering what Dieu et Mon Droit meant.

'Young lady, are you or are you not, Cleopatra Kelly?' asked the Chairman of the bench.

Cleo said nothing. Her eyes were still fixed on the coat of arms behind the man's head.

'Answer me, girl!'

She slowly transferred her gaze and gave him her look of benign imbecility. One of Ant's favourites.

The chairman leaned over to the clerk and enquired, 'Do we know if the girl is mentally enfeebled?'

'According to her school reports, she's quite bright, your Worship.'

'Is she really?'

The magistrate examined her over the top of his glasses and Cleo suspected she hadn't passed muster when he remarked, sternly, 'We must take your insolence into consideration when judging this matter.'

She transferred her gaze to the coat of arms once again and eventually worked out that Dieu meant God. She'd heard Ant, who had taken French at school, say 'Mon Dieu' loads of times and he'd once explained what it meant.

'My God.' Cleo mouthed the two words to herself.

'Speak up, girl!' demanded the magistrate, who must have thought Cleo was speaking to him.

Cleo ignored him. *Tell the buggers nothing.* She wasn't much good at speaking to grown-ups in authority. Some of her unenlightened teachers took this to be surliness but they couldn't have been more wrong; she might be a lot of things but surly wasn't one of them. The case continued without any contribution from her. Cleo had no representation. Horace spoke against her:

'I've done me best by the girl, yer Worship,' he said.

The clicking of his loose teeth was accentuated by the hollow acoustics of the court. It brought a smirk to the face of an otherwise bored court reporter.

'Many's the time I've stayed me hand when she's given me cheek,' Womack went on. 'But yer'd need the patience of a saint not ter give her a bleedin' crack now and again.'

The chairman's face froze at this expletive and only thawed when Horace issued a swift apology.

'Begging yer pardon, yer Worship. I'm a bit past meself with all what's been goin' on.'

'Quite,' conceded the magistrate, who talked

through his nose as if he had a cold. The combination of this and Womack's clicking teeth set the young court reporter giggling to himself. An usher caught his eye and frowned him into silence.

'You're not on trial, Mr Womack,' said the magistrate. 'Corporal punishment has its place in our society. Bringing up children is difficult enough when they're your own, but to bring up someone's else's child is doubly difficult.'

Cleo smiled at the young reporter, who smiled back, taken with her. Then she transferred her attention to the magistrate who seemed to have her future in his hands. Nothing about him was impressive or reassuring. He was very old, at least fifty, with a fat face and an Elastoplast stuck to his chin. Whatever was under the plaster was of more concern to him than the girl in the dock, whom he spared barely a single glance. He kept fingering the plaster, in between wiping his nose with a large, white handkerchief. There was a long silence in the court as he studied the case notes. Then he looked over his glasses at Horace and said, 'I understand her older brother…' then back through them at his notes, 'Antony Kelly, has run away from home.'

'That's right, yer Worship,' confirmed Horace. 'Took a knife ter me and ran away.' He winced and tried to raise his wounded arm. 'I'm still not back at work.'

'I suspect the boy is something of a worry to you.'

'As God is my judge, yer Worship, there's not a night goes by without me and the wife worrying ourselves sick about the lad.'

Horace turned to look at his wife for her confirmation. Cleo looked at her in the vain hope that just for once in her life she'd do the right thing and condemn him for what he was – a bully and a liar. Cleo was willing her to stand up and shout out the truth about him. To tell the world what a rotten awful pig of a man he was.

Nelly knew her daughter's eyes were on her, but she fixed her own gaze on Horace and nodded, dutifully, without sparing Cleo a glance; as though her own daughter wasn't important enough for her to look at.

'Thank you, Mr Womack, you may return to your seat.'

As Horace went back to join Wet Nelly, the chairman shuffled a few papers then began to deliver his verdict without looking up at the court.

'I think it's reasonable to assume that by setting her home on fire and running away, this young lady has proved herself to be beyond parental control,' he droned. Then he took off his glasses and wiped them on an unused part of the same handkerchief he'd earlier wiped his nose with. 'And in view of her insolent behaviour in this court I don't think we need to retire to consider this verdict.' He held his glasses up to the light to check for smears, then put them on and glanced over the top of them at his two colleagues for their agreement, which he got. He then turned his attention to Cleo.

'Cleopatra Kelly. You have proved yourself to be a dishonest, dangerous and ungrateful child. It is the decision of this court that you be held in secure accommodation until you prove yourself fit to be released into decent society. The term of your custody will be not less than two years.'

The magistrate was lowering his gaze when he caught sight of her hand in the air. He looked up and glared at her, almost putting her off asking her question; the one Ant would have wanted her to ask.

'What is it, girl?'

'Mister, where I'm going, will they be cruel to me like they are at home?'

Tell the truth and shame the devil.

The magistrate followed her gaze and looked to where Nelly and Horace were shuffling in their seats with embarrassment. Someone tittered and was silenced by the clerk of the court. The magistrate didn't know what to say at first.

'Your persistent insolence has been noted,' he sniffed, eventually. 'You'll be placed in the care of someone who will teach you how to conduct yourself.'

Cleo knew he wouldn't answer her question, but she was optimistic that life couldn't be any worse where they were sending her.

'Thank you, mister,' she said. 'I'm sure it'll be very nice.'

She looked at her mother, who now returned her gaze. Cleo had seen warmer eyes on a fishmonger's slab. The policeman's hand on her skinny shoulder held more affection than her mother had ever shown her. The constable knew that justice wasn't being served here. It wouldn't have taken a genius.

'Come on, love,' he muttered. 'Before yer get yerself into more bother.' He fingered a set of handcuffs dangling from his belt. 'Yer not gonna give me any trouble, are yer?'

Cleo looked up at him. 'No mister,' she said, and at the time she meant it because he seemed such a nice man.

With the constable by her side she walked out of the Juvenile Court and headed for the Bridewell in Leeds Town Hall where she was to be held until transport arrived. At the other side of the road was Ant, his legs dangling loosely from a bicycle. He casually flicked away a cigarette he'd been smoking and pointed to the Ladies' toilets a few yards away. Then he winked at her. He didn't need to paint a picture, Cleo knew exactly how his mind worked.

'Can I go to the lavvie, mister?' Cleo asked.

'When we get ter the station, lass.'

'Sorry, mister. I'm burstin' for a wee.'

She ran in the direction of the toilets, leaving the policeman more cross at her insubordination than worried that his prisoner was escaping. It wasn't until she suddenly darted to one side and mounted the saddle of Ant's bike that the policeman, with a roar of vexation, set off in pursuit – by which time it was too late. Ant was standing on the pedals and working up sufficient speed to carry them away from the pursuing constable. They flew around the corner of the Town Hall and away towards the Headrow and freedom.

Ant rode straight through red traffic lights in

front of the Town Hall and turned right down East Parade, then left along Infirmary Street and into City Square, where he turned right against the flow of traffic. He was dodging in and out of hooting, oncoming cars as they passed the Majestic Cinema which, Cleo noticed, was showing *Dial M for Murder* starring Ray Milland and Grace Kelly. Cleo was adding Grace to her list of preferred names when the front wheel caught in the tramlines and threw them in front of an oncoming tram, which Cleo thought was very careless of Ant, under the circumstances. Even she knew not to cycle anywhere near tramlines. To be fair he did push her clear of one line while he rolled clear of the other and waited with bated breath for the tram to pass between them so he could see if his sister had survived, which of course she had. Cleo was sitting on the ground rubbing her knee as the tram scraped to a halt just beyond them, mangling the stolen bike beneath its wheels.

Ant winked at her and said, 'Nearly.'

'Nearly?' Cleo said. 'How d'you mean, nearly? That was really stupid, that was. Are you all right?'

He'd banged his elbow, grazed his knee and torn his trousers into the bargain, but he was obviously so relieved that he hadn't killed her that he shook his head and grinned, as though it was all a great big joke. That was one of the things about him that made her mad. When someone nearly kills you and they think it's funny – that's really annoying.

'I don't know what you think's so funny, we

could have been flippin' killed.'

'I know, but we weren't,' he pointed out. 'So that's good, isn't it?'

Ant had a weird sense of logic. A gathering crowd of spectators and a hooting of horns urged them to their feet. Ant grabbed her hand and virtually pulled her up the steps and through the doors of the Queen's Hotel, past a snooty-looking woman in a fur coat and a commissionaire who was coming down the steps to open the door of a Rolls-Royce.

They tried their best but it was difficult to look as though they belonged there. Well, impossible actually. Cleo was limping and dusting the road dirt from her clothes on to the plush carpet, and Ant's equally dirty trousers were torn and bloodied at the knee. A man wearing a morning suit and a very sour expression looked at them as though they were something nasty he'd trodden in. He lifted the flap on a reception desk and headed towards them.

'Smile at him,' whispered Ant.

She did as he asked but this man was obviously trained not to respond to such as her. Her brother spotted this and also spotted a door marked Station Exit. He led his limping sister across the carpeted foyer and through this less public door. Within a minute they were mingling with the people in the station.

'Come on,' said Ant. 'We need ter buy a couple of platform tickets.'

'Where we going?' Cleo was examining her knee as Ant studied the destination board. 'I could do with a plaster.'

'London,' he said. There was no doubt in his voice. He was studying the train times, rubbing his chin like an old man. 'Eleven forty-five sounds okay to me. Gets in at four-fifteen – just beats rush hour.'

Cleo didn't know whether to believe him or not, but he'd done okay so far, and she supposed her grazed knee would heal quicker without a plaster. They sat and drank strong tea in the station café; neither of them liked strong tea but it was the only variety on offer. Strong tea and curly sandwiches that looked to have been there since the old king died.

'Where'd you get the bike?' Cleo asked.

'Borrowed it ... sort of. From Morton's bike shop.'

'You mean you nicked it.' She disapproved because she didn't want Ant to become a thief; he was too good for that.

'I had no choice.'

'What happened to *your* bike?' she asked.

'Sold it the day I ran away to a bloke coming out of a pub. He gave me two quid for it. I asked for ten but I wasn't in a position to argue.'

'Two quid, was he drunk?'

'Hey! Don't be so cheeky. It was a good bike was The Black Panther.'

Cleo couldn't help but grin, he saw her and joined in. 'Wasn't much like a panther, was it?' he admitted.

'Not much,' Cleo said. 'But it was clever the way you made it all yourself.'

They sat in silence for a while until she asked him, 'How come you knew everything that was happening to me?'

He winked at her and touched the side of his nose, knowingly. 'I kept ringin' old Foxy Foxcroft,' he said. 'He said he'd keep an eye on what were goin' on. He did an' all.'

It explained everything. Ant used to do a paper round for Foxcroft's Newsagents.

'He's all right is Mister Foxcroft,' Cleo said.

Ant's gaze seemed to lose its focus. He did that a lot when his mind got crammed with all his weird ideas. Cleo had something on her mind as well, so she stared at him until he remembered she was still there.

'What's up?'

'Thanks for coming to get me,' she said. 'But you shouldn't have left me – not with him.'

He lowered his head and looked down, and at first Cleo was glad he had. Ant had permanently cheerful eyes and a mouth that was only ever a flicker away from a grin; although few people in the world had less to grin about than Ant Kelly. Cleo bent her head down so she could see his face and noticed a shine in his eyes, the sort of shine you get when you're about to cry. She'd made him feel rotten and she didn't really want that.

'I know I shouldn't have left you,' he said. 'I'm sorry ... I didn't know what to do for the best.' Then he asked, 'What, erm, what did he do to you?' He didn't look up at her. It was as though he was afraid of the answer.

'He locked me in the bogey hole. I nearly froze to flippin' death.'

Ant nodded, without looking up. He'd spent

many days and nights under the stairs himself. He reached out and took her hand. 'Owt else?' he said. 'Did he ... did he do anything else?'

'Well, he gave me a good hiding before he locked me up.'

'A good hiding ... just a good hiding?'

'How d'you mean, just? He thumped me black and blue.'

'Was Mam there?' he asked.

'Oh aye, she were useless as usual. I was there for five days then they went out and the flippin' house caught fire.'

He looked up and wiped his eyes quickly so his sister wouldn't notice, but you can always see where tears have just been and she knew those tears were for her. He'd been crying for her.

'It burned right down,' she said, pretending she hadn't noticed. 'Best thing that could have happened to it. I reckon it was because they didn't put the fireguard up, dozy sods.'

'I thought *you'd* done it,' Ant smiled. 'I laughed like hell when I heard. Best thing I'd heard for ages.'

Cleo looked at him, scornfully. 'How could I set the house on fire when I'm locked in a cupboard? I only got out by the skin of me flippin' teeth. If them stairs hadn't been droppin' to bits I'd have been roasted alive.'

'Is that how yer got out?'

She nodded. 'Kicked one of the stairs out then I got out through our bedroom window – like you used to do.'

It was as though he hadn't realised how close he'd come to losing her. He hung on to her hand until she felt uncomfortable. There's a limit to how long a brother should hold a sister's hand.

'Oh heck!' she said, looking outside.

Ant followed her gaze and the two of them immediately turned their backs to the window. She'd seen two policemen striding across the station concourse; one was quite tall, his colleague about a foot shorter. Under other circumstances they'd have found something funny to say about them.

'D'you think they're looking for us?' Cleo asked. 'We put on a bit of a performance just now. Two kids riding a bike – it shouldn't take much figuring out.'

'Could be,' Ant said. 'We'll have to split up. You latch on to someone.'

'How d'you mean, *latch on?*'

'Just find some grown-ups and walk as though you're with 'em. Follow 'em on to the train. Make your way to the dining car and wait outside. I'll find you.'

'Why the dining car?'

'When the ticket collector comes, we'll be standing looking dead fed up. He'll ask us for our tickets and we say our mam and dad have got them and they're in the dining car and will he tell them we're bored and we've gone back to our compartment?'

'Can't we just hide in the lavvies?' Cleo asked.

'This way's better,' he assured her. 'More comfy than a lavvie.'

'Will it work?'

'It always has for me. Once he's seen your face he won't ask for a ticket again. Sometimes they ask if you've found your mam and dad. You just say yeah, then they go away. Most of 'em don't know who's got tickets and who hasn't. They just like to let on they know what they're doing. That's what most grown-ups do when you get to know 'em.'

An echoing voice came over the loudspeaker and announced that the train now standing on Platform Five was the eleven forty-five to King's Cross. Ant looked at the station clock. Eleven thirty-five.

'You go first at about twenty to,' he told her. 'I'll be a couple o' ticks behind you.' Then he gave her one of his smiles. 'Don't worry, our lass, it'll be okay.'

As the clock moved on to eleven-forty an elderly couple came rushing from the ticket office, both of them carrying what looked like heavy cases. The man was looking at his watch, then he beckoned to a small boy who was trying to keep up with them. The boy was struggling with a bag that was nearly as big as him.

'I'm coming as quick as I can, Granddad.'

Ant almost pushed his sister into action. 'Latch on to them,' he said.

Within seconds Cleo was walking two paces behind the struggling grandson. As she turned on to Platform Five the two policemen came into view, about fifty yards away. The tall one looked straight at her and nudged his colleague to do the same. Then the small officer nodded and they both headed in Cleo's direction with their arms behind their backs. She knew that Ant would be following close behind, and for her to hesitate at this point would land them both in it. Then she thought back to what happened in the bogey hole and how she'd escaped certain death; and she knew she had the confidence to try absolutely anything. Nothing she'd ever faced in life would be as bad as that. She picked up her pace and caught up with the elderly couple.

'Excuse me, missis,' she said, politely, in a voice that didn't carry to the approaching policemen.

The woman, who had a kind face, looked down. Cleo smiled up at her and took the bag from the boy. 'I'll give you a hand, missis,' she said. 'If you like.'

The boy's grandmother seemed hesitant but Cleo's smile won her over and she said, 'Thank you, dear.'

As they walked past the two policemen Cleo was chatting away as though she'd known the old lady all her life. The constables stopped and Cleo could feel their eyes burning the back of her neck, but she didn't look round. A porter was walking down the length of the train, slamming doors.

'Oh dear,' said the woman.

Cleo ran forward, still carrying the bag, and waved her arms. 'Wait for us!' she shouted, pointing back at her temporary relatives. This seemed to decide things for the two coppers, who went on their way. Cleo chanced a backward glance to confirm this, then she turned and smiled at the porter who was standing by an open door; one hand on the handle, the other hoping to collect a tip for his chivalry. Granddad obliged by dropping a coin into the man's hand.

From the edge of her vision Cleo saw Ant walk past, then from over the porter's shoulder she saw him carefully opening the door to the next carriage, which had just been closed.

'Thanks, mister,' she said to the porter as he helped her with the bag. 'My grandparents are a bit slow on their feet.'

Her 'grandparents' were fortunately out of earshot.

'Any time, love,' he said, impressed by her smile.

Ant was now safely on board. Cleo stepped clear of the door as the porter slammed it shut, then she handed the bag back to the boy, who was told to say 'thank you' by his grandmother.

'That's all right, missis,' Cleo said. 'I wish I had a nice grandma like you.'

She don't quite know why she'd said this, but she meant it, and it brought a smile to the old woman's face so it was worth the effort. A guard blew his whistle to confirm all was clear and the train began to move off.

Cleo leaned out of the open window and watched Leeds go past to the quickening clatter of train wheels and the odd blast of steam and she felt a joy she'd never known before. Somehow she knew they'd get to London. After that nothing could be worse than her life up until now. Surely.

Chapter Three

Her first sight of London was Trafalgar Square, where they emerged after an interesting, but much longer than necessary journey through the Tube from King's Cross. In order to get the most value out of their tickets Ant took her on what he called the scenic route, although Cleo didn't actually see any scenery, just place names she'd only ever visited on a Monopoly board. At the top of the escalator a paper boy was selling the *London Evening Standard* beside a placard which read 'Meat Rationing Ends'. This meant little to her and her brother who had never been fed their full ration, not at home anyway. Meat was the last thing to go off ration. It had taken nine years since the end of the war for the ration book to become obsolete; a lot longer than most people had anticipated back in 1945.

They dodged the rush-hour traffic and crossed the road into the Square where Cleo stared up at the statue of Nelson which she'd only ever seen on the pictures before. The sky was bright and breezy with cotton-wool clouds rushing past Nelson's head and after a few seconds she had to look down because it made her feel dizzy. A pigeon landed on her shoulder, assuming she was a regular tourist who would have food about her person. It was joined by others and soon she was enshrouded in birds, much to her consternation and her brother's amusement. She ran around in a small circle and sent them flapping away. Ant climbed on one of the stone lions and Cleo climbed on behind him, then a policeman appeared from around the fountain and shouted at them and just for a moment she thought they were done for. They climbed off, which seemed to satisfy the constable, but it took a while before her heart stopped pounding.

'We shouldn't do anything to annoy coppers,' she said to Ant.

'Give over, you daft ha'porth, we're two hundred miles away. They'll not be looking for us down here. We're not international gangsters you know.' The scorn in his voice annoyed her, but she thought he was probably right. He did get some things right. Quite a lot of things actually.

The ticket collector had fallen for Ant's routine exactly as he had forecast, although her brother was pushing it a bit when he asked the man if he would come with them to look for their parents. 'I'm sure yer mam and dad'll find you when they're good and ready,' the man had said. 'Sometimes mams and dads need time to themselves, especially on trains. They know yer'll come to no harm.'

It occurred to her that if this were the case, most parents weren't much better than theirs. Leaving kids to their own devices on a train. When she mentioned this to Ant he assured her that the man was saying anything, just to get rid of them. 'Grown-ups'll allus take the easy road out. All you've got to do is pretend to cause 'em trouble an' you won't see 'em for dust.'

It was perhaps a warped philosophy, but his life had given him no reason to doubt the truth of it.

Cleo saw Big Ben in the distance and dragged Ant down Whitehall until they stopped in front of a street sign that said Downing Street SW1.

'Is that it?' Cleo asked. 'Is that where Mr Churchill lives?'

He nodded, knowingly, and pointed to a policeman standing outside a door, about fifty yards up the street on the right. 'That's his house,' he said. 'Number Ten Downing Street.' Ant announced the fact with pride, as though basking in Downing Street's reflected glory. 'What d'you think?' he asked.

Somehow Cleo thought Number Ten Downing Street would be much grander, basically it was just a house in a street. She couldn't think of anything to say except, 'I wonder where he keeps his dustbin?'

The two of them sauntered up the famous street and took up position at the opposite side of the road from Number Ten, along with a group of colourfully dressed tourists who were taking flash photographs of a po-faced policeman guarding Mr Churchill's front door.

'Yanks,' whispered Ant.

'Oh,' Cleo said, wondering how he knew.

'Just go along with what I say, we'll make a few bob.'

'Right.'

'Excuse me, mister,' said Ant to one of the tourists.

Cleo noticed a marked change in his accent, from Leeds to what an American might well mistake for Cockney.

'We was wonderin' if you'd like me sister to be in one of your photos. She's a genuine Cockney kid born wivvin the sarnd of the Bow Bells.'

Cleo was annoyed at being exploited like this. Anyone else would have mentioned it to her first. All Ant did was dig her in the ribs by way of telling her to go along with him. She gave the tourists one of her better smiles. Her brother spotted how impressed they were.

'Our Rosie is the most famous Cockney kid in London, what wiv her famous Cockney sparrer smile which most kids ain't got. Most Cockney kids ain't got enuff teef ter give a decent smile wiv. Most Cockney kids got teef like a row o' bombed houses.' He turned to Cleo. 'Go on, Rosie, give 'em your famous Cockney sparrer smile.'

Cleo could have kicked him where it really hurt but she smiled all the same. In response to urging from the tourists she crossed the street and stood next to the policeman who, to her, looked about seven feet tall in his helmet. Cleo chose not to speak to the constable, nor he to her. He was fed up of being photographed with tourists and snotty-nosed kids.

'As many photos as you like for a quid,' Ant was saying from behind a shielding hand. He didn't want the policeman to know he was party to an illegal commercial transaction. The cameras flashed for a full two minutes with Cleo, at one stage, having to hold the policeman's very reluctant hand. She wasn't too keen herself, owing to her problem with the law.

'Is Mister Churchill in?' she enquired, politely, just for something to say.

'You don't sound like any Cockney kid I've ever heard,' he muttered from the corner of his mouth. 'And no, he's not in ... and before you ask, I don't know where he is, neither. He don't let me in on his whereabouts.'

The Americans were considering an offer from Ant to show them around London where they could pose with his Cockney sparrer sister in front of Buckingham Palace, Big Ben, Nelson's Column and the statue of Eros; special price, two quid the lot. The tourists eventually declined his offer but thanked them both profusely and gave them each a pound. The policeman smiled through gritted teeth and refused the pound note he was offered, although he could have done with it. Ant followed the Americans down the street and said he'd take the policeman's pound and give it to him when he came off duty. His suggestion was rewarded with another pound note.

'I hope you do give it to him,' Cleo said after they'd waved goodbye to the departing tourists. 'Otherwise it's stealing.'

Ant looked at her and shook his head despairingly. 'So, you want me to get that nice copper into trouble, do you? Honestly, what d'you think Mister Churchill'd say if he saw a member of the public slipping one of his bodyguards a quid?'

'Well, you shouldn't have taken it off them.'

'They've got loads o' dosh,' he said. 'An' they'll go back home to America an' tell all their friends how they gave the Prime Minister's personal copper a quid, plus a quid each to two starvin' Cockney sparrers.'

'A quid each – is that what you charged them?'

'That's what they gave me, an' it'd be rude for me to argue with 'em.'

'Blimey, it's money for nothing down here. Is it like this all the time?'

'I wish it was, our young 'un. Mostly it's hard graft an' common sense, especially in the buildin' game.' He tapped a finger to his forehead. 'And you've got to keep your wits about you. Find out more than the bloke you're workin' for. That's how you get on.'

'Is that what you're doing?' Cleo asked.

'It's what I intend to do. I've signed on for night school. I'm doin' a six-month sandwich course in building construction just to find out what it's all about.'

As they walked across Parliament Square her gaze was transfixed by Big Ben and the ornate architecture of the Houses of Parliament. When all you've ever seen are pictures, the real thing becomes even more impressive. Then her thoughts turned to other things.

'Why did you call me Rosie to those people?'

He touched the side of his nose. 'Tell the buggers nowt.'

'If I'm going to have another name I'd prefer to be called Grace,' Cleo said, having mulled the name over on the train journey.

'Grace Kelly?'

'It's better than Cleopatra.'

'Actually,' said Ant, 'I've allus liked Cleo. It sort of suits you.' He thought for a while. 'What if I slip up an' call you Cleo instead of Grace – where will we be then?'

Cleo didn't know where they'd be. She just shrugged.

'Best stick to Cleo for the time being,' he advised. 'Nobody will be looking for you down here. Just keep your head down an' things'll work out.'

'What will I be doing down here?'

He put his arm around her shoulder and gave her a squeeze; the sort of squeeze her mother should have given her now and again, or even Horace if he'd had an ounce of decency in him.

'I've got no idea, our lass. First things first, that's what I always say. We'll get some grub then I'll take you to me digs. See if Stan can fix you up with a room.'

'Who's Stan?'

'He's me landlord. He's a Pole but he's all right.'

Stanislaus Pacholski was a former RAF corporal who had settled in London after the war and bought a rundown boarding house south of the river. Most of his clients were Irish construction workers, originally employed to put right the damage caused by the Luftwaffe and now finding work on the new roads being constructed in and around the capital. They left the house at seven each morning after a good breakfast of bacon, eggs, mushrooms and a fried slice. Stan would provide each man with clean sheets once a week and a packed lunch every working day except Saturday. Only a few returned before ten at night, most of them spent their evenings in the Crown and Anchor, just around the corner. The men slept four to a room and paid Stan two pounds ten shillings a week; which was approximately one-fifth of their wages. Some would send money home to Ireland, some would save anything up to five pounds a week, but most would have spent up well before pay day and be borrowing off Stan, who always obliged. He catered precisely to their needs, no more, no less. Occasional bouts of unruly drunkenness were dealt with by the men themselves, who placed a high value on a good lodge such as Stan's. It was almost seven in the evening when Ant turned up with his sister in tow.

'Hey up, Stan!'

Stan found Ant's Yorkshire greeting amusing; that's why Ant used it. Cleo had never heard him say it before.

'I've brought me sister to stay with me for a bit. D'you think you could make a bed up in that little room on t' top landing.'

Cleo smiled up at Stan, who coloured slightly.

'Er, I don't know. Is only small room for brushes and stuff.'

'I don't take up much room, Mister.'

'And she could be very useful,' added Ant, persuasively. 'She's ever so good at cleaning and cooking. You've allus said you need help.'

Up until now he'd said nothing to Cleo about cleaning and cooking. She pulled a face at him.

'You want her to work for me?' said Stan. 'But she is too young.'

'She's fourteen, nearly fifteen. She's left school,' lied Ant, much to his sister's dismay. He'd just added two years on to her age.

'She look very small for nearly fifteen.'

'She's from Yorkshire, we don't get much to eat up there. We're very much like Poles in that respect,' Ant pointed out.

Stan nodded, then studied Cleo carefully. 'She has run away from home.'

It wasn't even a question. Ant shrugged and nodded. 'Okay, so she's run away from home. If she'd stayed there the bugger would've killed her, that's why she ran away. Do you want to see her bruises?' he asked.

Cleo was hoping Stan would say no, as most of her bruises had gone. She was relieved when he said, 'It is not necessary. I believe you. But she cannot stay here for good or I will get into trouble with–'

He was wavering under Cleo's steady gaze even as he spoke.

'Thank you, Mister,' she said. 'My name's Cleo and I won't be a spot of bother.' She turned to Ant. 'He's a very kind man, isn't he?'

'Very kind indeed,' said Ant.

Stan followed them up the stairs, no doubt wondering what he'd let himself in for.

The Irish lodgers didn't question her right to be there, nor her right to a room of her own. In fact none of them expressed any curiosity at all as to where she'd come from; it was none of their business. Cleo helped Stan with the cooking and the shopping and she cleaned the house with such enthusiasm that Stan decided to pay her ten shillings a week on top of her free board. Within a week she had made herself indispensable. Cleo had learned one of the great secrets of a successful life.

Ant was working for a firm called Sharkey and Mullen, which specialised in sewer work. He laboured for a bricklayer called Chas Devlin who spent all of his time building brick manholes and grumbling about his bad back. Chas was always happy to sit back and offer advice to Ant who never turned down an opportunity to try his hand out with the brickie's trowel. After four months Ant reckoned he was nearly as good at laying bricks as the tradesman himself. 'It's all common sense, Cleo,' he said to her one evening. 'Once you've learned your bonds it's all plain sailing.'

'What are bonds?'

'It's the way yer lay bricks. There's English Bond and Flemish Bond and Double Flemish, an' headers an' stretchers an' frogs an' bits of bricks called king closers an' queen closers.'

'Sounds very complicated.'

'That's what they like you to think, but it's dead easy really, once you've got the knack of it.' He tapped the side of his head as he often did. 'Bullshit baffles brains, our lass. An' Chas Devlin's the biggest bullshitter of 'em all. He's off back to Ireland next month an' I'm gonna ask the gaffers if I can do some bricklayin'. They know I can do it.'

'Will you get proper man's wages?'

'I will if I can do the job. Dunt matter ter them if I'm fifteen or fifty. If I make a mess of it I'll be back on lad's money, but I'll not mess up. It's all cash in hand as well.'

'What does that mean?'

'It means the gover'ment dunt take nowt off me. We're on the lump. We're all supposed to pay our own tax at some time or other. Most of the lads go back to Ireland every so often an' come back usin' another name.'

Cleo hadn't a clue what he was talking about, but it sounded illegal, which was okay by her. All that stuff in court had been legal. It was apparently legal to beat kids up and lock them in cupboards while they nearly burned to death.

Her time at the lodgings was a happy time, happier even than the remand home she'd just left. The Irish lodgers treated her with humour and respect; occasionally paying her to scrape the heavy mud off their boots, or take a hard clothes brush to their donkey jackets, or wash their work clothes; and sometimes to write letters home for them, often explaining why so little money was being sent that week. Cleo disapproved of this and gave them her most censorious gaze, which made them feel guilty and often resulted in an extra pound or two, which had been earmarked for the Crown and Anchor, being sent home to a deserving wife or mother. Cleo accepted all their jobs and their money, and so long as she did the work asked of her by Stan, he didn't mind.

Stan was a creature of habit. At nine o'clock each morning, after he and Cleo had cleared away and washed the breakfast dishes, but before they had tidied the rooms, he would give her a pound note and send her to the shops for groceries.

'Take care. Is unsavoury neighbourhood,' he always warned.

She took care by sticking the note in her sock and taking it out when she got in the shop. The journey from the lodgings to the shop was pretty much all the fresh air she got. Ant had advised against going out too much in case a school board man was on the lookout for truants.

'It's school holidays in three weeks. You'll be okay for six or seven weeks then,' he'd said. 'After that we'll just have to think o' summat.'

Not having to worry for nearly two months was an eternity compared to the short span of her existence so far. Cleo made the journey to and from the shop with great care, often walking the other way when a policeman or someone looking like a board man came into sight. Although never having seen a board man meant her having to make many such diversions, and the half-hour round trip often took twice as long.

Cleo liked the streets of London. There was a decrepit grandeur about them. Everything seemed bigger and more solid than in the streets of Leeds; and the people didn't seem as friendly, which suited her down to the ground. Friendly people often turned out to be nosey people, asking: 'Why aren't you at school?' and 'Where are you from?' and 'Have you lived round here long?' There were mysterious faces with dark, hooded eyes and sharp, thin mouths which spoke foreign words as she hurried past them; and coloured faces ranging from light brown to jet black with the whitest teeth she had ever seen; mostly smiling, as if happy to be in the big city. In the distance she could hear the sound of river traffic and Cleo made up her mind to ask Ant to take her on a boat ride come the summer holidays, when it was safe. She had never been on a boat, except for an occasional stolen ride on an abandoned rowing boat in Roundhay Park lake back in Leeds; abandoned because the customers had overstayed their allotted time and had chosen not to pay the excess. There were many cheap ways for kids to enjoy themselves, especially if you had a brother like Ant.

During her second week in London two local children, a boy and a girl, had been watching her money-in-the-sock routine. They were roughly the same age as her and no doubt they could have pointed out the board man, had Cleo asked.

She was as happy as she'd ever been the following Monday morning. The summer sky was diamond bright and at the end of that week the school holidays would start, so her time for subterfuge was drawing to a close. Cleo was halfway to the shop when the two children stepped out of a doorway and blocked her path.

'Hello,' said the girl.

She was grubby-looking with threadbare clothes, jagged, mousy hair and an expressionless face. But there was no threat in her voice nor anything to suggest a problem, so Cleo smiled and said hello back to her.

'What's yer name?' asked the girl.

'Cleo, what's yours?'

The girl's expression turned ugly and unpleasant. 'What's it got ter do wiv you? Anyway, what sort of a name's Cleo?'

Cleo was taken aback and didn't answer. The boy grabbed her by the front of her dress and pushed her against a wall.

'She asked yer a question. Are yer bloody deaf or somefin'?'

'It's short for Cleopatra, if you must know,' Cleo was annoyed that he'd got it out of her so easily, but she could hardly breathe so she had no option. 'Let go, you're choking me.'

The boy let her go. His face creased into a nasty smirk.

'Cleopatra? Stupid name fer a stupid tart.'

'What school do yer go ter?' enquired the girl.

'What's it got to do with you?' Cleo muttered. After all she'd been through recently it would take a lot more than a couple of kids to trouble her.

'It might have a lot ter do wiv us,' said the girl.

'Can I get past, please?'

The boy held out his arms and pushed her backwards. He had close-set eyes, not much forehead between his eyebrows and his hairline, a pinched face that looked a lot older than his body and, like the girl, he was shabbily dressed and dirty.

'Give us yer pound note first,' he said. 'Then we might let yer go.'

'How did you...? I haven't got a pound note.'

'Liar!' The girl spat the word out, making Cleo jump. 'Yer've allus got a pound note ter go shoppin' wiv – it's in yer sock. We've been watchin' yer.'

'Is that what you are, then?' Cleo said. 'A couple of thieves.'

'Who're you callin' fieves?' snarled the girl. She contorted her face into an expression of ugly hatred and thrust it right into Cleo's.

Cleo looked away and decided to say nothing. Aggravating them wasn't a good idea.

'Yer talk bleedin' funny. Where yer from?' asked the boy. 'Timbucbloodytu?'

The girl cackled but Cleo didn't give them the satisfaction of a reply. *Never argue with idiots, Ant* had once told her. *It means you're as daft as them.*

'If yer don't give us yer quid yer ain't goin' nowhere,' the boy said.

'S'not my money,' Cleo blurted, worried now.

'Snot!' howled the girl. 'Is that where yer from? Snotland.'

Cleo spun on her heels and ran, gaining a few yards' start before they gave chase. She had scarcely rounded the corner at the end of the street when she ran straight into the arms of a policeman.

'Whoa!' he said.

Her pursuers stopped in their tracks a few yards away. The policeman looked at them through narrowed, suspicious eyes and held on to Cleo as she tried to pull away.

'What's goin' on?'

'Nuffin',' said the boy.

'Why aren't you lot at school?'

'Holidays.'

'School holidays don't start till Friday,' said the constable.

Silence from all three children.

It was Cleo's guess that the policeman was about to let them go with no more than a ticking off when the girl, who was much more spiteful than her friend, said, 'She wants lockin' up, she does. She's a bleedin' tea leaf.'

Cleo hadn't a clue what the girl was talking about.

'We seen her rob a dear old lady, didn't we, Bernard?'

Bernard nodded, uncertainly.

'I didn't rob anyone,' Cleo protested. 'They were trying to rob me.'

'Liar!' snarled the girl. 'I bet if yer search her she's got a pound note stuck inside her sock. That's where she put it when she robbed it off the dear old lady.'

'I did not!'

The policeman shook his head. Cleo looked a lot more trustworthy than her two accusers, who were backing away now.

'Here,' he called out. 'You two stay where you are until I sort this out.'

'Nuffin' ter sort out,' shouted the girl. 'She's a bleedin' tea leaf. Her name's Cleopatra an' she comes from Snotland.'

The constable was holding on to Cleo as the boy and girl ran off, laughing.

'All right, young lady,' he sighed. 'Let's have a look inside your sock.'

Cleo had no option other than to take out the pound note and show it to him. 'I was only goin' to the shops, mister,' she said. 'I haven't done anything wrong. I didn't steal it or anything.'

The policeman took the pound note and examined it as though it might contain some incriminating evidence, such as a dear old lady's blood. Satisfied that it was just an ordinary banknote he gave it back to her.

'It's money for shopping,' Cleo explained. 'I didn't steal it off an old lady or anything. I go every day about this time and I always stick my money in my sock. Them kids must have seen me do it.'

'Every day, eh?'

Cleo could have kicked herself for being so stupid as to admit to going shopping when she should have been at school. The policeman spoke to the top of her head.

'I think I'd like to know who you are and where you live.'

Her heart sank. Giving away information like that would be bad for both her and her brother. Very bad indeed. She racked her brains trying to think of a local street name, but nothing came to mind.

'My name's Mary,' she said, looking at her shoes so he couldn't spot the lie in her eyes, 'and I live at Seventeen Baxter Terrace.'

Baxter Terrace was in Leeds but Cleo hoped the policeman wouldn't know that.

'Hmmm ... Mary,' he mused, with a rub of his chin. 'I didn't think it'd be Cleopatra. Baxter Terrace, eh ... where's Baxter Terrace?'

Still looking down, Cleo waved a limp hand in the direction she'd come. Had this been Ant he'd have got away with it, but she was useless at lying.

'How long have you lived on Baxter Terrace?'

She hesitated, things were getting complicated. 'All my life,' she said.

'That long eh? Maybe it'd be best if you and me take a walk to this Baxter Terrace – where ever it is – and find out who you belong to.'

Thus it was that, only two weeks after arriving in the capital and the freedom it had offered her, Cleo found herself heading back to Leeds, and captivity.

Stan became increasingly worried when Cleo didn't arrive back at the time she usually did, and at lunchtime he took a bus to the site where Ant was working. The two of them searched all the streets around the lodging house until, in the late afternoon, Stan placed a decisive hand on Ant's shoulder.

'We have to tell police.'

'I know,' agreed Ant, whose worry for his sister far outweighed his need for self-preservation. 'Might as well get it over with.'

She was coming down a flight of stairs, accompanied by a policeman as Ant and Stan entered the station. Her brother was opening his mouth to greet her when Cleo stuck a thumb up, mimed 'I'm okay' without actually looking at him, and walked past with no sign of recognition. The policeman had a tight grip on her arm as he marched her to the front desk where a sergeant commenced taking down her details. A passing WPC told Ant and Stan to sit down on a bench to await their turn.

'He won't be long,' she assured them.

Cleo put her hands behind her back where only Ant and Stan could see them and jabbed her thumb at the door, signalling them to go. Her brother ignored this. He needed to know what was happening. The sergeant was asking her questions but Cleo was saying nothing.

'Her name's Cleopatra Kelly, Sergeant,' said the constable. 'She's escaped custody in Leeds a couple of weeks ago. That's as much as we know. She won't tell us where she's been in the meantime. It's taken me God knows how long to find out who she is. If I hadn't have had this brainwave about her name being Cleopatra and her being from up north we'd still be none the wiser.'

'Brainwave eh?' said the sergeant. 'Not many of them in this station. We'll have to see about a medal for you. Although I don't think they hand out medals for workin' out the obvious.'

'Cleopatra's not an obvious name, Sarge,' protested the arresting officer.

'It wasn't much of a brainwave, mister,' said Cleo. 'One of the other kids told him my name.'

The sergeant smiled at her, pleased to have her on his side.

'I prefer to be called Cleo,' she went on, 'and I never did anything wrong. I keep getting locked up for doing nothing wrong. I'm getting a bit fed up of it, to tell you the truth.'

'And are you going to tell us the truth about where you've been staying for the last two weeks and how you got down here from Leeds?' asked the sergeant.

'No, mister, I'm not – because you can't get me into any more trouble than I'm in already. And I've never done anything wrong to anybody.' Cleo was acquiring a new-found confidence in the face of authority. They would call it cheek.

The desk sergeant stared at her, and Cleo returned his gaze with a soulful smile. For two pennies he'd have let her go there and then; he hadn't joined the force to lock up kids like her. He glared at the constable who had put him into this predicament, then he looked down at his ledger.

'I'm sorry, love,' he sighed, more to his ledger than to her. 'We'll have to keep you overnight – them's the rules, such as they are. Someone's coming down from Leeds in the morning to collect you.'

Behind her back, Cleo's thumb was jabbing urgently at the door. She was becoming worried that Ant might do something stupid which would get him locked up and sent back to Leeds as well; not to mention the trouble Stan might get into. The pair of them looked on, helplessly, as Cleo was taken past them through a door.

'Right, what can I do for you gents?' enquired the sergeant.

Two pairs of eyes were still fixed on the heavy door which was being ominously locked behind her.

'Er, excuse me?' said the sergeant.

Stan was the first to look at the policeman. He got to his feet, nudging Ant with his elbow as he did so.

'We've come to report a lost dog,' said Ant.

The sergeant let out a sigh which seemed never ending. 'We don't do lost dogs here, sir. We don't do lost cats, horses, mice or buffaloes. Why don't you try the RSPCA?'

Ant stared at the policeman, then at the door through which his sister had just been taken out of his life, and he couldn't believe how much it hurt him. Tears stood in his eyes.

'Are you all right, lad?' the policeman asked, guilty that his flippancy might have caused the young man to become upset.

'He love his dog very much,' explained Stan. Then to Ant he said, 'Come, we go to SRPCA.'

'RSPCA,' corrected the sergeant. 'It's in Bascombe Street, turn left out of the door, second on your left.'

'Thank you,' said Stan, leading Ant into the street. They walked back, slowly, to Stan's lodging house where Cleo had spent the two happiest weeks of her life. Suddenly Ant stopped in his tracks. Stan had taken another two paces before he stopped and looked back at the mortified face of his young lodger.

'What is the matter?' he asked.

'What date is it today?'

Stan thought for a second. 'Seventeenth of July ... why do you ask?'

'It's her birthday,' said Ant. There were tears both in his eyes and in his voice. 'She's thirteen today.'

Chapter Four

Out of the one hundred and thirty-one inmates at Whitley Grange Girls' Home only about a quarter of them deserved to be there. The others were either misfits or children of inadequate parents or abused former residents of children's homes, sent there for being disruptive. In the main the girls were victims rather than criminals; victims of a system that had neither the knowledge nor the willingness to put right the obvious wrongs. Unfortunately, most girls, upon being so unjustly stigmatised, decided to act in accordance with the label that society had stuck on them, and if they weren't delinquents when they entered the home they most certainly were when they left.

Some were simply mentally disabled kids who had been dumped by parents who couldn't be bothered, and through a series of mishaps and misunderstandings had ended up in a reformatory. Beryl Lister, better known as Blister, was one such girl. The only thing she and Cleo had in common was arson. But Blister was a genuine arsonist who had set fire to the special school her parents had dumped her in.

'D'yer smoke?' were the first words she said to Cleo. She was an enormous girl with a cleft palate, which affected her speech. ''Cos I've gorra light,' she added.

She struck a match and Cleo wondered what the girl was talking about. Maybe it was leading up to some sort of strange induction ritual. One of the other girls brushed past her shoulder and knocked the flickering match to the floor.

'She's not s'posed ter have bloody matches. She'll set the bloody place on fire.' Then to Lister she said, 'If yer've got any more, give us 'em, Blister!'

Blister backed away, sullenly.

'I said, give us 'em!'

There was a rush of girls from behind Cleo. They dragged Blister to the floor, pummelling her, searching her pockets and pulling off her shoes and her socks. They even searched her navy blue knickers with some distaste before throwing them out of the window. One of the girls looked up at Cleo and explained:

'She set fire to her bed last week. She'd burn the bloody place down if we let her ... and us in it.'

'There's no need to hit her.'

'You don't know Blister like we do.'

A half-empty box of matches was found somewhere on Blister's person and the searchers left her shoeless, sockless and knickerless on the floor, sobbing to herself. Cleo knelt beside her.

'Are you okay?' she asked.

'Leave Fat Freak alone!'

Cleo looked up and saw Dobbs for the first time. She was at the far end of the dormitory, shouting at her. Dobbs was a tall girl of around fifteen with mean eyes and a turned-down mouth like a haddock's (and matching breath as Cleo found out later). She stood in the company of three equally unpleasant-looking girls.

'I was just seeing if she was all right,' Cleo said.

'Course she's not all right, she's bloody barmy. I know one thing, she shouldn't be in here wi' us. We're not safe wi' nutters like that around. What's yer name, any road?'

'Cleo Kelly.'

'Cleo ... that's a daft name. What's it short for?'

'Nothing. It's just Cleo.'

'What yer in for?'

After witnessing the trouble Blister was in for setting fire to things, Cleo decided on discretion. 'Stealing,' she said, 'and absconding from court.'

'Absconding?' Dobbs seemed impressed. 'Where d'yer abscond ter?'

'London.'

This earned her a nod of approval from Dobbs.

'I once went ter London. Big Ben's a big bugger innit?'

'Yes,' agreed Cleo. 'It's very big.'

'Very big? I'll say it's very big. It's only the biggest bloody clock in the world,' said Dobbs to those around her. 'Hey!' she called out to Cleo. 'Give Fat Freak a kick from me, I can't be bothered comin' down there.'

Cleo looked down at the girl cowering at her feet, then back at the four girls at the far end of the room. This was obviously one of the deciding moments in her life. It seemed that kicking Blister would get her in with the girls who mattered, and make her life easy. Then she remembered how Horace used to kick her for no reason. Horace the coward.

She held out a hand and helped the big girl to her feet. It was more of a symbolic gesture than of any physical assistance, such was Blister's size.

'You shouldn't muck about with matches,' Cleo said, quietly. 'It's not worth it.'

'Okay.'

'What's your real name?' Cleo asked. She'd been called enough stupid names in her time to know the hurt a nickname could cause.

Blister gave her a smile that displayed a mixture of gums and erratic teeth, wedged in at all angles. 'Blister,' she said. 'Everybody calls me Blister.'

'Right,' Cleo said. Behind her new friend she could see Dobbs and her cronies muttering to each other and Cleo knew she'd booked a difficult ride for herself. But it was exactly what Ant would have done, so she felt some solace in that. 'I'll call you Blister then.'

Blister was big, clumsy, bespectacled and fourteen. She occupied the bed next to Cleo in the Wetherby Wing dormitory, where she annoyed everyone within earshot with her snoring, flatulence and mumbling in her sleep. She went to lessons in the special class for girls of so-called sub-normal intelligence, whereas Cleo attended ordinary class and came to be regarded as one of the brightest girls there, which wasn't the accolade it sounds. So, for different reasons, Blister and Cleo were picked on. One for being stupid and annoying, and the other for being the stupid and annoying girl's friend. Backward girls without friends tended not to last long before they withered under the constant taunting, and degenerated into gibbering wrecks and got sent to the loony bin – the last outpost on the road to isolation and despair. But with Cleo being her friend it made the job of getting rid of Blister much harder, so the girls stepped up their efforts; especially Dobbs and her three stooges.

The Home consisted of a main building which had once housed a family of some wealth and position, and four prefabricated dormitory blocks which were called wings. In the main building were the classrooms, workshops, dining rooms, kitchens and staff accommodation. The grounds were extensive and well tended, but no perimeter walls held the girls in. They wore no identifying uniform and were free to wander abroad between certain hours but subject to harsh punishment if they didn't attend classes, work or roll-call. It would have been considered a strict regime by any normal standards but most of the girls were used to worse; much worse. The home was run by a governor and fifteen house parents, seven of whom were also teachers. They were divided into five classes, strictly in accordance with age – ability was of no account; with the exception of the girls in the special class. A week or two in the special class was also used as a punishment for any girl who committed a minor misdemeanour. The stigma this inflicted on the permanent special-class girls, such as Blister, would have been unbearable if they'd had more awareness, but most of them dumbly accepted their lot in life almost from birth. The world looked down on them and that was that. However, there was a corner of Blister's brain that wasn't sub-normal – quite the opposite in fact. Blister, who hadn't the motor skills to put pen to paper with any degree of success was a genius at mental arithmetic.

Some of the girls who had witnessed what they called her 'party tricks', simply regarded her as a freak. The teachers had either failed to spot her talent or simply weren't interested. Cleo had been there several weeks before she became aware of it.

In the dormitory, she and Blister shared a table with two other girls, on which they did their homework, read books, played games or wrote letters home (in Cleo's case to Mr Foxcroft who would send them on to her brother).

Ant would write back to the newsagent, whom Cleo managed to visit about once a month. Their letters weren't censored as they might have been in other institutions, but Ant took no chances. Cleo missed him and wished he'd take a risk and come up to see her; but if they caught him they'd probably lock him up for his part in her escape, if not for stabbing Horace.

He told her to keep her head down and keep out of trouble. He was working as a bricklayer in his own right and was on man's money and bonuses. Every month he sent her a pound note which supplemented her pocket money of a shilling a week – well earned for sweeping all the outside footpaths twice a week. Apart from a gaberdine raincoat, supplied by the Home, their clothes were supposed to be the responsibility of parents or guardians. Cleo bought her own.

She was sitting at the table, muttering to herself

how anyone could be expected to work out the square root of a stupid number like 7,569, when Blister said, 'Eighty-seven.'

Cleo looked at her, then purely out of curiosity, did the multiplication of these two numbers, and stared at the result with some disbelief. Blister was scrawling an illegible letter to her parents.

'How did you do that?' Cleo asked.

Blister shrugged and continued with her writing. 'Don't know,' she said.

''Cos she's a bloody freak!' said a girl sitting opposite.

'I wish I was a freak,' Cleo said. 'I'd be able to do my homework a lot faster.' She looked at Blister who had returned to her letter. Her tongue was poking out of the corner of her mouth in intense concentration. 'Blister,' Cleo asked. 'What's forty-seven times ninety-three?'

'Four thousand three hundred and seventy-one.'

The answer came almost before Cleo had finished asking the question. Blister didn't even look up. Cleo did the multiplication, as did the girl opposite.

'She's wrong,' said the girl.

'No she isn't,' said Cleo.

The girl went back to her calculation and after several minutes she grudgingly conceded that Blister might be right. 'She's a bloody freak,' the girl muttered, and got up to leave.

Good teachers could get jobs anywhere and Whitley Grange provided a challenge that most of them didn't need. The live-in house parent aspect of the job appealed to some but not to many; consequently the standard of teaching wasn't high. Which was a pity because some of the girls had potential that would never be realised.

For months Cleo had watched, helplessly, as Blister became the butt of cruel jokes and comments – her too for being the big girl's friend. But Cleo's friendship with her only served to slow the inevitable decline in Blister's spirit at the hands of Dobbs and her stooges. The autumn of 1954 turned to winter, and winter to the spring of 1955, by which time the tide of Blister's flagging spirits was at its lowest ebb.

For Cleo, the time at the Home wasn't too bad. Ant's letters cheered her up, as did his pound notes. But she'd have swapped them all for just one glimpse of his cheeky smile. He'd completed his building course and was doing well as a bricklayer. Cleo got on with her own lessons because she was given no option and gradually realised that she was quite clever; and better still, she enjoyed learning. She made no close friends, other than Blister, but most of the girls tolerated her and drew her into any circle which didn't include Dobbs. Cleo could put up with trouble from the nasty minority, mainly Dobbs's pals. Intellectually they weren't much in advance of Blister and it was easy to turn their own jibes against them and make them the butt of their own humour. Eventually they gave up on her, but not on Blister.

Nasty remarks and painful slaps were part of the big girl's daily life. She was clinging to what remained of her sanity a lot longer than the bullies had anticipated; which annoyed them. The rest of the girls were either against her or remained neutral. Everybody needs somebody, so the song goes, and Cleo was Blister's somebody. She'd once had five desolate days of having no hope and no one to turn to, so she had an inkling of how Blister felt. But Cleo could only offer friendship and sympathy; protection was what Blister really needed.

For all her shortcomings she had the most generous spirit of any person Cleo had ever met. When she told Blister the story of her time in the bogey hole the big girl's face crumpled with pity and she took Cleo in her arms and squeezed her so hard she could hardly breathe. Cleo escaped her clutches with as much tact as she could manage and then had to comfort Blister because she was weeping copiously on Cleo's behalf. As if she didn't have enough troubles of her own.

One of the ploys of Dobbs and her stooges was to follow Blister to the lavatory then lock her in with a broomstick jammed through the door handle. This caused her to miss lessons and roll-calls; consequently being punished for it. Eventually, Blister became too scared to go to the lavatory and started wetting herself and, on one occasion, even worse; much to the disgust of the staff and the amusement of the girls.

Miss Phelps seemed to be one of the more approachable teachers. One day, after class, Cleo stepped from the orderly line of departing girls to have a word on Blister's behalf.

'Excuse me miss, can I say something to you?'

'What's the problem, Kelly?'

There wasn't much friendship in the teacher's voice. She knew that the girls would take advantage of any sign of weakness. Friendship was considered a weakness.

'I haven't got a problem, miss. It's Blis ... er, Beryl Lister, miss.'

'Lister?'

'Yes, miss.'

'Has she been bothering you?'

'No, miss, she never bothers me. She never bothers anyone, doesn't Lister.'

The teacher arched her eyebrow. It was a thin, pencil line just above where her real one had been plucked out and it gave her face an unnatural look. Why anyone bothered to do this had always baffled Cleo.

'Really?' Miss Phelps said. 'You do surprise me. It seems you're one of the few people here who hasn't had trouble with Lister.'

'She's very nice when you get to know her, miss. But I'm very worried about her.'

'In what way?'

'She's forever being bullied by the other girls and she seems to be getting very sad.'

'Bullied?' The teacher seemed surprised.

'Yes, miss. They lock her in the toilet and things.'

'She's a very big girl to be the victim of bullying.'

'I know she is, miss, but she gets bullied all the time. It makes her cry, miss.'

Miss Phelps had been filling her briefcase with books during the conversation. 'I'll look into it,

Kelly,' she said, 'but I must say it's the exact opposite of everything I've heard about the girl up until now.'

'Maybe you shouldn't believe all you hear, especially in this place, miss.'

The teacher stopped what she was doing and glared down at Cleo, who had obviously overstepped the line. Questioning authority was not allowed in this place. Without blind obedience the system would collapse. Cleo had already spotted her mistake, which she quickly put right.

'I'm not trying to be cheeky, miss – it's just that the girls in this place don't always tell the truth. And I think someone must be telling lies about Lister, miss.'

The teacher's frown relaxed. The mask of authority she wore was simply that, a mask; underneath it she was softer than most (or so Cleo thought at the time).

'Maybe you're right,' she said.

Cleo saw the chink in the woman's armour and decided to get everything in while she had her attention. 'Did you know Beryl Lister's very clever with sums, miss?'

Miss Phelps was struggling to fasten a strap on her bulging briefcase. 'Damn this thing! ... what? ... I believe she has some unusual ability, yes.'

'Oh,' Cleo said. 'I didn't think anyone knew, miss ... with them not bothering about it.'

'We know most things about you lot.' The teacher paused in her efforts and regarded Cleo, quizzically. 'I know enough about you to make me wonder why you're in here, Kelly. You're much more of a mystery to me than Lister is.'

'Me and Beryl Lister are very much alike in some ways, miss.'

'Are you now, in what way?'

'We both get picked on and we never get any visitors. Only I don't get picked on anywhere near as much as Lister, miss.' Cleo waited for the teacher to comment, but when nothing seemed forthcoming she continued: 'It just seems a shame she's in the special class, miss, when she's so much better at arithmetic than anyone in the school. Don't you think so?'

Miss Phelps shook her head. 'It's not quite as simple as that, Kelly. Apparently it's such an isolated talent that it's doubtful it can be put to good use ... more's the pity, I suppose. I'll look into the bullying thing. Although God knows what I can do about it ... there!' She muttered most of the last sentence to herself as she managed to fasten the strap with an exasperated pull.

'Thank you, miss,' Cleo said. 'Oh, and by the way, miss,' Cleo called out after the departing teacher. 'I'm in here for something I didn't do.'

It probably wasn't the first time Miss Phelps had heard that from a girl but Cleo didn't think it would do any harm for her to hear it again. Whether or not she believed it was up to her.

Chapter Five

'What's four hundred and twenty-two times seventeen?' It was Dobbs asking the question.

'S ... seven thousand ... one hundred and s ... seventy-four.' Blister could scarcely get the answer out for sobbing. She was standing on a table in her bare feet.

'Wrong,' said Dobbs.

'I bet she isn't,' Cleo called out. She was being held down by two of the three stooges.

'Who the 'ell asked you?' snapped Dobbs.

'Ouch!' said Cleo.

The stooges were hurting her arms. Cleo threw out a challenge.

'I bet you a bob she's right.'

Not taking a bet was a sign of weakness among the girls. The stooges relaxed their grip and looked at their leader, who looked at Cleo and snarled, 'Let's see yer money.'

Cleo pulled one of her arms free and took a shilling coin from her cardigan pocket. 'There!' She slammed it down on the table and with a challenge in her voice, said, 'Let's see yours.'

Her idea was to give Blister some respite. Maybe even give her an opportunity to jump down off the table and run away. But to take such an opportunity you need presence of mind, and Blister's mind wasn't exactly present.

Dobbs turned to one of her gang. 'Put a bob on

t' table,' she ordered. The girl went through her pockets and came up with a sixpence, a threepenny bit and a penny, which she laid on the table saying. 'That's all I've got.'

'That's tuppence short,' Cleo said. 'The bet's off, you can get down, Blister.'

Cleo knew she was clutching at straws but it was worth a go.

'Stay where you are, Fat Freak!' roared Dobbs, as Blister made to get down.

Dobbs took two pennies out of her own pocket and laid them beside the stooge's tenpence.

'The bet's on,' she said.

Every time Blister got a question wrong Dobbs stubbed a cigarette on her foot. No one was checking her answers, Dobbs was the only adjudicator. There were three burns on the big girl's left foot and she was whimpering in distress and pain. Her chubby face seemed to have collapsed like last night's party balloon and was damp with tears. Most of the girls in the dormitory were looking on silently; not approving but unwilling, or too plain scared, to intervene. They all thought Blister was a nuisance and they had all teased and taunted her at some time, in the hope she might one day be taken off their hands and put where she belonged – in a loony bin. But they knew she didn't deserve this. Dobbs was a big girl with a violent and sadistic streak that none of them could match; in fact most of the girls thought Dobbs belonged in a loony bin as well. Some of them might have tried to stop it but one look at Cleo's bloodied mouth put them off. That's what she'd got for her efforts. Dobbs relit her cigarette and asked for a pencil and paper.

'What did you say the answer was, Fat Freak?'

'Seven thousand one hundred and ... s ... seventy-four.'

Blister was wetting herself with fear. Urine ran down her left leg and on to the foot scarred with cigarette burns.

'Hey!' screamed Dobbs. 'Don't go pissin' on yer left foot, Fat Freak. That's foot's my property till I say different.' She took a deep drag on the cigarette, quickly scribbled some numbers down on the paper then showed it to one of her stooges, who nodded.

'Wrong,' said Dobbs, pocketing all the money. She stubbed the cigarette out on Blister's foot, causing her to howl with pain once again.

'You're a liar and a cheat!' Cleo shouted. 'And a *coward*. You're only brave when you've got your daft pals with you.'

Dobbs went pale with anger and took a step towards her. She was a lot taller than Cleo and a good two stones heavier.

'Fancy yer chances, do yer?'

Cleo didn't fancy her chances one bit, fighting wasn't her strong suit. She tried pouring scorn on Dobbs instead.

'Trust a coward not to pick on someone their own size.'

Being beaten up by Dobbs wouldn't have helped anyone, least of all her. Maybe that made her a coward as well.

'How about the Fat Freak?' Dobbs sneered. 'Is she big enough?'

Cleo said nothing, but it seemed she'd

unwittingly challenged Dobbs on Blister's behalf. She looked up at her friend, half hoping the worm might turn, but the cowed and frightened look on Blister's face told her otherwise.

Dobbs pulled at one of her ankles, bringing Blister crashing from the table. As she lay on the floor Dobbs swung a kick at her stomach causing her to curl up in agony. Cleo felt sick with fear for her friend and tried to pull herself free so she could somehow help her.

'Right, Fat Freak,' snarled Dobbs. 'Gerrup an' fight.'

Blister remained in a ball, distressed and blubbing. Dobbs kicked her, viciously, again and again. The other girls in the dormitory turned their heads away and someone called out, anonymously, 'Leave her alone, Dobbsy.'

Cleo was trying to get to her friend but was held back by Dobbs's sniggering stooges. The bell rang for evening roll-call which meant they all had to get there on the double, or else. Dobbs was giving Blister a couple of final kicks as Cleo was being frogmarched out by the stooges, forced to leave her friend in a sobbing heap on the floor. It was the last memory Cleo had of Blister. She never saw her friend alive again.

Roll-call was always held in the school gymnasium at 6 pm. The governor, Mr Forrester (known to the girls as Bushy because of his facial hair), usually attended. The register would be read out by one of the house parents and any girl not answering first time without a good excuse would be considered absent without permission; a serious offence.

Generally speaking this was the only contact the governor had with the girls on a day-to-day basis. Because punishments were always sanctioned by him he was held in some fear and had decided that this fear was best maintained by remaining distant, unapproachable, unpleasant and stone-faced.

The name Lister was being called out when one of the girls shouted, 'Fire!' The governor got to his feet as the girls surged towards the window. Dense clouds of black smoke were billowing past; they could smell it from inside.

'Remain where you are,' shouted Bushy. Then to the woman calling the register he said, 'Stay with them.' He stepped down from the podium, told someone to phone the fire brigade and motioned the other staff members to follow him outside.

The very nature of the girls made it impossible for just one adult to control the curiosity of the 126 who had made it to the roll-call (the others being either sick or in detention) and had packed the gym to capacity. The ones at the front, furthest from the doors, began to surreptitiously edge backwards, crushing those at the back, until the latter had no option but to open the doors and retreat outside; happy in the knowledge that they couldn't be punished for self-preservation. Not even Bushy could blame them for that.

By the time Cleo got outside, the Wetherby Wing was ablaze from end to end and no one was making any attempt to put out the fire; it would have been useless. Cleo ran to where Miss Phelps was standing.

'Blister's in there, miss!' She was screaming in panic.

'Who?'

'Beryl Lister ... she's in there.'

'Prob'ly her what started it,' chortled Dobbs, who was standing close by.

Cleo flew at her, knocking her to the ground and punching wildly at Dobbs's face until she was dragged off, kicking and screaming, by members of staff. Dobbs lay there with blood pouring from her nose and mouth. Cleo was completely out of control, calling Dobbs a bloody murderer.

'If she dies it's you who murdered her. I hope they bloody well hang you!'

Dobbs blanched as such a possibility struck home. The fact that they didn't hang girls of her age didn't immediately register with her.

Windows began to explode, sending shards of glass shattering outwards and spraying across the tarmac towards them.

'Get back, everybody!' Bushy shouted. 'Someone get those two into the detention room. I'll deal with them later.'

'Blister's in there, sir!' Cleo screamed. 'Somebody do something!'

The authority on the governor's face crumbled. 'Are you sure, girl?'

'I, I ... I think so, sir.' Cleo was stammering now, still upset, but realising that she might be wrong and that Blister might have set fire to the place and run away. Please let it be the case, Cleo thought. Please let Blister be okay.

'Let her be,' said the governor to the woman holding on to her. 'Come here, girl. Tell me what you know. Is anyone in there or not?'

'Beryl Lister was there when we left,' Cleo sobbed. 'Dobbs had been kicking her, sir. She was lying on the floor, sir.'

'Oh shit! What a mess!' The governor turned to the girls. 'I want everyone to search the grounds for Lister. No one is to leave the grounds. Do you hear me?'

There was a desultory, 'Yes' from the girls who would much rather watch the fire than look for Lister. They moved off in small groups with no enthusiasm for the search which took them away from the excitement of watching the Wetherby Wing burning down. A clanging bell signalled the arrival of the first of three fire engines. Cleo didn't move to join the search, somehow she knew exactly where her friend was.

And she was right.

They slept in the gymnasium that night. It was unusually quiet, apart from Cleo's crying until the early hours. Dobbs was confined in the detention room; mainly to keep the two of them apart until the truth was known. Blister's body had been found in the charred ruins of Wetherby Wing. It was burned beyond recognition. The police were hovering around but not asking too many questions until the fire investigator's report was finalised. At the moment the dead girl was the main suspect, which suited the governor.

Cleo was off her head for a while; condemning Dobbs as a bully and a killer. Dobbs was everything in her life that Horace had been. Maybe she was venting her hatred of her stepfather on Dobbs, but she certainly didn't care who knew what she thought of her; to the extent of her becoming a potential embarrassment to the Home. She was called to the governor's office before lessons the following day. Miss Phelps was there too, sitting at the side of the governor's desk. Cleo walked in and stood smartly, as was required of her.

'I asked Miss Phelps to come along because she knows something of the history between you and Beryl Lister,' said the governor.

It was the first time Cleo had heard anyone in authority call a girl by her first name. Maybe that was a privilege accorded only to the dead. She remained silent, as she hadn't been asked to speak, yet.

'You were friends, were you not?' he went on.

'Yes, sir.'

'And you called her Blister.'

'Yes, sir,' Cleo said. 'Everybody called her Blister.' Then Dobbs came to her mind. 'Well, nearly everybody, sir.'

'As far as we can ascertain,' said the governor, 'your friend was the butt of a silly practical joke. Something to do with her unusual ability with mental arithmetic. Do you understand this?'

'Yes, sir.'

'Good.'

Bushy seemed relieved that Cleo wasn't proving stubborn or stupid. He was a morose-looking man with small eyes lost under heavy eyebrows, a wiry moustache and beard that began high up his cheeks and was evenly trimmed to form a dense rim around his lower face, with a sharp nose poking through the middle of it all; like a rat looking through a lavatory brush, Cleo thought. What she didn't know at the time was that if the truth came out, that Lister had been a victim of persistent bullying, it would reflect poorly on the staff, not least the governor; and he was much more interested in his own career than the welfare of the girls. The death of a girl as inadequate as Blister was unfortunate, but hardly enough to merit an enquiry.

'So,' he said, leaning forward on his desk, 'if and when the police ask you what happened, that's what you will say. That the girls had been having a bit of a joke with Beryl Lister and maybe she'd taken it the wrong way.'

'She was being bullied, sir.' Cleo was unaware of the problem she was causing him. 'Dobbs had been stubbing cigarettes out on Blister's bare feet. It was a very cruel thing to do ... sir.'

Bushy gave an exasperated sigh and sat back in his chair; then he glanced across at Miss Phelps as if for inspiration. Nothing was forthcoming.

'Now look, Kelly,' he said. 'With you being Beryl's friend I must commend your loyalty to her. Loyalty to a friend is an excellent quality. But for you to go around accusing Dobbs of murder is ... well, I'd say it's taking things a little too far, wouldn't you? I would suggest less hysteria and more common sense.'

Hysteria? Cleo thought she was being surprisingly calm and reasonable under the circumstances.

'I don't know what to say, sir,' she said. 'Dobbs pulled Blister off the table and started kicking her; then the bell went for roll-call and that's the last I saw of her.'

'Kelly, how do you think the fire started?' enquired Miss Phelps.

'I don't know, miss.'

'Oh, I think you do.'

Cleo thought for a long minute as she tried to think of a reason that didn't implicate Blister in the fire. She couldn't. 'Well, I imagine she started it herself,' she conceded. Then added, 'But if she did, it's only because she was so upset with all the cruel bullying that's been going on. I did tell you about it, miss.'

Bushy looked daggers at Miss Phelps, then he drummed his fingers on the desk and asked, 'Was it just Dobbs who did the bullying?'

'No, sir. Most of the girls picked on her ... but Dobbs was the worst. Do you think she committed suicide, sir?'

The governor fixed her with a stare. 'I don't suppose we'll ever know, Kelly.' Cleo noticed she wasn't on first-name terms with him, unlike Blister.

Then Miss Phelps said, 'You have to understand, Kelly, that girls such as Dobbs have different values. What you see as bullying, Dobbs sees as horseplay.'

'Yes, miss.'

'She has the occasional psychotic episode, which is only to be expected. Most of the girls here have problems.'

'I suppose so, miss,' Cleo conceded, uncertainly.

To her, the term 'psychotic episode' sounded a bit too intellectual for Dobbs, who was just a thick bully. Bushy's eyes glared at her from way behind his eyebrows and Cleo still hadn't a clue why she was there. She didn't know she was being coerced into changing her damaging story.

Miss Phelps pressed her point home. 'Take your friend, Beryl, for example. No doubt she seemed a simple and innocent girl to you ... perhaps a kind and gentle girl.'

'Oh, she was when you got to know her, miss ... ever so kind and gentle.'

'I'm sure she was,' said Miss Phelps, not unkindly. 'But in point of fact, Beryl Lister was a dangerous arsonist. This is a sad truth we cannot overlook.' She paused and leaned over to her, challenging her, 'Can we, Kelly?'

'No, miss.'

The governor nodded his agreement and eagerly picked up the thread of Miss Phelps's new approach. 'We're lucky no one else got hurt in the fire,' he said. 'Otherwise, your friend Beryl might have been remembered as a killer. You wouldn't want that, would you?'

'Oh no, sir, I definitely wouldn't want that.'

'So, do we understand each other?'

'I think so, sir.'

'You only think so?'

'No, sir ... I mean, yes sir, I understand.'

Actually, Cleo didn't understand, but he was a figure of high authority and she didn't want him to think she was stupid. For her to have suspected their motive would have meant her genuinely believing them to be dishonest and self-serving. After all the rubbish that had been thrown at her by people in authority she should have seen straight through them, but she didn't, she trusted them. The only excuse she could offer for such stupidity was that she was only thirteen.

The governor glanced upwards for a second and drew his hands together as though offering up his thanksgiving that at last he'd got through to this dense girl. He drummed the tips of his fingers together as he spoke and his words dripped out like treacle:

'Of course Dobbs will be punished for horse-play and we should punish you for fighting, but under the circumstances I think we can overlook that.' He added the last bit with what he hoped was a kindly twinkle in his eye.

'Thank you, sir,' Cleo was fingering her swollen lip as she spoke; which made her think of Dobbs. 'But Dobbs was definitely bullying Blister. It wasn't horseplay, sir.'

Bushy exploded. 'Oh Jesus Bloody Christ! Save me from stupid children!'

Miss Phelps stepped in, quickly and calmly. 'Kelly, you remember I said we know most things about you girls?'

'Yes, miss.'

'Well,' she said, 'and this doesn't go beyond these four walls, Kelly.'

'No, miss.'

'Dobbs had a dreadful childhood,' she said. 'She inherited her nasty ways from a very abusive stepfather and uncaring mother who treated her like an animal. We have to try and make allowances for girls who come from less fortunate circumstances than ourselves. When you leave here you'll go home to loving parents; Dobbs has no one. That's why she's like she is.'

Cleo looked at her, dumbfounded.

'Do you understand?'

'Um, er...'

'You see,' said Bushy, giving Cleo one last try, 'we take a lot of the time and trouble to check the background of the girls so we can act in their best interests.'

These words sounded so hollow that it made Cleo realise what they were up to. Everything they'd said to her suddenly made sense, and she wasn't going to let them get away with it. Her best friend in the place was dead and all they were worried about was her keeping her mouth shut and not rocking the boat.

'My parents treated me like an animal as well, sir,' Cleo said. 'They locked me in a cupboard for five days. Then they told lies about me and got me sent here, even though I hadn't done anything. But I don't go round bullying people, sir.'

Bushy's pale face went pink, the veins in his neck stood out and Cleo thought he was going to hit her, but she felt better for having said her piece. She took a step back as he slammed his fist down on the desk with a force that made all the objects on it jump in the air. An expensive-looking fountain pen dropped on to the floor, nib first, adding to his exasperation.

'Oh for God's sake, you stupid little bitch! Just keep your bloody mouth shut. Now ... get out of my sight!'

On her way to class, Cleo had made up her mind to abscond that very day. Life in that place was so unfair. Nice people were killed and no one cared.

She had over two pounds saved up, mainly from Ant's monthly money. That should go a long way. She wouldn't go to London, not straight away. That would be the first place they'd look and although they didn't have Ant's address, he was still living quite near the police station where she was taken that day. No, she'd head for the coast, get a job, and look after herself for a bit.

There was no one in the classroom when Cleo got there. Lessons didn't start for ten minutes. A few minutes later, Dobbs and her three stooges followed her in. Dobbs pushed her face right into Cleo's. There was still dried blood around her mouth.

'Can't keep yer bloody trap shut, can yer?' she snarled. 'Tellin' Bushy I were bullyin' Blister.'

If Cleo had had time to think, she'd have asked Dobbs how she knew what she'd just said to Bushy. But the next thing she knew she was on the floor protecting her face from Dobbs's kicks. The bully dragged her to her feet and head-butted her, catching her just below her right eye. Down Cleo went again and Dobbs knelt astride her, going through her pockets as the stooges held on to her arms and feet. She found her purse containing two of Ant's pound notes.

'What's this?'

'It's mine. Give it back.'

'Yours? How come yer've got two quid? Yer must've stole it. I'd better report this ter Bushy.'

'It's mine.'

Cleo pulled an arm free and made a grab for the purse but Dobbs held it away from her and slapped her with a free hand. 'Now, now,' she sneered. 'They can't have thieves like you in a respectable place like this. What shall we do with her, girls?'

Cleo heard sharp, evenly paced footsteps approaching along the corridor, it could only have been Miss Phelps. Thank God for that. Dobbs got up and stuck Cleo's money into her pocket and threw her empty purse back at her.

'I haven't finished wi' you, yet,' she hissed. 'Keep yer trap shut or yer'll end up like Fat Freak. And I'll report yer ter Bushy fer thievin'!'

Several girls came into the classroom just behind the teacher. Cleo couldn't really complain about the theft of money she wasn't supposed to have, but she hardly needed to tell Miss Phelps she'd just been beaten up by Dobbs and the stooges. The evidence was plain to see. Victim, culprits, blood on her face, her on the floor. Miss Phelps looked down at her.

'Been in the wars, Kelly?'

She asked the question with one raised eyebrow and no compassion. It was obvious what had been done to Cleo and who had done it, but she chose not to pursue it. She glanced, briefly at Dobbs, who was smirking all over her face. Then Cleo realised what was happening. If Bushy and Miss Phelps couldn't shut her up, they knew someone who could. Cleo couldn't fight that.

'I fell, miss,' she said.

'Perhaps you should watch your step in future.'

'Yes, miss.'

That afternoon Cleo absconded from the Whitley Grange with a black eye, various bruises and the emergency half-crown she always kept hidden in the hem of her green cardigan. It was the same cardigan the police had found for her the night their house burned down. The beating and the threats and the indifference the staff had shown towards Blister's death, and the way they'd let Dobbs beat her up didn't really trouble Cleo. She expected no better from these people who, to quote Ant, weren't worth a bloody light. What troubled her deeply was that she had let Blister down. Cleo knew that somehow she should have prevented her friend's death. She didn't know how, but she knew she should have.

Although her absence was noted at evening roll-call it wasn't reported to the police until the following day. Bushy wanted to give her a head start. Capturing a loose cannon such as Kelly during the enquiry into the fatal fire wouldn't have helped matters one bit.

Chapter Six

The weather was quite pleasant and Cleo's step was light, having unburdened herself of the wretchedness of Whitley Grange. She headed east, which was where the nearest coast was. At one stage she was tempted by a bike leaning against a lamp post outside a grocery shop. Ant wouldn't have thought twice, but Cleo wasn't him; nor did she consider herself a good enough cyclist to guarantee a clean getaway. A few minutes later the bike passed her, erratically ridden by a wheezing old man with a shopping bag over the handlebars. He smiled and said, 'How do,' to Cleo as he rode by and she was glad she hadn't stolen it.

Keeping the sun more or less behind her right shoulder was a good way of heading in the right direction and after a while she saw a sign for York. By nightfall she was several miles outside Leeds on the A64, York Road, where she found a deserted bus shelter littered with empty bottles and obscene graffiti, and with a wooden seat carved with dozens of names, which made her wonder where all these people came from. It wasn't the most comfortable bed she'd ever slept on, but the next morning she was fast asleep when the six twenty-seven, East Yorkshire Special pulled up to let a passenger off. The conductor spotted her.

'Are yer wanting this bus, love?' he called down.

He grinned at the startled expression on her face as Cleo stared around her, trying to orientate herself. From somewhere she found the presence of mind to say, 'Yes please,' although she hadn't much of a clue where the bus was going.

There were just three people on board, including her and the conductor. Cleo gave him her half-crown and asked how far it would take her.

'Half fare? Three stops short of Scarborough bus station.'

'That's where I want to be, please.'

As she'd no idea what three stops short of the bus station looked like, and as the conductor didn't tell her, the bus station was where Cleo ended up.

'Officially, yer owe me sixpence,' he said, as Cleo was getting off.

'I'm sorry, I haven't got sixpence.'

'In that case, young lady, yer leave me no option. Yer'll just have ter get off here.'

Cleo stared at him until his face broke into a grin and she realised he was joking. She wasn't used to adults joking with her.

'Thank you,' she smiled. 'Could you tell me where the sea is, please?'

'Keep walking downhill till yer feet get wet.'

'Thank you.'

Cleo had never seen the sea in her life and her first glimpse of it wasn't all that thrilling. There was a sea fret hanging over Scarborough Bay which merged into the grey of the water, and she couldn't tell where the sky finished and the sea began. She could just make out the lighthouse at the end of the harbour wall and a shadowy boat chugging out to sea, disappearing, mysteriously into the mist. Maybe that was her future, a life on the ocean waves; but who ever heard of ships taking on cabin girls? Life was a lot tougher for a girl on the run than a boy.

It was early April, not quite Easter, and the season hadn't really got under way. At that time of year the old folk outnumbered the young and were already parading along the sea front, shivering women wearing cardigans and headscarves, linking arms with blue-nosed men wearing flat caps and frowns. The amusement arcades began to blare out pop music and ice-cream vendors rolled up their shutters. A dark-skinned fortune teller, who looked to have originated from a lot further east than Scarborough, unlocked the door to her tiny booth which had a sign saying, *Madame Zora – Eastern Mystic. Fortunes told 1/6; Palms read 1/-; Pensioners half price.* She was calling out a greeting in broad Yorkshire to a man in the neighbouring candy-floss stall before, hopefully, adjusting her accent to that of the mysterious East as she sat down behind her crystal ball to await her first customer.

Cleo wrapped her navy blue gaberdine coat around her to keep out the morning chill and set foot on a beach for the first time in her life. The tide was in and the beach was empty apart from an old man leading a line of dismal-looking donkeys. Then a tractor pulling a trailer full of deckchairs drove down a ramp and pulled up next to where Cleo was standing. A woman jumped down and winked at her. She lit a cigarette and immediately bent double with a fit of coughing, which made Cleo wonder why she bothered smoking. After her experience in the bogey hole and watching what Dobbs did with a cigarette, smoking was a vice she'd never indulge in. The woman looked to be well into her thirties, with masses of dark curls and dark rings under her eyes as though she didn't sleep too well. After she finished coughing she called out to Cleo:

'Instead of just gawping, you might want to gimme some help with me chairs.'

The woman gave the impression of having been around, seen a few things. She had the fading beauty of a former man-killer and she intrigued Cleo instantly. There was no malice in her voice and she was probably not expecting Cleo to take her up on her offer.

'Okay,' Cleo said. She was hoping there might be some payment at the end of it.

'Help me stack 'em an' I'll give you a bob,' the woman said.

'Okay.'

A shilling would buy a half-decent breakfast.

'Here, you climb on the trailer and pass 'em down.'

'Okay.'

'Is that all you can say, "Okay"?'

The woman's grin was cheerful and genuine. Cleo prided herself on being able to see that in a person. She was no threat to her. Cleo climbed up on the trailer and passed down a deckchair.

'I can say all sorts of things,' Cleo said. 'I could

say, give me ten bob and I'll help you all day.'

Where she got the cheek from she had no idea, but the woman was the type of person who made her feel instantly relaxed. Cleo accompanied her request with a smile which the woman returned with ten per cent interest. Cleo had never met anyone who could smile better than she could, except Ant of course. The woman turned the offer over in her head and then said:

'Seven and six.'

'Okay,' Cleo said. 'Seven and six.'

The woman spat on her hand and held it out to her. Cleo spat on hers and did the same.

'My name's Flo Dunderdale. What's yours?'

'Cleo.'

Flo didn't question Cleo's name, like most people would have, but she did take a precaution that showed she had some sense of responsibility.

'Will it be okay with your mam an' dad?'

'I haven't got a mam and dad.'

Flo scrunched her face. 'Sorry love ... me and my big mouth.'

'It's okay,' Cleo said. 'I'm staying in a children's holiday home.' She'd heard of such places and assumed there'd be at least one in Scarborough.

'Aye, there's a few of them round here,' Flo said. 'Not bad places neither. Some of the kids can be a bit rough, though.' She was looking at Cleo's bruised face. 'Looks like you've been in the wars.'

'Bit of a disagreement with one of the girls,' Cleo explained.

Flo took Cleo's hands in hers and examined her knuckles; grazed from her attack on Dobbs.

'I hope you gave as good as you got.'

'Not really,' Cleo said. 'I was caught off-guard.'

'You mean you've been bullied?'

'Something like that.'

Flo studied her for a while, then said, casually, 'I thought high school holidays didn't start till next week.'

Cleo thought quickly, aware that she was being tested. 'They have different holidays in York,' she said. 'We break up same time as the little 'uns.'

'Never thought of that,' Flo said. 'Nice place, York. It's sort of ... old.'

Cleo agreed that York was old and hoped Flo wouldn't ask her any questions about a place she'd never been to. The deckchair offloading went on in silence for a while, then Flo said, 'Easter comes round quicker every year. It doesn't seem two minutes since it were Christmas.' She looked at her watch. 'Give it half an hour an the tide'll turn.' Then to the sky, she added, 'Take this lot with it most likely. Could be a nice day.'

Cleo stared upwards and saw a suspicion of blue behind the blanket of mist. 'Is that what happens,' she asked. 'Does the tide always take the mist with it when it goes out.'

'Takes this stuff,' Flo said. 'They call it a fret.'

Almost as she spoke the mist began to clear, revealing a clear blue sky above and everything looked so much better, as if someone had opened the curtains and let the daylight in; and all of a sudden Cleo felt really optimistic about everything. She looked upwards and let the sun warm her face. Whitley Grange and the bogey hole seemed a million miles away.

Flo grinned at her. 'That's the ticket, girl. Take your coat off. Get yourself a proper Scarborough suntan to take back to York with you.'

It was one of her better days. All Cleo had to do was hand out the deckchairs as Flo took the money. By lunchtime there were plenty of people on the beach, the tide was out, and they only had half a dozen chairs left, including the two on which Flo and Cleo were sitting. Flo bought them fish and chips from a sea-front café. It was the first meal Cleo had eaten for twenty-four hours, and she was ready for it. Flo had only eaten half of hers when Cleo was wiping her mouth with the paper. Away to their right a bunch of kids were laughing at a Punch and Judy show.

'Do you mind if I go and watch?'

'Be my guest,' Flo said. 'I'll stay here and mind the shop.'

Cleo had never seen a Punch and Judy show before; she only recognised it from pictures she'd seen in comics. She ooohed with the rest of them as the crocodile appeared and stole the sausages; she laughed when Judy battered poor Punch over his head with a club, and imagined her doing that to Horace. The policeman arrived to arrest Mr Punch and he served to remind Cleo of her own predicament, which seemed a million miles away on this happy afternoon.

A young boy darted forward and jumped up at Mr Punch, trying to grab him. A woman, presumably the boy's mother, looked round and grinned at anyone who was bothered to take notice.

'Yer can't fool my Norman,' she said, winking and tapping her temple. 'He knows it's not real.'

'I think they all know it's not real,' muttered a red-haired woman standing next to Cleo, under her breath.

Norman was an overweight child who also looked to have been overindulged, something Cleo wouldn't have minded a bit of.

'He's only seven,' said the mother, proudly, as the boy ran around the back of the flapping booth and tried to get inside. 'Yer wouldn't think my Norman were only seven, would yer?'

'Norman needs a crack round his ear'ole,' muttered the redhead.

The puppets disappeared from view as the Punch and Judy man dealt with the intruder. He still had a Mr Punch squeaker in his mouth as he told Norman to piss off. Fortunately, the squeaker served to obscure the expletive, at least from the children's ears. The boy re-appeared and ran around the front to tell his mother it was really a man inside. As the puppets took to the stage once more, the boy picked up a handful of sand and threw it at Mr Punch, who looked around and squeaked, 'Who did that?'

All the children pointed at the boy and shouted, 'He did.'

The boy's mother swelled with pride as her son began kicking at the curtain. There was a cry of pain from inside; Mr Punch forgot himself and squeaked, 'Ouch! ... ooh, you vicious little bastard!'

This swear word came out loud and clear and the audience were gob-smacked at such profanity, especially coming from Mr Punch. A small girl began to cry and the boy's mother shouted, 'Don't you call my son a little bastard, yer bastard!'

Young Norman foolishly lifted the curtain and looked inside to see what damage he'd caused. There was a loud smack and he emerged in tears with a red weal on one of his fat cheeks. Some of the watching adults clapped, the red-haired woman cheered, and Norman's mother hurled herself at the booth, punching at the curtain and the child molester within. The booth collapsed, the Punch and Judy man crawled out and delivered a kick at the cursing woman, who was entangled in striped cloth and punching at fresh air as her son bawled at the top of his voice and adults arrived to hurry their children away from the mayhem.

Cleo watched from a distance with one eye out for any approaching policemen. The irate woman took her weeping child away with a promise of an ice-cream and doughnuts as the white-haired Punch and Judy man surveyed the damage she and her son had wrought. He looked up at Cleo, the one remaining spectator.

'It's not the first time this has happened, you know,' he bemoaned. 'You'd think they'd show an artiste a bit more bloody respect, like.' Without the squeaker he had a Geordie accent.

'Do you need any help?' she asked.

He smiled at her and shook his head. 'No thanks, pet. I'm packin' up an' gannin' on home. Termorrer's another day.'

'It is, isn't it?' Cleo said, wondering what she'd

be doing tomorrow. For all that happened afterwards she would remember that day as a happy day. She went back to where Flo was sitting.

'What on earth was all that about?' Flo asked.

'The Punch and Judy man called one of the kids a bastard.'

'Sounds like old Ronnie. He can't stand kids.'

'But why–?' Cleo began.

'He's an old pro,' Flo explained. 'Used to be a song and dance man till he got gout – and he never did have much of a voice. We all have to do what we can to get by,' she said.

Cleo nodded as she thought about how she'd get by, then she dismissed these worries and asked, 'Do you mind if I go for a paddle?'

'They're your toes, love. If you want to freeze 'em off it's up to you.'

Cleo took off her shoes and socks and strolled down to the sea which was breaking gently in the light breeze. Her feet left footprints on the damp sand, which was a great novelty to her. She was almost fourteen years old and she'd never seen her own footprints in the sand. She hopped on one leg, then the other, making a single, deeper print; then she tried to retrace her steps so as to leave a mysterious dead end. Cleo had once read about footprints that stopped in the middle of nowhere. She ended up falling backwards, laughing at her own clumsiness and grinning up at a passing woman who must have thought she was a loony on a day out.

When she took her first steps into the water she realised what Flo meant about the temperature of the North Sea in April; it took her breath away and she had several attempts at acclimatisation before allowing the waves to lap up to her knees. White-sailed yachts raced across the bay; and a pleasure boat called the *Scarborough Belle,* all decked with coloured bunting, headed for the horizon. There were squawking seagulls gliding above the waves, diving into the sea and surfacing with a fish supper. What a life. Cleo stood on frozen legs and marvelled at the hardiness (or stupidity) of the people who were actually swimming in the icy sea and she laughed at a small dog as it barked at the retreating water then yelped and ran away as breakers tumbled towards it. Cleo had always wanted a dog, any kind of dog would have done, although she did favour the collie from *Lassie Come Home*. Neither her mother nor Horace would allow it, which was probably a stroke of luck for the dog; knowing Horace they might well have ended up eating it.

Behind her, on the wet, flat part of the beach there was an old man with no teeth, wearing a Kiss-Me-Quick hat and rolled-up trousers. He was kicking a ball to a chubby little girl who giggled a lot and had her dress tucked into her knickers. It briefly crossed Cleo's mind to do the same with her dress so that she could venture deeper into the sea. But only briefly. A boy was flying a kite. As Cleo watched it, dipping and weaving across the bright sky, her thoughts drifted ahead once again, on to where she would stay that night. With the weather being quite warm she could sleep in the open somewhere and let tomorrow take care of itself. Maybe Flo would need her to help again. This thought was very much on her mind when Cleo got back to where her new friend was sitting. Flo smiled at her and asked if she'd enjoyed her paddle. Cleo said she had, and then, as if she'd been reading her thoughts, Flo said: 'It's only a one-off is this you know, love. I hope you're not expecting to be doing this every day.'

Cleo sat down and said, 'That's okay.'

'I'm feeling a bit knackered today,' Flo explained, 'and your help didn't come amiss. But I should be okay tomorrow.'

'I hope you are.'

Flo lit another cigarette; her tenth since the one that set her off coughing, then she turned to Cleo and gave her the once over. 'I must say, love, there's something about you – did you know that?'

'Something about me? I'm not sure what you mean.'

'I'm not sure I do meself,' Flo grinned. 'Take no notice of me. I'm a silly old sod.'

Cleo closed her eyes and sank down into her chair, disappointed that she wouldn't be needed tomorrow because she was beginning to like this woman.

'By the way,' Flo said. 'I don't think you're staying in any children's holiday home.'

Despite the warmth of the sun, Cleo felt herself go cold. Without opening her eyes, she asked, 'What makes you think that?'

'Because I used to get sent to 'em when I was a kid,' Flo told her. 'And it used to get on me nerves that they wouldn't let me out of their sight for more than two minutes.'

'Maybe things have changed since your day.'

'Aye, maybe they have ... and maybe you think it's none of my business.' Cleo could sense Flo sitting up, looking at her. 'But it *is* my business if it gets me into trouble with the council. If I get in trouble with the council, bang goes me deckchair pitch.'

Cleo wasn't quite sure what she meant, but she didn't want to get her into trouble with the council. Flo was one of the few nice people in her life. Cleo got out of the chair.

'I'll go then, shall I?'

'I'm right, aren't I?' Flo said.

'I never said that. But I'm not staying where I'm not wanted.'

Flo squinted up at her, shading the sun with one hand. 'Just tell me what's what, love, then I'll see.'

Cleo gave her offer lengthy consideration. 'Okay,' she said, sitting down again. 'But you could get me into trouble if you tell on me.'

'Well then, you'll just have to trust me, won't you?'

Cleo looked at her to confirm she could definitely trust her, then she said, 'Shall I start from the beginning?'

'Always a good place to start,' Flo said.

Her story came out like a bursting dam, unleashing a torrent of words. Cleo told her all about her mother and Horace and the bogey hole; and how Ant had taken her to London. Then she told her about Whitley Grange and how brilliant Blister was; and about Dobbs and Bushy and how Blister died (at which point the tears arrived); and how Miss Phelps had turned on her.

Her story-telling was disturbed by a man returning a couple of deckchairs. He handed them to Flo, then he glanced down at Cleo's tears and said, 'Oh dear.'

'Boyfriend trouble,' Flo explained.

The man gave Cleo a sympathetic smile and walked away. Flo Dunderdale was such an easy person to tell the truth to. What's more she believed Cleo, despite her previous deception. It took her a long, tearful time to tell it from the beginning but it gave her a wonderful feeling of release.

Another customer arrived just as she was finishing her tale. Flo touched her hand and got to her feet. Cleo remembered that touch; it told her she wasn't on her own; it told her that Flo understood everything she was going through. She watched as Flo dealt with a sudden flurry of returned chairs; some people were leaving the beach to go for lunch. When she sat down again, Flo smiled.

'I never saw me dad,' she said. 'He was killed in France in 1916, three months after I was born. Me mam died o' flu two years later.' She took a deep drag on the cigarette and had to clear her throat before she continued: 'I'm telling you this because I've run away from more children's homes than you've had hot dinners.'

'Oh,' Cleo said. 'What'll happen to me?'

Flo shrugged. 'It's hard to say. If you go back of your own accord they'll be worried about you opening your mouth about that lass what were killed. They don't like owt like that. Especially if it gets in t' papers. So you've got one up on 'em in that respect.

'I don't want to go back there.'

'I can't say I blame yer,' said Flo. 'There's some right nutters in them places. I took a lot o' stick meself an' I were never in an actual reformatory.'

'There was actually only one nutter there,' Cleo said.

'Dobbs?'

'Yes. If she hadn't been there I could have stuck it out.'

'Shame you had to be there in the first place, by the sound of it.'

'It was better than living at home.'

Cleo looked around her at the simple happiness the beach was providing for the holidaymakers. Smiling faces, blue sky, warm sun, jangling music coming from the arcades. From her perspective it seemed like paradise.

'I'd like to stay here,' she said. 'At least for the summer. Maybe by that time they'll have forgotten about me.'

'They'll not forget about you, love. You'll be a name in a black book until you're found. And a name like Cleopatra isn't one they'll overlook in a hurry.' (Cleo had owned up to her full name in the telling of her story.)

'I'm going to change it to Grace.'

'Grace Kelly? I think it's been done, love. Besides, Cleo's not a bad name – better than mine.'

'What, you mean Florence? What's wrong with Florence?'

'Nothing, only me name's not Florence.'
'What is it, then?'
'Promise you won't laugh?'
'Course I do.'
Cleo had had enough people laughing at her to know what it was like.
'It's Floribunda,' Flo said. 'Floribunda Rose Dunderdale. Apparently it was me dad's bright idea – I'd change it otherwise. He sent a letter from France as soon as he found out he'd got a little girl. Liked his roses, you see.'
'Floribunda Rose ... that's a beautiful name.'
'Try Floribunda Dunderdale.'
She checked Cleo's face for signs of mirth and Cleo had trouble job keeping it straight. Her lips were trembling with silent laughter until she couldn't hold it in any longer. Flo gave her an admonishing tap on her wrist.
'You said you wouldn't laugh.'
Maybe it *was* that funny, or maybe Cleo was just releasing all the misery she'd endured over the years in one uninhibited bout of hysterics. It was definitely the most she'd laughed in her life. Cleo was doubled up on the deckchair with people staring at her. Flo eventually joined her and Cleo suspected it wasn't the first time she'd laughed at her own name. Not many people can do that, but Flo wasn't like anyone she'd ever met. It certainly made Cleo feel a bit better about being called Cleopatra.
When they'd calmed down, Flo nipped her cigarette out between her fingers and flicked the end into a nearby waste bin. 'It won't be easy you know, they'll always be on the lookout for you.'

'Then I won't let them find me. I look fifteen, I'll get a job and look after myself.'

She narrowed her eyes, assessing her. 'How old are you, really?' she asked.

There was no use lying to Flo. 'Thirteen,' Cleo said. 'Fourteen in July. But I'm tall for my age.'

'You *might* just pass for fifteen,' she said. 'But you'll need a job where you don't pay tax or insurance or anything. And you'll have to give a false name and address.'

Cleo didn't really understand the tax and insurance part, other than it was a way of working favoured by Ant.

'And you'll need a place to live.'

'I suppose I will.'

Cleo hadn't thought that far ahead. Flo was alternately scratching her head, rubbing her neck, looking at Cleo, then at the sea.

'By heck, it's taking some thinkin' about is this, love.'

She seemed to have taken full responsibility for Cleo's predicament and Cleo was more than willing to hand it over. Then another customer arrived and it seemed to change the direction of Flo's thoughts because she began to ask about Ant and how he was managing to live on his own in London at such a young age.

'If you knew him, you wouldn't have to ask,' Cleo told her. 'He's always three steps in front of everyone.'

'Do you miss him?'

'Yes I do.'

She chose not to elaborate on her answer, although Flo seemed to want more. 'If he's as capable as you say, it's a pity he can't look after you.'

The thought of Ant looking after her made Cleo smile. 'We could look after each other,' she said.

Flo took her hand again. 'Aye, lass,' she said. 'I've no doubt you could. No doubt at all.'

She stayed with Flo until the sun was low in the sky. Most of the deckchairs had been returned and Cleo knew her day with this woman was about to end. They had spent the afternoon talking about this and that.

'I assume you're not married,' Cleo said.

'Why would you assume that?'

'Because you wouldn't be Floribunda Dunderdale any more.'

It brought a dry laugh from Flo. 'Ah,' she said. 'For a while I wasn't. I was Floribunda Millichip. At least I thought I was. But then it turned out I wasn't.'

'Oh,' Cleo said, not understanding.

'It's a long story,' said Flo. 'The top and bottom of it is that Sid Millichip's in jail for bigamy and theft.'

'So, you married Sid and...'

'And Sid was already married, but he never thought to tell me. Men can be very absent minded when they want to be. He was also a thief. Stole a lot of money off his proper wife. I never saw any of it, but the bookies and the pubs did ... plus a few women I didn't know about. He was the most plausible spiv you've ever come across, called himself a commercial traveller. He certainly did a lot of travelling. Never have anything to do with a man whose job takes him away from home for days on end, Cleo. Men who take jobs like that are not to be trusted.'

'I'll remember that.'

Cleo mulled over the idea of someone being tricked into a bigamous marriage and wondered if Flo's problems had been worse than hers. No matter how bad things are, there's always someone worse off than you. Ant once said this to her, and Blister was a prime example.

'Did you love Sid?' she asked.

'Sid was a lifelong shit.'

'But did you love him?'

Flo took her time to reply. She knew the answer even as Cleo was asking the question, but it was something she didn't want to admit to herself. 'He had ... he had entertaining ways,' she said, 'which counts for a lot in a man. He was never cruel, not intentionally anyway, and he made me laugh. And, you know, although he wasn't exactly the Errol Flynn type himself, he somehow made me feel pretty.'

'But you are pretty.'

'Maybe I was once, but there's a difference between *being* pretty and *feeling* pretty. I always felt pretty when I was with Sid.'

'So,' surmised Cleo, 'you loved him, then.'

'I suppose I must have,' Flo admitted. 'God, he hurt me. Don't ever let a man get close enough to hurt you, Cleo. Unless you're absolutely sure of him.'

Flo changed the subject and for the remainder of the afternoon she seemed keen to glean every speck of information about Cleo's life so far and, as Cleo had never unloaded her thoughts and her hopes and dreams on to anyone, she wasn't exactly backward in coming forward. They stopped chatting as Flo puffed on her seventeenth cigarette; she seemed to become engrossed in her thoughts. Then, with an air of someone who had just made a reluctant decision, she pushed herself up from her chair.

'Could you mind the shop for a bit, love. There's only a few left to come in.' She looked at Cleo, sideways. 'You *will* still be here when I get back, won't you?'

'Course I will.'

Flo took off her money bag and hung it around Cleo's shoulders. 'There's a tanner deposit back on every chair,' she said.

'Right.'

Cleo looked inside the heavy bag. It contained every penny of the day's takings – close on seven pounds. Such a sum would tide her over for quite some time, and Flo knew this. She lit her eighteenth smoke and said she'd be as quick as she could. Then she wandered off.

Cleo was telling herself that honesty was a virtue she could ill afford. Her brother would have run off with the money without giving it a second thought. In fact Ant would have assumed Flo had done this on purpose to facilitate his escape without her actually being involved. This did cross Cleo's mind and she wondered if Flo was secretly watching her from somewhere, wondering what sort of an idiot she was for not taking the money and running.

It was two hours before she got back. Cleo had

wrapped her coat around her as the warmth had gone out of the day. Her thoughts were taken up by where she should sleep that night and what help Flo was going to give her, if any. She had learned not to expect too much from people and was half planning what to do if she and Flo parted company. The beach had emptied quickly the instant the sun disappeared behind the Grand Hotel, and all the deckchairs had been returned. Cleo somehow knew that Flo was away on business which concerned her, so she wasn't overly concerned about the length of her new friend's absence.

'Told you she wouldn't do a bunk with me money.'

Flo's voice came from behind. Cleo spun round, and had never seen a more guilty look on anyone's face. Flo was standing between two policemen. Cleo's heart sank. Her friend had betrayed her.

'If she was as bad as she were painted she'd have done a bunk with me money,' Flo was saying. 'Nine out o' ten kids would have been away on their toes the minute me back was turned.'

With her heart in the pit of her stomach, Cleo took off the money bag and handed it to Flo, without saying a word. She was dumbstruck at this awful turn of events. One of the policemen walked forward and stood beside her, with a hand on her arm.

'There's no need for any strong-arm stuff,' Flo said. 'She'll not give you no trouble.'

Cleo found her voice at last. 'Flo, why are you

doing this to me?'

'Because it's for the best, love,' Flo said. 'What I didn't tell you was that I'm a magistrate.'

'A magistrate?'

Cleo compared her to the magistrate in Leeds and the comparison didn't stand up. At that moment she preferred the Leeds magistrate, at least she knew where she stood with him.

'I know it's hard to believe but we come from all walks o' life,' Flo added, lamely.

At that moment Cleo hated her with a passion she had hitherto reserved for Horace Womack and Dobbs. She hated Flo not for what she was doing to her, but for not being the person Cleo thought she was; for not being her much-needed friend. Flo saw it in her eyes.

'Don't look at me like that, Cleo, love. If I'd told you what I was doing, you wouldn't have been here when I got back.'

She's dead right there, Cleo thought.

'I've had a few words with people over in Leeds,' Flo told her, 'and I've put 'em straight. Things'll be better for you. You mark my words.'

Cleo didn't want to mark her words. She pulled her arm free and ran towards the sea, with the two policemen in pursuit and Flo shouting for her not to be so daft. Why she ran into the sea she would never know. Perhaps the sea represented the edge of the world and she just wanted to get off. She ran until she was in too deep to run any more, then she fell forward. Her tears mingled with the salt water and she didn't feel the cold. An icy wave crashed over her head and knocked her off her feet, and Cleo couldn't swim. The force of the wave made her take a sudden breath, but there was no air for her to breathe, only water. It was her worst experience since being in the burning bogey hole. The end of her life seemed imminent. Lack of oxygen made her black out and she only vaguely felt the hand that grabbed at her hair. She came to on the beach with a policeman pumping water from her lungs. Flo was looking down at her, trying to apologise with her eyes, and in between retching and coughing, Cleo returned as much venom as she could from her own eyes in Flo's direction. There was nothing else Flo could do but turn and walk away. It had been one of those days.

Chapter Seven

Cleo spent the night in St Thomas's Hospital being guarded by a policeman who took her off to a Scarborough police station the next day as soon as a doctor had given her the all clear. Just after lunch she was led away, in handcuffs, to a waiting car. The two people in the car, a man at the wheel and a woman, were unknown to her. Neither wore a uniform and both seemed very friendly, albeit somewhat personal.

'Have you been to the toilet? Because you won't be able to go on the way,' the woman asked. She had an efficient face and hair in the style of a bun loaf.

'I'm okay, thank you.'

'I don't think she needs these, constable,' the driver told the policeman, indicating Cleo's handcuffs.

'With her track record for running away she's lucky not to be wearing leg irons, sir,' said the policeman. He was the one who saved Cleo's life and to her subsequent shame she never thanked him. 'I'll have to clear it with the boss,' he said, going back inside.

'It'll be all right,' said the woman, who was sitting next to Cleo in the back. 'I've got a file in my handbag.'

They were obviously trying to put her at her ease, but Cleo didn't trust them. She gave the woman a brief smile to tell her she understood her little joke, but she didn't ask who the woman was or where they were going (although Cleo had a good idea about the latter), nor did either of them enlighten her. They could have been kidnappers for all Cleo cared. She just settled into her own thoughts. The treachery of Flo Dunderdale still rankled with her. Never before had Cleo been so wrong about anyone. It had taught her not to trust a friendly adult; certainly not these two strangers in the car, whoever they were. Far better a genuine scowl than a treacherous smile.

The policeman came back and unlocked her handcuffs with a warning to the woman, who appeared to be the senior of the two: 'We're handing her into your custody. She's no longer our responsibility.'

'She's a thirteen-year-old girl, not Al Capone,' pointed out their driver.

This amused Cleo. Even if she didn't trust these people a sense of humour is an attractive trait, even in a kidnapper. Including two stops, the journey back took over three hours. Cleo wasn't allowed out of the car during these stops but they did bring her tea and a sausage sandwich. They took the long route across the North Yorkshire Moors, dawdling at times to admire the scenery, especially the view from the top of Sutton Bank. It gradually occurred to her that they might not be going back to Whitley Grange. Her heart lightened.

'Where are we going?' she asked.

'Whitley Grange.'

Cleo sank back into depression. They tried to talk to her but she was monosyllabic with her replies.

'I get the strong impression that you've lost all faith in authority,' the woman said, as they drove in through the gates of the reformatory.

Cleo didn't answer. It seemed as though all the joy of yesterday had curdled into a leaden ball of misery which sat painfully in the pit of her stomach. Several men were working among the charred ruins of Wetherby Wing. A builder's wagon was parked nearby and a man wearing a hard hat and a donkey jacket was in deep discussion with a man in a smart suit and trilby; they were standing right where Blister's body had been. Just looking at the spot brought a tear to Cleo's eye.

They pulled up in front of the main block alongside a car Cleo had never seen before. Out of all the staff, only the governor and two of the male teachers had cars, and it wasn't either of theirs. Their driver got out and walked into the building, leaving the woman with her.

'Cleo,' she said. 'I'm placing you on trust not to run away.'

'Why, miss?' Cleo probably sounded really sullen.

'Do you mean, why am I placing you on trust? Or why shouldn't you run away?'

'Both, miss.'

The whole place was getting her down. If this woman knew how bad Cleo felt she wouldn't be asking her such stupid questions; she'd be taking her somewhere safe.

'Cleo,' she said. 'The very worst thing you can do is try and run away. You must have faith in me.'

Cleo didn't have any faith in her but she still said, 'Yes, miss.'

The woman got out of her side of the car and waited for Cleo to join her. That was the point where she could have run away. The fact that she didn't seemed to justify the woman's trust in her.

'So far, so good,' the woman said. 'Now I understand there's some sort of common room.'

'Yes, miss. They call it the Day Room.'

'Right, well, if you'd like to wait in there I'll come and get you when we're ready.'

'Yes, miss.'

Cleo's heart was drumming as she made her way to the Day Room. Classes were over for the day and most of the girls looked to be out and about in the grounds, although Cleo hadn't seen anyone from Wetherby Wing. As she opened the door and came face to face with the girls from her dormitory all action became suspended in a frozen moment of surprise. There wasn't a single word of friendship or greeting as Cleo scanned their faces and noticed one missing. Dobbs.

'If yer lookin' fer Dobbsy she's with Bushy and them other lot,' grunted one of Dobbs's stooges.

'I wasn't looking for her,' Cleo said. 'I don't make a habit of looking for murderers.'

'She'll murder you when she gets back,' sneered the stooge.

'We've all had ter see Bushy,' called out one of the other girls. 'There's some bosses in with him. He didn't look so suited.'

'He had a face like a smacked arse,' commented another girl.

'Yer'd better 'ave all kept yer gobs shut!' the stooge threatened. 'Or else Dobbsy'll 'ave yer.'

'Oh yes,' Cleo said. 'And what's wrong with telling the truth?'

The stooge, without Dobbs, didn't scare Cleo who stared at her and waited for an answer to her question. The stooge lowered her gaze. 'Just wait till Dobbsy gets here, that's all,' she muttered.

The door burst open and Dobbs stood there. Her face was still bruised from where Cleo had hit her two days earlier. 'Did I hear my name being taken in vain?' she said. Then she saw Cleo. 'Bloody hell fire! I thought they were supposed ter shoot yer on sight.'

'How d'yer go on?' asked the stooge who had been doing all the talking.

Dobbs shrugged. 'Just told 'em what we all agreed. We were havin' a bit o' fun and she must have taken it the wrong way. Isn't that right, girls?'

She addressed her question to the whole room, and received desultory murmurs of assent. Dobbs nodded her approval.

'I'm glad we're all agreed, girls, because that's what Bushy wanted to hear.'

She then turned her attention to Cleo. As she approached, all three of her stooges fell into line behind her. She pushed Cleo with both hands, causing her to stumble backwards, then, as she regained her feet Dobbs pushed her again; she repeated the exercise until Cleo's back was against the wall. Two of Dobbs's cronies pinned her arms by her side.

'No ... one ... goes ... round ... callin' ... me ... names!'

Dobbs emphasised each word by slapping each of Cleo's cheeks in turn. Cleo kicked her on her shin and made Dobbs howl with pain and rage. Then Cleo howled with pain herself as Dobbs kicked her back. Without the two girls holding her Cleo thought she might have given a better account of herself.

'Why don't you fight me on your own?' she challenged. 'Without your monkeys to help you. I'll tell you why – it's because you're a bloody coward!'

She was yelling at Dobbs with a tear-streaming, futile anger; unbelievably depressed at her situation, not just at that particular moment (which was bad enough), but in general. Whatever courage Cleo was showing was born of desperation; fighting one had to be better than fighting three. Even if she came off worst she should be able to get a couple of blows in. There was a murmur of agreement from the watching girls. Dobbs was a lot bigger and older than Cleo and she shouldn't need any help.

'That's right,' someone shouted. 'Fight on yer own Dobbsy.'

Just for an instant Cleo spotted the fear in Dobbs's eyes. She had so much more to lose. For her to be beaten by a skinny thirteen year old would end her reign as the 'cock o' the school' in the most ignominious fashion. Then the fear vanished as she thought of a way out.

'Who said owt about fightin'? This isn't a fight,

this is punishment for squealin' on yer mates.'

'Bloody coward!' Cleo shouted.

Dobbs punched her in her stomach so hard that Cleo thought she'd never breathe again. It was less than a day since she'd nearly drowned and here she was being punched in the stomach. So much for trusting that bloody woman who had brought her back. The woman who had told her to wait in this room. She was obviously as treacherous as Bushy and Phelps ... and Flo. Cleo was gasping for breath and crying, not so much from pain or fear but from sheer despair at being let down so often by adults. The stooges struggled to support her as she became a dead weight in their grasp. Dobbs grabbed her hair and yanked her head up. She was about to punch her in the face when a voice shouted, 'Stop that!'

Through her fogged brain Cleo recognised the voice of the woman in the car. The stooges let go of her and she dropped to the floor like a sack of potatoes. The woman rushed to her side.

'I'm sorry, Cleo,' she was saying. 'We didn't mean this to happen.'

It took Cleo several minutes to regain her breath and get to her feet. Dobbs was wearing handcuffs similar to the ones Cleo had been wearing earlier in the day. The three stooges were standing, crestfallen beside her. All of them were flanked by two large policemen. Miss Phelps stood to one side. The woman turned to face Dobbs, whose face was white now.

'Are these the ones, Miss Phelps?' the woman asked.

'These are the four in question.'

The woman inclined her head towards Dobbs. 'And I assume this young lady is their ringleader?'

'That one's Dobbs,' confirmed Miss Phelps.

'My name is Henderson of Her Majesty's Prison Service. The four of you are being transferred to Peterlee,' the woman announced, crisply. 'As of right now ... and I doubt if you'll be doing much bullying there!'

There was a gasp from the other girls in the room. Peterlee was a closed detention centre, renowned as one of the toughest girl's reformatories in the country.

Dobbs looked at Cleo with hatred in her eyes, which became shock as the news sank in; then she joined her stooges in weeping, copiously. And Cleo realised that, like most bullies, Dobbs wasn't hard, just bad.

'And as for you,' Miss Henderson turned to Cleo and softened her tone. 'You and I have some people to see.'

Bushy passed them in the corridor, his inflexible face was more rigid than usual. He spared neither Cleo nor her companion a glance.

'We have just accepted his resignation,' said Miss Henderson in a low voice. 'Effective as of now.'

'What about Miss Phelps, miss?' Cleo asked.

'She was a great help to us.'

'She wasn't much of a help to me, miss.'

'You can't win them all, Cleo.'

Another of life's lessons learned. Miss Phelps, it seemed, had saved her skin by turning on Bushy when things began to look tricky.

They entered the governor's office without knocking. There were five people in there. Three of them Cleo didn't know, one was their car driver and the other was Flo Dunderdale. She gave Cleo a huge smile then went over to hug her.

'What are you doing here?' Cleo asked, bewildered.

'I thought you might need a bit of help,' Flo said. 'Most of the girls corroborated your story.'

'Oh,' Cleo said. 'I didn't think they would.'

'Well they have, and Miss Dobbs is in very deep trouble.'

'Oh,' said Cleo, once again; still not sure where Flo fitted into all this.

'Oh? Is that all you can say after all the trouble I've been to?'

'Well ... I don't know what to say.'

'You could say, thank you,' said Miss Henderson. 'She twisted a lot of arms did your friend Flo, who is a most unusual lady.'

'Yes,' Cleo said. 'I suppose she is.'

'On top of which, *they* all believe your story,' said Miss Henderson, turning to the three strangers in the room.

The two men and the woman all nodded their agreement. Cleo never found out who they were but they all looked very important, and having important people believe in you is always a good thing.

'I gather you didn't speak up for yourself in court,' Miss Henderson said. 'The magistrate had no option but to find you guilty.'

It seemed Miss Henderson felt she had to defend the juvenile penal system.

'I was only twelve, miss. I didn't know what to say to them.'

'Quite.'

'The reason they're more inclined to believe you now,' Flo explained, 'is because your stepfather was jailed last week for assaulting a boy. He got six years.'

'It wasn't–'

'No, it wasn't your brother. We're not quite sure where your brother is. Although I suspect you could enlighten them if you wanted to.'

'I don't want to.'

So, Horace was in jail. So much justice in one day was hard to take. But Cleo wasn't entirely convinced – her fortunes had a habit of going belly-up.

'What will happen to me?' she asked.

Flo looked at Miss Henderson, who said to Cleo: 'I'll get a photographer to document your bruises, just for our records. I'm arranging for your status to be adjusted. Hopefully we can transfer you to Priory Hall which is actually outside our jurisdiction but more suitable to your needs. We'll keep a discreet eye on you, of course, while your conviction remains on file.'

Other than the fact that she was being moved, Cleo didn't really know what all that meant.

'I'm not sure I want to be moved.'

She was thinking in terms of better the devil you know. Whitley Grange without Dobbs would be easy enough to bear.

Flo explained. 'Priory Hall's just an ordinary

children's home near Leeds. When I say "ordinary", it's one o' the good ones I'm led to believe. In the meantime I'm going to make it my business to get your sentence quashed.'

'Will my brother be able to visit me without being arrested?'

'I'll do what I can,' Flo assured her. 'Under the circumstances I doubt if anyone will trouble him. They'll have me to deal with if they do. I wouldn't mind meeting him myself.'

'You'll like him.'

'I already like him,' Flo said, 'and I haven't even met him.'

It was very much an afterthought when Cleo asked, 'What about my mother?'

'No one knows where she is, love.'

Cleo nodded. It didn't matter to her. The only person in the world who mattered to her was in London.

'Is there anything else you want to know?' Flo asked.

'Yes,' Cleo said. 'Where's my seven and six?'

Part Two

Chapter Eight

Priory Hall, near Leeds, was like a holiday camp compared to Whitley Grange. Cleo went to the local secondary modern school and prospered both physically and mentally; staying on beyond the optional leaving age of fifteen to take six O Levels. Cleo only got four, but from her starting point she was more than pleased. Ant came up from London half a dozen times a year; on one occasion in an old banger he'd borrowed after passing his driving test. They went to Scarborough in it and Cleo introduced him to Flo, who fell in love with him and very much regretted being old enough to be his mother. Flo visited Cleo every month without fail. Cleo's case was reheard without any contribution, this time, from Horace Womack and her conviction was quashed.

She stayed at Priory Hall until the week after her sixteenth birthday, when she left school. They said she was free to go, provided she had somewhere safe to live. By this time Ant had been living and working back in Leeds for several months and had just rented a house. For the two of them.

Priory Hall restored her faith in human nature. There were no exciting happenings to talk about, just the normal 'kids growing up' stuff. As it was a children's home there were a few oddballs about, but none so odd as Blister or as nasty as Dobbs. Cleo didn't get into any scrapes. She was one of life's victims, never a perpetrator.

Ant collected her from Priory Hall in an old pickup truck he'd recently bought. It was the last Monday in July 1957, as Cleo said her tearful farewells to the friends she had made and to the people who had looked after her and treated her like a human being. Whitley Grange was a distant memory, and Cleo had no interest in the whereabouts or well-being of her mother, much less Horace Womack.

By sheer chance (and Flo Dunderdale) Cleo had managed to spend the two most formative years of her life in the care of decent people; but was she wise in choosing to spend the most interesting years of her life in the care of Ant Kelly, who was both a victim and a perpetrator (in equal measures) of life's injustices? Much as she loved her brother she was unsure about this from the start.

Ant gave her a huge grin as she climbed into his truck, then he thrust two fivers into her hand.

'What's this for?'

'Call it a "welcome to the world" present,' he said. 'We all need money to get by.'

It was the most money she'd ever had and she mumbled an inadequate 'thank you'.

'I need to call at the office on the way home,' Ant said.

'Office, what office?'

'Jimmy Dickinson's, the firm I'm working for. They owe me seventy-five quid, but they'll only pay me sixty.'

'Why's that?'

'They say it's twenty per cent retention to be paid in three months, but when the time comes, they'll find something wrong with my work and I won't get it. They do it to everyone.'

'So, why do you work for them?'

He grinned. 'Well, I didn't know about it when I priced the job and they always pay me a month in hand, so if I walk away I stand to lose a lot of money. I just pretend I don't mind and make it up in other ways. I do okay, don't worry about me.'

'I see.'

Cleo didn't really, but she didn't want to know. It was a beautiful day in many ways and she felt a new life beckoning. Ant wasn't going to spoil that.

'You can come and work for me, if you like.'

'Me ... what doing?'

'Brickie's labourer.'

He said it as though a sixteen-year-old girl working as a bricklayer's labourer was the most natural thing in the world.

'I could pay you three bob an hour and I work a sixty-hour week so it's worth nine pounds a week. Which is twice as much as you'd earn anywhere else.'

'Ant, I'm a skinny girl, not a big Irish navvy.'

'Being strong's not everything, you just have to be fit.'

'It'd kill me.'

'Not when you get used to it.'

Cleo was actually thinking of applying for an

office job, but she had already been offered an alternative.

'Flo's offered me a job in Scarborough,' she said. 'I told her I'd think about it.' Working for Flo on Scarborough beach sounded a lot more attractive than working on a building site.

'On the chairs?' Ant asked.

'Maybe. She's got an ice-cream stall as well – and a few donkeys.'

'Sounds as if she's going up in the world.'

'Flo's been up and down in the world more times than Blackpool Big Dipper.'

'I like Flo,' he said. 'Anyway it's up to you.'

Cleo sat back and chose not to think about it for the time being. They were driving south along the Wetherby road and had crested a hill when the panorama of Leeds spread out below them. Despite the blue sky above there was a grey pall hanging over the city centre and its southern suburbs where all the heavy industry was. Under that umbrella of smog the people of Leeds worked, played, suffered from catarrh and plodded cheerfully on with their lives as best they could. This would never be enough for Cleo. She could even see the gasometer that had cast a dark shadow over her childhood, albeit not as dark as the shadow cast by Womack and Wet Nelly.

'Whereabouts is this house you've rented?' she asked, hoping it would be nowhere near the gasometer. He pointed almost directly at it.

'Over there, Hamblin Terrace.'

'Oh,' Cleo said, with no enthusiasm whatsoever. She knew Hamblin Terrace. It was half a dozen streets away from their old house. A vastly superior street, but in the same neighbourhood, with all its memories. Scarborough was becoming more attractive by the minute.

'Mam's not there any more,' Ant said, as though in mitigation. 'Nobody knows where she is.'

'So, you bothered to ask then?'

'Not really. Some people hoped I might know where she is so they could chase her for money. She owed Foxy for six weeks' papers. I paid him, but I didn't pay anyone else. I told 'em I didn't know where she was and I didn't care.'

'I'm glad you paid Foxy... What about Horace?'

'Still inside as far as I know – he attacked a kid, you know.'

'Yes, I know.'

They had never discussed Horace Womack or their mother on Ant's visits to Priory Hall. Almost to himself, Ant said, 'I reckon there's more to that than came out in court or they'd have thrown the key away.'

'Oh, such as?'

He went quiet, as if regretting he'd brought the subject up. Cleo could have sworn he was blushing as he said, 'Nothing.'

The headquarters of J Dickinson Ltd consisted of a yard and a long wooden building, part of which was an office; the rest was storage sheds. Ant parked the pickup outside the office door.

'Come in with me,' he said. 'Might as well start learning the ropes straight away.'

'Ropes, what ropes?'

She hadn't agreed to work with him yet, and she certainly hadn't agreed to be a bricklayer's labourer. But she didn't argue, after all it was one of her good days and she'd had few enough of them. They entered a narrow passage where Ant knocked on a sliding-glass window. It slid open and a pretty face smiled at him. Jenny Smith looked a few years older than Ant but her eyes lit up when she saw him.

'Is he in?' Ant asked.

Jenny pressed a button on her telephone. 'Mr Kelly's here, Mr Dickinson. He wants to know if you're in.'

She held the phone away from her as a stream of vitriol poured through the earpiece. 'He hates me doing that,' she said to Ant, 'but he can't get anyone better for what he pays me.'

Cleo moved into view and the woman's expression froze for a second, perhaps assuming Cleo was a rival. 'This is my sister, Cleo.' Ant said. Then to Cleo, 'Cleo, this is Jenny Smith.'

Jenny extended her hand through the small window and Cleo shook it.

'Pleased to meet you, Cleo. I've heard a lot about you.'

Cleo gave her brother a look that asked if he and Jenny were a couple.

'I wine and dine her now and again,' he said, in response to her unspoken question. 'Don't I, Jen?'

'He takes me to the Tomato Dip every other Tuesday,' Jenny told Cleo. 'One of these days he'll splash out.'

'Not if he keeps knocking me money down,' Ant grumbled.

At that moment a door further along the

passage opened and a middle-aged man stepped out. He wore a frown and a tired suit that somehow matched the rest of him.

'Ant,' he said. 'What are yer doing here? I thought yer'd be grafting away on site.'

'I've been to collect my sister. I did tell you. Anyway, while I was passing I thought I'd pop in and pick up my money.'

The smile on the man's face dropped. 'Right, lad,' he said. 'Yer'd best come in. You as well, love. Let's get a good look at yer.'

Cleo didn't like him. He was trying to patronise her, but she followed Ant into the office.

'By heck! She's a right bobby dazzler. I wish I were ten years younger.'

Cleo was thinking, try forty, as she gave him one of her smiles.

The man sat down and drummed his fingers on the desk. 'Right, where did I put yer invoice? That lass's filing system's a bloody mystery ter me.'

'I've got a copy of it here,' Ant said, bringing a sheet of paper from his pocket and placing it on the desk. 'It's all agreed by your surveyor. Seventy-five pounds.'

'Right, lad ... so that's how much, after retention?'

'Sixty,' Ant said. 'But I've got three lots of retention due to me for stuff I did over three months ago. Do you want me to make out a separate invoice or will you just pay it?'

'Once I've knocked the cost of the remedial work off, I reckon you'll be owin' me brass,' said Dickinson, without looking up to see Ant's reaction.

'Right,' Ant said – giving in very easily, Cleo thought. 'I just thought I'd mention it.'

The contractor wrote a cheque out for sixty pounds. 'I've dated it Friday,' he said, 'because yer'll not have time ter take it ter yer bank before then, with all yer've got on.'

'That's very thoughtful of you, Mr Dickinson,' said Ant. But his sarcasm fell on deaf ears.

'Thinking's all part of my job,' said the contractor, happy now that he'd deprived Ant of another fifteen pounds. 'Your job's ter graft. I'll do the thinking.' He turned his attention to Cleo and she couldn't decide whether he was smiling or smirking.

'I don't suppose yer can type, can yer?' he asked. 'Cos if yer can, there's a job goin' for yer here. That lazy cow's days are numbered, believe you me.'

'Give over,' grinned Ant. 'There's only Jenny knows what's going on round here.'

'No harm in swapping her for a newer model,' said Dickinson. 'Especially one what looks like your lass. I wouldn't climb over your lass ter get ter my missis, I'll tell yer that for nowt.'

Ant's face had turned to stone and Cleo thought for a second that he was going to give Dickinson a well-deserved mouthful. But he just picked up his cheque and muttered something about having to be off. Cleo went out of the door in front of him. Jenny called cheerio as she walked down the passage and Cleo felt like telling her what a pig her boss was, but she guessed Jenny already knew that. Ant was a few steps behind; he leaned in through Jenny's window.

'I'll give you a ring,' he said.

'Pigs might fly, but I can dream.'

Cleo suspected that Jenny's tongue was in her cheek when she said it but she liked her and couldn't get over the fact that this attractive woman obviously fancied her brother.

'Will he have had to do any remedial work?' she asked Ant as they drove off.

'No.'

'Why did you let him get away with it?'

'Because it keeps me in work. Most brickies leave him as soon as they twig what he's doing. I just make up for it in other ways. I'll show you, if you like.'

Ant drove her to a line of lock-up railway arches about a mile away from the centre of Leeds. He opened one and switched on a light inside to reveal an Aladdin's cave of building materials. Bags of cement piled to the roof, bricks, pipes, timber and many things Cleo couldn't put a name to.

'I don't work exclusively for Dickinson,' Ant told her. 'But he does supply me with most of the materials I use on other jobs – at a very good discount.'

'You mean you steal this stuff off him?'

'No, I transfer it from his sites to here and pay for it with the money he owes me. He doesn't know it, but that's only a technicality.'

'I doubt if the police would see it as a technicality, if they ever find out.'

'Why would they find out? Dickinson never misses it ... besides.' He gave Cleo one of his grins.

'Besides what?' she asked.

'I've got his written permission to do it, just in case.'

'Then how come he doesn't know?'

'Because he never looks at what he's signing. If push came to shove it'd be a civil matter, not a criminal offence. And he wouldn't have a leg to stand on.'

'Jenny,' Cleo guessed. 'You've got Jenny involved in this?'

'The letter was her idea,' Ant admitted. 'She typed it out one day and stuck it under his nose. He's so slack about paperwork, he'd sign his own death warrant rather than read it. That's one thing you've got to keep your eye on in business – paperwork. It's paper that builds a business, not bricks and mortar.'

'What does Jenny get out of it?'

'My undying gratitude – plus a few quid now and again.' He shook his head at his sister's disapproving look. 'Cleo, I do a damn good job for Dickinson – so everybody's happy. It's the way things work in this world.'

'Is there anything else I need to know?' she asked.

Ant rubbed his nose, guiltily. 'Well, there's some developers that Dickinson does a lot of work for – they're going to give me their next job.'

'Dare I ask why?'

'Well, my price is a bit cheaper, and they know my work's good.'

'I suppose Jenny told you what Dickinson's price was?' Cleo was learning fast.

'She might have mentioned it. Cleo, everybody's at it. Dickinson's as bent as a nine bob note. He'd never shop me to the police in case it opened a can of worms he'd rather keep the lid on. The worst he'd do is sack me.'

It had a kind of twisted logic. Maybe it was the way the world had treated them that helped Cleo accept her brother's way of doing things.

'You know, it's a good thing Dickinson fiddles you out of money,' she said.

'Oh, why's that?'

'Because you'd never be able to live with your conscience otherwise.'

'You're right there,' said Ant. But he didn't sound convincing.

They were back in his truck now, heading for Hamblin Terrace, and her surroundings were becoming increasingly familiar. This instilled a gloom into her that didn't make sense but she couldn't shake it off. She tried small talk.

'Is Jenny Smith your girlfriend, then?'

'Jenny? No she's too old for me, she's just a mate.'

'Too old? I bet she's only twenty-one.'

'Twenty-three.'

'So, you took the trouble to find out, then? I bet you know what colour her eyes are, and her birthday.'

Ant didn't answer, which told Cleo she was right. 'Have you got a girlfriend?' she asked.

'Not as such.'

Not as such? What was that supposed to mean? she wondered.

'You never talk about your girlfriends,' she

pressed. 'I bet you've had loads.'

'A few.'

He was so non-committal it could have meant anything, but Cleo could read Ant better than anyone and she got a feeling that he hadn't had a proper girlfriend ... ever; which was odd, considering his age, his looks and his personality. She didn't pursue the matter.

'What about you?' he asked. 'I bet you've been beating lads off with a shovel.'

'A few,' she said.

'How many?'

'Mind your own business.'

'You want to be careful,' he said. 'Lads take advantage.'

He sounded more like a father than a brother, Cleo thought, maybe that's the way he felt towards her and maybe she should be grateful.

'I know how to take care of myself, thanks very much.'

'Don't get your knickers in a twist.'

There was a slight atmosphere between them now, and they drove in silence for a while, eventually stopping outside Number Twenty, Hamblin Terrace.

'That's it,' he said. 'Number Twenty. It'll do till I get properly on my feet.'

It was a palace compared to their last home, but Cleo wasn't at all sure she wanted to live there. She loved Ant, but the idea of them living together didn't feel right; and she certainly had reservations about becoming a brickie's labourer, even for nine pounds a week.

Within a couple of days of moving in with Ant she knew one thing for certain, she couldn't live with him. The brother she'd known had matured into something she didn't understand. Their relationship had become awkward. He was constantly on the defensive when she asked him anything marginally personal. If she tried to talk about Jenny or girls in general, he'd clam up. In fact he didn't seem to have a social life at all; his world revolved around his work. He also seemed to keep more of a physical distance between himself and Cleo. In the past he'd often put an arm around her shoulders and squeeze her, or give her a playful push or a gentle punch on her arm (sometimes not all that gentle). But he'd stopped doing all that. There was no more teasing and no more friendly fights. All the things Cleo missed about having a brother seemed to have gone. He was still funny and kind and he still loved her, but he treated her with too much respect. She didn't want respect from him; she wanted him to be good, old, scatterbrained, incorrigible Ant, the brother she'd so desperately missed having beside her when things were going wrong.

This wasn't the reason she gave him for wanting to go and work with Flo. She told him she fancied an easy life for a bit before she started growing up. Flo had offered to put her up in her house and Cleo sensed an adventure in the offing. There was a depth to Flo that Cleo wanted to explore, a past she wanted to know about, and lessons to be learned from this woman. Lessons Ant couldn't teach her.

Her brother took her over to Scarborough on Friday after work and stood there like a lemon as Cleo said goodbye to him. The old Ant would have been hugging the life out of her. So she took the initiative and hugged him, as Flo looked on with her arms folded and the inevitable cigarette in her mouth.

'Come over whenever you want,' Flo said to him. 'I've got bags of room.'

'I'll do that,' he grinned. 'See you, Cleo, thanks Flo.'

He climbed back into his truck and drove away and Cleo somehow felt that the thread that had bound them together as kids in common adversity had suddenly snapped. And it made her cry.

Chapter Nine

Looking out of her dormer window, across a jumble of rooftops, Cleo could see the sea from her room in Flo's house. It was a tall, narrow building in grey stone and she lived just under the pantiled roof. Had it not been such a pretty room the sloping ceiling might have been reminiscent of the bogey hole, but there the similarity ended. Cleo knew the instant she opened the door that it would take wild horses to drag her back to Hamblin Terrace.

Her room was chocolate-box pretty with white walls and a bright floral cover on a bed which she knew would swallow her up and send her to sleep with a head full of pleasant dreams. On the floor was a well-worn, but clean, carpet, and on the dressing table was a vase of fresh flowers. There was a small wardrobe and a comfortable-looking chair and best of all there was a deep window seat where she could sit and dream and watch the boats out in the bay. A passing seagull peeled off from a screeching, marauding flock and flapped to a halt just outside the window, where it perched on the sill, looking through the window, expectantly.

'Don't feed 'em,' Flo warned. 'You'll never be rid of 'em. That bugger must have a long memory. Somebody must have fed him at some time.'

She opened the window and the bird took off, flew around in a wide circle and returned in a stately glide past; with a beady eye out for any food being put out on the windowsill. Then it gave what sounded like an insulting squawk and flapped away. Flo turned to Cleo.

'What do you think?'

'I think it's beautiful.'

'It used to be a very popular room when I let this place out,' Flo said. 'More bother than it's worth, that game. Better off hirin' out deckchairs. You don't have to make deckchairs breakfast or let 'em in, blind drunk, at midnight. Deckchairs are a lot less trouble than people.'

It was a philosophy Cleo had some sympathy with. 'How much will it cost me?' she enquired.

'Pound a week off your wages,' Flo said. 'All found.'

'And how much are my wages?'

'Four pound a week.'

It seemed generous enough. Certainly a pound a week board and lodgings was; and four pounds a week was the most a sixteen-year-old school leaver could reasonably expect.

She still had four pounds left from the money Ant had given her, having splashed out on make-up and a hair cut – the first time in her life she'd ever been to a proper ladies' hairdresser's. As a girl her mother used to cut it, always finishing with the immortal words of amateur hairdressers the length and breadth of the country, 'There's only a fortnight between a good haircut and a bad 'un.' In Whitley Grange it was cut by a visiting hairdresser with blunt scissors (Cleo always assumed this was part of the punishment), who gave them all the same cut, once every two months. Priory Hall was marginally better, with the haircutting being done by one of the house parents who had actually trained as a hairdresser.

But Blanche Nuttall (of Rome, Paris and Leeds) was the first hairdresser ever to *style* it for her, and Cleo thought she looked the bee's knees. Seamus Jaques thought so as well.

She met Seamus on the beach. Flo had given her a deckchair pitch of her own up on the North Shore. At first it was a bit lonely until she found out she could talk to people. With her recent, institutionalised background she'd found that keeping her mouth shut and ears open was the best way to be. *Tell the buggers nothing.* But she was now dealing with the public and, to her surprise, she found she could deal with them very well, especially the boys. In fact it amazed her when a girl of around nineteen confronted her with blazing eyes and arms akimbo and accused her of flirting with her boyfriend.

'I thought I was just being polite,' Cleo said.

'Well I reckon yer were flirting.'

'I wasn't,' Cleo protested.

'If I catch yer smilin' at 'im again, I'll knock yer bloody block off!'

Cleo never saw them again, but it didn't stop her smiling, especially when there was someone worth smiling at – such as Seamus Jaques.

He was a local lad of twenty, who drifted from

job to job; mainly fairground or building work, although his father had a fishing boat on which he occasionally helped out. He had two older brothers who took precedence in the family business. This suited Seamus, who couldn't stand the smell of fish – one of the few things he and Cleo had in common. Seamus was dangerous to women insofar as he was good looking and had charm, humour and the body of an athlete; or to be more precise, the body of a footballer. Seamus played left half for Scarborough Town reserves and was as fit as a fiddle. And like a lot of the young men who worked the fairs, he wore his long dark hair in a ponytail, which fascinated Cleo. Flo had known Seamus for some time and she didn't trust him as far as she could throw him, which cut no ice with Cleo. When you're sixteen you need to find these things out for yourself.

The first time Cleo saw him was on a sunny Saturday. She'd been there a fortnight and he was suddenly standing in front of her asking for two chairs; one for him, one for the girl who was standing just behind him. Two minutes later he came back on his own, leaving his girlfriend struggling to put the chairs up.

'You know, you're the bonniest bird on the beach,' he said.

Cleo didn't know how to handle compliments yet. 'Shouldn't you be helping your girlfriend?'

'That's not my girlfriend, that's er ... my sister.'

His hesitation told her he was probably lying, but he said it with such an innocent look in his baby blue eyes.

'I think your er ... sister needs your help,' she said.

His 'sister' was looking daggers at him. It was the day after Cleo had been threatened with having her block knocked off and she didn't want it to become a habit.

'Are you here every day?' he asked.

'Weather permitting.'

'Maybe I'll see you tomorrow then?'

'Maybe you will.'

Their first date was to the pictures where they sat on the back row to watch *The Bridge on the River Kwai.* At least they watched the first half of the film and, long before Alec Guinness and his British POWs had finished building the bridge, Cleo and Seamus were building bridges of their own and were locked in a deep embrace, which was broken only by the usherette's torch. It caught Seamus's hand wandering across Cleo's blouse where it stretched over her breast. She turned her face away, embarrassed, but Seamus just grinned and said the usherette was only jealous. On the way home he took her up a dark alleyway where they kissed again; this time his hand became more adventurous.

'No,' Cleo said, half heartedly.

Seamus sensed her lack of conviction and ignored her, expertly unfastening her bra strap. Cleo's heart quickened as his hand gently massaged her breast, her nipple hardened to his touch. She felt him hardening against her and knew she had to make a decision.

'Please,' she said. 'No further.'

'I wasn't going to go any further, you brazen hussy,' he said. 'What do you take me for?'

His tongue was in his cheek but she was grateful. Had he been more persistent she might have given in to him; and she wasn't ready for that. Whenever and wherever that happened it had to be special. Preferably on her wedding night in some plush honeymoon hotel on the French Riviera. No harm in dreaming.

'Fancy going to a dance on Saturday?' he asked, later. 'My mate and his girlfriend are going, we could make up a foursome.'

They were standing at the door of Flo's house, inside which Flo was resisting the temptation to peep through the curtains.

'I'm not very good at dancing,' Cleo said.

'Neither am I,' said Seamus. 'We can teach each other.'

Flo was watching television as Cleo came in. 'Had a nice time?' she asked. She really wanted to know if that Jaques lad had tried it on, but she didn't want to patronise Cleo. The girl had had a lifetime of that.

'Yes thanks.'

'Good film,' Flo commented. 'Did you like the ending?' It was as though she knew what Cleo and Seamus had been up to.

'Yeah,' said Cleo, then hurriedly changed the subject. 'We're going dancing on Saturday.'

'Are you now?' Flo failed to hide the disapproval in her voice. Cleo picked it up.

'What's up, don't you like Seamus?'

'It's not that I don't like him. He's quite a lot older than you and...'

'And what?'

'Experienced,' Flo said at length, nodding to herself to confirm she'd chosen the right word. It wasn't the first word that came to her mind when describing Seamus Jaques but it would have to do.

'In what way?' Cleo asked.

'Well he's got a bit of a reputation that's all.'

'Reputation?'

'With the girls ... and don't ask me to elaborate because I'm only saying what I've heard.'

'He's very good company,' Cleo said.

'Oh, I'm sure he is. I'd just like you to be careful, that's all.'

'I wouldn't mind a new dress.'

Flo smiled. 'I've got a wardrobe full,' she said. 'See if there's anything that takes your fancy. I might have to take one or two of them in, but I was your size once, believe it or not.'

'Won't they all be–?' Cleo was trying to be tactful.

Flo finished her question off for her. 'Old fashioned? Don't judge till you've had a look. Some of 'em cost an arm an' a leg, and class takes a long time to go out of fashion. You mark my words.'

The dress Cleo chose needed no alteration. It was a knee-length, halter neck, black and red dress with a daring slit up the side and would have cost her a month's wages to buy it new. Flo reckoned she looked 'bloody spectacular' in it.

As Cleo walked into the Crescent Ballroom she could almost feel the eyes of the men as they stared at her. She felt good in her dress but took an instant dislike to Seamus's friend, Kev, and his girlfriend, Anita. Kev was very coarse and looked to be several links down the food chain from normal people. They sat around a table for four as Seamus went for the drinks.

'I reckon yer were brought up in a children's home,' Kev said.

'For the last couple of years, I was.'

'Where did yer live before that?'

Cleo had unwisely confided in Seamus about Whitley Grange. 'My parents split up,' she said. Then to change the subject, she asked Anita, 'Do you still live with your parents?'

Anita ignored Cleo's question. 'Seamus reckons yer were in a reform school before that.'

'Does he now?' said Cleo.

'He tells me yer burnt yer house down.' Both Anita and Kev burst out laughing. 'I don't wonder yer mam and dad split up if they had nowhere ter live!'

Cleo was becoming annoyed when Seamus got back with four glasses of Kia-Ora orange juice on a tray. Licensing laws dictated that only soft drinks were sold in such places, so both Seamus and Kev had persuaded the girls to each smuggle in a half bottle of gin in their handbags, some of which was now added to their drinks. Cleo sipped at hers and could barely detect the tang of Gordons. She remained the topic of Anita's barbed conversation and was grateful when Seamus got her up to dance.

He had been lying. Seamus Jaques was the best dancer on the floor whether the band played modern, old time or rock and roll. Cleo's only experience had been at a youth club near Priory Hall, where she had learned the fundamentals but had acquired no real expertise. A night dancing with Seamus altered that.

He whispered in her ear that she was a quick learner and held her to him as they circled the dance floor under the twinkling mirror ball. 'And the best-looking girl here.'

'I had a good teacher,' she whispered back. 'And you're not so bad yourself.'

He kissed her, gently, and she knew the lessons would continue on the way home. She was enjoying herself now and wished they'd come on their own and not in a foursome.

'I don't think Anita likes me,' she said.

'Take no notice. She can't stand competition, that's her problem. It's the same every time we come out in a foursome. I reckon she only goes out wi' Kev ter get ter me.'

'And has she ever got to you?' Cleo enquired.

'Don't be daft,' he said. It wasn't much of an answer, but she didn't press him on it.

Cleo glanced over to their table and thought she saw Kev topping up her glass with gin. When they got back she took a tiny sip of her drink to confirm her suspicions.

'Hmmm,' she said, 'nice.' It tasted lethal.

She put her glass down beside Anita's drink which had hardly been touched. Kev and Anita smirked and looked away, not noticing when Cleo picked up Anita's glass instead of her own. But they watched as she drank it in one go.

'Thirsty work, dancing,' commented Seamus, who was not in on the trick. 'Your round,' he said to Kev, who sniggered:

'I think yer might be on a promise ternight, mate.'

'Don't be so crude,' said Seamus.

'I'm only sayin' what's on yer mind that's all. There's nowt unnatural about it.'

'There's something unnatural about you!' said Seamus, annoyed that his chances with Cleo were being jeopardised.

'Unnatural? Shaggin's not unnatural, is it Nita? It's how the 'uman race came ter be 'ere.'

His girlfriend glared at him then drank the swapped gin and orange in one go. Cleo waited for her to comment on its strength, but Kev's embarrassing crudity had distracted her. Anita just took a sharp intake of breath, plonked the empty glass down on the table and said, 'Do summat useful, monkey brain, and fetch us some more drinks!'

Kev got to his feet and pulled a monkey face at her. He hung his arms loose and scratched his armpits.

'Suits yer!' Anita snapped. 'You act like a bloody monkey most of the time.'

'That's exactly me point, innit?' said Kev. 'We all come from monkeys.'

'You haven't come very far, have you?' said Cleo.

Seamus laughed out loud. 'He's like one of them baboons. Hey, Kev, does yer arse go red when yer feelin' randy?'

Kev wandered off, bemused, and Anita's eyes blazed angrily at Cleo.

'He's my bloke,' she said. 'I'll thank yer ter keep

yer snide bloody remarks ter yerself.'

'I was just agreeing with you,' retorted Cleo. 'It was you who called him monkey brain.'

'Yer cheeky bloody mare! Anyroad, what room have you ter talk? A bloody reformatory lass.'

'Whoa, girls!'

Had Seamus not put his arm around her at that moment, Cleo would have got up and left.

'Come on, Nita,' he said. 'She was only kidding.'

Cleo was dying to say she wasn't, and returned Anita's stony stare with a better one of her own. There was an awkward silence between them until Kev came back with the drinks, Anita took a large gulp from hers then stood up.

'Come on, Kev,' she said. 'We're dancin'.'

Seamus turned in his seat to watch them go. 'Kev's a bit thick,' he said, 'but he's harmless.'

Cleo was topping Anita's drink up with gin as he spoke. Then she poured some of her own drink into Kev's half-empty glass. Flo's parting words as she left to meet Seamus were still ringing in her ears. 'There'll be alcohol about, Cleo. Raises the libido and lowers the resistance. You mark my words.'

'You do realise she's as jealous as hell of you, don't you,' Seamus said, returning his attention to Cleo, who had finished what she was doing and was smiling, innocently. 'You look too good. That's why she's being so catty.'

'Is that a compliment?'

'It's a statement of fact.'

In between dances, during the course of the next couple of hours, Cleo managed to top up

Anita's glass several more times while avoiding drinking much alcohol herself. As the evening wore on, Anita's general attitude became more and more aggressive. The band went into a rock and roll session and she dragged Kev, roughly, to his feet.

'C'mon, yer big useless bugger. Less show 'em how iss done.'

'She sounds a bit tipsy,' Cleo commented as Anita and Kev tried a few unco-ordinated dance steps.

'I know,' said Seamus. 'Funny that. She's had no more to drink than anyone else, including you.' He gave Cleo a suspicious look. 'Trouble is,' he said. 'She gets very ratty when she's had a few.'

'Really? I hadn't noticed,' Cleo said.

The two of them watched as Kev and his tipsy girlfriend eventually picked up the rhythm and whirled around to 'See You Later Alligator'. Kev stepped on Anita's foot, and he was no lightweight. She spat out a mouthful of expletives and a woman dancing nearby called her a 'Common cow!' The woman received a very common mouthful for her trouble and was about to give as good as she got when her partner skilfully steered her away. The second time Kev stepped on Anita's foot she reacted with a scything punch to the side of his face which sent him sprawling. Then, as though hitting her partner was all part of the rock-and-roll experience, she pulled him to his feet and yanked him into action once again. She was in mid-turn when she vomited all over herself and various nearby dancers. The floor cleared within seconds and the music came to a halt. Kev quickly deserted his girlfriend, who now stood, white-faced and hapless, inside a circle of sick and a larger circle of muttering people. Cleo felt almost as good as she had when Dobbs was clapped in handcuffs. Justice came and went in this world, you just had to take what was on offer and forget the bad times.

A grumbling man with a mop and bucket arrived to clean up the mess and Anita, who was obviously drunk and very much *persona non grata,* was asked to leave. Kev grudgingly went with her, leaving Cleo and Seamus to enjoy what was left of the evening.

'Funny how she got blind drunk and you didn't,' Seamus commented. 'I must be careful not to cross you.'

She looked at him, and knew he knew.

'Very careful indeed,' she said. 'Or I might just come and burn your house down.'

She had been the focus of many jealous eyes all evening, and not just Anita's. But Seamus only had eyes for her, which made her feel special. There was a magnetism about him that lowered her resistance, but she knew she mustn't weaken. By the time the last waltz came to a close and everyone was standing for 'God Save the Queen' she had planned her strategy to forestall him in his ultimate carnal ambition.

They made their way home along a clifftop path, with nothing but the sound of an occasional insomniac seagull and the crashing waves to disturb their conversation. A bright moon shone its shimmering light on the bay and the night sky was huge and dense with stars. Seamus was easy going and fanciful. He told her about his ambitions, which Cleo thought were a bit pie-in-the-sky. They included him one day playing First Division football and climbing the steps at Wembley to receive the FA Cup from the Queen. This seemed a big step from Scarborough Town reserves. But everyone should have their dream and she had no right to belittle his. Their walk took them past a cricket pavilion, to which he had a convenient key.

'I play for them now and again,' he explained, as he unlocked the door.

Once inside, he took her in his strong arms and kissed her, and she knew she had a fight on her hands if she wasn't to lose her virginity that night. Within five minutes her dress was around her ankles, her brassiere on the floor and Seamus was easing her pants over her suspender belt and stockings and down her thighs. But her fear of going all the way overcame her arousal. Just. Cleo undid his trousers and took him in her hand. It was the first time she'd ever done this with any man, and she gave a shudder of excitement as she felt him instantly harden to her touch. His breathing quickened and his hands were now running frantically over her naked body, across her breasts and between her legs as she brought him to a climax. Then she clung to him as the passion drained from his body and rose in hers.

Cleo was now frustrated to the point of tears. She was virtually naked, her pants and stockings around her knees, and she felt cheated. Wanting what she'd just given him but aware she only had herself to blame. Silently she adjusted her clothing, as he did the same.

'Phew!' he said. 'That was er ... are you okay?'

Cleo didn't quite know what he meant and neither did he probably, but she said she was okay and maybe she should be getting back or Flo would be worried.

But Flo had more to worry about than Cleo. He had walked through the door less than an hour after Cleo had left for the evening. Flo thought it was her.

'You're back early. What happened?' she asked, without turning away from the television.

'I got parole. Time off fer good behaviour.'

His voice came from behind her. Flo froze, but she didn't look round.

'You slimy sod! What are you doing here?'

'Where else would I go?' he said. 'This is me home.'

She turned to look at him now. His prison pallor took little away from that face. His gnomelike smile was still intact and as wide as ever. Two rows of tombstone teeth gleamed like old piano keys beneath a cauliflower nose that had suffered much damage, probably from the fists of irate women. He had an explosion of wiry hair which was greyer now; but otherwise, Sid Millichip hadn't changed in the last three years.

'I hope you're not expecting to stay here,' she said.

'It's just for a night, until I sort meself out.'

'You can sort yourself out a bed and breakfast,' Flo told him, firmly. 'You're not staying here. I'll ring the police if I have to. I'll tell them you've been harassing me. They'll find you a bed for the night.'

He held up his hands and smiled. 'Okay, yer Worship, you win.'

There was a time when that smile might have broken down her defences, but not any more. Not after it became public knowledge that her marriage to him had been a mockery.

'No doubt you got a big kick out of telling all your convict pals how you'd bigamously married a magistrate.'

Sid put his hand on his chest. 'Hand on heart, Flo. I never mentioned a word to anyone about yer. I always had the greatest respect for yer.'

'God! You're such a liar!'

'It's true ... and I never stole anything from yer. Come on, Flo, credit where credit's due.'

'You stole my dignity.'

'Oh, well – I'm sorry about that.' He thought for a moment, then said, 'Didn't stop yer bein' a magistrate though, did it?'

'I stayed on the bench to spite you! No way was I going to let a thieving liar like you destroy my life. And it wasn't easy.'

'That's what I liked about you,' Sid said. 'You always had spirit.'

'So did you, anything you could pour down your throat.'

Sid gave the pun a bigger laugh than it deserved, but Flo didn't weaken.

'I thought you'd have gone back to your proper wife in Huddersfield,' she said.

'She divorced me.'

'That wouldn't stop you.'

'I always preferred you, Flo, you know that. That's why I came to you and not to her.'

'So, if I pick up the phone and ring her up, she'll confirm you haven't been there.' Flo's hand was hovering over the phone.

'Well, naturally I called in ter pay me respects and offer me apologies. But that's all it was, as God is my judge.'

Flo moved away from the phone and picked up a pack of cigarettes, deliberately not offering him one. 'It was the best news of my life when I found out I wasn't really your wife.' She blew a cloud of smoke his way. 'Saved me a messy divorce.'

'Now, yer've hurt me, Flo,' Sid said. 'I've paid me debt to society and I know how yer once felt about me.'

'Once,' she admitted. 'But once bitten, twice shy.'

'Fair enough,' he said, graciously. 'I'll not force meself on yer.' He turned to go, then paused halfway to the door, and said without turning round. 'Yer do know this house is half in my name?'

'You bastard!' she fumed. 'I've paid the mortgage on this house since the day we bought it. You haven't paid a brass farthing. So don't you dare think you've got any claim on it!'

'I just want me rights, that's all,' he said.

'After what you did, you haven't got any bloody rights!'

'Yer probably right,' he accepted, reasonably. 'But if yer don't mind, I'll just check with a solicitor ter be sure.'

With that, he left. Flo sat down and buried her head in her hands, just like she'd been burying her head in the sand these last three years. She should have known he'd come back, like the bad penny he was.

Chapter Ten

'Are you and Seamus going steady now?' Flo was making conversation rather than taking an interest.

'I suppose so,' Cleo said.

It was the day after the dance and they were on the beach. Flo had checked with her solicitor to find out what claim Sid had on her home. The news wasn't good so she stuck her head back in the sand once again. This was unlike Flo, but the only way she could handle the spectre of Sid Millichip was not to think about him and hope he'd go away.

'What are you going to do about Sid?' Cleo asked.

'Oh, I don't know,' Flo sighed, staring out to sea. A breeze ruffled her hair and the bright morning sun made her half close her eyes against the glare off the water. 'It crossed my mind to have him back just for the fun of it, but he's such a reprehensible little shit. I always fall for the same type.' Glancing at Cleo she added, 'You mind your step with Seamus Jaques.'

'Seamus is okay.'

'Has he tried it on, yet?'

Cleo blushed flame red and said no he hadn't. Flo said it was only a question of time and when that time came, Cleo must be ready.

'Ready for what?' Cleo asked.

'Ready to repel boarders.'

'You make him sound like a pirate.'

'Plundering a girl's virginity is very much an act of piracy, Cleo. And with his ponytail he fits the part. They call them ponytails because when you lift one up there's usually an arsehole underneath.'

'I'm surprised Sid hasn't got one,' Cleo retorted, annoyed at Flo's comment about Seamus.

A family arrived to hire six chairs. As Cleo dealt with them, Flo lit up a cigarette. Cleo had thought about the previous night continually. Sometimes wishing she'd let Seamus have his way and then feeling relief that she hadn't. She knew she'd done the right thing, but what would happen next time?

'To be honest, Flo,' she said. 'He did try it on a bit.' Cleo remembered the 'bit' she was talking about and felt excited at the memory.

'Did he get past the giggling strip?'

'Giggling strip?'

Flo grinned and explained. 'It's what boys call that strip of flesh between the top of your stocking and your knickers. The theory is, if you get past that, you're laughing.'

'Ah,' said Cleo. 'Well he didn't get past that.'

She could have mentioned that Seamus approached things from the opposite direction but she didn't.

'Good girl,' said Flo. 'I expect he wanted to go all the way.'

'Probably, but I er ... I stopped him in his gallop, so to speak.'

Flo laughed out loud. 'There's always that ...

stopping them in their gallop works every time. Trouble is, they lose interest after that and you feel like a spare part.'

Cleo was non-committal, but the expression on her face showed that she agreed with every word her friend had just said. 'If you must know,' she said. 'Going any further scares me.'

'My advice is to stay scared,' Flo said. 'You're a normal young woman, with normal urges. The trouble is that normal young men have much bigger urges and far less self-control. Once they've got what they want you won't see 'em for dust. In my experience, giving in too easily can lead to big trouble. In fact, giving in at all can lead to trouble if he doesn't use a wotsit.'

'Wotsit? ... oh, right. What would you do if you met someone you really liked and he wanted to ... you know?'

'Me?' Flo laughed out loud. 'At my age I'd be grateful. At your age you should be very careful.'

Cleo laughed as well. 'You shouldn't put yourself down so much,' she said. 'You're a good-looking woman.'

Flo smiled. A compliment from Cleo carried much more weight than all the gush she'd heard from men over the years.

'Thanks,' she said. 'Promise me you'll be careful.'

'I promise.'

Flo studied Cleo's expression with a slow nod. Then, satisfied that her young friend was serious in her promise, she said, 'Right. I've got ice-creams to sell and donkeys to annoy. See you tonight.'

Cleo watched her friend as she left the beach and noticed the eyes of several men follow her. Many of them were young men. Cleo smiled to herself and tried to picture Flo twenty years ago. Whatever it was, Flo still had it.

Cleo never knew whether or not her keeping her promise to Flo made Seamus go astray. They had a good time, he was amusing company and he was the first man she ever loved. Physically they went so far and no further. She always stopped him taking that final step. Maybe she was worried about Flo's 'you won't see 'em for dust' warning. They had been together for nearly two months and Cleo was giving serious consideration to giving in to him, purely as an expression of her love. All her life she'd never had anyone to hold her and to love her. Ant would give her a squeeze now and again but it wasn't the same. She had missed the love of a daddy or a proper mother. Maybe giving herself fully to Seamus would make up for all that.

What brought their courtship to an end was the girl Cleo had seen him with on the beach that first morning – his 'sister'. She had never challenged him about this obvious lie; back then she had no claim on Seamus and she didn't want to embarrass him.

It was early October; Scarborough had been enjoying an Indian summer but the season was coming to a close. Cleo was on the beach, packing up for the day, when the girl came up to her and asked whose turn it was to go out with Seamus that night.

'I've lost track,' she said, brazenly. 'I normally see him on the nights he's not seeing you and I'm buggered if I can remember if he sees yer on a Wednesday.'

'You're a liar!'

The girl feigned innocence. 'Oh, heck! Yer don't know, do yer? Me and me big mouth. Look, don't tell him I told yer, will yer? It's just that he reckons he's not getting his end away wi' you, so I just help out in that respect.'

Cleo couldn't make out if she was teasing or telling the truth. The girl slapped a hand to her head as if remembering something.

'I remember now,' she said. 'It *is* my turn. Yer see, there's a party at Nita's house ternight, her mam and dad are out. Have yer ever been there? She's allus havin' parties is Nita.'

'No,' Cleo said. Suddenly she felt like an outsider among Seamus's circle of old friends.

'She lives in that white house up Sandsend Road – number forty-six.'

'Does she now?'

'Come if yer like. Nita won't mind – she'll prob'ly be too pissed ter know who's there. But yer'll have ter bring another feller. Seamus's all mine ternight ... and I'm all his, if yer know what I mean.'

She gave a mime which left no doubt in Cleo's mind what she meant. Words failed her as the girl wandered off, having inflicted as much damage on Cleo's emotions as she'd suffered in a long time.

Cleo was sitting in a chair staring at a blank

television screen when Flo came home. She had been crying and wasn't far off starting again. Flo sat in the chair opposite.

'Problem with Seamus?' she asked, gently.

Cleo nodded, distantly.

'Want to tell Auntie Flo about it?'

It took Cleo some time to form her words. 'I think he's seeing someone else.'

'Oh.' Flo took out a packet of Players and muttered something about having to cut down; then she offered one to Cleo. 'Might calm your nerves,' she said.

'No thanks.'

'Quite right, bad habit. Do you know this other person?'

'She came to see me this afternoon to tell me she goes out with him on the nights I don't see him.'

'She sounds a right catty little bitch,' Flo said. 'Do you believe her?'

'I don't want to believe her. She says she's going to a party tonight with Seamus. I can go if I like but I can't be with Seamus because he's with her tonight.' She ended the sentence in a flurry of tears.

'Well, the little madam! Have you asked Seamus about this?'

Cleo shook her head and sobbed, 'I don't know how to.' She looked up at Flo. 'I've never felt like this before, Flo. I can't stand the thought of him ... you know, *doing it* with anyone else.'

'So, you think he's doing it with her?'

Cleo nodded, dismally. 'I never let him. Do you think it's my fault? Do you think I should have let him and that's why he's going with her?'

'Cleo,' said Flo. 'I don't know what to think. All I know is that some men have very little control over what's in their trousers and if Seamus's one of 'em you might as well ditch him before he really hurts you.'

'Ditch him? How do I do that?'

Flo shrugged. 'Go to the party and see for yourself. She could be lying.'

'Would you come with me?'

Flo pulled Cleo to her feet and took her in her arms. 'If you like, love,' she said. Then she stepped back and held Cleo at arm's length. 'Actually, I might have a better idea. You've never met my nephew, John, have you? He lives in Seamer.'

'I've never met any of your family.'

'I'll give him a ring, maybe he can take you. You'll make more of an impression going with him.'

'Is he nice?'

'Oh yes,' Flo assured her. 'He's very very nice.'

John Dunderdale was in his early twenties and looked to have stepped out of a cinema screen. He had a bright red MG sports car, impeccable manners and an androgynous beauty that took Cleo's breath away. He was tall, tanned, athletically slim and looked like James Dean's better-looking brother. Cleo had borrowed another of Flo's frocks and as a couple they looked stunning. When John first saw her, he looked from her to Flo, and then back.

'Auntie Flo, I'm not sure I want to go out with

anyone who's prettier than me.'

'Just bring her back in one piece, young Dunderdale,' Flo instructed him. 'Emotionally and physically.'

John touched a servile forelock and replied, in a mock Cockney accent, 'The coach awaits wivout, me lady.'

'Wivout what?' said Flo.

'Wivout the bleedin' 'orses.'

Aunt and nephew giggled at their much-repeated joke and Cleo felt a little better about the task ahead – if in fact there was to be a task.

John suggested leaving it until around ten o'clock before Cleo made her entrance.

'By that time everyone who's going should be there, so there'll be no need to hang about if Seamus isn't there.'

There was something so capable and understanding about him that she'd never experienced in a man before. They killed time by taking a drive out in the country and stopping off at a pub. Cleo was still too young to drink legally, but no one asked any questions, and had it not been for the cloud hanging over the evening she would have thoroughly enjoyed John's charming and witty company. At half past nine he looked at his watch.

'Ready?' he said.

'As I'll ever be.'

He didn't disturb her thoughts with idle chatter during the drive back to Scarborough, but as he helped her from the car outside Nita's house he placed a hand on her shoulder.

'If there's anything to cry about in there,' he advised, gently, 'I suggest you save your tears until later. Don't give him the satisfaction.'

'I'll try.'

'Good girl.'

A girl was being sick on the lawn and two shadowy youths appeared to be relieving themselves in the rose bushes as Cleo and John walked up the driveway.

'It's obviously a society do,' John remarked.

Cleo's mind was on other things. She desperately hoped she wouldn't find Seamus inside with the girl. Either way, she just wanted to get it over with. Elvis was singing 'All Shook Up' as they walked in. The house was packed with young people, many of whom were too young to be drinking the alcohol they had brought; especially in such quantities. Every boy's head turned as Cleo walked by, as did the girls when John followed. They went into the kitchen where John handed a bottle of whisky to a spotty adolescent who was preparing a lethal-looking punch. The youth said 'thanks.' unscrewed the top and poured it all into the bowl.

'Should give it a bit of a kick,' he explained.

'It was actually a single malt,' John said.

'Not ter worry, pal,' said the youth, giving John a wave of benign absolution. 'Nobody'll know the difference. They're too pissed ter notice what crap goes in ... so long as it does the job.'

Elvis gave way to Lonnie Donegan's 'Gamblin' Man' as Cleo went to the kitchen door and peered into the dancing throng, looking for Seamus.

'Any sign?' John asked, ladling out two glasses of punch.

'Not yet.'

She took a sip and said, 'Wow!'

John followed suit. 'Jesus! Another hour and this lot'll be paralytic.'

A girl ran out of the house, alternately sobbing and swearing, closely followed by an apologetic youth in a teddy boy outfit who was trying to assure her that he'd only been having a bit of a laugh and 'It didn't mean owt, 'onest.' Another young man was swaying around, threatening to 'chin the next twat what mucks about wi' me bird'. He collapsed in a heap on the floor. A girl, presumably his bird, stepped over him, left the house and returned with the teddy boy; whom she led by the hand up the stairs to enjoy carnal pleasures her unconscious boyfriend was now incapable of providing. A large vase was knocked off a sideboard and smashed on the floor and Cleo recognised Nita's voice, shouting, 'Oh bollocks, me dad'll go bloody mad!'

'Diana' had been at Number One for five weeks and it was playing when Cleo caught her first glimpse of Seamus. She hated the record ever since. He was with *that* girl – the catty little bitch, to quote Flo. They were on a settee, practically eating each other. Seamus had the girl's blouse unbuttoned and was brazenly unclipping her brassiere, not caring who could see. Cleo's immediate reaction was one of anger and disgust. John had followed her gaze and was up with events without being told.

'I er ... I assume that's him,' he said.

Cleo took John in her arms and moved into a close dance as Paul Anka's voice sang from the radiogram, which was turned up to full volume. Seamus's ladyfriend had now spotted her. Her eyes were following Cleo around the room while her lips were sucking at Seamus's face.

Someone shouted 'Throw a bucket o' water over 'em!'

Seamus had her breast out of her brassiere now and was stroking it. Cleo's distress at this sight was tinged heavily with anger.

'Give over, Seamus!' scolded the girl, making no attempt to replace the exposed bosom. 'Everyone can see.'

'Lerrem,' Seamus slurred. 'Yer norra ashamed of yer tits are yer? I'm not ... I've gorra soft spot fer your soft bits.'

As Seamus laughed at his joke, the girl pushed her exposed breast back inside her bra and pulled him to his feet, glancing sideways all the time at Cleo, whom Seamus hadn't noticed.

'C'mon, yer drunken pig,' she said. 'Let's go upstairs an' do it properly.'

A few leers and shouts of 'Get stuck in, Seamus' came from the boys in the room as Seamus allowed himself to be dragged up the stairs. Cleo made to follow them, to reveal her presence to him, but found herself being ushered into the kitchen by John.

'He's too drunk to listen to reason,' he said. 'And there's no point letting him see you upset. I think we should go.'

Kev came in to the kitchen and recognised Cleo. He grinned, drunkenly. 'He's a right randy sod is Seamus. Have you an' him split up, like?'

'Yes,' Cleo said. 'I'm with John now.'

As if to help her prove it, John took her in his arms and kissed her. She responded enthusiastically, for the few seconds the kiss lasted. The youth nodded at John and said, 'Nah, then.'

Cleo thought for a while, then said to Kev, 'I'm a bit surprised *you're* still friends with him.'

Kev stared at her, stupidly. 'Yer what?' he said.

'In fact I'm surprised any of the lads here are still friends with him. Still it takes all sorts.'

'What's she on about?' Kev asked John, who shrugged.

'I split up with Seamus,' explained Cleo, 'because I found out he'd been having it off with Nita.'

'My Nita? Give over.'

'I noticed that time at the dance,' Cleo said. 'She fancies him like mad. You must have noticed yourself.'

'Mebbe,' Kev admitted, 'but he wouldn't shag his mate's bird. Mind you,' he admitted, glumly, after giving the matter some thought, 'most o' the birds fancy 'im.'

'That's the problem,' Cleo went on, warming to the theme. 'There's not a lad here whose girlfriend hasn't been with Seamus at some time or other during the last six months. He must have mentioned it to you.'

'Well, I know he puts it about a bit,' muttered the youth. 'An' yer reckon he's shaggin' my Nita?'

'I know he is,' Cleo assured him. 'Definitely. That's why I finished with him.'

Without another word, Kev turned and made

his way back into the living room where his girlfriend was.

'Is that true?' John asked.

'It's not beyond the bounds of possibility,' Cleo said.

Raised voices were heard above the music. Cleo and John went to the door and heard Kev berating Nita, who was giving as good as she got. Other guests were sniggering. Kev turned on them.

'I don't know what you bloody lot are laughin' at!' he shouted, sullenly. 'He's shaggin' every lass in this room ... and I know that fer a fact.'

Not every girl had the immediate presence of mind to protest her innocence, indicating an element of truth in Kev's outburst – enough truth to condemn the innocent ones as well as the guilty. More arguments followed and more drink consumed until everyone was too drunk to speak with any degree of reason. Before long, tears, screams and insults were flying back and forth. One angry girl pushed her boyfriend backwards against a glass coffee table laden with drinks, scattering them all over the floor, breaking the glass and cutting the boy's hand. He got to his feet and flung himself at the girl, who neatly side-stepped him so that he knocked another youth over. The other youth began swinging punches at anyone within range and mayhem ensued. Furniture was upended, bottles and glasses smashed against the walls; boys began fighting with each other, and girls with girls. Boastful confessions were made, with boyfriend trying to outdo girlfriend with the extent of their infidelity, and vice versa; virility and sexual prowess was brought into question; revelations made about organ size, or lack of it. At one point Kev became so incensed at Anita's taunting, that he picked up the television set, hurled it at a window, climbed out through the shattered glass and disappeared into the night.

Then one youth shouted, 'Let's get shaghappy Seamus!'

This was a popular suggestion and soon the stairs were packed with young men trying to get at Seamus.

Cleo and John stood, dumbfounded, in the kitchen doorway as Seamus was passed down the stairs, naked, above the heads of his irate and drunken friends. He had been disturbed at a critical moment in his passion, his penis was still erect and adorned with a condom which hung limply off the end like a chef's hat. He was protesting loudly and trying to thump downwards at those who were passing him over their heads. They, in turn, thumped him back.

Seamus was carried, almost ceremoniously, into the garden and hurled into a rose bush where he howled with pain as the thorns made a hundred holes in his naked flesh.

Cleo made her way through the crowd and stood over him as he tried to extricate himself from the bush. He did a double take of her and attempted a smile.

'Have I caught you at a bad moment, Seamus?' she said. Despite her sarcasm she felt a measure of pity for him in his obviously painful and embarrassing predicament.

His lover leaned out of the bedroom window, naked and frustrated. 'Tell 'em ter stop messin' about, Seamus love, an' come back ter bed,' she shouted.

Seamus tried to say something to Cleo but could only come up with a series of 'oohs and ouches!' as the thorns dug deeper into him. Cleo stared at him for a second, then shook her head and turned away. John was escorting her back to his MG just as a police car arrived, summoned by an angry neighbour. Another car pulled up behind the police and a middle-aged couple got out. The man didn't look pleased.

'What the hell's all this about?' he shouted.

'It's a disturbance, sir,' said a policeman, donning his helmet. 'Have you any idea whose house this is?'

'Yes,' fumed the man. 'It's my bloody house!' He glared at Cleo and John as they hurried past.

'I think we should make ourselves scarce,' whispered John. 'By and large, I think it's all gone rather well.'

They were scarcely in the car when Cleo broke down into floods of tears. John offered no words of comfort. Not so soon. He just drove around until the tears had subsided.

'All done?' he asked, after a while.

Cleo just nodded, not trusting herself to speak just yet.

John handed her a handkerchief and asked, 'He's obviously a lout. Did you actually ... love him?' He couldn't hide his incredulity.

She shrugged and gave the question some

thought. 'I thought I did. Maybe I don't know what love is, just yet.' She dried her eyes and managed a smile. 'I'll survive,' she said.

'You had a lucky escape.'

'Do you think so?'

'A lot luckier than Seamus,' said John. 'Hell hath no fury like a woman scorned, eh?'

Cleo managed a laugh, then said, 'I think I need a hug.'

John leaned across and hugged her to him.

'Did you mean it when you kissed me?' she asked, turning her face to his. Her lips were almost brushing against his cheek, and she desperately wanted him to kiss her again. This man was seriously attractive.

'I was acting a part,' he said. 'As per Auntie Flo's instructions.'

'Oh, thank you very much. I didn't realise I was so repulsive.'

'Cleo,' he said. 'I assumed you knew.'

'Knew what?'

He paused before saying, 'I'm homosexual.'

'Oh heck!' She moved away from him in a mixture of embarrassment and confusion. 'John, I'm ever so sorry.'

'Don't be. I'm not.'

'Flo never said anything.'

He grinned. 'Sometimes nothing is the best thing to say.'

'What?'

'It's one of Auntie Flo's many sayings. Would you have taken me along if you'd known?' he asked.

Cleo gave a rueful smile. 'I *should* have known,'

she said. 'You're a bit too good to be true – and when something's too good to be true you can bet your boots it isn't true. By the way, you kiss very well, for a–'

'For a queer?'

'I didn't say that. I'd never call you that. It's just that I find it hard to believe you don't like girls.'

'I do like girls. I love girls. I don't want to jump into bed with them, that's all – any more than I want to jump into bed with my sister.' He started the car. 'Tell you what, it's a lovely night, we'll go for a spin to wind the evening down.'

Cleo went quiet as the car zipped along the coast road. It was a situation she and thousands of other girls had dreamed of. The sky above was abundant with stars, the sea reflected the moon and she was in a sports car with the most handsome man she'd ever clapped eyes on.

'I don't suppose there's any chance you might have made a mistake about what you are?' she asked, hopefully. 'I mean, we all make mistakes.'

He laughed. 'Cleo, if there's a cure for homosexuality I think you're it. If I can't summon up any lust for you, what hope have all the other girls got?'

'I think you'd better take me back,' she said.

Chapter Eleven

Grey, autumn rain pattered against the window of Cleo's room. She was looking out across the rooftops towards the limp sea, which was as invisible to the eye as it had been the first time she arrived in Scarborough. The shipping forecast would have put the visibility in shipping areas Tyne, Dogger and Humber at around 100 yards. There was a quiet knock on the door and Flo popped her head round.

'It's like a ghost town in winter,' she commented as she joined Cleo on the window seat.

'What do you do to keep yourself busy?' Cleo asked.

'Pub work, mainly.'

Cleo gazed through the window. 'I wonder if there are any real, genuine men out there. Or are they all like Seamus or Sid ... or John?'

'They're out there all right,' Flo said. 'Trouble is, most of 'em are married. All the ones I've met are. It's good fun looking, though – well, it is at your age.'

'Seamus wrote to me,' Cleo said. 'Apologising. He said he got drunk and didn't know what he was doing. He says he loves me.'

'I hope it didn't block the toilet when you flushed it down.'

'It's okay,' Cleo smiled. 'I know he's a rat.'

'That's an insult to rats,' muttered Flo.

'It's a pity John's ... you know. I was quite taken by him.'

'Pity's not the word. It's a crime that someone like him has to be wasted on other men. Men don't deserve a man like him.'

'I suppose I'll have to go back to Leeds,' Cleo said, changing the subject. She missed Ant, but she still wasn't looking forward to living with him.

'I'll come with you, if you like.'

'What?'

Flo laughed. 'Don't sound so surprised. I'm not tied by hand and foot to Scarborough, you know. I've lived all over the country in me time. Not just this country, neither.'

Cleo had heard some of Flo's story. About her being a band singer, touring all over the country and abroad.

'What will you do in Leeds?' she asked.

'I'll be sixty odd miles away from Sid Millichip for a start,' Flo said.

'What about you being a magistrate?'

'I'm giving it up. I've done it seven years, which is long enough.' She lit a cigarette.

'That's something you should be giving up,' Cleo said. 'It gives you cancer, you know.'

'It's an old wives' tale,' scoffed Flo. 'I've heard 'em all. If all the smokers were laid end to end around the world do you know what would happen?'

'What?'

'Two-thirds of 'em would drown.'

It raised a smile from Cleo. Flo could always manage that.

'There's always some killjoy trying to stop people doing things they like,' Flo went on. 'It's a wonder we're still allowed to have sex. Not that it'd make any difference to me at the moment.'

'So,' Cleo said. 'You're running away from Sid?'

Flo sighed. 'Yes, I am. If I stay, he'll suck me in. He has a way about him and I'm so weak when it comes to certain men – and Sid knows this. I wouldn't mind so much if he was good looking. He's got a nose like a blind cobbler's thumb and I've seen whiter teeth on a ragman's horse. He can live in the house so long as he pays the mortgage – which should be a first for him.'

'Where will you live?'

'With you, I hope – unless you want to go and live with your brother, which doesn't sound like a good idea to me.'

A slow smile travelled across Cleo's face. 'Flo, I'd love that. I'll ring Ant and tell him to find somewhere for us to live.'

'Actually, that won't be necessary,' said Flo. 'I've been invited to take a tenancy on a pub. You and me can live on the premises. You can stay for a fortnight or for ever, whichever takes your fancy.'

'Somewhere in between sounds good.'

Chapter Twelve

In April 1961 Yuri Gagarin was orbiting the earth in Vostock 1 just as Ant Kelly was orbiting the former offices of Jimmy Dickinson with his sister. Cleo was wondering what she was doing there and Ant's head was bursting with triumph at having bought the failing Dickinson firm out at a knock-down price. During the past four years Ant had worked all hours and saved most of the money he made. Cleo had been happy enough working at the Bird in the Hand with Flo. Boyfriends came and went, some for Cleo some for Flo, both of whom sought the other's approval before embarking on anything serious. Such approval had yet to be granted with any enthusiasm.

'Well,' Ant said, after they'd done a full circuit. 'What do you think?'

'I've seen it before. The day I came back to Leeds, remember?'

'I remember Dickinson being a pig to you,' Ant said. 'And I remember making up my mind to screw him into the ground the first chance I got.'

'Well, you did that all right. I think Jimmy Dickinson can consider himself well and truly screwed.'

'He had it coming. He'd turned into a real cowboy. I might be many things Cleo, but I'm no cowboy. When I do a job, I do it right.'

'Was it absolutely necessary to shop him to the council so he'd have to get out from under before he went bust?'

'Hey, I just told the council what I thought he was up to. It was my civic duty,' Ant said, innocently. 'It was them who refused to pay him until he put the job right.'

'Which he couldn't afford to do. Which you knew because Jenny told you. You knew his financial affairs better than he did himself.'

'It's business, Cleo. Do unto others before they do it unto you first – it's in the builder's bible. You know what he was like. Blimey, he was fiddling me out of money from the first day I worked for him, you know that.'

'You mean he *thought* he was fiddling you out of money.'

'Amounts to the same thing,' Ant grinned broadly. 'Hey, he still thinks I did him a favour by buying him out before his creditors managed to issue a winding-up notice. How thick can you get? My solicitor advised me to get in quick, although he'd deny he ever said any such thing – he's a bit of a wide boy is Collins.'

'Why would Collins deny it? Was what you did legal?' Cleo asked.

'Sort of. I had an invoice saying he owed me six thousand pounds for work done so Jimmy signed his premises, land and stock over to me in lieu, and his creditors will have to go and whistle. According to Collins, when they find out he's got nothing they won't even bother to go for compulsory liquidation. It'd be like throwing good money after bad.'

'But he didn't owe you six thousand pounds. Any money from the sale should have gone to his genuine creditors,' pointed out Cleo, who was studying business administration at night school.

'Cleo, after the taxman and solicitors and accountants had taken their sticky fingers out of the pie, there wouldn't have been much left to go round,' explained Ant. 'And no one could ever prove Jimmy didn't owe me money. Jenny adjusted the books to suit and Jimmy won't be around for anyone to argue with. He went off to Spain this morning.'

'How much did you actually give him?'

'Two thousand in cash, practically every penny I had. Which is two thousand more than he'd have ended up with.'

'What about Jenny?'

'I gave her a nice few quid. Enough to send her off on holiday for a month until the dust settles. And when she comes back she gets a rise. That's why I need you to help out in the meantime.'

'Me? I've got enough on at the pub.'

'Flo said she could spare you.'

'Flo's in on all this as well, is she?'

'She likes me,' Ant said.

Cleo nodded and strode up and down the yard, assessing her brother's purchase.

'So, you got all this for a third of its value,' she said.

'Shhh,' said Ant. 'As far as anyone knows, it cost me six thousand, which was the going rate for it.' Then he grinned. 'Actually it's a bit better than you think. There's a big piece of land at the end of the yard that Jimmy couldn't find a use for. I checked with the planning department months ago and I reckon I can get permission to build five pairs of semis on it, once I've negotiated access through someone's back garden.'

'Which you've already done,' Cleo guessed.

'Which I've already done.'

'You crafty monkey.' Cleo said it with grudging admiration.

'Believe it or not,' Ant said, 'Jimmy didn't know it could be done. Honestly, if his brains were dynamite–'

'He wouldn't have enough to blow his cap off?'

'Correct,' Ant said. 'It never occurred to him to pay someone over the odds for a bit of access. That's what comes of being a tight sod.'

'How long have you been planning this?' Cleo asked.

'On and off, ever since he insulted you that day. There's only one person allowed to insult you and that's me.'

'I'm not sure about this, Ant. None of it sounds right.'

'Cleo, trust me. It happens all the time in this business.' He looked at his watch. 'Anyway there's a valuer coming round in ten minutes, I'm putting the whole thing up as security to the bank. I need money to get this firm working for me. There'll still be a job for you even after Jenny gets back. I need people I can trust.'

By the time Jenny got back from holiday, Cleo was well ensconced in the business, but was glad of someone who could type and do shorthand. She assumed the title of office manager while

Jenny was happy to do what she had always done – the donkey work, as she put it.

The Bird in the Hand was a small, old-fashioned pub in the northern suburbs of Leeds. During the three and a half years of Flo's tenancy it had acquired the reputation of selling the best pint of Tetley's outside the town centre, well on a par with the cluster of Tetley pubs that surrounded the brewery; and as such, it became what Flo called a boom pub. Flo had taken on a new permanent barmaid to replace Cleo.

'You run a good bar, Cleo,' she said, when Cleo told her of her decision to work for Ant permanently. 'And you've had a big hand in making this pub what it is. But you were destined for greater things.'

'I'd still like to live here, if it's okay with you.'

'Be my guest,' Flo said, and pulled them each a half of bitter to celebrate the next stage in her young friend's life.

'Ant wants me to become a partner,' said Cleo. 'But it doesn't seem fair. He's done all the work.'

'He wants someone to share the responsibility,' Flo said. 'You're studying business.' She tapped her temple. 'Ant relies on his wits, hard work, and he flies on a wing and a prayer – you make a good combination. He also loves you.'

'I know, but he scares me sometimes. He seems obsessed with work. He never bothers with girls.'

'What about Jenny?'

Cleo shook her head. 'She'd marry him tomorrow if he asked her. She loves him as much as he loves work, but he doesn't seem to notice. You don't suppose he's–?'

'Like my nephew, John?' mused Flo. 'I shouldn't think so. Maybe he's just not bothered. Not everyone's sex mad you know.'

'Er, excuse me,' Cleo protested. 'I hope you're not insinuating anything. After my near miss with Seamus I lead the life of a nun, me.'

'Funny, that,' Flo said. 'You don't get many nuns going down to the Mecca every Saturday and being brought home by a different bloke every time.'

'I'm a bit choosy. I'm waiting for that bolt of lightning to hit me when our eyes meet across a crowded room.'

'It'll come,' Flo said. Then her eyes clouded over with deep sadness; something Cleo hadn't seen in all the time she'd known her. She'd seen anger and frustration when the subject of Sid Millichip cropped up, but never this.

'What is it, Flo?'

'Oh, nothing. Just a painful memory.'

'It's a memory you haven't told me about.'

'Cleo, I've got lots of memories I haven't told you about. Sometimes you're allowed to have private memories. Things you want to keep all to yourself.'

'Is it a man?' pressed Cleo, who had shared all her inner thoughts and fears with Flo.

Flo nodded, hesitantly. 'Was a man,' she said. 'Not any more.'

Cleo said nothing. They were sitting alone in the tap room during afternoon closing time. Flo finished her half pint and went to the bar.

'Brandy?' she asked, placing a glass to an optic.

Cleo rarely drank spirits but she said, 'Yes

thanks,' in order not to break the flow of the moment. Flo had a story to tell and Cleo wanted to hear it.

Flo came back with two glasses and set one in front of Cleo, who was still finishing off her beer.

'There's not much to tell, really,' she said. 'It was just your remark about eyes meeting across a crowded room. That's how I met Robert. Funny, he was always Robert to me – never Bob, as his pals used to call him.' Her voice tailed off.

'It's a nice name is Robert,' Cleo said, wanting to keep the story going. 'I think you should only shorten a name if it's silly, like Cleopatra.'

'Or Floribunda.'

Cleo laughed. 'You said it, not me. Come on, Flo. Tell me about Robert. What was he like?'

'He was handsome – tall, dark and handsome. Straight out of a romantic novel, only he was flesh and blood. He asked me to marry him.' She looked at Cleo, as if ready to challenge any doubt. 'He asked me the night before he went away.'

'Went away?'

Flo didn't reply immediately. She took out a cigarette, offered one to Cleo, who refused as she always did, then lit it and blew out a stream of smoke. 'He went back to his wife.'

'His wife? I see. He was married.'

'Cleo, don't sound so damn sanctimonious, these things happen.'

'I wasn't being sanctimonious ... sorry.'

'He was going to tell her he was leaving her for me. They had no children and there was nothing else to tie them together.' Flo inhaled deeply on her cigarette, as if drawing strength from it to carry on with her story. 'He lived in London and he was in Scarborough on some sort of business. Something to do with the RAF.'

'It was during the war?' Cleo asked.

'What? Oh, yes, I met him at a NAAFI dance. I was singing with the band.'

'And your eyes met across a crowded room?'

'Yes,' Flo said. 'As a matter of fact they did. He had the saddest brown eyes, but he had the loveliest face you've ever seen. He wasn't anything flashy like a Spitfire pilot or anything, although he was clever – and so funny.'

'I like men who are funny,' said Cleo, encouragingly. 'I'd rather have a funny man than a good-looking one.'

'Robert was both,' Flo said. 'He'd got married just before the war. Got bamboozled into it, to use his words. Some men are like that, you know. They're so nice they let themselves get bamboozled into marriage rather than upset the applecart. It's as if they don't realise marriage is for life.'

'Was he very young?' Cleo asked. 'When he got married, I mean.'

'Twenty-one,' Flo said, cynically. 'There should be a law against men getting married at twenty-one. They don't grow up till they're at least thirty.' She swallowed her drink in one go then went back to the bar for another.

'Not for me,' said Cleo, who hadn't started on her first brandy yet.

'It was a bomb,' Flo said. She had her back to Cleo as she refilled her glass.

Cleo was about to say, 'What was?' when she realised what Flo was already telling her.

'I didn't know about it for a fortnight,' Flo went on. 'He only had a weekend pass and when he didn't turn up for our date I thought he'd had second thoughts and decided not to go through with it. I cried every night for a week. Then I bumped into one of his pals in town and he told me Robert was dead. I collapsed in the street right in front of him.'

'Oh, Flo. I am sorry.'

Flo smiled. 'It's a long time ago. I'd only known him for three months but I can remember every second of every minute of the time I spent with him.' She went very quiet as if there was something more to the story that she couldn't quite bring herself to talk about.

'When I collapsed I was in such a bad way that I was taken to hospital. That's where I found out I was definitely pregnant. I'd been a bit worried but I didn't know for certain.'

'You had a baby?'

Flo's eyes misted over at the memory. Cleo had never seen this before. She went round the table and sat beside her friend, comforting her.

'I lost it in the hospital, Cleo. I was five weeks gone – didn't even know if it was a boy or a girl.'

Cleo wanted to hear the whole story but decided it was too much of an intrusion, so she didn't press.

'Do you know, I haven't even got a photo of Robert,' Flo said, at length. 'When I thought he wasn't going to leave his wife I ripped up the only one I had and threw it away.'

'What exactly happened to him?'

'He was out in the street during an air raid – helping an ARP man to get some people out of a burning building. He spotted Robert's uniform and asked him for some help. So naturally Robert didn't go down the shelter, he gave the man a hand. In fact he gave him more than a hand, he gave his life. A bomb dropped right on top of them, killed the two of them – and the people they were trying to rescue.'

'It must have been awful for you.'

Flo nodded, then said, 'Do you know the worst thing? I didn't know myself at the time, I found out later from one of his friends.' She sucked on her cigarette again, then stubbed it out, violently, in an ash tray. 'That's my last one, definitely. It was smoking that ruined my voice, you know. It improved Frank Sinatra's but it ruined mine. Luck of the bloody draw eh?' It was as though she'd lost the thread of her thoughts, but Cleo hadn't.

'What was it – this worst thing?' she asked.

Flo sighed and reached for the cigarette packet, but Cleo's hand stayed her.

'He never told her he was leaving her.'

'Oh,' Cleo said. 'Maybe he hadn't found the right moment.'

'No, he told this friend he'd changed his mind. They were on the London train together. His friend told me to stop me feeling guilty at the thought of him dying, having just hurt his wife because of me.'

'There's a sort of logic to it.'

'I know, I didn't want to hurt his wife – but why

did he change his mind? Didn't he love me after all?'

'Didn't his friend tell you?'

'His friend's a man. Men don't discuss things like that too deeply; they generally stick to words of one syllable, and not too many of them either. All he knew was that Robert had decided not to say anything to his wife. He was quite definite about it.'

'That could mean anything – it didn't mean he didn't love you.'

'Cleo, don't you think I haven't tossed the whys and wherefores over in me mind a million times. And I felt so guilty. Still do to a certain extent.'

'Guilty – why?'

'Well, one minute I'm beside meself because I think he's let me down and doesn't love me. Then I find out he's been killed, which was awful, but at least it meant he must have loved me after all – so I had that to hold on to; then I find out he didn't tell his wife so he probably didn't love me and I'm back to square one.' She looked at Cleo and smiled, 'I've lost you, haven't I?'

'No, not really,' Cleo said. 'But I still don't see why you should be feeling guilty. You can't help your feelings.'

'Cleo, can't you see? All I was thinking about was me, never mind him and his poor wife who might well have loved him as much as I did.'

'I think you're being hard on yourself. If you want my opinion I think he probably loved you but couldn't bring himself to tell his wife, who might well have had enough to put up with at the time. She *was* being bombed every night.'

'I know. The truth is, Cleo, he didn't love me *enough*. Not as much as I loved him, that's for sure. I've never loved anyone since, not like that.'

'There's still time, Flo. You still turn men's heads, I've noticed that.'

Flo patted Cleo's outstretched hand. 'Bless you for that, love. But it sort of ruined me for any decent kind of relationship with men. That's why I ended up with Sid bloody Millichip. Whatever you do, Cleo, don't end up with one of life's Sid Millichips.'

During the next few months Cleo's boyfriends came and went, none lasting more than a couple of weeks. Jenny still had her heart set on Ant, who had his heart set on business. The girls were at the Christmas Eve Dance at the Majestic Ballroom in Leeds City Square when an apparition in a bright red suit and Santa Claus hat tapped them both on their shoulders.

'Have a look round, girls,' grinned the apparition, who looked to be about seventeen, 'and when you realise I'm the best thing in this joint, I'll be waitin' at the bar wimme mate.' He nodded in the direction of another youth who was wearing an elf outfit, winkle-picker shoes and a drunken grin. The Santa Claus youth had virulent body odour.

'I think we'll just dance with each other until we get a better offer,' said Jenny, stepping away from him.

'God! If he's the best thing available, I'm going home,' Cleo grumbled, as they moved off to stand by the dance floor. 'Surely there's a man in here with more than one brain cell, who gets a bath now and again.'

The ballroom was packed to capacity with happy revellers as the Johnnie Wollastone orchestra alternated with the Dave Dalmour quartet. Seasonal inebriates sang drunken carols; an occasional scuffle broke out and was quickly resolved by patrolling bouncers. The early part of the evening was dedicated to modern dance: the waltz, the foxtrot and the quickstep, interspersed with novelty dances such as the conga and the hokey cokey. Later would come rock and roll, following by a dimly lit smooching session, for 'young lovers'; and the evening would end with the last waltz.

Cleo and Jenny attracted the attention of many a passing male dancer; to the annoyance of many a female dancing partner. Jenny was soon waltzing with a young man in an RAF uniform, to whom she'd been 'giving the eye' – much to her friend's amusement. The bandleader announced the hokey cokey and the dancers formed themselves into several circles.

A young man moved to Cleo's side and said, 'Did you know the man who invented the hokey cokey has just died?'

'Oh dear I'm sorry to hear that,' she replied, intrigued by this unique chat-up line.

'Oh yes,' he said, earnestly. 'And they had a devil of a job getting him into his coffin.'

'Why was that?'

'Well,' he explained. 'No sooner had they got his right leg in than it came out again, then they put his left leg in...'

Cleo was giggling now.

'Would you do me the honour of not having this dance with me?' he said. 'I can't stand the hokey cokey – far too rough for a delicate lad like me.' He looked a cut above the rest. Tall and slim, with unruly fair hair and a pleasant smile, and smelling of expensive aftershave.

'It would be a pleasure,' she laughed.

'My name's Jeff,' he said, reaching into his pocket. 'Would you like a cigarette?'

'I don't smoke.'

'Good for you, filthy habit.' He lit one for himself and said, 'You can tell me your name if you like.'

'Cleo,' said Cleo, waiting for the usual question about her unusual name.

'As in Cleo Laine?'

'Yes, but there the similarity ends. I'm no singer.'

'I'm no John Dankworth either.'

'Are they still married?'

'As far as I know,' said Jeff. 'If they've split up they haven't told me.'

He was pleasant and easy to talk to – and more intelligent than most. She was interested enough in him to check his credentials. *Always check their credentials,* Flo had advised her. *If he's a travelling salesman tell him to keep travelling.* The hokey cokey ended and the band went into a quickstep. Cleo and Jeff, now happily acquainted, took to the floor.

'What do you do?' she asked him.

Jeff didn't answer immediately, then he said, 'I'm an accountant – of sorts.'

‘Of sorts – and what sort are you?’

He gave her an embarrassed grin. ‘Of the turf accountant sort.’

‘You mean you’re a bookie?’

‘Well, my dad is. I’m still learning the trade. There’s a lot more to it than you’d think,’ he assured her. ‘We do all the northern courses.’

‘Can you do tick-tack?’

‘Actually, yes.’

‘And what are the odds on you buying me a drink?’

There was a likeableness about him that she hadn’t seen in a man for a while. Not since John Dunderdale.

Chapter Thirteen

By spring of the following year all ten of the houses were built, sold and occupied at an overall profit of £6,200. Ant ploughed all the profit into a land purchase and, backed by an enthusiastic bank manager, had already started work clearing a site for twenty-seven bungalows in Ripon.

'I've just seen a site in Garforth that'll take over eighty, once I've got the planning permission changed to residential,' Ant told Cleo one morning as he made one of his rare visits to the office.

'Don't you think you're moving too fast? We're going to be stretched to the limit building the site in Ripon.'

Ant grinned and tapped the side of his nose. 'I'm not building the Ripon site. At least not the houses. I'm sticking a road in and selling off the plots individually, for people to build their own houses on. Each plot connected up to sewers and services, people go for that sort of thing. I've been doing a bit of homework – I'll get twice what I paid for it.'

'Have you told the bank?'

'Not yet. I only tell them what they need to know.'

It took Ant four months to sell all the plots at more than twice what he paid. The bank manager was put out at being left in the dark but conceded he might not have gone along with Ant's scheme had he known about it. But Ant now had over £12,000 in the bank and was proving to be a shrewd businessman. The manager had orders from on high to take a risk on him.

Ant had got his information about the Garforth site from a councillor who sat on the local planning committee. A man of experience in planning matters whose word carried a lot of weight where planning decisions were concerned.

'It's down fer industrial development at the moment, lad,' he had told Ant. 'But there's them as live nearby who don't want a load o' bloody factories built on their doorstep. Yer can pick it up for ten grand as it stands but if it gets changed ter residential it'll be worth a lot more than that.'

'How can I be sure it'll get changed?'

'Yer can't be sure o' nowt in this life, lad. If it dunt get changed yer'll just have ter sell it on. Yer'll not lose nowt by it. I reckon it's worth a bit of a gamble. Especially if I get one of the houses ... at a discount, like.'

'I'll sell you the first one half price if by some miracle the planning permission is changed,' Ant said.

'I'll shake yer hand on that, lad.'

By June 1963, Kelly Construction, despite a harsh winter, had completed fifteen houses on the Garforth site which had planning permission for eighty-eight and which Ant, with the help of the bank and the bent councillor, had bought for two-thirds of its value. His accountant valued his company at £36,000. Ant had promised himself one of the houses but every time a buyer came along he stepped aside, unable to resist a sale. He was still living in the rented house in Hamblin Terrace, much to everyone's amusement.

Cleo, Flo and Jenny were in London on a shopping spree, Ant's treat as a reward for Cleo finishing her business administration course and passing her driving test second time. This was one test less than Ant had taken, but he chose not to mention that. Not once in their lives had they been rewarded for doing something good; such as when Ant passed his scholarship or when Cleo played hockey for the school. Birthdays had come and gone without much celebration – a birthday card if they were lucky. So they made up for it now. For Ant's twenty-fourth birthday Cleo had taken him to Church Fenton Air Display where she'd booked him a thirty-minute flight in a two-seater Spitfire. The best half-hour of his life, he'd told her.

Jenny had heard of a new dress designer called Mary Quant who had opened a shop called Bazaar in King's Road.

'Might treat meself to something,' Flo said. 'I wonder if she caters for forty-five year olds.'

In the meantime, forty-five-year-old Horace Womack was back in Leeds, looking for work. Nelly Kelly was just an unpleasant memory, as were those brats of hers. In his opinion life had been unfair to him. He needed money, which meant work or thieving. The latter sounded attractive, but not when set against a swift return to jail. He'd been out for a few years now but his time inside had been hard. Being locked up for attacking a child was no joke and he'd spent most of his sentence in isolation for his own protection. A lot of building was going on in Garforth to the north of Leeds but the sign saying Kelly Construction meant little to him other than it might provide a source of work. It was knocking-off time for the week and most of the men were packing to leave when he walked on to the site. Womack was now a grey-faced man with a tangle of blue veins in his neck and looked as if he hadn't an ounce of hard work left in him. The only outstanding thing about him was his insignificance. His arms didn't swing much as he walked and his gaze was angled towards the ground. He stopped and looked up at a passing labourer.

'Are they settin' men on?' he asked.

The man jabbed a thumb towards the site hut. 'Do no 'arm to ask,' he said.

'What's t' gaffer's name?'

The man directed Horace's gaze to the sign board. 'He's gorrit written up there, so's we won't forgerrit.'

'Kelly,' read Horace. 'That's 'is name then, is it?'

'If that's what it says up there, it must be.'

'What's 'e like?'

'He's a bloody 'ard taskmaster, but he pays good money.' He looked Womack up and down, then added, pointedly, 'To them as can earn it.'

'Is 'e in?' asked Womack, ignoring the disparaging inflection in the man's voice.

'Aye, lad.'

Without so much as a thank you, Horace

headed towards the site hut and left the labourer grinning to himself as he tried to picture the expression on the gaffer's face when this useless lump turned up looking for work.

Ant paused in what he was doing and looked out through the cabin window with some satisfaction. Two weeks ago there had been several days of rain that had set back his progress. But he'd made it all back and was now ahead of schedule with fifteen houses completed, and holding deposits taken on another twelve. His bank manager had agreed in principle to help Kelly Construction buy a portfolio of land now that the firm was becoming established. Ant had seen a two-and-a-half-acre site with outline permission for twenty-eight semi-detached bungalows – bread and butter bungalows as he called them. He had put in a last-minute tender to the selling agent, which he already knew was the best bid, albeit by the narrowest of margins. Having a man on the inside who would divulge information for a few pounds was an invaluable business asset. He wouldn't tell Cleo of course, he hadn't told her about the Garforth councillor yet, but he'd have to come clean when she asked why the first house had been sold so cheaply. Despite her one-third ownership of the company she just didn't understand the cut and thrust of business like he did.

His thoughts turned to his sister having a good time in London and it brought a smile to his face. Leaving her to the mercies of Womack all those years ago had scarred his conscience. He should have gone back to face the music. Ant knew that at the time, but he didn't have the guts. Sometimes he thought of Cleo locked in the cupboard under the stairs as the house burned down around her and marvelled at her courage and presence of mind in escaping. Most kids would have curled up and died under those circumstances. She coped with life her way, he did it his way. One day he'd be a millionaire, the biggest builder in Yorkshire. He'd learn to fly, one of his life's ambitions. Maybe buy himself an old Spitfire and fly it at air shows like the one at Farnborough; and Cleo would come along for the ride. She was good for his business. Everyone loved Cleo Kelly, she had that sort of face. The bank manager doted on her and he hadn't a man working for him who wouldn't leave his wife and run away with Cleo at the drop of a hat. It troubled Ant sometimes that he couldn't summon such passion for a woman. Deep down he knew the reason, but a sense of irrational guilt wouldn't allow him to admit it. Even to himself.

He'd given Cleo £100 to spend, with instructions not to bring any money back with her. No doubt Flo and Jenny would help her out if she had a problem. He liked them both, especially Jenny. But he couldn't rationalise his feelings towards her, nor to any woman for that matter. He was almost twenty-four years old and had never so much as kissed a woman with any passion. What the hell was wrong with him? Maybe he was a latent homosexual? Ant watched a strapping young labourer climbing down a ladder, stripped to the waist, and he smiled to himself. No, nothing there. He was neither one thing nor the other. Never mind, there was always work. He'd need to keep working to give Cleo the life she deserved.

The assistant in Bazaar looked at Cleo, who was trying on a knee-length skirt, while dancing to 'From Me To You' by the Beatles. Now at number one in the charts.

'Let me show you something shorter,' the assistant said. 'It's a sin to cover up legs like yours. One of these days Mary reckons she's going to make skirts so short they'll set men's eyes popping, but I don't think the world of fashion's ready for it just yet.'

'It's not the only part of a man it'll set popping by the sound of it,' commented Flo, drily. 'You haven't got a nice, knitted twin set in powder blue, have you?'

'I'm sorry.'

'Take no notice,' Cleo laughed. 'She's younger than any of us, inside.'

'I thought as much,' said the young assistant. 'It's inside that counts, especially when the figure's still intact like yours is, madam.'

'If you're trying to butter me up, love, you've succeeded,' said Flo. 'But the Dunderdale thighs will remain hidden from the world.'

The Beatles gave way to Gerry and the Pacemakers singing 'I Like It', but Cleo preferred the Beatles, particularly John Lennon because, like Seamus Jaques, he was dangerous. She had a thing about dangerous men. Pity Jeff Warrilow wasn't a bit more dangerous – or was that being unfair to him?

As Womack knocked on the cabin door, Ant had returned his attention to the plan for the new site, trying to work out how to get another pair of bungalows on it.

'Come in,' he called out, absently.

Womack entered and stared at the back of the figure hunched over a desk. 'I er, I were wonderin' if yer were settin' men on.' He still had the same false teeth, only now the clicking was worse when he talked. Ant recognised the voice instantly. It had been nearly ten years but it still made his flesh crawl to hear it. Of course it might not be Womack, just someone who sounded like him. Without turning round, he asked, 'What's your name?'

'Horace Womack... I'm a good labourer.'

All doubt was eliminated. The man who had damaged his life in such an awful way was standing behind him, asking for a job. Slowly, Ant turned round to confront him. To see what he had to say for himself. Womack didn't recognise him. Not straight away.

'Well,' said Ant.

His stepfather seemed to have aged twenty years. He had lost most of his hair and a lot of weight, but it was him all right. He had lost none of his unpleasantness. Ant could still detect that. An aura of intense foulness had pervaded the cabin.

Womack stared at him, blankly. Kelly was a lot younger than he'd expected, a lot younger. Then he realised he must be talking to the wrong man.

'I'm lookin' fer t' gaffer,' he said in a manner which was less respectful than before.

'I'm the gaffer.'

'Oh, right.' Womack's manner reverted to respectful. There was something familiar about this young man. 'Do I know yer from somewhere?' he asked.

'I don't know, you tell me.' Ant's voice was cold, without emotion.

Then Womack put the name and the face together. 'Bugger me!' he gasped. 'It's you ... it's bloody you. The young pillock what stabbed me!'

'You mean your stepson? Don't you remember being my stepfather?'

'Oh aye, lad, course I do.' Womack's manner was now conciliatory. 'I suppose I still am, now yer come ter mention it. We never got divorced, yer know, me an' yer mam.' He figured there might be an advantage here, with this lad being family, more or less. 'Although me an' 'er split up, as yer prob'ly know. God knows where she is now.'

'I'm not interested in where she is.'

'No, lad. I don't bloody blame yer, neither. God, she were rough. Rough as a bear's arse. It wouldn't surprise me if she's died o' clap in some back alley.'

Ant stared at Womack for a while as he recollected his memories; memories he'd locked away in a part of his mind he had hoped he would never have to visit again.

'How long have you been out of jail?'

'Oh, you 'eard then? Put-up bloody job that were. I 'ardly touched the lad. He ran off yellin' like I were Jack the bloody Ripper.'

'Did you do the same to him as you did to me?'

'What? Nay, lad. Me an' you 'ad a bit o' fun sometimes. Larked about like lads and their dads do. Mind you, yer were a rum 'un. Liked yer own way. I 'ad ter knock some sense into yer now and again if me memory serves. You and that sister o' yours.'

'Why did you lock her under the stairs that time?'

'What?... Is that what she told yer. My God, she 'ad a way wi' t' truth did that lass.'

'You locked her under the stairs for five days. Then you went out and let the house catch fire.'

'She's been tellin' yer lies, lad. She set t' bloody house on fire, that's why she got locked up.'

Ant shook his head in contempt and looked away. 'Why did you do all those things to me?' He'd had enough of looking at Womack and switched his gaze to out of the window; his voice was almost inaudible, as though he couldn't bear to hear his own words. 'I was only a kid, for God's sake!'

'Do what, lad?'

'You know what you did to me, you bloody pervert!' Ant turned his head and confronted the man; his eyes blazed with hate, as dark and painful memories flooded back.

Slowly, the old look came over Womack's face; that mask of evil that Ant remembered so well. Womack knew there was no chance of a job so there was no point in being polite to this little shit any more. He began to snigger.

'Didn't yer like it, then? I must say, I've 'ad

better meself, but it was either that or sticking it up yer mam. Never knew what yer'd catch, stickin' it up her. So I never bothered.'

'I never understood why you married her.'

Womack smirked. 'Well, it were nowt ter do wi' true love, lad. It were a condition she made before she agreed ter go out on t' streets, workin' fer me. She reckoned she wanted respectability.' He laughed out loud. 'Wet Nelly Kelly, the respectable prozzy.'

Ant felt sickened. How come he never knew? 'You're a liar,' he said, angrily. 'If she'd have been a prostitute I'd have found out.'

'She weren't at it long enough fer anyone ter find out,' Womack explained. 'She were bloody useless at it, like she were at everythin' else. Punters never paid 'er and I ended up lumbered with 'er – and 'er two brats. I went out ter work ter feed and clothe you two, did yer know that?'

'I don't remember being fed much – and you didn't spend much on clothes. God you're sick!' Ant stared at his stepfather with revulsion, then asked, 'Did you do it to the boy?'

Womack shrugged. 'They never got me for that. Just fer knockin' 'im about a bit.'

'You did though, didn't you? You did it to him, you sick-minded bastard! The poor kid was probably too ashamed to admit it.'

'What about you?' Womack sniggered. 'I bet you didn't go round shoutin' about it.'

Ant shot him a look of intense disgust. 'You pile of filth! Why don't you do the world a favour and shoot yourself? I would, if I thought I was like you.'

Womack ignored these insults, he'd heard worse. 'Yer weren't much good at it,' he sneered. 'Mind you, yon lad were even worse at it than you. God he were an ugly bastard! Kids nowadays – they don't know their arse from their elbow.' He laughed uproariously at his own joke.

Ant felt bile surging up his throat. 'You sick bastard!' he hissed. His hand was gripping the handle of a spade; his sense of reason had completely deserted him, and he didn't want to hear this voice any more. He didn't want anyone to hear it.

'What happened ter that sister o' yours?' Womack sniggered. 'I thought about givin' 'er one as well, but girls don't do much fer me – never 'ave. Mind you, it'd 'ave taught the little bitch a lesson she'd never forget.'

It was the thought of him doing this to Cleo that made Ant jab the spade at the grinning man's throat to cut off the source of all the filth. A thick stream of blood squirted, almost horizontally, out on to Ant's shirt. Womack made a ghastly choking sound and slumped to the floor, his face frozen in a look of surprise.

Ant gasped, 'Oh, Jesus!' He dropped the spade from his trembling fingers as he watched the life drain out of his stepfather. Womack's throat rattled as he tried, desperately, to breathe through the blood bubbling from his mouth and neck. There was a look of terror in his eyes as he realised he couldn't, and was therefore about to die. All he'd done was to come looking for work and now he was going to die. The rattling and choking stopped and his eyes went blank, but blood still poured from him, and would until his heart stopped beating, which wouldn't be long. From outside someone called out:

'See yer Monday, boss.'

Ant shouted back, with astonishing calmness, 'Don't be late.' Then he kicked the door shut to hide the gruesome sight from the outside world. The world that didn't know what he'd just done. And must never know.

It had been the best weekend Cleo could remember. Her time working in the pub with Flo had been interesting, and in many ways carefree, but this had been her best time ever; better even than her first day in Scarborough when she met Flo. That had started out well but had been tainted by Flo's betrayal – albeit well meant and with its ultimate happy ending. But as Cleo relaxed in the first-class compartment, occupied only by her and her two friends, she knew nothing could spoil this happy time. Everything was going just right. Back in Leeds she even had a boyfriend who showed great promise.

Flo had 'copped off' with a youngish man in a club the night before; re-appearing, flushed, dishevelled and guilty, in the hotel just before breakfast, and subjected to intense cross-examination by her two companions. She fielded all the intrusive questions with a couple of 'mind your own businesses' and an 'I don't ask you what you get up to with boys' and went to bed until lunchtime when she emerged just in time to check out.

'Are you seeing Jeff tonight?' Jenny asked Cleo

as the train slowed down in Peterborough.

'Not till Wednesday,' Cleo said. 'He's away at a race meeting in Lancashire somewhere. I'm calling in to see Ant tonight to thank him.'

'Better say thanks from us two as well,' Flo said.

Ant had paid for the train tickets and the hotel.

'He never spends much on himself, does he?' Flo mentioned. 'I mean he's a lovely lad but he's not exactly a man-about-town, is he? It's a shame he doesn't have much time for girls.'

'Oh, I don't know,' Jenny said. 'He took me to the Tomato Dip again last week. That's twice in a month. By Ant's standards that's going steady.'

Cleo laughed, although she did wonder about her brother herself at times. 'Leave him alone. He's too busy making his first million to spend time with girls – and that suits me fine.'

'A new suit wouldn't go amiss,' Flo said. 'I'm sure he can afford a new suit.'

'I know, I'm going to frogmarch him to Burtons next week if it flipping kills me,' Cleo said. 'And throw that old sports jacket into the bin. Even his elbow patches are wearing out.'

'Tell him I might let him take me out if he plays his cards right,' Jenny said. 'He can wine and dine me properly, like he's been promising for years. Tell him I'd like to go somewhere where they have tablecloths and saucers. It'll make a nice change to look at him across a table with a candle between us and not an HP sauce bottle.'

Waiting people surged across the platform towards their carriage; then they noticed the First Class sign on the window and cast a variety of jealous and admiring glances at the three beautiful and wealthy-looking women inside, before heading further along the train to the carriages reserved for the common herd. Cleo felt a mixture of superiority and guilt; Flo smiled at her, as though she were reading her thoughts.

'Is your working-class conscience coming to haunt you?'

'Something like that. I feel a bit of a fraud.'

'Rubbish,' said Flo. 'Everyone needs luxuries now and again.' She placed a cigarette in a long holder, her idea of filtering out nicotine, then she rested her feet on the opposite seat and added, 'Especially me.'

'Was last night one of your little luxuries?' enquired Jenny, as the train moved off.

'There was nothing "little" about last night,' Flo said. 'And yes, it was very luxurious – so don't ask me any more.'

Both girls were consumed with curiosity, but Flo's wagging finger warded off further interrogation. Cleo's mind went to Jeff Warrilow, who had proposed to her two days ago. She'd promised him an answer on Wednesday and she still didn't know what that answer would be. They'd been together for six months now. He was funny and decent and considerate, more cavalry twill than mohair; and he wasn't unreliable or unpredictable like Seamus – or dangerous like John Lennon. Flo had instantly classified him as good husband material and advised Cleo to set her cap at him as good men are hard to find. Cleo hadn't told Flo or Jenny about his proposal; she didn't want outside influences affecting such a decision. On balance she was inclined to say 'Yes' to him as she knew he'd give her a happy and contented life. He didn't light any fires inside her, but was she asking too much? Maybe that sort of thing only happened in films.

Ant didn't sleep that Saturday night. The image of Womack was too vivid in his mind; the horrific sight and sound of death. Paradoxically, his stepfather's death had released him from the internal torture he had suffered every time he thought of Womack and his disgusting perversions, but the release had come at a price. Perhaps too great a price for Ant to cope with.

He was still there. Or rather *it* was still there – Womack's body. Ant had stared at the lifeless remains of his tormentor until the horror of what he'd done had gradually sunk in. He had padlocked the cabin door and run in a tearful panic to his van. Once home he had ripped off his clothes and burned them on the fire. Then he sat there, naked and stunned, watching his bloodsoaked garments go up in flames and he knew he was a murderer. He needed Cleo now more than he had ever needed anyone. His mind was empty of ideas, which wasn't like him at all. Cleo would know what to do. He'd wait until she got back. She would get him out of this mess.

For hours he walked around the house, completely naked, talking to himself; at times convincing himself that it hadn't really happened and all he had to do was go back to the site and there'd be nothing there, and everything would be all right. But deep down he knew the truth. Womack was dead. He'd killed him and what was worse he was glad Womack was dead. Womack had been a repulsive spectre who had haunted his life, and now that spectre was dead. Which was good. So why did he feel so bad? He felt bad because he felt good. What sense did that make?

When Cleo arrived on Sunday evening Ant hadn't eaten or slept since the previous morning. He was in his dressing gown, sitting in front of a roaring fire despite it being a warm summer's evening. He didn't look up when she came in. Things needed to be said but he didn't have the words. Not yet.

She greeted him with a cheerful, 'Hiya,' then plonked her bags down, before plonking herself down in the chair beside him. 'We had a great time. Flo and Jenny told me to say thanks.'

His gaze was still concentrated on the flames. Thinking.

'Are you okay?'

He pulled a face that could have meant anything.

'You're not, are you?' she said. 'Look, if you're feeling poorly you should be in bed.'

'I killed Womack.'

His words made no sense to Cleo, so she dismissed them and got to her feet to place a hand on his forehead.

'You're very warm. Mind you, sitting in front of this fire probably accounts for that. Are you feeling fluey or something?'

'He's in the cabin. I don't know what to do.'

'Ant, what are you talking about?'

His words still weren't panicking her. They made too little sense. Ant turned and looked at her, and she was shocked by the profound misery etched into his normally cheerful face.

'What is it?' She was panicking now.

'I killed Womack.'

'Horace?'

'Yes, Horace Womack. I killed him and I don't know what to do. How many more times do I have to tell you?'

Ant returned his gaze to the fire. Cleo stared at him for a while, wondering if he'd had a breakdown or something. These things happen to people who work as hard as Ant.

'I think you've been working too har–'

He spoke over the top of her. 'I've got to get rid of him.'

'What?'

'I killed him with a spade,' he said. 'He came on site. He didn't know it was me. He asked me for a job ... and I killed him with a spade. And I've got to get rid of him or I'll get done for murder.' He turned to her again. 'Do they still hang you for murder? There's been a lot of talk about stopping hanging. It was in the papers.'

'Ant, you're frightening me.'

'When they sentence you to death they've got to leave it for three clear Sundays before they can hang you. Did you know that?'

'I'm going to ring for a doctor.'

'It was the way he was talking,' Ant said.

'How do you mean? Talking about what?'

Ant's face coloured bright red when he realised his sister was on the verge of prising his hideous secret from him. A secret he'd kept to himself all these years.

'Dirty,' he said. 'He was talking dirty stuff about you so I hit him with a spade. I didn't mean to kill him. At least I don't think I did. Oh, Cleo, I'm in terrible trouble.'

He held out his arms for her to hold him, the first time she'd ever known him do this. There had been times when they were kids when he'd hugged her and told her not to worry. She knelt beside his chair and held him tightly.

'Oh God, Ant! You're serious aren't you?'

Ant nodded. 'I killed him, just like I said I would when we were kids. I knew I'd do it one day ... and I have.'

'Where is the er ... where is he now?'

'In the cabin. He came in the cabin looking for work. That's where I killed him.'

'Did anyone see you?'

'No ... I don't think so.'

'When did it happen?'

'Yesterday dinner time.'

'And he's still there?'

'Yes.'

Cleo exhaled a long, slow breath as she tried to take in the enormity of the situation. 'Well, you can't tell the police, that's for sure.' She still didn't trust the law after what it had done to her. 'We'll have to get rid of him.'

Ant nodded again, then he came to a decision. Cleo's presence seemed to give him the strength he'd been lacking during his ordeal. He pulled himself together and got up from the chair.

'I don't want you involved,' he decided. 'This is my problem.'

'No,' she said, with finality. 'It's *our* problem.

And I think from a practical point of view, you'll need help.'

He thought about this for a while, then conceded she was right. 'We can bury him or dump him,' he said. 'What do you think's best, burying or dumping?'

'We'll bury him,' Cleo decided. 'If we bury him, no one will miss him.'

'They won't, will they?' he said. 'They'll miss him about as much as they'd miss a dead rat. We could bury him on the site, or maybe take him to the yard and bury him there.'

'The yard's better,' Cleo decided.

'We'll have to move him tonight,' Ant said. His brain was ticking over again. 'We can move him into the yard tonight and hide him somewhere. I'll bury him tomorrow night when I've decided where's a good place for him.'

'Somewhere deep,' Cleo suggested. 'Very deep.'

Justice had been done as far as she was concerned. She felt no guilt at her callousness, just concern for her brother; who had been forced by circumstances to put an end to a worthless life and to have it on his conscience. Womack's existence had been so harmful that his death should be on no one's conscience. Least of all her brother's.

Ant went into the cabin first. His heart was racing at the thought of what lay behind that door. He and Cleo had stood outside for several minutes as he summoned up the courage to go in. It was dark and beyond the range of any street lights, but a half moon provided enough illumination for him to unlock the padlock on the door.

They had decided not to use a torch which might attract the attention of a passer-by, a policeman even. Risks must be kept to a minimum.

As he pushed the door open the smell told them that the warm summer weather was hastening the putrefaction of their stepfather's body. Ant had reversed his van almost up to the hut to minimise the effort. He glanced inside, worked out his plan of action and came back out.

'Wait here a minute,' he instructed Cleo, who was in no hurry to begin the gruesome task.

Her brother took a sack from the van and went back in the cabin. He slipped it over Womack's bloodied head and shoulders and tied it at the neck with string.

'Okay,' he called in a low voice. 'I'm ready now.'

Cleo took a deep breath and went inside with her hand cupped over her nose and mouth and her head half turned away from the shadowy corpse on the floor.

'I've covered his head,' Ant said. 'So there's nothing to see. If you can take his feet, we'll lug him out and put him straight in the van.'

They carried out the operation in silence, each one of them concentrating hard on not throwing up; trying to distance their thoughts from the horror of what they were doing. Heavily congealed blood was still sticky beneath their feet as they carried the body outside. Womack's body weighed no more than eleven stones but it felt like half a ton. The term, 'dead weight' was apt. Ant tried to close the van doors but they stopped against Womack's feet and he had to open them again and try to bend the body's legs at the knee to get the feet properly inside. But the knees wouldn't bend. He looked to Cleo for help, but she turned away, not even wanting to watch, so he went to the passenger door and pulled the seat forward; then he pulled at the sack-covered head to clear the feet away from the doors. As he tugged, the body gave a moan as the last vestiges of fetid gas were expelled from within it. Ant leapt back and ran from the van. Cleo, who had also heard the moan, followed and flung herself into his arms.

'Oh, Jesus!' she said. 'What the hell was that?'

'I don't know,' he said hoarsely. 'I just hope the bugger's dead, that's all.'

They stood there for several minutes trying to summon up the courage to go back. Ant went first. He reached inside the van and tentatively touched Womack's hand. It was cold and stiff, as was the rest of him.

'He's dead all right,' he said, closing the doors on the now silent corpse. 'The bugger's still trying to make our lives a misery, even after he's dead.'

By the light of the moon, Cleo noticed dark stains on her hands. Womack's blood. She immediately vomited, causing her brother to do the same. Then she wiped her mouth with her sleeve and said, 'We need to finish off here.'

'Finish off what?'

'Cleaning up the blood. We can't leave the cabin in this state. We'll need water and some cloths and–'

Ant had walked away from her, over to a store shed. He re-appeared with a can. 'It's paraffin,' he said. 'You get in the van.'

Cleo nodded her approval of his plan. 'Is there anything inside the hut you really need?' she asked.

'Probably, but I'm not going in there again.'

Two minutes later the hut was blazing from end to end, and within half an hour, they had deposited their stepfather in his temporary tomb, an old storage shed to which Ant had the only key.

For Cleo it had been a poor finish to a good weekend.

Chapter Fourteen

Ant woke at ten-thirty to the sound of the telephone. It was unheard of for him to sleep in and Jenny needed to speak to him. It took him a few seconds to come round, and to remember what he'd been up to these last two days. His hand reached out from under the bedclothes and accidentally knocked the phone off its hook and on to the floor.

'Oh, bugger!' he mumbled.

'Ant?'

He could hear Jenny's voice coming from somewhere beneath him.

'Yeah!' he called out.

'I can hardly hear you.' Her voice squeaked out of the phone, like Tom Thumb speaking from a matchbox.

He managed to put it to his ear. 'Hiya, Jen... I slept in. Not feeling too good.'

'Oh dear ... erm, there's been a bit of a fire on the site, I'm afraid. Your cabin burned down. The police reckon it was vandals. I assume we're covered by insurance?'

'I er ... I think so. Anything else damaged?'

'No, just the cabin.'

'It'll be kids,' he said. 'See if you can order me another one as soon as poss.'

'Will do. I need some cheques signing.'

'Cleo's got the authority to sign cheques.'

'Cleo's not coming in today,' Jenny told him. 'She rang first thing. I can call round if you're not up to coming in either. Oh, and the Water Board have turned up a week early.'

'Water Board, what do they want?'

'Ant, don't tell me you've forgotten. They're coming to put a new connection in, like you've been nagging them to do for the last three months.'

'Ah, right.'

'I think they must have got their schedules mixed up but I told them it was okay. Hope I did the right thing. Looks like they're going to make a mess of the yard for a few days, but the sooner they start the sooner they're gone. They say a few days, but you know what they're like.'

'That's all I bloody need.'

'Should I have told them to come back? They've started digging now and they've brought all their equipment in.'

'No, no, it's okay,' Ant assured her. 'We need a proper supply to the yard.'

'They said they're putting a bigger main in for future requirements, whatever that means. Apparently you don't have to pay for it.'

'Good ... er, I'll be in later.'

He put the phone back on the hook and disappeared back under the blankets, trying to work out the implications. It didn't make much difference. He wasn't going to bury the body until dark, by which time the Water Board men would have gone home.

'Do you get a lot of vandalism round here?'

enquired the clerk of works from the Water Board. 'I gather you had a bit of trouble on one of your sites last night.' Ant had already been to the site and noted with some satisfaction that the fire had obliterated all traces of Womack's blood.

'Now and again,' he said, without thinking. His eyes were continually drawn to the storage shed containing his late stepfather's rotting body.

'Hmm,' said the clerk of works. 'We've got some valuable materials coming on site. I hope the little sods don't pay us a visit. Best have a word with the office.'

'Yeah, right,' Ant said, not taking much notice of what the man was saying. His eyes were scanning the yard, looking for a suitable burial plot; one that would never be disturbed. There was a Priestmann Cub mechanical digger on the building site that would do the job in minutes and Ant was just about proficient enough to drive it himself. He made a mental note to have the Priestmann brought into the yard that night for 'security' reasons and decided on an area beneath which he planned an extension to his sheds; a place that would be concreted over within days of the burial. He would bury Womack good and deep, ten feet at least. Maybe some future palaeontologist might theorise about the bones, but Ant would be long gone by then. He even managed a smile. He'd killed a human being, but this was outweighed by the fact that this particular human being was Womack, and his demise was beginning to lift a heavy weight off Ant's shoulders. He felt freed of the man's dark influence on his life. After it was over, maybe he'd take Jenny out for that meal he'd been promising her. He looked at her through the office window and caught her eye. She smiled at him and somehow he saw her in a different light for the first time.

It was late afternoon and Ant was on the top lift of the scaffold when he saw the Water Board van come on to the site. The clerk of works got out and called up to him.

'I've arranged for a night watchman back at your yard.'

'Good,' called back Ant.

Then he cursed to himself as the implication hit him. He wouldn't be able to bury Womack until the Water Board had gone. It shouldn't make too much difference in the long run, but it wouldn't be over until Womack was ten feet under and concreted in. 'How long do you think you'll be?' he called back.

'We should be finished by Tuesday,' the man called back.

'Which Tuesday?' shouted a bricklayer. 'Next Tuesday or Pancake Tuesday?'

'You keep yer nose out, clever sod!' said the clerk of works. 'All you brickies think you're clever sods. A week tomorrow, we'll be all done and dusted.'

'Two days' work in just over a week, eh?' taunted the brickie. 'That's not bad for the Water Board. The gas lads would've taken a fortnight.'

'It'd take you a month at the speed yer've been layin' them bricks,' retorted the clerk of works.

Ant tried to muster up a grin at the banter.

Eight days before he could bury the body. Eight days before he could rest easy.

The following afternoon, Cleo was in the office she shared with Ant when the police came. Jenny tapped on her door and poked her head round.

'There are two coppers here. I think it's about the fire. They want to speak to someone in charge.'

Cleo nodded and felt a heavy weight in her stomach as she braced herself to lie to the police, not for the first time. She looked at her watch and wondered if she should ask them to wait until Ant got back. He was a much better liar.

'Did Ant say what time he'd be back?'

Jenny shook her head. 'Not to me he didn't.'

'Okay,' Cleo decided. 'Send them in.'

She got up and walked to the window from where she could see the four Water Board men digging a trench by hand. A police car was parked about twenty feet away from the shed containing Womack's body, and a dog belonging to one of the Water Board workers was sniffing around the site. There was a tap on the door. Jenny came in and introduced two uniformed policemen, a middle-aged sergeant and a young constable.

'This is Sergeant Openshawe and PC Walker ... this is Miss Kelly,' she said. 'One of our directors.'

Cleo waited for one of them to remark that she was very young to be a company director. The sergeant obliged.

'Put it down to nepotism, Sergeant,' smiled Cleo. 'My brother's the boss.'

'We don't get much nepotism in the force,' said the constable, 'do we, Sergeant?'
'Er ... no.'
The sergeant didn't seem sure what nepotism was. His subordinate colleague knew it, and gave Cleo a smug grin.
'Sit down,' Cleo invited them.
'It's all right, miss,' said the sergeant. 'We've just got one or two loose ends to clear up about the fire at your site.'
'Oh? What loose ends are they?'
'Well er, will you be claiming on your insurance?'
'We haven't decided, Sergeant. It affects our premiums and on balance it might not be worth claiming.'
The sergeant took out a pocket book and wrote something down. Then he looked up at her with a puzzled expression on his face. 'The thing is, someone rang the station to say they'd seen a van with your firm's name written on the side leaving the site just before the fire.'
Cleo shrugged. 'I don't know what to say. We've only got one van and my brother drives that.'
'And this informant saw two people in the van.'
Cleo felt herself going cold. Playing dumb was the best bet. That's what Ant would have done. *Tell the buggers nothing.*
'I see,' she said. 'What does all this mean?'
'We were hoping you could tell us, miss. If not you, then maybe your brother could. You see we're investigating a crime of arson and we need to get to the bottom of it.'
'Are you saying my brother set his own site hut

on fire, Sergeant? Why on Earth would he want to do that? It's caused more problems than enough. He's been out all afternoon trying to get replacements for all the plans and paperwork that were destroyed. Insurance doesn't cover that sort of thing.'

'I don't imagine it does, miss. Where can we get hold of this brother of yours?'

His tone was patronising which got Cleo's back up. She lost her smile and went on the attack.

'I've got no idea, Sergeant. I'll ask him to give you a ring, as and when he can find the time, shall I?'

The constable grinned from behind his sergeant's back. He was very taken with Cleo. Given the opportunity he'd ask her out, but not right now.

'If you would, miss,' said the sergeant, gruffly.

They turned to go and Cleo followed, wanting to see them off the premises as soon as possible. This was a twist in events she and Ant could have done without, the sooner the police got off their backs the better. Her heart sank when Ant's van drove into the yard. He parked beside the office and got out.

'What's this?' He was grinning and Cleo didn't know how he could manage it. 'They haven't caught up with you at last, have they, Cleo?'

'Are you the proprietor of this company?' the sergeant asked, officiously.

'If that means, "Am I the boss?" Yes, I am.'

Ant was maintaining his smile. Cleo was impressed. The dog appeared and began to sniff around his van. The sergeant walked over to the vehicle, opened the door without asking, and looked inside.

'Phew! What have you had in here, dead rats?'

'It's a chemical smell,' said Ant. 'We use it to clean old masonry. Stinks to high heaven. I sometimes think we're better off using good old-fashioned elbow grease.'

He was hoping the policeman wouldn't ask for further enlightenment. The dog was now trying to get inside the van.

'Clear off, dog!' Ant aimed a pretend kick at the dog, which sent the animal scurrying away. Cleo watched with horror as it ran towards the hut containing Womack, and began barking again.

'What's the problem?' Ant asked the policemen.

'Someone saw your van leaving the site just before the fire,' Cleo told him. She'd had time to think of a plausible reason for him being there. 'I expect you were doing one of your checks.'

'That's right,' Ant said. 'I've taken to calling on site every night just to check that everything's all right. The kids round here are little buggers. They must have been waiting for me to leave. I blame myself, Sergeant. I didn't even bother to get out of the van to take a proper look. Live and learn eh?'

The sergeant grunted and looked at his notes. 'It says here that the informant saw a woman in the passenger seat, sir. It might help if we could speak to her.'

'I was on my own,' Ant said. 'I had a big sack of scaffolding clips on the passenger seat.'

'I suppose that would explain it, sir,' said the sergeant, grudgingly. 'I know a woman with a face like a sack of scaffolding clips.'

'I hope you're not talking about your wife, Sergeant,' said Cleo, relieved that her brother had talked his way out of it.

The sergeant sniffed the air and grimaced. 'My word! It carries does that smell, doesn't it, sir?'

'I think it's on my clothes, Sergeant,' Ant said.

The dog was barking frantically at the hut. The young policeman walked over to it to calm it, then retreated with his hand to his nose. 'Oh, Jesus! I can see what he's barking at. I'd bark myself if I was a dog!'

The sergeant joined his young colleague, then turned to look at Ant.

'It's the same smell as the one in your van, sir,' he called out. He tried the hut door but it was locked. Cleo's heart raced, but Ant maintained his grin.

'That's where we keep the stuff,' he said. 'Regulations say we have to keep the hut locked – it's a hazardous chemical. Get some on your uniform and they wouldn't let you back in the station.'

The policeman nodded and walked towards his car. 'I expect they wouldn't, sir. Anyway, I've enough on my plate without getting involved in other people's bad smells.'

Ant sat opposite Cleo drinking coffee. They were in the office.

'Bloody coppers,' he groaned. 'I hate coppers.'

'Oh, I don't know,' Cleo mused. 'The young one was rather nice. He kept smiling at me – I think he fancies me.'

Ant wasn't listening. 'I'm going to get rid of the

bugger tonight,' he said. 'My nerves won't take any more of this.'

'How are you going to do that with the watchman hovering over you?'

'You're going to take him to the pub for a drink, that's how,' Ant said.

'And how am I going to do that? He's old enough to be our great-granddad.'

'Ah, but he wears his medal ribbons, so he'll like to talk about the war. I'll tell him I'm working late at the yard so if he fancies a swift half at the pub I'll cover for him. Then you come over and offer to go with him, tell him you'll treat him to a couple of pints providing he tells you about the war. The old soldier hasn't been born who could resist an offer like that.'

'Which war? The Wars of the Roses or the Crimea?'

'Just do it, Cleo.'

Persuading the night watchman to go to the pub was as easy as Ant said it would be. Ant pretended to busy himself stacking bricks until they were out of sight then he started up the excavator and trundled it over to Womack's burial site. Within ten minutes he had dug a trench ten feet deep.

He got out of the cab and wrapped a scarf around his face to ward off the smell that made him retch, even though the hut door was still closed. When he opened it the real smell hit him like a pungent wall and Ant wondered if this was normal or it was because foul people like Womack smell worse than normal people when they're dead. He dragged the body by its feet as fast as he could to the hole. Another few minutes and it would be over. He'd join Cleo and the night watchman in the pub to wash the nasty taste from his mouth. To celebrate even. Three torchlight came on at once, and a shout of, 'Stop right there!' came from the darkness.

Cleo was listening without interest to a story from the First World War trenches. Her thoughts were on her brother.

'It was broad daylight,' said the night watchman, 'but yer couldn't see yer hand in front of yer face there were that much smoke about. If yer saw yeller smoke yer knew ter put yer gas mask on. Me, I just kept me eyes shut and kept on goin'. Then I fell in a bloody 'ole and broke me bloody leg. I were thankful, I can tell yer. I'd sooner have a broken leg than a bloody big 'ole in me 'ead.'

'Miss Kelly?'

Cleo was grateful for the distraction. It was the young policeman she'd seen earlier.

'Yes?'

She assumed he was asking her for a date. She'd read the signs and knew he liked her.

'I wonder if we could have a word?'

'Nay,' said the watchman. 'She's wi' me. Yer can't go tekkin' 'er off me like that.'

'Sorry, sir.'

'What is it?' Cleo asked, without too much concern. He looked pleasant enough. It would make a change to go out with a policeman.

'We've just arrested your brother, Miss Kelly, and we think you might be able to help with our enquiries.'

She saw a WPC hovering behind him and Cleo felt like her stomach had hit the floor.

'Arrested, what for?'

'We'd like you to come to the station.' said the WPC, unpleasantly. She had a wide nose and a plain face scattered with moles of different sizes.

Tell the buggers nothing came once again into Cleo's head. She got to her feet and went with them. As they got outside the young constable told her, 'The sergeant thought he recognised the smell and it wasn't anything to do with chemicals, but without a search warrant or a good reason for one, we couldn't open the hut. So we've been watching the yard all evening. I, er we ... followed you here. We've just got word over the radio to say a body's been found and your brother has been arrested.'

Ant let go of Womack's feet and shielded the light with his hands. There was nothing he could do. Torches were shining at him from all angles. He was on the ground now, with his arms jammed up his back as handcuffs were put on him, then he was roughly dragged to his feet. The torches now shone on Womack's body. The sergeant pulled the sack off the head and recoiled at the gruesome sight. Womack's white, bloodless face made a grisly contrast with the dark, congealed blood around his neck. One eye was partly open and reflecting in the torchlight and his mouth was frozen in the terror of his last living moment.

'Antony Kelly,' the sergeant said, when he recovered his composure. 'I'm arresting you for murder. You do not have to say anything but anything you do say may be taken down and used in evidence against you. Do you mind telling me who this is?'

Ant said nothing.

Cleo maintained her silence and got in the car. The young constable got in beside her and the policewoman got behind the wheel.

'Your name's Cleopatra, isn't it?' asked the constable who didn't look any older than herself.

Cleo paused then nodded.

'Cleopatra Kelly,' he said, awkwardly. 'I am arresting you for murder. You do not have to say anything, but anything you do say may be taken down and used in evidence against you.'

The words meant little to Cleo. Her mind was full of what was happening to Ant. The constable took out a pair of handcuffs and put them on her. 'I didn't want to embarrass you by doing this in the pub,' he explained.

'That's very thoughtful of you, but it's no way to ask for a date,' was the only thing Cleo could think of saying.

In the rear-view mirror she could see disapproval in the eyes of the plain policewoman who had been all for handcuffing her in the pub. She thought women as pretty as this prisoner had things too easy. No doubt she'd led a cosseted life, born with a silver spoon stuck in her gob, probably. People like that needed a bit of humiliation.

Cleo had been formally charged, fingerprinted and locked in a room for over two hours before the sergeant and the young constable came in to interview her. They were both already well into overtime and looked tired.

'Right, young lady,' said the sergeant. 'We've interviewed your brother and he's told us everything, so we just need you to confirm his story. Tell us in your own words the events leading up to the body being locked in the hut.'

'What you told me earlier,' Cleo said to the constable. 'Did you mean it?'

The young man shifted uneasily in his chair. 'What did I tell you?'

'You told me I don't have to say anything – did you mean it?'

'Well yes,' he said. 'It's the standard caution. But for your own benefit–'

Cleo interrupted him. 'Good. I'll take your advice. I won't say anything.'

'It wasn't advice.'

'What was it then?' Cleo asked, innocently.

'For God's sake, woman!' the sergeant butted in. 'You've been charged with murder. If it's a solicitor you want, you'd better say so.'

'Who have I murdered?'

'We don't know who–' began the constable. He stopped when the sergeant glared at him and took up the questioning.

'Your brother was about to bury a dead body which he had hidden in a shed in his yard. You were obviously covering for him.'

'Why's that?'

'Young lady. We ask the questions.'

'Your constable advised me not to say anything so I won't. And I want a solicitor.'

'We'll continue this in the morning when you've had time to consider the folly of your actions,' the sergeant said. 'Take her to a cell, constable.'

Ant had had all night to consider his strategy. He knew Cleo had been arrested and, like him, she wouldn't have said anything. But he also knew it was only a question of time before the body was identified and the connection made to the two of them. He waived the right to a solicitor and asked to be interviewed again.

'Well?' said the sergeant. 'What have you got to tell me?'

'I've come to tell you my sister had nothing to do with the body being there.'

'That's for us to decide.'

'All you know is that I was about to bury a dead body. You don't know whose body it is and you don't know who killed him. For all you know I might have found him dead in my yard and decided to bury him rather than go through a lot of questioning.'

'Only an idiot would do that.'

'I know, Sergeant. But it's not a crime to be an idiot. You've got me on unlawful burial and nothing else. I haven't got a criminal record and I'm not a violent person. Plenty of people will vouch for that.'

'Never heard of circumstantial evidence, Kelly?'

'You need more than you've got,' Ant challenged. 'You'd need to identify the body and make a connection between him and me. You'd need a murder weapon with my fingerprints on and you'd need to place me at the scene of the murder. You don't even know where it took place.'

'We can put both you and your sister away for

a lot of years on what we've got. If both of you are unco-operative in court the judge will take a dim view of it and advise the jury accordingly.'

'Drop the charges against my sister and I'll tell you all I know.'

'I can't do that.'

'Yes you can,' Ant insisted. 'Your pathologist will give you an approximate time of death. You'll find that Cleo was in London when it happened.'

'Be that as it may. Your sister has made a full statement.'

'Rubbish!'

Ant knew for certain that this was a lie. Cleo would have *told the buggers nothing.*

He smiled at the sergeant. 'Cleo doesn't know anything, so that's what she'll have told you. Nothing. She'll be keeping quiet because she doesn't want to say anything that might incriminate me. If you want to wrap your case up, let my sister go without charge.'

The sergeant sighed and got to his feet. He told the constable, who had been taking notes, to stay there. Then he left the room without saying why.

'How come you know so much about the law?' the constable asked.

'I read a lot,' Ant said. 'Where do you think he's gone?'

'To have a word with the inspector about Cl ... your sister.'

'She fancies you,' Ant told him. 'Did you know that?'

If there was card to be played Ant would play it. Getting Cleo out of trouble was the only thing on his mind. It was important that all charges against her were dropped before they identified the body without Ant's help and he lost his trump card.

'Who is he?' the constable asked. 'The body, I mean.'

Ant said, mysteriously, 'You'll never find that out in a million years, unless I tell you. Go tell the sergeant that – and tell him I want a solicitor to verify that all charges have been dropped against my sister before I say another word.'

Cleo had been awake all night, trying to make sense of what had happened. Ant hadn't fully explained why he'd killed Womack, only that he'd lost his temper and lashed out with a spade. But this wasn't like Ant; he hadn't got much of a temper. The night he'd stabbed Womack in the arm it wasn't done out of temper, but to save her from harm (although it ended up doing her more harm than good). Despite the trauma that life had thrown at them both, Ant was the one who seemed to handle it with the greater equanimity. He was the one who could shut problems out and get on with things – such as his business. There was more to this than he was letting on.

And what was her punishment to be for aiding and abetting a killer to escape justice? She knew Ant would do his utmost to take all the blame himself but the police weren't *that* stupid. They must know she had lured the night watchman away so that her brother could dispose of the body in secrecy. Could forensics somehow identify the burned-out site hut as the scene of the murder? And could they somehow prove she'd helped move the body? No doubt the evidence would be piling up against her by the minute. Police like to leave their customers to stew in a cell for a while; such confinement tends to induce paranoia and an unburdening of guilt. But Cleo had been left to stew in much worse places than this. *Tell the buggers nothing.*

Would Jeff have misgivings at having just proposed to a woman accused of murder? She still hadn't decided on her answer. It would be a true test of his love for her.

It was mid-morning and she was dozing fitfully beside a cold and untouched breakfast when the cell door clanked open and a custody sergeant told her she was free to collect her things and go because all charges against her had been dropped.

'What about my brother?'

'Your brother's not going anywhere. He's made a full confession.'

'I'd like to see him, please.'

'I'm afraid that won't be possible. Not at the moment anyway.'

'What's he been charged with?'

She was ever hopeful that Ant had been crafty enough to get off with a minor charge.

'He's confessed to murdering your stepfather. I assume you knew whose body it was. If you didn't, I'm sorry.'

Cleo was bursting to release a torrent of invective and words mitigating Ant's crime, but she knew to keep her own counsel on the matter. Such an outburst wouldn't do her any good.

'Don't be sorry,' she said. 'My stepfather was a very evil man. When they bury him, make sure they bury him deep, preferably in a lead coffin.'

Flo handed Cleo a drink to settle her nerves. 'You've been through a bad time. I can't condemn you for what you've done – I'd probably have done the same in your shoes.' The pub wasn't open yet and they were sitting in the spacious living room above the lounge bar. 'If they'd found out you helped him hide the body you'd have got a custodial sentence.'

Cleo sipped at her drink. 'If it had helped Ant,' she said, 'I wouldn't have minded. I've been locked up before.'

'Not in a proper prison you haven't. Besides, you owning up won't make any difference.'

'What will they do to him?'

'It all depends on the circumstances. If he pleads guilty it'll help. Then he'll have to plead mitigating circumstances. He needs to have had good reason to have lost his temper and killed his stepfather.'

'I think he did,' Cleo said.

'Let's hope the judge agrees with you.'

'Jeff asked me to marry him,' Cleo said.

Flo had managed to steer the conversation away from the killing to more cheerful things. 'Did he now? Well, under the circumstances,' she commented, 'I'd say it proves something about him. It proves he's not a man who'll run away when things get tough.'

'He asked me before all this happened. Before we went to London.'

'Oh,' said Flo.

'I'm seeing him tonight. I'm going to say yes.'

Flo smiled at her troubled friend. 'He seems a good man. The type to keep you on the straight and narrow.'

'So, you approve, do you?'

'Yes, I do, Cleo – and I'm pleased for you.'

'I've decided something else as well,' Cleo told her, almost defiantly. 'After I've told him ... I'm going to ... do it with him. I think I've been a virgin long enough.'

Flo hugged her. 'You do right, love. Make him take you somewhere nice. Have a night to remember.'

Jeff's smile seemed awkward when they met under the Guinness Clock outside the Corn Exchange, their usual meeting spot.

'How are you?' he asked.

'Okay ... you?'

'Me?' he said. 'Oh, same as usual.'

'Did you make any money at Aintree?' she asked, trying to sound interested.

'Not too bad. Took a bit of a hammering when the favourites came in on the first two races, but we made it up.'

'That's good.' Cleo smiled and vowed to herself to take more of an interest in racing now that they were about to become engaged. 'Where are we going?'

'Do you fancy the pictures? *Dr No's* on at the Majestic – it's supposed to be brilliant.'

'Okay,' she said.

He took her hand as they walked along Boar Lane towards City Square. There was an uncomfortable silence between them and she found herself looking down as they walked, thereby noticing his shoes; brown suede and comfortable looking – a bit like their owner.

'Did you get some new shoes?'

'Yeah,' he said. 'Hush Puppies. Thought I'd treat myself.'

'They're nice.'

They were behaving like a couple on their first date, testing the water with each other, which was odd because they didn't usually indulge in small talk. Why was this? – of course! Jeff was nervous about her answer to his proposal of marriage. He probably didn't know what had happened. He wouldn't have had time to read the papers or listen to the news. If so, she didn't want to have to broach the subject. Cleo was considering having a night out that didn't include any talk about Ant or the killing of Horace Womack. But was it sensible to say 'Yes' to him and let him make love to her if he didn't know what had happened? Did she have a duty to tell him?

'Bad do about your brother,' he said, solving that particular dilemma.

'Ah, you heard then?' she said.

'Yeah. I've only met him a couple of times, but I never thought he was like that. Fancy killing someone with a spade... Ugh! Doesn't bear thinking about.'

'He's not like that. Our stepfather was an animal.'

'It's in all the papers,' Jeff said. 'They make it sound gruesome.' He looked at her, keenly. 'Some of the papers said you were involved.'

'Really? I haven't read any papers today.'

She became aware of all the people hurrying past. Did they recognise her? Were they staring at her? A seafood vendor outside Trinity Church shouted his wares and looked straight at her. She lowered her eyes and jumped when he shouted, almost in her ear.

'Get yer luvly prawns 'ere! Only a tanner a bag.'

Jeff stopped and bought a bag, probably from force of habit. They often shared a bag of prawns together in the street. It was one of their things. Cleo refused his offer of one. They walked a little way, then she stopped.

'Do you think I was involved?' she asked.

'I suppose if you were involved, you wouldn't be here,' he said.

'No, I don't suppose I would.'

She was hoping for more support. If he'd known all about it, why hadn't he flung his arms around her when they met? Why hadn't he told her he'd do everything in his power to help her through it? Why was he just chewing and trying not to look her in the eye.

'Jeff,' she said. 'Would it make any difference if I was involved. Even if the killing was justifiable?'

'What sort of a question's that? You weren't involved ... were you?'

'Jeff, you asked me to marry you last week and I don't want a husband who'll run at the first sign of trouble. It's important that you answer my question.'

'Sounds to me as if you *are* involved,' he muttered, through a mouthful of prawns.

'What if I am? Will you stand by me?'

'Be fair, Cleo. How could I stand by you if you're

locked up in prison? What sort of a marriage would that be?'

'Not much of a marriage,' she said. 'Not much of a marriage at all.'

She walked away from him. Jeff stood there for a few seconds then hurried to follow her. But the distance she'd put between them was more than just physical. He didn't love her *enough*. Maybe it was for the best – she probably didn't love him enough either. Maybe she had only decided to say 'Yes' to bring some light back into her life.

'I don't want to marry you, Jeff,' she said when he caught her up.

'Oh.' There was both sadness and relief in his eyes.

She gave him a wan smile and kissed him on the cheek. Perhaps it was a bit much burdening a man with all her problems; but she knew that when the right man came along it would be someone who would love her above and beyond the call of duty; someone who would carry her safely across the unpredictable steeplechase of life. Jeff the bookie's son had fallen at the first fence.

Chapter Fifteen

Cleo had a good view of her brother from her seat in the public gallery. His normally tanned face had grown pale during his three months on remand in Armley jail pending his trial at Leeds Assizes. Ant had left his plea of guilty to the last minute.

'If the bank thinks I'm definitely going down they'll shut up shop on me,' he had told Cleo, 'and the creditors will be hammering on the door. As it is, the bank won't want to be seen pre-judging the issue. As soon as I plead guilty they'll freeze the accounts and I want you to be ready with cash put to one side. Right now, I want you to tell the bank I'm innocent and it's all a big mistake and that you're going to carry on as best you can until I get back, which won't be long. Tell them about you passing your business exam with flying colours, lay it on thick.'

'I don't need to lay it on thick. I got a distinction.'

'Good,' said Ant, who wasn't normally impressed by academic achievement. 'Tell the bank that. We'll transfer my Cortina into your name so no one can get their grubby hands on it.'

Ant's last-minute plea of guilty meant she wasn't called to give evidence that might incriminate her. For that reason he had refused to accept her as a character witness, either for him or to tell the court about Womack's cruelty to them as children.

'These barristers are crafty, Cleo,' he explained. 'They can trip you up without you realising it. The next thing you know you're in a cell being charged as an accomplice. I'll be all right.'

When asked if he had anything to say before sentence was passed Ant took a deep breath and read out his prepared statement in a faltering voice:

'Horace Womack was the cruellest man I have ever known. When my sister was twelve years old he locked her under the stairs for something I had done, only I had run away so he couldn't punish me. He and my mother went out one night and the house caught fire because they hadn't put the fireguard up and my sister was nearly burned alive. Any other child wouldn't have got out. Then he blamed her for starting the fire and got her sent to a reformatory.'

He looked up at Cleo and tried to smile. She was in floods of tears. Jenny and Flo, on either side, each put an arm around her. Ant looked down at his sheet of paper and continued:

'In 1956 a court found out the truth and the verdict was quashed. At that time my stepfather was in jail for assaulting a young boy. When we were children he hit us every day. On the day he came to the site hut he started talking dirty about my sister. I lost my temper and I hit him with a spade. I tried to bury him myself because I knew this would happen if I reported it to the police.'

He stopped and there was a silence, as the court didn't know if he had finished or not. Ant folded up his paper, put it in his pocket and stood with his arms behind his back. The judge cleared his throat and nodded his head to himself as if confirming what he was about to say. He stared into space for a few seconds as the court held its breath, awaiting his pronouncement.

'Antony Kelly,' he turned to face Ant. 'You have just told me that you killed your stepfather out of revenge. I accept that the act was not premeditated and that it was committed on the spur of the moment. But I am also satisfied that you had an accomplice; if not in the crime of murder, but in attempting to conceal the evidence. I must take into consideration your refusal to reveal the identity of this person.'

He paused and looked directly at Cleo, and she all but got to her feet to tell the world she was that person and would the judge go easy on her brother. Flo, who knew this would do no good, gripped her arm, tightly.

'Steady,' she whispered. 'It won't make any difference.'

'Your crime,' the judge went on, turning back to Ant, 'was motivated by revenge for the way you perceived Mr Womack treated you and your sister when you were children...'

'What's he on about?' said Flo in a voice loud enough to be heard across the court. 'It wasn't revenge. He just lost his rag like anyone would have done.'

'Silence!' shouted the judge, banging his gavel.

Flo pulled a face and shut up. Ant's barrister shook his head. He had advised Ant what to say in mitigation, but the lad reckoned he knew best.

If he'd thrown himself at the mercy of the court and maybe summoned up a tear of remorse for what he'd done it would have gone in his favour. But the lad would have his own say and it was now going to cost him dearly.

'Antony Kelly,' continued the judge, 'I have no option other than to sentence you to life imprisonment.'

He stared at Ant for a second as if trying to gauge his victim's reaction, but Ant was just numbed by the sentence. It was too enormous for him to take in. The judge got to his feet, then said to the two policemen guarding Ant, both of whom seemed unsure whether the judge had finished or not. 'Well, take him down.'

'No!' screamed Cleo, as her brother was led down the steps to the cells. 'You can't do this. It wasn't his fault. Don't you bloody idiots ever get anything right?'

The judge was already entering his chambers but he heard Cleo's insult quite clearly. He paused in his step, as though wondering whether to turn round and order her to be punished, then he thought better of it and closed the door behind him.

Chapter Sixteen

It just didn't feel right sitting in the comfort of The Bird in the Hand sipping brandy, while Ant was sitting in a cell in the bowels of Leeds Town Hall awaiting transport to jail. Cleo remembered the time Ant had rescued her from a similar situation. Maybe she should be waiting outside the door with a getaway bike. She told Flo and Jenny the story of what had happened that day and they both laughed. The three of them were sitting around a table in the tap room of Flo's pub, which was otherwise quiet at that time of day.

'He's the most enterprising lad I've ever come across,' Flo said. 'If he'd managed to stay out of trouble he'd have been a millionaire by the time he was thirty.'

'That was his ambition,' said Cleo. 'God knows what I'm going to do now. It's been hard enough keeping things going the last three months while he's been on remand. If it wasn't for Ant's architect helping us out I don't know what we'd have done. I suppose we'll have to sell up now. Without Ant there is no Kelly Construction.'

'He was the engine that drove it, all right,' Jenny agreed. 'Puts me out of a job, though.'

Flo looked at her, fiercely, and Jenny put her hand to her mouth.

'Sorry Cleo. That sounded a bit selfish.'

'You shouldn't have to apologise for losing your job,' Cleo assured her. 'I wish there was something I could do. Ant reckons the bank will freeze all our accounts.'

'The first thing you do is call a meeting with your architect, the bank, your accountant and your solicitor,' Flo advised. 'At the moment Kelly Construction is still a solvent company.'

'The trouble is it was Ant who made it solvent, and the bank know that,' Cleo said. 'A building company doesn't run itself and Ant won't let anyone else run it on his behalf. He told me as much himself.'

'He knows that someone else would run it into the ground,' Flo commented, 'after taking all they could get out of it. When push comes to shove there's no sentiment in business.'

It was a week before Cleo was able to visit her brother and she was shocked by his appearance. He looked empty and soulless; it was as if a light had been extinguished within him.

'How are you?' she asked.

'Okay.'

She wanted to tell him he looked far from okay, but what good would that do?

'I've brought you some stuff,' she said, handing him a carrier bag. 'They checked it all on the way in. They even opened the cig packets and took them all out.'

'Some people bring drugs in,' her brother explained. 'Anyway, I don't smoke. Why bring me cigarettes?'

'Flo's idea. She says it's a form of currency in

these places. If you don't smoke it's to your advantage.'

Ant nodded his understanding. 'I'm not up with the system yet. It hasn't sunk in that I'll be here for the best part of my life.' He was fighting the urge to indulge in a bout of self-pity, but that wouldn't do anyone any good, especially Cleo.

'I was going to ask you about the business,' she said. 'The bank withdrew our overdraft but Harry Radcliffe got them to reinstate it when he said he was going to help us run the site. I'd stuck a few hundred to one side just in case. Jenny and I have been struggling along. Harry's been a big help. He's a good architect, but he's not a builder. He's made a few cock-ups already.'

Ant scratched his head, trying to adjust his thoughts to affairs of business, and failing.

'I called a meeting with the bank and a few other people,' Cleo went on. 'Harry was there, and someone from your accountants. Oh and your solicitor. Didn't like him. He's all for liquidating the company.'

Her words were falling on practically deaf ears. 'We'll discuss it later,' she decided, 'when you've had time to think.'

'Right,' he sounded relieved.

'Flo's making enquiries about appealing against the length of your sentence,' she told him.

Ant just shrugged and looked at her. There was no hope in his eyes and the ready smile that was always on his lips seemed a million miles away.

'We'll have to come up with some convincing mitigating circumstances,' Cleo said. 'Flo reckons your barrister was rubbish.'

'I don't think it would have made much difference, Cleo. I killed him and that's that.' Ant's voice was flat.

His sister looked at him, steadily. There had been a doubt gnawing away at her ever since the time of the killing. Losing his rag in such a devastating manner just wasn't in Ant's nature, or so she had thought. She hadn't pressed him on it because there seemed no point. Pressing him wouldn't bring Womack back and if Ant had had some other reason for doing what he did, then surely he would have mentioned it in court.

'Can you think of anything at all that might go in your favour?' she asked.

Ant lowered his eyes and she could see him blushing.

'There is something, isn't there?'

He shook his head, but didn't look up. Cleo leaned over the table and tilted his chin up like an adult would do to a reluctant child.

'Ant,' she said. 'It's too late for secrets. If there's anything that might help, we need to know.'

He looked at her and his eyes misted over. 'There's nothing that can help,' he told her. 'Not now ... not now he's dead.'

'How do you mean?'

'Even then it would have been my word against his,' he said. Tears were tumbling down his cheeks now but his voice was steady and controlled, only loud enough for Cleo to hear. 'I just wanted to forget about it,' he said. 'Forget about all that stuff he did to me.'

'He did it to me as well, Ant. Maybe I didn't cop it as much as you, but being locked under the stairs wasn't a picnic–'

'I know it wasn't,' he said. 'If you'd died under them stairs I'd have killed him anyway ... but he didn't do to you what he did to me.' He looked at her. 'At least I hope he didn't?'

There was a question in his last sentence that Cleo didn't understand ... at first. The realisation dawned on her.

'Do you mean he…?'

The look in his eyes gave her his answer. There was shame and guilt there. 'I don't want you to tell anyone,' he whispered. 'He didn't do anything like that to you, did he? I once asked him and he said you weren't his type.'

She slowly shook her head and for the first time appreciated why Ant had killed Horace Womack. 'Oh, Ant. I didn't know... How long did it go on for?'

It took him a while to answer, then he had to force the words out, so painful was the subject. 'Practically all the time he lived with us. It's not something you go round telling people.'

'Is that why you didn't say anything in court?'

'There wasn't much point. For all they knew I could have just made it all up. They'd have asked me why I didn't say anything while it was going on. The truth is I felt dirty just thinking about it, I certainly wasn't going to tell anyone about it.'

Cleo had no words of easy consolation. She felt guilty relief that Womack's perversions didn't extend to him assaulting her.

If Cleo was going to enlist Flo's help she needed to break the vow of secrecy she'd sworn to Ant that very afternoon. So the sooner she got it over and done with, the better.

Flo listened with great concern to Cleo's story of how her brother had been a victim of Womack's perversions.

'He felt guilty, as if it was somehow his fault. He was too ashamed to tell anyone,' said Cleo, in tears now at the thought of all the torment her brother must have gone through. Too ashamed to tell even her. Until that day.

'I've seen enough of that sort of thing to know kids feel guilty when they shouldn't,' Flo said. 'And they keep their mouths shut because telling the truth only gets 'em into more trouble. I've had many an argument with people who are too ready to take an adult's word against a kid's.' She looked keenly at Cleo. 'He didn't touch you, did he?'

'Not in that way, thank God.'

'I wonder if your mother knew?'

'She wouldn't have done anything to help Ant, even if she did know.' Cleo's voice was heavy with contempt.

'She might now he's dead,' said Flo. 'If we can get her to testify that Womack sexually assaulted Ant when he was a child, it'd make a big difference at the appeal.'

'Why would she do that?' Cleo asked. 'If she knew what was going on it makes her as bad as Womack. Couldn't she be locked up for aiding and abetting or something?'

'Not if she's granted immunity from prosecution,' Flo said. 'Anyway she's all we have.'

'God help my brother then.'

Wet Nelly Kelly seemed to have vanished off the face of the earth. Cleo even employed a private detective to try and track her down, but to no avail. After a month, the only information he did come up with was unsavoury.

'The last anyone heard of her she was er, working the streets. She'd become a erm...' he hesitated to say the word in front of Nelly's daughter. Cleo helped him out.

'Prostitute?'

'Er, yes. She was last arrested in Leeds three years ago. Since then no one has heard of her. I think you might have to take into consideration the fact that she might be, er ... deceased.' He chose the word carefully, hoping to lessen the blow. 'People disappear without trace all the time, especially...'

'Prostitutes?'

The thought that Nelly might be lying at the bottom of the River Aire wrapped in heavy chains didn't strike much of a pain in Cleo's heart, more a sense of disappointment at her mother not being around to help Ant. But it had always been a long shot.

Cleo put the phone down and looked at Jenny. She'd just asked the bank manager for an extra £500 on the company overdraft to tide them over until some house completion money came through.

'Five hundred quid for one week,' she grumbled. 'You'd think I'd asked them to pay off the national flipping debt. Six months ago they couldn't do enough for us.'

‘Briggs’s have put us on their stop list,’ Jenny told her. ‘No more bricks until we pay off October’s invoice.’

‘I’ll call out on site and see what the brick situation is,’ Cleo said. ‘Then I might ring Briggs’s up and tell them to stuff their order and I’ll get the rest of the bricks from somewhere else.’

‘I don’t know where,’ replied Jenny. ‘Word’s gone round that we’re struggling. Most people can’t understand how we’ve managed to keep going this long.’

It was mainly because of Cleo that the men had remained loyal and helpful. She spent almost as much time on site as Ant had, with the men helping her to fill the large gaps in her knowledge. Harry Radcliffe was a help, but all this wasn’t enough. What the firm needed was a builder who knew what he was doing. One such man had been and gone after making a cock-up that had taken several days and a lot of money to put right. Cleo had felt bad about sacking him and was reluctant to gamble on a replacement.

‘We could stick an advert in the *Construction News*,’ Jenny suggested. ‘Try to find another building manager.’

‘All the good blokes will want some guarantee of permanence,’ commented Cleo, gloomily. ‘We can’t see beyond next week. Trouble is, everybody knows that. The accountants reckon if we sell now we can just about come out without owing anybody anything. If the bank foreclose on our overdraft we could be declared insolvent.’

‘Do you think you should have a word with Ant?’ Jenny asked. ‘Tell him how things are.’

'At the moment,' said Cleo, 'I think my brother's got enough to worry about.' She took out a packet of cigarettes and offered Jenny one. It was a habit they'd both recently succumbed to because of the pressure they were under. 'On paper, we can carry on,' she said. 'If only people would let us. The houses have been selling well, that's one good thing.'

'Lets hope the buyers don't start going off,' remarked Jenny.

'I don't even want to think about that,' said Cleo.

A young couple were on site when Cleo arrived later that morning. They were looking at a partly built house. Cleo recognised them as having reserved it a month ago.

'It should be finished in about six weeks,' she said.

'That's what your foreman told us,' replied the young man. He looked, earnestly, at Cleo. 'We're supposed to be signing the contract today and to be honest we're a bit worried.'

'Oh?' said Cleo, pretending she hadn't a clue what they were talking about. 'Worried about what?'

The couple looked at each other, then the young man said: 'We've been hearing rumours that your firm's in trouble. If we sign a contract and you go bust we might lose our ten per cent deposit money.'

'And we can't afford that,' said the young woman. 'We're getting married next month.'

Faced with this dilemma, Cleo knew she

couldn't lie to them. Even Ant wouldn't have put their money in jeopardy. 'The only problem we've got is this stupid rumour,' she told them. 'But we'll come out of it okay, no fear of that. I'll tell the solicitor to hold your money in a client's account. It won't be passed on to us until the house is sold to you. That way your deposit is safe. We don't need your ten per cent, we just need the rumours to stop. Your house will be finished on time, don't worry about that.'

The young man nodded. 'Thanks,' he said, and took his fiancée's hand. 'We'll sign the contract this afternoon.'

Cleo thanked them and walked away. She would have to notify all the other prospective purchasers that their deposit money wasn't in jeopardy. This was another blow. She'd taken the ten per cents into consideration when working out her financial strategy.

A week later Cleo found herself staring at the completion statement from the solicitor; in her other hand was the banker's draft it came with. The house had sold for £2,700 and she expected payment of around £2,600, give or take a few pounds. Instead she'd been paid £1,235.8s.6d. Attached to the statement were another two sheets, listing charges for appointments, phone calls and letters. Cleo picked up the phone and dialled the solicitor's number. A woman's voice answered.

'Could I speak to Mr Collins please?' Cleo said.

'Who shall I say is speaking?

'Cleo Kelly of Kelly Construction.'

There was a pause then muffled voices, as though the woman had her hand over the mouthpiece. 'Could you tell me the reason for your call?' said the woman eventually.

'Yes,' Cleo said. 'I've received a completion statement for a house sale on our Garforth site and the payment's about £1,400 short. I want to know why.'

Another pause, more muffled voices then, 'Mr Collins is with a client at the moment. Is there anything *I* can help you with?'

Cleo sighed. 'I just want to know why I wasn't paid the full amount. If I go to the bank with this they'll go potty.'

The woman cleared her throat, nervously. 'I understand that all our charges are listed in detail, Miss Kelly. Apparently we've been overlooking certain charges and this statement just brings us fully up to date.'

Cleo saw what was happening. 'You mean Collins has heard we're struggling and he thought he'd screw us out of as much money he could before we go under.'

'It's er, it's standard solicitor's practice,' said the woman, uncertainly.

'According to this statement,' Cleo said, trying to control her anger. 'You've charged us every time we've had any contact with you. Isn't this covered by the conveyancing fees?'

'The conveyancing fee doesn't include the items on your statement.'

'Just let me speak to Mr Collins,' Cleo shouted. 'I'd like to hear this from him. If I'm going to be cheated, I want to hear what the crook has to say for himself.'

'I'm afraid Mr Collins isn't available right now. If you have a complaint I suggest you put it in writing, thank you.'

The woman put the phone down, leaving Cleo seething with rage. She stormed into Jenny's room and told her the story.

'I've been half expecting this,' Jenny said. 'Two writs came in this morning's post for invoices we've only had a couple of weeks.'

'They can't do that,' Cleo said, 'can they?'

Jenny shrugged. 'Seems they can. I think it's vulture time. Look, if it's any help you don't need to pay me till you get back on your feet.'

'God, Jen! I hope it hasn't come to that.'

'Cleo, with the extra five hundred the bank let us have, that cheque still leaves us well overdrawn.'

'Yes, but it brings us under our credit limit.'

'Only just,' Jenny pointed out. 'And if the bank call in their loan, we've had it.'

'I promised them two thousand six hundred,' groaned Cleo, looking at the banker's draft. 'What do you think will happen if I take this in?'

'I dread to think,' said Jenny.

Cleo stared at the bank note in her hand. 'I wish this was cash,' she said. 'We could just do with this right now. It seems a shame we have to give it to the bank for them to swallow it up and give us nothing back.'

'We er ... we don't actually have to do that,' said Jenny. 'We could pay it in to another account.'

'What other account?'

Jenny looked embarrassed and took out a

paying-in book with the name Scottish Thistle Bank Ltd on the cover. 'Ant made me promise not to tell you about it ... sorry.'

Cleo took the book and flicked through the pages. The account name was Anthony Kelly trading as Kelly Construction. Small amounts had been paid in, but nothing for over a year.

'You know what Ant was like,' Jenny said. 'He had little ways of his own that he thought you might not approve of. And he didn't want to worry you. As far as I know the account's still open.'

Cleo thought for a while, then gave Jenny the banker's draft. 'Pay this in to the Thistle Bank, Jen,' she said. 'And draw it all out in cash. If our proper bank ring, tell them we haven't been paid for the house yet ... it's sort of true when you think of it. It'll keep the vultures at bay and pay the wages for a bit. There's another house just about ready. Once we get the money from that, it should put us in front ... for a while.'

Chapter Seventeen

High in the Pennines, west of Huddersfield, the old man didn't hear the knock on his door above the sound of November rain hammering against his cottage window. An unenthusiastic fire flickered in the grate, taking the chill off the room but little else. He wore an old trilby hat, an overcoat and gloves with no finger ends to enable him to hold a knife and fork and turn the television off when *Coronation Street* finished. It was the only thing he liked, everything else was a waste of the electricity that had only just reached his part of the world.

He sometimes fantasised about Elsie Tanner becoming stranded on the bleak moors outside his door and him gallantly putting her up for the night in his cottage with its one bedroom – and one bed. He laughed at Elsie's son, Denis, who was up to his old tricks with his pal, Jed Stone. The old man was still laughing when two men walked in. Vincent Pascoe threw a wad of notes on the table, making the old man jump.

'Five hundred quid,' he said, 'as we agreed.'

Pascoe was a large, bullet-headed, bulbous man. Every part of his body seemed to be trying to break free from his clothes. His fat neck was squeezed into a shirt collar that looked to be choking him, his belly overhung the waistband of his trousers like a waterbag and his leather watch strap appeared to be cutting into his fat wrists, stopping the blood supply to his gold-encrusted fingers. He had a cauliflower left ear, a florid complexion and small, piggy eyes.

The old man looked up, bemused at first, then he suddenly remembered where he'd seen this man before. Pascoe leaned over him and glared in to his face.

'We've come for the deeds ter the land we talked about.'

'Flamin' Norah, that were ages ago!' grumbled the old man. 'I thought yer'd forgot about it.'

'Forget? We never forget,' Pascoe said. 'Nor do we go back on a deal. We shook hands on it, remember?'

'I remember sellin' it ter someone else,' muttered the old man. 'I mentioned you, an' he said he knew yer an' that yer'd bought another piece o' land instead.' He wiped a dewdrop from the end of his nose with a bony finger as he recalled the conversation he'd had with Ant. 'That's right. He said yer'd bought a piece near 'alifax, and yer wouldn't be needin' mine.'

'I hope this is some sort o' bloody joke!' roared Pascoe. 'Because if it's not I'm going to ring yer scrawny bloody neck!'

The old man shrank back in his chair, terrified of the big man's rage.

'Steady on, Vinny,' cautioned Pascoe's companion. 'What's done's done. We'll have to track this other chap down.'

Pascoe stood for a while, opening and closing his fists. A vein throbbed in his thick neck as he tried to control his temper. 'This other man,' he rasped. 'Who is he, and where do I get hold of him?'

The old man was too scared to think. Pascoe slapped him hard around his head, knocking him from his chair on to the floor. Then the big man dragged him to his feet by the scruff of his neck.

'I won't ask yer again, yer cheatin' old bastard!'

'I don't remember,' sobbed the old man. 'Yer confusin' me.'

'Let him be,' advised Pascoe's companion. 'Let him think.'

The old man sat down in his chair. Blood was running freely down his face, which he wiped with the sleeve of his overcoat. 'Kelly,' he said. 'He's a builder.'

'Builder?' bellowed Pascoe. 'It's not buildin' land. What's a builder want wi' it?'

'Maybe when he realises that he'll let us have it for a reasonable price,' soothed Pascoe's companion.

'Reasonable price!' roared Pascoe. He grabbed the old man again. 'If it costs me a penny piece more than what I agreed wi' you, yer cheatin' owd bastard, I'll be back. Where can I find this Kelly?'

The old man's eyes dropped. 'I were readin' about him in t' papers,' he muttered, nervously. 'He's in jail fer murder.'

Pascoe exploded and stomped around the room. 'Jail? That's all I bloody need. How am I supposed ter buy land off someone what's in bloody jail.'

He lashed out at the old man again, knocking him unconscious. The second man took Pascoe by his arm.

'Look, Vinny,' he said, placatingly. 'I think I know who he's talking about. I read about him myself. Just calm down and let's think it through before you find yourself sharing a cell with our Mr Kelly. If he's in jail for murder the land's not much use to him. I'm sure we can persuade him to sell it.'

'You're supposed ter be a solicitor,' Pascoe snarled. 'I reckon you should sort it out.'

'Perhaps if you'd bought the land earlier, like I suggested, none of this would have happened.'

'Oh, so all this is my bloody fault, is it?'

The two of them left the cottage still arguing. The old man opened a cautious eye, rubbed his bruised cheek and went over to a dresser where he opened a cupboard containing a tin box.

'Me a cheatin' bastard?' he muttered, taking out a bundle of notes from the box. 'I'd say it's you what's a cheatin' bastard, offerin' me five hundred when the other feller says it's worth a lot more. An' yer can come back when yer like, it's time I were movin' on. This is Kelly's place now – not that he'll have much use fer it.' He cackled to himself as he counted the fifteen hundred pounds that Ant had given him for the land and the cottage.

Vincent Pascoe pulled his Bentley to a halt outside Kelly Construction's offices. His solicitor companion wasn't with him this time, instead he was accompanied by one of his quarry managers, Fat Eric – a man even larger and more menacing then Pascoe himself. It was the morning after he'd paid the old man a visit. Pascoe had business to settle and waiting for solicitors to help with negotiations wasn't his style. Time was money, especially in this particular instance. The two of them stared at the wooden building and saw a woman walk past a window. Pascoe grinned at Fat Eric.

'If I can't make a stupid bint part wi' a bit o' land, my name's not Vinny Pascoe.'

'Word has it that the firm's on its uppers,' his companion said. 'I reckon if yer offer her a grand, Vinny, she'll grab yer hand off.'

'She gets five hundred, not a bloody penny more.'

'Suit yerself, Boss. But we need ter be makin' a start before somebody else steps in and gets that stone contract.'

'There's nobody can undercut us,' Vinny snarled contemptuously. 'My quarry's less than two miles front t' motorway in some parts. Us delivery costs'll be less than half everyone else's.'

'That's why yer should offer her a grand and be done wi' it.'

Pascoe got out of his car and slammed the door, angrily. Eric was talking sense but five hundred quid was five hundred quid. He'd brought a thousand with him, but if it cost him that he'd go back and take the other five hundred out of the old man's hide. He was still angry when he hammered on the office door. Jenny looked out of the window and spotted Pascoe's car.

'There's a Bentley parked outside,' she said to Cleo. 'Who the hell have we upset now?'

Cleo opened the door with some trepidation, expecting an irate creditor waving an unpaid invoice at her. Pascoe's menacing face took her aback but she relaxed when he attempted a smile. Fat Eric smiled as well, although it was obviously something he wasn't used to doing.

'I'm looking for Miss Kelly,' Pascoe said. His voice was brutal, despite him trying to sound pleasant.

'That's me.'

'My name's Pascoe of Pascoe Quarries. I understand you're running the firm in your brother's er ... absence?'

'That's right.'

'In that case,' he said. 'I've a proposition yer might be interested in.'

'Oh?' Men with propositions were not men to be trusted. She made no move to allow him through the door. 'What sort of proposition?'

'A proposition that'll make yer five hundred pounds better off just fer selling me a scrap of land that can't possibly be of any use ter yer.'

Cleo still didn't budge. But £500 wasn't to be sneezed at, not in her position.

'What land?'

'If we can come in we can discuss it properly. I might even go up ter seven fifty.'

He had already made his mind up to go to the full thousand his quarry manager had suggested.

Cleo considered this for a second. 'I don't actually know what land you're talking about,' she said. 'But if you've just come ahead of all the other vultures to get some easy pickings I'm afraid you'll be disappointed.'

She didn't like the look of Pascoe at all. The smile dropped from his face as he sensed this wasn't going to be an easy ride.

'I'll go to a thousand,' he said. 'And that's me final offer.'

'A thousand – what exactly for?'

Jenny was looking over Cleo's shoulder. 'Perhaps we should discuss this inside?' she suggested.

'Good idea, lass,' said Pascoe.

Cleo reluctantly stood to one side and allowed the two big men to walk past her. Jenny led them down the short passage and into Ant's office. Cleo sat behind the desk with Jenny hovering at her shoulder.

'Right, gentlemen,' said Cleo. 'What's this all about?'

Pascoe looked at his quarry manager who took a plan from his pocket and spread it out on the desk. An area of land had been outlined in red. Pascoe stabbed a fat, nicotine-stained finger at it.

'This land here,' he said. 'I understand yer brother bought it recently.'

Cleo frowned. 'Not to my knowledge he didn't.' She twisted her head to get a better look. 'Whereabouts is it?'

'Far side of Huddersfield. Half an acre o' moorland – no good fer buildin' or nowt.'

'And you say my brother bought it?'

'Cheated me out of it, if the truth be told,' Pascoe said, forcefully. 'I'd arranged ter buy on the shake of me hand and yer brother stepped in an' bought it from under me nose.'

'I wonder why?' mused Cleo.

'Never mind why,' said Pascoe, impatiently. 'It's no use ter you and I'm offerin' a thousand quid fer it, here an' now.' He took a thick wad of notes from his pocket and placed it on the desk. Cleo glanced at it. The money would come in handy, no doubt about that, but it didn't answer two important questions. Why had Ant bought the land, and where were the deeds?

'I can't take it,' she said.

'Can't what?' Pascoe was angry now. He'd never come across a problem that money or threats wouldn't solve. Leaning across the desk he thrust his face into hers, causing her to flinch. 'I think yer'll find yer can, lass,' he said, giving her a menacing wink. 'Because I think yer'll find yer don't want ter get on t' wrong side o' me.'

'I don't want to get on any side of you, Mr Pascoe,' Cleo retorted, evenly. 'But I can hardly sell you land that you say belongs to my brother – on top of which, if you *are* right in what you say I haven't a clue where the deeds would be. I'll be seeing him on Friday, you'll have to wait until after then.'

Pascoe picked up the money and stuffed it back in his pocket. 'I hear yer runnin' this firm on yer own now yer brother's inside,' he snapped. 'So don't give me a load o' crap about not knowin' where stuff is.' He placed a huge hand around Cleo's slender neck and gave her a leering grin that made her shiver with revulsion.

'Nobody cheats Vinny Pascoe. You tell that murderin' brother o' yours I want that land and if I don't get it, he's responsible fer what happens ter yer. In fact, don't bother, I'll get word to him meself.' The two men walked to the door, Pascoe turned round.

'I'll back on Saturday mornin' with a solicitor. Have them deeds ready!'

Ant was already sitting at the table when she walked in to the visitors' room. His grey face almost merged into his prison uniform.

'How are you?' she asked.

'Okay... How are you?' There was concern in his eyes.

Cleo shrugged. 'I'm okay, why shouldn't I be?'

'Because I've heard something, that's all,' Ant said. 'Pascoe's been to see you, hasn't he?'

She tried to appear nonchalant. 'You mean the loudmouthed chap from the quarry?'

'Cleo, he's a nasty piece of work. Don't cross him. Sell him the land.'

'Okay,' she shrugged.

The worry went from Ant's face. He smiled, probably for the first time in months. 'I tried to pull a fast one on him,' he explained.

'I don't understand any of this,' Cleo said. 'Except that he came in the office trying to scare the life out of us.'

'Us?'

'Me and Jenny.'

'He didn't hurt you or anything, did he?'

'He's just a big man with a big mouth,' Cleo said, with more confidence than she felt.

'He's got a bad reputation,' Ant warned her. 'I was takin' a risk myself, but it would've been worth it.'

'Ant, how come you bought the land without

me knowing? I thought I was supposed to be a partner.'

He gave her an embarrassed grin. 'I bought it with funny money,' he said. 'You wouldn't have approved.'

'You mean stolen money?'

'I don't rightly know where it came from,' Ant admitted, in a low voice. 'I did a private job for a bloke who paid me in cash. It's just that he's a bit of a dodgy character. It was him who told me about Pascoe. There's a bit of bad blood between them. The bloke reckoned I could buy the land for a grand and sell it to Pascoe for ten.'

'A thousand? Is that what you paid for it?'

'I could have. In the end I gave fifteen hundred and the old bloke who owned it threw in his cottage. Cleo, let Pascoe have the land for a thousand and you keep the cottage. It's no use to him.'

'We could use a thousand right now,' Cleo said. 'Everyone's breathing down our necks. We're holding on but I don't know for how long. The bank's being awkward.'

'All banks turn awkward just when you need 'em,' Ant said. 'They'll give you an umbrella when the sun's shining and take it away when it starts to rain.'

'Collins paid us fourteen hundred short on the last sale,' Cleo told him. 'He sent a statement to cover it. He's charged us for every phone call, every letter, every time you've ever spoken to him.'

She expected Ant to blow up with anger. He just shook his head, philosophically. 'My fault,' he said. 'I should have seen it coming. He's as bent as a nine-bob note. No wonder the bank's getting awkward if you paid them fourteen hundred short. It's a wonder they didn't call in the overdraft.'

'They don't know about it yet,' Cleo said. 'They just think it's a delayed completion. I paid the cheque in to the Thistle Bank and drew it all out in cash.' She folded her arms and sat back, as if waiting for an explanation.

He gave an embarrassed grin and said 'Ah ... Jen told you about that, did she?'

'Yes, she did. Pity you didn't let me in on your secret bank accounts – me being your partner and all that.'

'Sorry, must have slipped my mind. Look, make sure Pascoe pays you cash as well.'

'Ant, is there anything else I need to know about your private business dealings. Any other bits of land? A bank account with a few thousand pounds in it would come in handy.'

He shook his head. 'I wish there was. But that's about it. Are the lads behaving themselves?'

'The men have been great,' Cleo assured him. 'They couldn't be more helpful. But I honestly don't know how long we can keep it going.'

'I've thought about that,' Ant said. 'And you need a builder to help you.'

'Don't think I haven't tried to get one. But who wants to work for a firm that might go under any minute?'

Ant grinned. 'I know a bloke whose been studying building for years. He's got his Higher National Certificate in Building Construction and all sorts of other stuff. You name it, he knows it. He's forgotten more about building than I know.'

'Sounds like we can't afford him,' Cleo grumbled.

'Oh, you can afford him all right. He's never set foot on a proper building site in his life.'

Cleo shook her head. 'Go on,' she said.

'He's my cellmate, comes out on Friday. They put him with me because they thought I might be able to give him some advice. He's done all his studying inside. Whenever there's been any building going on in here they let him get involved. He's a good bloke, even the screws like him.'

'What's he in jail for?'

'Manslaughter.'

'Great.'

'Don't look like that. I'm in for murder, which is worse.'

'I know, but...'

'But nothing. Rocky's a good bloke.'

'Rocky?'

Ant grinned. 'His real name's Rodney Diggle, but he used to be a boxer.'

'I see.'

'So he calls himself Rocky Diggle. He used to be a good middleweight.'

'Don't tell me, he could have been a contender.'

'He *was* a contender. He'd have been British middleweight champion if he hadn't killed his trainer.'

'Bad move for a boxer,' said Cleo, who didn't like the sound of Rocky Diggle one bit.

'Honest, Cleo. He's as soft as they come. If we give him a chance he'll never let us down, I promise you that.'

Ant using the words 'we' and 'us' gave her hope. It meant he hadn't given up.

'You're the boss,' she smiled.

'Remember, his name's Rocky, he hates being called Rodney.'

'I'll try,' she said. 'I must introduce him to Floribunda Dunderdale, they'll have a lot in common.'

They both laughed and for that moment it felt like old times. There had been many occasions when, as kids, they'd had little to laugh about, but had still managed to find something. She looked into her brother's eyes and saw the old resilience still there.

'By the way,' Cleo said. 'I'm trying to track Mam down so we'll have grounds for appeal against your sentence.'

'What grounds for appeal?'

'She can back up your story of how Womack used to abuse you. Surely she must have known?' Cleo made this sound like a question and looked at her brother for the answer.

He stared at her for a while, remembering. 'Yes,' he said in a low voice, 'she knew all right. I once asked her if she could get him to stop messing about with me. It took some doing, but I thought she'd help me.'

'What did she say?'

'Nothing. It was as though she hadn't heard me. I never asked her again.'

Cleo's eyes misted over with tears and she felt

disgust at her mother surging from her stomach like bile. Ant took her hand, as if to say, don't worry.

'But she definitely knew about it?' she said, at length.

'Yes, she definitely did.'

'In that case,' said Cleo, 'all we have to do is find her and you'll be out in no time.' She didn't mention the dead end she'd come to in her search for their mother.

'I won't hold my breath,' Ant said. 'If I keep my nose clean I'll be out in twelve years, and I've accepted that.'

Cleo saw the old Ant smile flicker across his mouth.

'In a way I feel sort of...' He hunted for the right word. 'Sort of cleansed, now that he's dead. In a way I feel better. I never felt like a proper man with him still walking about somewhere. But he's not there any more.' He sat back in his chair and pondered for a while, examining his feelings. 'I'm not sorry I killed him, Cleo,' he seemed to decide. 'I was shocked at first, but not now. And if this is the price I have to pay, then I'll just have to get on with it. At least I'll not be looking over my shoulder for the rest of my life.'

The thought of her brother spending all those years inside for ridding the world of vermin like Womack depressed Cleo no end. She couldn't allow this to happen. People like Ant shouldn't be caged up; the world needed good people like him.

'Will you tell a solicitor what Womack did to you, just so it's down on record somewhere.

Swear an affidavit or something.'

'I'm not telling Cuthbert Collins.'

'Well, tell another solicitor then. I'll get you one if you like. I just want someone else to know, so we can be properly advised about where to go from here.'

'It's a waste of time, Cleo.'

'Will you do it?'

'I suppose so. I've got nothing better to do.'

'I'll get you out,' she vowed. 'One way or another.'

'Don't worry about me.' He took her hand and squeezed it tight. 'I'll survive. Oh ... the deeds for the land are in your name.'

'My name?'

'I needed to be a bit devious ... as it happens it turned out for the best. The accountant's got them – only he doesn't know what they are. Tell him I said to ask for envelope number three – he'll know what you mean.'

'Envelope number three? It all sounds very cloak and dagger.'

Ant smiled at his sister. 'There's two separate deeds inside. One for the land, one for the cottage. Hey! ... and don't haggle with Pascoe. Take what he offers and smile.'

'If you say so.'

'I do say so,' Ant said. 'I've heard a lot of nasty rumours about him. They reckon people who cross him end up buried in one of his quarries.'

'It didn't stop *you* taking a chance though, did it?' Cleo had a glint in her eye that her brother didn't see.

She left the prison with no intention to take

what Pascoe offered with a smile. The bad people of this world had messed her about enough. Ant hadn't explained why the land was so valuable to Pascoe, but she knew a man who would know.

'I've done some checking,' said Harry Radcliffe, taking off his glasses and rubbing his eyes after poring over Cleo's deed plans. 'And I do know that Pascoe's just bought forty-five acres of land adjacent to your bit, and he's got permission to quarry stone from it, good stone as well by the sound of it; and with this new M62 about to start, he's right on the doorstep. He'll be able to undercut everybody.'

'So, why does he want my bit of land?'

'It's the old story,' Harry explained. 'His land's not much use without yours. He's got to cross yours to get to the road, there's no other way. I can't understand why he didn't buy your bit first.'

'He seems to think Ant cheated him in some way,' Cleo said. 'Ant got some information from a bloke who hates Pascoe and bought the land from under his nose.'

'So, what are you going to do with it?' Harry asked.

'Ant wants me to sell it to him for a thousand.'

'Could be a wise move. It'd help with your business as well.'

'If it was anyone else but Pascoe, I wouldn't hesitate,' Cleo said. 'If he'd been nice about it and told me what a rotten trick Ant had played on him I'd have felt guilty and sold it back to him, but he's such a bully.' She thought, fleetingly of

Dobbs and Horace Womack. 'I hate bullies.'

'Maybe your brother wouldn't have done it to a decent bloke.'

'I *know* he wouldn't,' Cleo said.

'So, what are you going to do?'

'I think I might ask Flo,' she decided. 'She's never short of a good idea or two.'

Pascoe turned up with his solicitor. After delivering his message to Ant via a prison inmate he felt confident Cleo would give him no trouble. Normally he only had to deliver such a message once to get the required result. He was considering reducing his offer to £500 to compensate himself for his troubles.

Flo was sitting by Cleo's side when Jenny showed him into the office. They were both engrossed in the *Daily Mail*, reading about President Kennedy's assassination the previous day. It was an event of such magnitude that it put the threat posed by Pascoe into the shade. Eventually Cleo looked up. She pretended she'd forgotten his name.

'Mr...?'

'Pascoe,' grunted Vinny. 'And this is my solicitor. He's got all the documents we need, so let's get it sorted out, I've got work ter do. And by the way, because yer've caused me all this bother yer'll only get five hundred. Where's the deeds?'

'You mean the deeds to the land?'

'Listen, lass, don't piss me about!'

Pascoe's face was going red and his solicitor was hoping he wouldn't vent his rage on Cleo the same as he had the old man. This time there was a witness.

Flo folded her arms and inclined her head to Cleo. 'I'm not happy with his negotiating technique,' she commented.

'Oh aye, and who are you when yer at home?' rasped Pascoe.

'This is Miss Dunderdale,' said Cleo, evenly. 'She's my adviser.'

'Well the best bit of advice she can give yer is ter get yer bloody finger out an' hand me them deeds!'

'I gather you need the deeds for access to a quarry?' Flo said, opening a file and perusing it intently. Pascoe twisted his head to see what she was looking at. Flo folded it shut before he could see she'd been studying a file full of sundry letters that had nothing to do with the land.

'Don't come too close, Mr Pascoe,' she said. 'I'm allergic to bad smells.'

Pascoe's mouth opened and shut as he tried to think of a retort. He wasn't quick enough.

'How many tons of stone do you expect to get from it?' Flo asked him.

Pascoe exploded. 'Never you bloody mind!'

'We estimate it at around a million tons,' she went on. Harry Radcliffe had briefed her well. 'You should be able to turn it into decent quality crusher run that will sell for at least six shillings a ton – especially to the motorway contractors – and still undercut the competition by a shilling a ton.' She looked up and met Pascoe's venomous gaze. 'But without access from the quarry to the road, you can't move a single shovelful. And threatening Miss Kelly won't help your cause.'

Pascoe slammed a fist down on the table and roared. 'I'll not let a couple of stupid bints stop my wagons moving.'

'I doubt if *we* could stop you, Mr Pascoe,' said Flo. 'But a court injunction could. Disobey a court injunction and you go to jail.'

'Miss Dunderdale's a magistrate,' said Cleo, stretching the truth. 'So she knows about these things.'

The solicitor took Pascoe's elbow and whispered something into his ear that made his client calm down. Pascoe nodded, reluctantly.

'All right,' he said. 'Have it yer own way. I'll give yer a thousand an' no more.' He looked at his watch. 'I've gorra a meetin' in half an hour, so can we get on with it please?'

'A thousand pounds, so you can get access to three hundred thousand pounds worth of stone,' Cleo said. 'Do you think that's fair?' She turned to Flo. 'It doesn't seem fair to me, what do you think?'

'It seems a bit on the low side,' Flo agreed. 'I think maybe he's missed out a nought.'

'You'll have to do a lot better than a thousand, Mr Pascoe,' said Cleo. 'Or your quarry won't be worth tuppence.'

Pascoe's face swelled with rage. He was a man with a very short fuse. Reason had now deserted him, as had his solicitor, who didn't want to witness any bloodshed. The lawyer was halfway out of the building when Pascoe made a grab for Cleo, who flung herself backwards from her chair. Neither she nor Flo expected such violence. A fierce shouting match perhaps; much banging around and threatening behaviour, which both of them could just about cope with – but not a physical assault. She now realised what Ant meant when he made her promise to sell the land to Pascoe. He came at her from over the desk and fell in a heap on top of her. Flo picked up a paperweight and hit him with it, but with little effect.

A pair of hands came from nowhere, grabbed Pascoe by his shoulders and yanked him to his feet. The women heard the quarry owner's screams of rage, then several thuds followed by a louder thud as though someone had hit the floor, heavily. A man's head peered over the desk at where Cleo and Flo were cowering.

'Miss Kelly?' the man enquired, politely.

'Yes.'

The man came round the desk and held out a hand. 'Rocky Diggle ... your brother said you might have some work for me.'

Cleo and Flo got slowly to their feet. Pascoe was lying in a heap by the filing cabinet.

'Ant said you might have a bit of trouble from someone this morning,' said Rocky. 'And I said I'd help out if I could. I hope I did the right thing.'

The events of the past minute had rendered Cleo and Flo speechless with shock. Heroes like this didn't come along every day. All he needed was a white charger.

'Did he tell you about me?' Rocky went on. 'I've got my Higher National Certificate in building construction.'

He spoke with the manner of a man attending

a formal job interview. On the floor was a cheap briefcase which he had obviously dropped prior to dealing with Pascoe. He picked it up and took out a certificate which he handed to Cleo, who stared at it in amazement.

'I've also got my City and Guilds in Municipal Works.'

He took out another certificate which Cleo took from him.

Flo's dropped jaw remained in place throughout. Pascoe moaned, blood poured from his nose and expletives from his mouth. Rocky urged him into silence with his boot as he waited for Cleo's appraisal of his job presentation. Cleo looked from the certificates to Rocky, and down at Pascoe. Not quite knowing how to react to such a situation.

'Well, I er ... this all seems to be very er, satisfactory,' she said.

'I haven't had much experience on the practical side but I'm a quick learner.'

'My brother spoke very highly of you.'

Rocky smiled. 'Did he? That's good of him. He's a good bloke is your brother.'

'You bastard!' said Pascoe, struggling to his knees.

'Do you want him to leave?' asked Rocky, grabbing the cursing quarry owner by his coat collar.

Cleo found her voice at last. 'Er, yes ... in fact no, not just yet. I'd like a word with him.'

Rocky pulled Pascoe to his feet and said to him, firmly but politely, 'Now, the lady wants to talk to you ... so behave yourself and listen properly, or

I'll have to give you another slap.'

Pascoe turned an amazed face to Rocky who was smaller than him, but so much stronger. 'Who the hell are you?' he said. One of his teeth dropped out of his bloodied mouth as he spoke.

'I work for Miss Kelly,' Rocky told him. 'I'm her new building manager.' He grinned, hopefully, at Cleo. 'Isn't that right, Miss Kelly?'

'Er ... well, yes, I suppose so.'

Flo was still too dumbfounded to add to the conversation, as was Jenny, to whom Rocky had just introduced himself when the commotion started. Cleo gathered her wits sufficiently to address herself to Pascoe.

'I *won't* sell you the land, Mr Pascoe but I will sell you legal access over it, so you can work your quarry. My price is ten thousand pounds and you pay all the legal costs. Ask your solicitor to call back and we'll sort out the details. I'd prefer not to have to deal with you.'

Pascoe stiffened, as though he was about to launch another attack, but Rocky's grip tightened on his collar.

'Would you like him to leave now, Miss Kelly?' Rocky asked.

His pleasant face belied his capabilities. Flo thought he was the most attractive man she'd ever seen, Cleo still reserved this accolade for Flo's nephew, whose looks were wasted on men. But she certainly thought Rocky was easy on the eye. So did Jenny.

'Yes, please,' Cleo said. Then to Pascoe she added, 'Please don't try and bully us again, Mr Pascoe, or I'll call the police.'

As Rocky escorted Pascoe off the premises, Flo and Jenny turned to Cleo.

'Have I just dreamt this?' said Jenny.

'Who the hell is that?' said Flo.

'Ant recommended him,' Cleo explained. 'He came out of jail yesterday.'

'What was he inside for?' enquired Flo.

'Oh, nothing much,' said Cleo, who didn't want to spoil the moment. 'He used to be a boxer,' she handed Rocky's certificates to Flo. 'And he seems very well qualified for the job, but he's never been on a building site ... so I'm not entirely sure he can actually do the job.'

'I shouldn't let that put you off him,' said Flo, quickly.

'Minor detail,' agreed Jenny. 'I think he's just what we need.'

Cuthbert Collins was on the phone when Cleo walked into his office, unannounced. She hated confrontations such as this. Ant may well have thrived on them, but Cleo preferred a quieter existence.

She remembered Flo's advice. 'Let him know you've got money behind you. That's the only thing these people understand. To a man I like Collins, money is power.'

Taking a deep breath, Cleo plonked herself down in the chair opposite the solicitor and fixed him with an unfriendly glare until he terminated his conversation prematurely by saying. 'Can I ring you back? Something's just cropped up?'

It had been an eventful week since Cleo first met Rocky. His reputation had preceded him on to the site and despite his lack of experience the men took no liberties with him. A visit to Ant had brought certain information about Collins to her attention. Information she now wanted to draw to *his* attention. Behind Cleo stood Collins's secretary.

'She just barged straight in, Mr Collins, I couldn't stop her.'

'That's all right, Mrs Brooke,' said Collins, brusquely. 'I'll deal with Miss Kelly.'

The solicitor waited until the door had shut before addressing Cleo. He made a show of looking at his watch and, very slowly, lit a cigar. 'I can spare you just two minutes, Miss Kelly, so say what you have to say.' Stale cigar breath accompanied every word.

'You're a crook,' said Cleo, drawing strength from the anger she felt at the gall of this man.

Collins frowned and drummed his fingers on the desk, nervously. 'You feel you've been badly done to, I can understand that. But I'm afraid that's business. It's a rough world, it's–'

'Dog eat dog?' suggested Cleo.

Collins nodded. 'Exactly,' he said. 'Dog eat dog.' He picked up a cup of steaming coffee and took a sip. 'We can't let sentiment get in the way. The fact is ... that your brother's company can't possibly carry on with him in jail and I obviously have to make up my losses before the liquidator moves in.'

'What losses, Mr Collins?'

He waved his hand dismissively and said, 'It's business, you wouldn't understand.'

'Try me.'

She placed her elbows on his desk and leaned towards him with her chin resting in her cupped hands. 'I studied business administration,' she said. 'Maybe I'll surprise you.'

Collins was embarrassed and looked away from her gaze. 'I invested a lot of time and effort into your brother's business activities. Things that can't be seen on paper.'

'Is that why you had to invent all the items on your invoice, Mr Collins, so no one would know the truth?'

'Like I said, Miss Kelly. It's just business. I'm sure your brother understands.'

'I must admit, my brother didn't seem *surprised* at what you did,' Cleo told him, 'but I wouldn't go so far as to say he understands. He says you're as bent as a nine-bob note.'

'I think this discussion is over, Miss Kelly. If you're here for reimbursement I'm afraid you're in for a disappointment. Good day to you.'

He got up and walked to the door, which he opened and waited for her to leave. She remained where she was and spoke without turning round.

'Tell me about the building society scam, Mr Collins,' she said, lighting up a cigarette. 'Sorry, do you mind if I smoke? Always vowed I never would, but it's a bad habit I picked up with all this worry. I believe it was the Gledhow Building Society, wasn't it?'

Collins closed the door, cleared his throat and muttered, 'I don't know what you're talking about.'

It was the reply Cleo had predicted, word for word. This made her smile.

'Then I'll help jog your memory,' she said. 'According to my brother you have a crony who works for the repossessions department of the Gledhow Building Society. I believe you've been buying repossessed houses at knockdown prices.'

'Using inside information isn't against the law,' Collins protested. He went back to his chair, picked up his coffee and sipped it with false nonchalance.

'Hmm,' mused Cleo, blowing a cloud of smoke at him. 'I think it might be if you're getting the houses at considerably less than market value. I wonder what the Law Society would say about it? Or the directors of the Gledhow Building Society for that matter?'

'Did your brother tell you he was involved in a couple of these house purchases?' Collins tried to put a sneer into his voice. 'If you get me into trouble you get him into trouble as well.'

Cleo's face broke into a broad beam. 'Are we talking about my brother who's serving a life sentence for murder? How the hell can he get into any more trouble?'

She allowed the smile to subside then said, flatly, 'I want every penny you owe us plus twenty per cent for all the trouble you've put me through, Mr Collins. Shall we say a round seventeen hundred pounds? Oh, and by the way, you'll be pleased to know that Kelly Construction isn't going under – check with our bank if you don't believe me. I deposited ten thousand pounds into the Kelly Construction account yesterday, so we're reasonably solvent. Sales are going well, we've just employed an excellent construction manager... Oh, and we've just got rid of a bent solicitor.'

Having convinced him that she was speaking from a position of financial power, Cleo got to her feet and extinguished her cigarette in his coffee.

'I'll give the name of our *new* solicitor to your secretary,' she said. 'Could you have all our files sent across with your bank draft?' She looked at her watch with the same flourish that he'd looked at his. 'No rush. Any time within the next couple of hours will do, otherwise I'll ring up the Law Society and the Gledhow Building Society. If they put you in the same prison as my brother you'll be able to pay him the money yourself.'

'It's only a question of time before you go under,' Collins blustered. 'You're a girl in a man's world.'

'Let me worry about that,' said Cleo, looking at her watch. 'If I don't hear from you by two o'clock I'll assume you're calling my bluff. Only it's not a bluff, believe me, Mr Collins.'

The solicitor had heard enough of Cleo's history to know she wasn't bluffing. 'I'll need longer than that to arrange a bank draft and get all your files over to you,' he grumbled.

'I'll make it four o'clock, then.'

He nodded, sullenly, and Cleo got to her feet to leave. She hated what she was doing. Against her better judgement she'd been drawn into the world of business, and as Collins said, it was dog eat dog. She had won a couple of battles, but could she survive the war?

Chapter Eighteen

Ant had been right about Rocky. In order to learn the ropes and get a feel for the job he spent the first three months as a labourer-cum-site manager. It was a combination of jobs only a man with his physical capabilities could handle without being taken advantage of by the men. Rocky was amiable but not weak.

One young joiner, new on the site, told everyone in the men's cabin, in graphic detail, exactly what he'd like to do to Cleo. Rocky took him outside and persuaded him to speak with respect about his boss. The joiner came back in, white faced with shock, and never spoke another word about Cleo; although, like most of the men, he still fantasised about her. Rocky had no control over that.

'I've had word that Collins isn't too pleased with you,' Ant said to his sister.

'It's his own fault for telling lies about you,' retorted Cleo.

It was spring 1964 and Ant had learned to accept his new existence. He was simply paying for ridding himself of Womack. Nothing comes free in this world, Ant knew that better than most. Despite his violent death Womack didn't even exist as a ghost, not even a dark shadow of him ever flickered across Ant's conscience. In some ways his jail sentence was a fair price to pay for this – and maybe he needed to pay that price, or Womack's ghost might appear. It was this sort of thinking that kept him sane and focused – cheerful even. Cleo was still determined to free him sooner rather than later. She took her optimism with her on every visit and shed it on the way home. Nelly, upon whom Cleo pinned all her hopes, seemed to have vanished off the face of the earth. Cleo knew she might be dead but didn't allow the possibility to cloud her determination. Surely if her mother was dead someone would know and would have got word to her. Or would they?

'He shouldn't have told me you were involved with his building society scam,' she said.

'Screwing the system's one thing,' Ant replied. 'But screwing people who can't afford to pay their mortgage isn't my style. You should have known that.'

'I do know that.'

'It was a bit rough reporting him to the Law Society,' Ant commented. 'And no building society will touch him with a bargepole now.'

'Oh dear! My heart bleeds for him. Anyway, how come you know all this?' Cleo asked. 'I never told you I'd reported him.'

Ant grinned. 'I'm in with the right crew,' he told her, touching his nose with his finger. 'We get to know stuff in here before the papers do. Some of the villains in here are running their businesses more successfully than they were on the outside. Nothing else to do, you see.'

'I wish you could run our business from in here.'

'Why? Is Rocky not doing so well?'

'Rocky's okay,' she said, 'but he's not you. I've no doubt he'll see the site through to the bitter end without too many cock-ups, but he's not a businessman and that's what we need.'

'I assumed you'd handle that side of it.'

'You assume a bit too much at times, Ant Kelly,' she said. 'When this site's finished I haven't a clue what to do next. Neither does Rocky.'

'It's obvious,' he said. 'You invest the profits in more land and carry on building.' Ant made it sound so simple. 'In fact you should be looking round now.'

'Ant, I don't know what to look for. I might end up buying a pig in a poke.'

'You just look for land in a popular area.' He smiled at her uncertainty. 'Look Cleo,' he explained. 'There's no great mystery to it. When land comes up for sale, take a look at it, get a feel for it, take photos, check round the area for schools and shops, then ask yourself if it's a place where you'd like to live. If you're still interested, bring me all you've got on it and we'll get a land surveyor and Harry to give it the once-over. I'll do the sums in here. If it all adds up, you can take it to the bank as if you've done all the work. Although with the money we're making on Garforth we might not need the bank too much.'

'You make it sound easy.'

'It *is* easy. The trick is not to let everyone else know that, or they'd *all* want to be builders.'

'Okay,' she said. 'Oh, by the way, I think I've got another lead on Nelly.'

'Good.'

He didn't believe her so he didn't press for details. She was glad of this because she was lying. One day, though – one day she wouldn't be lying. One day she'd get him out.

'Watch out for Collins,' Ant warned. 'He can be a spiteful prat when he wants – and he's got good reason to hate you. So has Pascoe for that matter. Screwing him for ten grand was great. I just hope he didn't take it too badly.'

'Did you hear anything?' Cleo asked; she did have the occasional sleepless night thinking about Pascoe.

'Not a peep. He'll be making money hand over fist from that quarry, maybe he's forgotten about you – written you off as a business expense.'

'I hope so.'

'Just watch your back, Cleo.'

'I will, don't worry about me. Just keep your spirits up till I get you out.'

'How's Jen?'

He'd taken to asking about her a lot recently – and Jenny had been paying him regular visits.

'Jenny's great,' she said. 'In fact she's as keen to get you out as I am. More maybe.' Cleo searched his face to gauge his reaction to her last remark. It seemed to please him. She'd report this back to Jenny. 'Maybe when you get out you'll treat her properly,' she commented.

'How do you mean? I always treated Jen properly.'

'I mean treat her like a woman. You do know she's potty about you?'

'Is she?'

The old Ant grin lit up his face. It was good to see.

'You mean you didn't know?' Cleo said. 'God! You are dense at times, especially about girls.' Her eyes searched his face for some reaction, but found nothing. 'You know, now that Horace is out of the picture, I was hoping that...' She left a long silence, hoping he might fill it.

'What?' he said, eventually.

She breathed a sigh of exasperation, then blurted out her question. 'Now that Womack's gone, do you feel differently about girls?'

'How do you mean?'

'God! You are an annoying sod at times. I think you know what I mean.'

Ant grinned at her annoyance, then gave her question some thought. He shrugged. 'Locked up in here I've no real way of knowing,' he said, 'but I know I don't feel ashamed any more.'

'Is that what frightened you off girls?'

He lowered his voice and leaned towards her. 'Cleo, I was never frightened of them, I just felt uncomfortable around them. It was the ... the sex thing I suppose. I always associated sex with something dirty – something to be ashamed of. I knew it wasn't, but ... I suppose I had a phobia about it.'

'*Had* a phobia – does that mean you don't any more?' she pressed, mentally filing the report she would be making to Jenny.

'I don't think so. Hey, and all this is confidential. I don't want you talking about it to Flo or anybody ... especially not to Jenny.'

'I won't. Why especially not to Jenny?'

'How are you and Rocky getting on?' he asked, by way of deflecting her question.

It was the first time anyone had linked her with Rocky – and it didn't trouble her. 'Me and Rocky get on fine, why?' She was wondering if Rocky had said something to him about her.

'Just wondered,' Ant said. 'He's a good bloke is Rocky.'

'I know.' She pondered for a while before asking, 'Ant ... do you know exactly what happened ... you know, to put him inside?'

Ant shook his head. 'It's not a question you ask in here. If someone wants to tell you, that's okay. Rocky never did.'

'Oh.'

'There's nothing to stop *you* asking, though,' Ant said. 'It's my guess the other bloke got what was coming to him, just like Womack.'

'I hope so.'

She was beginning to have disturbingly pleasant thoughts about Rocky, but he treated her like his boss. A little more friendship, affection even, and a little less respect would be nice. Maybe under the circumstances it was up to her to make the first move.

'I've a feeling there was a woman involved,' Ant remembered, after some thought on the subject.

'Oh?'

'In fact,' he went on. 'I think he was engaged once. He went on about her one night when I caught him at a weak moment. He was worried she wouldn't want to know him when he got out. I know she didn't visit him much. If at all.'

The fact that Cleo didn't want to hear any of

this made her realise that she had feelings for Rocky that extended beyond a boss/employee relationship. How serious these feelings were, she couldn't tell. Definitely more serious than her feelings for Jeff; even more serious than Seamus – but that ne'er do well was nothing to go on. She smiled to herself as she pictured him, naked, in the rose bush. But he *had* been fun.

She watched him from behind the wheel of the Cortina that she'd just driven on to the site. Apart from anything else, Rocky was too handsome for his own good. Were he the type, he could have had women queueing up for him, but she'd never seen him with a girlfriend, or heard him talk about women. Ant's revelation about him killing a man over a woman perhaps explained this, but Cleo needed to know more. She hooted the horn. Several heads turned but her eyes were on Rocky. He grinned and came walking over. Cleo wound down the window.

'I just wondered if you fancied a drink after work,' she said. 'I thought we could talk over a few things.'

'Suits me, boss.'

'Pick you up at six then?'

'I'll be in me muck.'

'Don't worry,' she smiled. 'We're not going anywhere posh.'

The tap room of the Bird in the Hand was a working man's room, always full of construction workers on a Thursday evening, the building trade's traditional payday. But today was

Wednesday and the room was as empty as the men's pockets.

Cleo and Rocky had chatted about work for a while. Things were going well. Rocky was learning fast, although he'd never have Ant's acumen. The sum total of their abilities didn't add up to one Ant Kelly, but it was pretty near; which, with Ant's coaching from in jail, was good enough to keep the company thriving. Rocky was on his third pint and feeling relaxed. Flo, who knew exactly what Cleo was up to, kept an inquisitive eye on them from behind the bar. She had advised Cleo on how to broach the subject.

'Don't go barging in like a bull at a gate – that'll frighten him off. Approach the subject from the side door.'

Cleo had worked out her tactics. 'Did Ant ever tell you why he killed our stepfather?' she asked him.

'He'll have had his reasons,' Rocky said. 'But he didn't tell me.'

'He bottled his reasons up,' Cleo said. 'It poisoned a part of him. If he'd just told someone, it might not have happened. Bottling secrets up doesn't do anyone any good in the long run. Even if you just tell one person.'

Rocky smiled at her. 'Like you, you mean?'

His smile melted her like no one else's had ever done, not even John Dunderdale's. It was the first time she'd had the exclusive benefit of it. She swallowed and managed to say, 'If you like. I think we're good enough friends for you to confide in me if you feel you want to get something off your chest.'

Rocky nodded, took a deep drink, and laid his glass slowly down on the table. 'I'm an orphan,' he said, unexpectedly.

'Oh? I didn't know. Sorry to hear that.'

'Don't be,' he said. 'I didn't have a bad childhood. I was brought up in a Barnardo's Home. It was okay, better than some kids had to put up with.'

He looked at her and she wondered how much Ant had told him about their childhood, such as it was.

'My dad was killed in the war and my mam died of TB about a year later,' he went on. 'I always thought losing him made her ... more vulnerable to stuff. She seemed to lose the will to live.'

'I can tell you come from parents who loved each other,' Cleo told him. 'It shows.'

This seemed to please him. 'Does it? That's a nice thing to say.'

'It's true,' she said. 'When I was at school I could always tell whose mam and dad loved each other. It comes out in the kids. Mostly, anyway.'

'How did *you* get to be so nice, then?' he challenged. 'Ant told me about your parents.'

'Maybe we're not as nice as you think,' she said.

'I think your stepfather might agree with that ... sorry!' Rocky buried his head in his hands for a second. 'I didn't mean that.'

'No, it's all right ... and you're right. Horace *would* agree with it. If he'd loved our mam he'd still be alive.'

Rocky looked at her and gave her another of those smiles, sadder this time. His eyes were a deep, liquid brown and his teeth white against his tanned skin. She gave him a smile of her own, which she hoped might match his. He spoke slowly in a low voice that only just carried across the table to her. She leaned towards him.

'Killing someone's the worst thing,' he said. 'The thought of having ended someone's life makes me feel sick to the pit of my stomach. God, he was such a bastard! Why did he make me do that to him?' He looked at Cleo, his eyes searing into hers. 'I didn't mean to kill him, you know.'

Cleo laid her hand on his. 'I know,' she said.

'How do you know?'

'I just do.'

'Thanks.'

Rocky drained his drink and made to get to his feet and go to the bar. He seemed to have ended his story before it had begun. She took him by his sleeve.

'Sit down,' she commanded.

He did as he was told.

'Now tell me about it,' she said. 'I'm not going to judge you. I'm just going to listen. You haven't told anyone about what happened, have you?'

'I told the court.'

'You pleaded guilty, just like Ant. If the court knew the truth about him they wouldn't have locked him up.'

Rocky was in tears now. It was a side of him she'd never seen. To everyone he was the ultimate hard man; frightened of nothing or no one, a nice bloke, but as hard as nails. He got to his feet and went to the Gents, leaving Cleo feeling guilty. Flo looked across at her, with the question, 'What happened?' on her face. Cleo shrugged and shook her head.

When he came back, Rocky had obviously washed his face – washed away both the site dirt and his tears. He stopped at the bar and ordered two more drinks.

'Orange juice for me,' Cleo called out, relieved she hadn't scared him off. 'I'm driving.'

He placed her drink in front of her and sat down with a resigned look on his face. Resigned to unburdening himself to Cleo, so she hoped. She caught Flo looking, expectantly, at her from behind him.

'This is between you and me,' he said, taking her hand. She felt his strength flow into her.

'Obviously,' she assured him. Flo would never hear what he had to tell her. No matter how hard she pressed.

'My girlfriend was a prostitute.'

He didn't look at Cleo when he said it. No one could hear but her and she wondered if she'd heard right, but she didn't want him to have to repeat it.

'Well, she gave it up when she met me,' he added.

Cleo felt like saying she wasn't surprised but it might have sounded flippant, so she didn't.

'She wasn't really like that, you see,' he said. 'She had no choice.'

Cleo had often heard about prostitutes who had no choice and she had never believed a word of it. Everyone had a choice.

'It's often the case,' she commented, not

wanting to hurt him.

'I was a boxer ... of course, you know that.'

'I heard you were good.'

'Yes,' he said without conceit, 'I was.' He took a drink of his beer. 'I had a trainer called Louis Gardner. One of the best in the country. He treated me like his own son. He was good to me.'

Cleo knew Louis Gardner was the man Rocky had killed. She made no comment.

'Jasmine used to wait for me in the dressing room. It wasn't her real name – her real name was Hilda – but she preferred to be called Jasmine.'

Cleo could well understand why – especially in Jasmine's line of work – but once again she kept her observations to herself.

'Louis never reckoned much to her. He reckoned she was out for what she could get. But I told him she loved me – she did as well. God, Cleo! you should have seen her. She was beautiful.'

Cleo had very mixed feelings about Jasmine/Hilda, but she felt she had no right to express an opinion. Maybe this reformed prostitute was a good woman underneath, she had to trust Rocky's judgement; but men can be so stupid where women are concerned – Seamus was living proof of that. Rocky's eyes glazed over with sadness.

'Louis said he could prove she was a bad woman. I told him to try if he wanted, but he'd only be wasting his time.' Rocky took another drink as if he needed it to get through his story. 'It was a title eliminator,' he said.

Cleo didn't know what it meant, but she was sure it was some of sort of boxing match.

'I won in the sixth – knocked him out. When I got back to my corner Louis wasn't there, which was unusual. Anyway, it took about five minutes to get all the formalities over and done with ... have you got a cigarette?'

'Of course.'

She got out a packet of Players and gave him one, lighting it for him and taking one herself.

'He had her on the floor.'

Rocky's eyes had misted over again as he spoke and Cleo hoped he wouldn't be vanishing to the Gents at such an important part of the story. His voice went up half an octave, but he carried on.

'He was ... doing it to her. As soon as she saw me, she started screaming at him to get off her. He said something about, "Not till I get me ten quid's worth." She screamed blue murder that he was raping her. Then Louis looked up and grinned at me – and he said, "Told yer she was still a slag." Jasmine was crying and asking me for help. What could I do, Cleo?'

'I don't know, love. What *did* you do,' she asked, gently.

'I pulled him off her and hit him. I hit him and kept on hitting him. She was yelling at me to make him pay for what he'd done to her and I kept on hitting him, even after he went down. Then someone dragged me off him ... but it was too late.' Rocky's face was wet with tears. He didn't speak for a while, then he said, 'I know what you're thinking.'

'What am I thinking?'

'You're thinking Louis was right. You're thinking Louis wasn't raping her. You're thinking she was letting him do it because he'd paid her.'

This was exactly what Cleo was thinking.

'But you didn't know her,' he said. 'If you'd known her you wouldn't be thinking that.'

'I'm not thinking anything, Rocky. Except I can understand why you killed him. What he did was inexcusable. Doing that to her when he knew you loved her. How on earth did he expect you to react?'

Rocky shook his head. 'I never saw her again, you know. She left before the police came to take me away and no one's ever seen her since. It bothers me does that. Not knowing where she is, what happened to her.'

'She didn't come to the trial?'

'No.'

'Pity,' Cleo said. 'If she'd told them she was being raped you might have got off. In fact you probably *would* have got off.' She resisted the temptation to add, 'But only if it really *was* rape.'

'You still love her, don't you?'

'I do,' he said. 'Even after all this time.'

'Even though she didn't thank you for saving her?' Cleo said. 'And even though she didn't come to court to speak up for you?'

'That's one of the things that bothers me,' he said. 'Her not coming to speak up for me. It wasn't like her. Something, or someone must have stopped her from coming.'

'Do you think she loved you?' she asked him.

He nodded. 'If you knew her, you wouldn't need to ask.'

She took his hand. 'She'd have been stupid not to.'

'I need to find her again,' he said. 'But I don't know where to start looking.'

'It's been a long time,' Cleo pointed out. 'She might well have found someone else.'

'I know, I've thought of that,' he admitted. 'But ... all I can say is I need to know the truth about her. To get her out of my system. If you knew her, you'd understand.'

Cleo doubted this very much, but said, 'I'll help you if you like.'

'Would you?'

'Of course.'

She had never felt less enthusiastic about anything, but she tried to sound sincere. Maybe, like Louis Gardner, she was trying to prove something to him.

Chapter Nineteen

Cleo opened the sixth of ten envelopes that contained details of building land. The response from the advert she'd taken out in the *Yorkshire Post* surprised her. She didn't know there was so much land available.

'I should have been a bit more specific,' she said to Jenny, who had just brought in coffee and biscuits. 'This one's for twenty-three acres near Hull and it's not even building land. The last one I opened was someone wanting to sell off their side garden. There'll be someone trying to sell us a window box next.'

Jenny picked up the advert that had produced these replies and read it out loud. 'House builder requires land suitable for housing development. Anything considered.'

'Ant's words, not mine,' Cleo grumbled. Then she imitated her brother. 'Cast your net as wide as you can. You never know what's out there.' She had her brother's voice off to a tee.

'If you cast your net wide enough you might catch yourself a Rocky Diggle,' Jenny said, without looking up.

'What?'

'Oh, nothing. Just thinking out loud.'

'He's got a fiancée,' said Cleo, sharply.

'You mean the ever-loving Jasmine?'

'He says he still loves her, Jen. I have to respect

that.' Contrary to her promise to Rocky, Cleo had confided in Jenny. She knew Rocky's secret wouldn't go any further and she needed a friend and confidante to help her make sense of it all. 'I just don't understand him,' she said. 'He thinks there's some great mystery as to why she did a bunk the minute things got rough. God! She couldn't have got her message over much clearer if she'd branded it on his backside with a red-hot poker.'

'I know,' sympathised Jenny. 'And he seems quite bright otherwise. Some of the men reckon he's the best boss they've ever had ... excluding Ant of course.' She added the last bit for Cleo's benefit.

'The two of them would make a good team,' said Cleo. 'If only...' Her voice tailed off.

Getting Ant out of prison was looking more and more unlikely. The odds were that their mother was dead, as Horace had suggested to Ant. Without Nelly's mitigating testimony Ant's chances of getting freed on appeal were nil.

'What are you going to do about helping him find the lovely Jasmine?' Jenny asked.

Cleo gave a wry smile. 'I wasn't going to tell you,' she said, 'and this is very strictly between you and me – but we went on tour of the red-light areas last night.'

'You what?' exclaimed Jenny. 'I don't believe this. You mean he took you out hob-nobbing with prostitutes to see if he could track down his old girlfriend. He sure knows how to show a girl a good time.'

'I wish I hadn't told you now,' Cleo grumbled.

'Rocky reckons she might have been driven back on the streets out of sheer desperation.'

'Oh dear, how sad – never mind.'

'It was awful for me,' said Cleo, ignoring Jenny's sarcasm. 'But it gave me the opportunity to ask some of the girls about my mother. I think there's a fair chance she's on the game as well – if she's still alive.'

'And...?' Jenny had a vested interest in Cleo finding Nelly. She was keen to get Ant out of jail as well.

'No one had heard of either of them,' Cleo said.

'Oh.'

'I even offered money for information. That's a bit of a shock to the system I can tell you. Offering money to a prostitute.'

'Did any of them take it?'

Cleo looked at Jenny and shook her head. 'What do you think? We're talking about women who are so desperate they'll do anything for money. All of them took it – and I know full well that none of them have any intention of helping.'

'So, why did you give them money?'

The phone rang before Cleo could reply. Jenny answered. 'Hello, Kelly Construction.'

'Is it you what's looking for land?' said the caller.

'Yes it is.'

'Well, I've got some.'

'Hold on a moment. I'll pass you over to Miss Kelly.' Jenny held her hand over the mouthpiece, raised her eyebrows at Cleo, and whispered, 'Someone with land for sale. Sounds like it could be the window box you've been waiting for.'

Cleo hurriedly gulped down the Garibaldi she was eating, wiped a crumb from her mouth and took the phone.

'Hello, who's speaking please?'

'Me name's Johnstone, Vic Johnstone.' The voice was gruff and indistinctive.

'I understand you have a win ... er, some land for sale, Mr Johnstone.'

Jenny's face trembled with silent laughter. Cleo glared at her then looked away, not wanting to be infected.

'That's right. I reckon yer could get fifty houses on it.'

'Does it have planning permission?'

'Aye, lass. Outline planning permission fer residential development. I saw yer advert in t' paper an' I thought yer might be interested.'

'Well, we're interested in anything. Whereabouts is it?'

'Wheatley.'

'Whereabouts is that, Mr Johnstone?'

'Leeds side o' York. About a mile off t' A64. There's about five acres wi' a road running right past it. I can let yer have it at a right price provided yer don't mess me about, like. I need t' money right quick.'

Cleo scribbled on a notepad as she spoke. 'I see. I can come out today if you like.'

'That'd be champion, lass.' There was a silence, then the caller added, 'Will yer be bringin' a surveyor or someone like that out wi' yer?'

'Not at this stage, Mr Johnstone. I'll probably come on my own. I might take a few photographs but I won't need a surveyor until I decide to buy.'

'How soon will I get me money?'

Cleo pulled a face at Jenny and held her hand over the mouthpiece. 'He wants to know when he can have his money,' she whispered.

'Humour him, you never know,' suggested Jenny.

Cleo nodded and took her hand away from the mouthpiece. 'I think I'd better take a look at it first, Mr Johnstone,' she said. 'If I'm interested I can push things along very quickly.'

'Right, lass. Yer'll want ter buy it all right. I can tell yer that fer nowt.'

'Could you give me the exact location, Mr Johnstone?'

'Aye, lass. Go through Tadcaster on t' A64 as though yer heading fer York. Yer'll see a sign fer Wheatley on yer left. About a mile or so down there there's a pub what's fer sale. It's empty but yer can get into t' car park. I'll meet yer there and tek yer ter t' land. Can yer be there at two o'clock?'

'I think so ... yes, two o'clock it is. I'll look forward to meeting you, Mr Johnstone.'

'Right, lass.'

Cleo put down the phone. 'It a big window box he's got,' she said. 'He reckons we could get fifty houses on it. Sounds genuine enough. On the other hand he could be a nut case.'

'I'll come with you if you like,' Jenny offered. 'I thought he sounded a bit odd.'

'No,' Cleo decided, after giving Jenny's offer some thought. 'I need you to hold the fort. After what I did last night this will be a breath of fresh air.'

Mr Johnstone's 'mile or so' turned out to be a three-mile drive down a poorly maintained country road that was too narrow for two cars to pass. An approaching tractor, the driver of which seemed to assume he had the right of way, almost forced her into a ditch at one point in her journey. Then she came to a ford that was blocked by an elderly looking cow taking a drink. Cleo hooted her horn, causing the animal to turn its head slowly and stare at her then, upon deciding she was of no interest or use, it continued with its drinking. Cleo knew little about farm animals but it was obvious this specimen had seen better days. It was an angular creature that didn't seem to have the wherewithal to dispense much milk or to provide a decent Sunday joint. Cleo got out of the car, approached the cow with some caution and slapped it on its bony hindquarters, before retreating quickly out of harm's way. Then she looked around to see if its owner was anywhere about. No one.

'Shoo!' she shouted, but the cow didn't budge. Cleo looked at her watch. She was due to meet Mr Johnstone in a few minutes and she hated being late for anything. Taking a pace forward she slapped its backside again. 'Clear off you stupid cow!'

'She'll go when she's good an' ready,' called out a voice. Cleo spun round and saw a young girl of no more than twelve standing where there had been no one just a few seconds before. Her grimy face, partly hidden beneath a flat cap, contrasted sharply with her even white teeth.

She wore flapping jeans, turned up several times and what would have been, had it any buttons, a khaki cardigan, made out of what looked like homespun material. Just for a second, Cleo saw herself ten years ago.

'No point slappin' 'er on 'er arse, missis.'

'Oh,' said Cleo. 'And who are you?'

'Me name's Elizabeth Rose Binks but everyone calls me Queenie 'cos I were born on the day Queen Elizabeth became queen – 6 February 1952. It's a crap name int it?'

'I've heard worse. Have you any idea how to move this er...' Cleo wasn't sure if it was a cow or a bull. 'This animal?'

'Mebbe,' said the girl. 'Is there a reward?'

'A reward? Cleo looked at her watch again, 'Oh ... I'll give you sixpence.'

Queenie held out her hand. 'Me dad says allus ter get payment in advance.'

'Does he now?' said a suspicious Cleo, handing the girl a coin.

Queenie splashed through the ford, past the cow. 'C'mon Agnes, yer big dozy bugger.' The animal followed her and stood patiently at the side of the road with its eyes on the girl, as though awaiting further instructions. Cleo got in her car and drove through the shallow water, stopping beside the girl and her well-trained bovine money spinner.

'I don't expect to have to pay on the way back,' she said.

'Depends on Agnes,' replied Queenie. 'She's a mind of her own.'

'I'll bet she has.'

Cleo was having serious misgivings about buying a piece of building land around here and had already decided to keep her appointment with Mr Johnstone only out of politeness. It might not do any harm to take a look at the land, having come thus far, but if she had no enthusiasm for this part of the world, neither would any prospective house buyers.

The faded sign on the Cock and Bottle creaked in the stiff breeze and Cleo wasn't surprised the pub was closed, with it being situated at the back of beyond. It had been a farmer's pub with its own brewery around the back, but modern transport and modem brewing methods had rendered it uneconomical. Most farmworkers now drank in the two John Smith's pubs in Wheatley. The Cock and Bottle was an empty shell, and attached to one of its crumbling walls was an estate agent's sign announcing that it was ripe for conversion into a family house.

Behind the pub was a small, gravel car park; the gravel only evident because of the faint crunching sound it made beneath her wheels – mostly it was hidden by a covering of weeds. Drawing the car to a halt she looked around for Mr Johnstone. Cleo had a mental image of him, formed from his voice over the phone. A rustic man in late middle age with grizzled features; probably a heavy smoker.

She arched her back and stretched away the discomfort caused by the bumpy road she'd just travelled, then decided to get out and stretch her legs. As she did so, a figure came out of the pub doorway and hurried around the back of the car. Cleo heard the last of the approaching footsteps and was about to turn round to greet Mr Johnstone when her world went black.

Jenny looked at her watch, 5.45 – fifteen minutes after her knocking-off time, but she suspected Cleo might call into the office on her way home. A vehicle pulled up outside. Jenny got up from her chair and took her coat from the hook behind the door. Rocky walked in, bringing a look of surprise to her face.

'What?' he asked.

Jenny smiled and secretly wished she was the lost girlfriend he was looking for. 'I thought you were Cleo,' she said.

'Why, where is she? I was hoping...' He decided against telling Jenny he was hoping Cleo would join him on a search of the red-light areas again.

'She went to see a man about some land,' Jenny told him. 'I thought she might call in on her way home. I should give her a ring later if you want her.'

'Maybe I'll do that,' Rocky said.

Flo was more annoyed than worried when Cleo didn't turn up for tea. Her young friend had a life of her own and she wasn't tied to Flo's dining table, still, it would have been polite for Cleo to have rung. Two pork chops were going to waste. Flo had done six but she could only eat four. She went to bed at midnight, with still no word from Cleo.

'I hope he's worth it, Cleo love.' Flo spoke to her reflection in the dressing-table mirror. 'And I hope his name's Rocky.'

Chapter Twenty

It took Cleo several minutes to orientate herself. There was an inky blackness about her and she had a splitting headache. The blackness, she eventually worked out, came courtesy of a blindfold which she couldn't take off, or even touch, because her hands were clamped behind her at the wrist, and she was squeezed into an uncomfortably small place which she quickly identified as the boot of a car, driving along a rough road, which was why the dark was doubly intense. The pain in her head took precedence over any fear she should have been feeling. All she wanted was for this pain to go away, then she'd cope with the rest.

Something was trickling down the side of her face, blood probably. Somebody must have hit her with tremendous force to have caused such pain. Why would anyone want to do that to her? Being in cramped, small places wasn't a new experience for Cleo but she hoped it wouldn't last long. Who the hell was doing this to her? The name Pascoe eventually came to her mind, making her shudder. Perhaps she was heading for one of his quarries. Now would be a good time to renegotiate her terms for selling the land. If only this headache would go away. Ant had warned her not to annoy Pascoe. God! How was she to know Pascoe would go this far? Was it too late to give him his money back? Mercifully the pain took away her consciousness, and with it her fear.

Her journey was short but she wasn't to know that. Two bouts of oblivion had removed any sense of time or distance. In fact, she had only travelled a couple of miles when the car came to a halt in the yard of a disused flour mill. Cleo regained consciousness as light pricked the edges of her blindfold and, by straining her eyes downwards, she could see her coat. It was important to be able to see her coat for it meant she hadn't been blinded by the blow; that possibility had been nagging her. Someone yanked at her arms, pulling her upwards, then hoisted her legs clear of the car boot.

'Okay ... out!'

The voice was gruff, as though the owner was disguising it. Why would he want to disguise it if he meant to kill her? Obviously he didn't. More relief.

'Who are you? Why are you doing this?'

Cleo's captor kicked her on her leg, sending her staggering forward. 'Shut yer trap or I'll shut it for yer!'

'Okay,' Cleo muttered. 'But if it's money you want you'd better tell me how much.'

Opening negotiations was preferable to being kicked, she decided.

'I said, shut yer bloody trap!'

Cleo tensed, awaiting another kick. Instead she was pushed, roughly, through a door, up two flights of metal stairs and into a room with an echoing wooden floor. There was a smell of dust in the air. Dust and mould. Whatever was binding her hands was metal, like handcuffs. This was confirmed when her hands were grabbed and she heard a key turn in a lock. One of the cuffs fell away.

'Over here,' growled the voice.

Cleo allowed her captor to lead her.

'Sit!'

The command could have been to a dog but Cleo knew it would be wise to obey. She felt a tug on her cuffed hand followed by a clicking sound as the other handcuff was attached to what sounded like a chain. Her captor was breathing heavily and Cleo could smell foul breath. She was now chained to something that felt like a radiator. A very substantial radiator. Her head throbbed with pain, but there was no relief from it. Never in her life, even under the stairs, had she felt so wretched. Under the stairs she'd had enough freedom to try and escape. Here she had nothing.

'What ... what do you want?'

Her question came out more as a sob and was answered by another kick. This time much more savage. No words, just a savage kick on her thigh that hurt like hell for a while, until the greater pain in her head resumed its dominance. She heard echoing footsteps moving away and a door closed, leaving her alone. Alone with the dust and the mould and the smell of bad breath up her nose. And suddenly she realised who was doing this to her.

The chain linking her to the radiator was quite short and meant her right hand was suspended at shoulder level. She pushed up the blindfold and looked around at her surroundings, but when she relaxed her handcuffed arm the steel handcuff dug into her wrist. She devised a method of sitting whereby she could rest her right hand and arm on her knees while leaning her body sideways against the radiator; all the time wondering how long she would have to endure this torture. She was in a large, industrial-looking room with rusty steel columns coming up through the floor and disappearing through a dilapidated ceiling with more holes than plaster. There were sixteen windows, eight on each opposite wall; all broken or cracked, one with some sort of gantry projecting outside with a winch attached, presumably for hoisting up heavy loads. The floor was dirty but relatively unlittered apart from a few old sacks and a pile of tins in one corner. Looking up she could see patches of sky, even though there was another floor above her. Hours went by. Cleo dozed and woke up with terrible cramp which she eased as best she could by stretching her legs. Her lips were parched, which contrasted with the fearful sweat moistening her skin. A drink would be welcome. She hadn't had a drink for hours and there wasn't much moisture left in her body. Cleo realised there was a good side to this, she didn't want to pee either. But that wouldn't last for ever, she knew that. Surely her captor would come back with food and drink and allow to her to go to the toilet. Then she remembered who her captor was and she held out little hope of this happening.

Night fell and Cleo arranged herself in as comfortable a position as she could in order to get some sleep and blot out her waking nightmare for as long as possible. It was the only way to survive. Sleep away the time. She'd done a lot of that in the bogey hole, which, she had to admit, was luxury compared to this. The pain in her head had eased to an aching numbness. So that was something.

She woke up in the middle of the night to discover that her bladder had relieved itself without her permission. How? This had never happened in the bogey hole. Had she lost control of her bodily functions? Her thirst was worse than ever now. There was a film of new sweat on her face. She was leaking liquid she couldn't afford to lose.

Dawn broke and heralded a sense of deep despair within her. It seemed a treacherous dawn that held out no hope, as dawns should. This was the dawn of a very bad day. Cleo was somehow sure of that.

Chapter Twenty-One

Rocky rang Cleo from the site the next morning, having rehearsed the words of his invitation over and over as he paced up and down the site hut. He hadn't had much experience with girls; being a guest of Her Majesty for all those years hadn't helped, and his youth had been dedicated to boxing. His relationship with Jasmine had been her doing, she'd made all the running. She'd lured him into her net, knocked off his rough edges, tried to teach him how to behave in a manner she assumed was acceptable to polite society and had then sat back to reap the rewards for all her hard work. Rocky killing his trainer hadn't been part of her plan.

'Is Cleo there?'

'No, she's not, Rocky. Was she out with you last night?'

'No.'

'Are you sure ... sorry, stupid question.' Jenny became vaguely worried. She looked at her watch – 10.35. 'I know she didn't go home last night, Flo's just been on the phone. We both thought she must be with you.

'She wasn't with me,' Rocky assured her. 'So, no one's seen her since she went off to meet that bloke yesterday.'

'Where the hell is she?'

'I don't know,' said Rocky, worried himself

now. 'I'm coming in.'

Flo was already there when he arrived. Jenny was trying to make sense of some scribbled notes Cleo had written on a pad as she had taken the directions from Mr Johnstone.

'Wheatley,' she read. 'Fifty houses. A64 out of Tad ... that'll be Tadcaster. Left to Wheatley. One mile ... closed-down pub. Two o'clock ... Vic Johnstone.'

'Do we know who he is, this Vic Johnstone?' Flo asked.

Jenny shrugged. 'Not really. He rang up yesterday telling us he had some land for sale. He wanted a quick sale so Cleo said she'd meet him at two o'clock. I thought he sounded a bit odd and offered to go with her.'

'You should have done,' chastised Rocky. 'A woman alone going off to meet a strange man, it's asking for trouble. I think we should ring the police.'

'Do no harm,' Flo said. 'Don't blame yourself, Jen. She's a mind of her own has Cleo, we all know that – at least we should by now.' She gave Rocky a hard glance.

'Sorry Jenny,' he said. 'It's just that...'

Jenny was already dialling the police.

'If we sent out search parties every time an adult went missing overnight we'd have no time left for proper policing,' said the constable who had arrived on foot three hours after Jenny's call. 'If it was a kiddie, now that'd be a different kettle o' fish.'

'But she's not the type to go missing,' Jenny

insisted. 'She has a business to run. She went off to meet a man she's never met before and she hasn't come back.'

'Well, I'll take her description and get a message across to the York and Tadcaster police and tell them to keep an eye out for her.'

'Thank you,' Jenny said, but there was no gratitude in her voice.

'And if she does turn up in the meantime, which is more than likely, you won't forget to give us a ring, will you?'

'No, constable, we won't,' Flo assured him. 'We don't want you working any harder than you have to.'

The policeman looked at Flo. The heavy cynicism in her voice hadn't escaped his notice.

'So, if I can have a description?' he said.

'We'll have to tell Ant,' Rocky said, as he watched the countryside go past Jenny's car window.

'All in good time,' said Flo. 'It's early days yet. She might have a perfectly valid reason for going walkabout. I've often fancied just clearing off myself and not telling anyone where I've gone. Cleo's been through a lot. Maybe this is her time.'

'Maybe,' commented Jenny. 'But it's not like Cleo. She'd know we were worried – she wouldn't do that to us.'

'I suppose not,' sighed Flo, who had momentarily cheered herself up with her walkabout theory. But she knew Jenny was right. Cleo would have rung. 'What the hell's that?'

Agnes the cow was in the ford. Jenny pulled the

car up and tooted the horn. Agnes ignored it. Queenie was sitting on a fence eating an apple.

'She's allus doin' that, missis,' she called out. 'Yer'll not be able ter shift her if yer don't know how.'

'Do *you* know how?' Jenny asked, impatiently.

'Is there a reward?'

Jenny looked round at Flo and Ant. 'Are either of you any good with cows?'

'I hate cows,' said Rocky.

'Give her some money,' said Flo.

'Okay, I'll give you threepence if you can shift her,' Jenny called out.

'Tanner,' said Queenie, 'in advance. Some people just drive away without payin'.'

'Oh, so it's a regular thing is it?' said Jenny, handing over the money.

Queenie smiled sweetly, climbed down from the fence and led Agnes out of the car's way.

'Do many cars come along this road?' Jenny called back to the girl after she'd driven through the ford.

'Not many, missis. It's a bugger of a road is this. It's people on bikes mostly. I haven't gorra bike. Me dad says he'd get me one if I passed me scholarship but I didn't. He says I'm a dunce. That's why I'm norrat school – no point if I'm a dunce is there, missis? Anyroad it's miles ter school an' there's no buses or nowt. Not from where we live. Me dad dunt know I'm knockin' off school. What time is it?'

'Twenty past two,' Jenny said. 'Did you see anybody yesterday about this time, maybe a bit earlier? A woman in a car – about my age.'

'Is there a reward?'
'Might be.'
'How much?'
Flo was out of the car now, speaking sternly to the girl. 'Listen, young lady. We promise not to tell your dad you're knocking off school if you tell us what we need to know.'
'Yer don't even know me dad,' replied Queenie, coolly, taking another bite from her apple and munching, loudly.
'A shilling,' offered Jenny.
'A bob's not much. Yer can't buy much wi' a bob. Not nowadays any road. Half a pint o' beer, five Woodbines, two Mars Bars...'
'All right!' Flo seethed. 'Half a bloody crown. And I can always make it my business to find out who your dad is.'
The girl splashed through the water and took the money from Jenny, exchanging it, cheekily, for her apple core which Jenny threw away in disgust.
'There were a woman came past about this time yesterday. She asked me who I was an' I told her me name's Elizabeth but everybody calls me Queenie 'cos I were born on the day Queen Elizabeth became queen.'
'Pleased to meet you, Queenie,' said Flo.
'That's what she said.'
'What sort of car did she have?'
Queenie shrugged. 'Don't know nowt about motors, missis. But she had a better motor than that owd banger.' The girl nodded towards Jenny's pre-war Austin Ruby. 'Agnes were blockin' road an' this woman slapped her on her

arse to try an' get 'er ter move. But it teks more than a slap on th' arse ter get Agnes ter do owt she dunt want.'

Jenny, Flo and Rocky all had a mental picture of Cleo slapping a woman's backside to get her to move. It didn't sound like Cleo at all.

'The woman in the car, what did she look like?' asked Flo.

'Like what yer said,' replied Queenie. 'She were about the same age as you only she had fair hair. I suppose she were quite pretty an' all.'

'Who's Agnes?' Flo asked, satisfied the girl was describing Cleo.

Queenie jabbed a thumb over her shoulder to where Agnes was grazing.

'Ah,' said Flo, enlightened now. 'Agnes is the cow,' she told Rocky and Jenny. 'Did you see this woman come back?'

The girl considered the question carefully. 'I saw t'car come back at a fair owd lick,' she said. 'I reckon it were her.'

'It was definitely a woman?' Flo said.

'Didn't bother ter look,' said Queenie. 'We'd have been run over if I hadn't got Agnes outa t' road in time. People mainly come down here on bikes. I know most of 'em, an' I hide 'cos they'll tell me dad I'm norrat school.'

'You should go to school,' Flo told her, not unkindly. 'Bright girl like you.'

'I'm not bright, I'm a dunce.'

'Believe me, young lady,' Flo assured her. 'You're not a dunce. You seem a bit unusual but you're far from being a dunce.'

Jenny stuck her arm out of the car window and

handed the girl one of the firm's business cards. 'If you hear of anything else about the woman would you ring this number, please?'

'Will there be a reward?'

'Yes,' said Jenny, quickly, before Flo could say anything.

There was not so much as a tyre track in the pub car park. The weeds saw to that. Rocky got into the building through a window and searched every room; calling out Cleo's name and getting no reply; dreading what he might find behind each door. Somehow he knew that if she was in this place she wouldn't be alive. It was with some relief when he finally poked his head through an upstairs window and announced to the women below that the place was empty.

'We found an old bike,' Jenny shouted back.

Rocky surveyed the surrounding countryside from his vantage point and tried to make sense of everything. What had happened to Cleo? And why this feeling of dread? His breathing was heavy, but not through any physical exertion. He didn't remember feeling quite this desolate about Jasmine's disappearance from his life – why was that? Was it different circumstances? Was it because Jasmine's life probably wasn't in any danger? Just beneath him the pub sign creaked away but not loudly enough to drown the drumming of his heart. *Please be alive, Cleo Kelly.*

He went downstairs and climbed back out through the window. 'She's definitely been here,' he said. 'Stands to reason that she's been here. So where is she? Is she in trouble?'

'I don't know, Rocky,' said Flo. 'I just hope she's–'

'Still alive?' said Jenny. 'Oh God, Flo, don't say that.'

'I'm not saying anything, love. I'm as worried as you are.'

'What about Pascoe?' said Rocky, voicing his thoughts. The women turned to him.

'What *about* Pascoe?' Flo asked.

'It's the sort of thing he'd do by all accounts.'

'*What's* the sort of thing he'd do?' enquired Jenny.

Rocky shrugged. 'Cleo made a fool out of him – and a lot of money. Men like Pascoe don't like being made fools of.'

Jenny and Flo looked at each other. Rocky's words had a ring of sense.

'I'll kill him!' said Rocky, who had now made his mind up. 'I don't care what happens to me; I'll kill him if he's hurt Cleo.'

There were tears of anger in his eyes. Flo put her arm around him. 'We don't know, Rocky. For all we know she'll be waiting for us when get back, wondering what all the fuss has been about.'

The office phone was ringing as the trio arrived back. Jenny snatched it from its cradle and voiced her hopes.

'Cleo?'

There was a snigger from the caller. 'It'll cost yer twenty-five thousand ter see Cleo again.'

Jenny put her hand over the mouthpiece and spoke to Flo and Rocky. 'I think she's been kidnapped.' Then she waved them quiet as the caller continued:

'If yer go ter t' police yer'll never see 'er again.'

'Mr Johnstone?' said Jenny.

'Never you mind who I am. I want me money termorrer. I'm only askin' what's due ter me. Stay on this number.'

The phone went dead. Jenny looked at it, then at Rocky and Flo. 'He wants twenty-five thousand pounds.'

'I'll ring the police,' Flo said.

'No!' Jenny placed her hand over the telephone. 'He said he'd kill her if we did that.'

'What did he sound like?' Rocky asked.

'Like the man who rang yesterday – Mr Johnstone. He sounds a bit odd, as though he's got something wrong with his voice.'

'Maybe he was disguising it,' Flo guessed.

'Which means it's someone whose voice we'd recognise,' deduced Rocky. 'Like Pascoe.'

'Could be,' said Jenny. 'Could be anyone's voice. He said he was only asking what was due to him.'

'How many people do we know who have got a grudge against Cleo and who reckon she owes them money?' Rocky pointed out.

'Twenty-five thousand pounds, though?' said Flo. 'Pascoe only paid ten for the land, where's the other fifteen come from?'

'These people charge their own rates of interest,' said Rocky. 'I know it's Pascoe and I'm going to pay him a visit.'

Both Jenny and Flo doubted the wisdom of this but their concern for Cleo's welfare overrode any worries they might have about Rocky. He was big enough to look after himself. Hopefully.

'Just be careful,' said Flo.

Rocky was already out of the door.

Pascoe's Bentley was parked outside the weigh-bridge office as Rocky drove into the quarry yard. It was early evening and the last of the wagons was leaving with its load of stone for the M62 site. All the machines were silent now and a cluster of dusty quarrymen were washing their hands under a cold-water tap; some splashed water on their faces and rubbed them dry with old rags that looked to have seen cleaner times.

In the distance Rocky could see Pascoe talking to one of the men. He sounded angry and was gesticulating wildly. The man shrugged, nodded and walked away, presumably to do his master's bidding.

'An' yer don't go till it's bloody finished!' Pascoe shouted after him.

'Is that how you frightened Cleo?' growled Rocky, walking straight up to the quarry owner and grabbing him by his collar. 'I bet you're good at frightening women.' He pushed Pascoe back-wards as he spoke. The man to whom Pascoe had just been speaking turned round and watched in amazement.

'What the bloody hell's all this about!' cursed Pascoe, loudly. 'Get yer bloody hands off me, yer bloody madman!'

The edge of the quarry was about twenty yards away. A vast hole in the earth. As though a dozen or more acres of ground had suddenly collapsed and left behind sheer cliffs of seamed stone; each seam representing a different era, a million years older than the seam above.

Rocky's eyes blazed with a wild anger as he forced the quarry owner backwards until the terrified man could see, over his shoulder, a sheer ninety-foot drop.

'What have you done with her, you bastard?'

Pascoe had made it his business to find out about Rocky Diggle and he didn't like what he heard. The man was a convicted killer.

'I don't know what yer talkin' about, lad. Honest I don't!'

'Liar!'

Rocky pretended to push him over, then pulled him back. Pascoe let out a squeal of terror. Men were gathering at a distance. None of them had any great liking for Pascoe, but he was their bread and butter and if he went over the edge of the quarry their jobs might well follow.

'Think o' what yer doin' lad,' called out one. 'No matter what he's done it's not worth gerrin' hung for.'

'I haven't bloody done anything!' howled Pascoe. 'What's this all about?'

'It's about you wanting twenty-five thousand pounds to give us Cleo back!' roared Rocky, so that everyone could hear. 'Where is she?'

'I don't know. For God's sake somebody get this bloody madman off me!'

The men inched forward and Rocky pushed Pascoe outwards so that the only thing between him and certain death was Rocky's grip on the quarry owner's coat.

'Tell me where she is or I'll let go!' he threatened.

There was such truth and determination in his voice that Pascoe thought his end had come. One of the men nudged his companion and whispered that Pascoe had just 'pissed his pants'. A spreading stain on Pascoe's trousers confirmed this.

'Don't kill me,' he pleaded, crying like a baby. 'I don't know where she is. Honest, lad, I don't know. If I knew don't yer think I'd tell yer.'

'He doesn't know,' called out a man. Others voiced their agreement. 'Leave him be, lad. He knows nowt.'

Rocky held on to Pascoe for a few more seconds as he weighed this advice up. Then his sense of reason returned. What the hell was he doing, trying to kill yet another man? He pulled Pascoe back and hurled him to the ground before storming off. The quarry owner curled into a ball and sobbed as his men gathered round him to watch – and to gloat a little.

'Shall we call the coppers, boss?' asked one.

Pascoe got to his feet and tried to regain his composure, which was not easy. Just a minute ago he was certain he was going to die. His voice was light-blue as he said, 'Just leave it. Just, just ... go away from me.'

The men dispersed, knowing full well that their boss wanted as little to do with the police as possible and wondered if he might seek personal retribution against this madman. Perhaps not. Pascoe was a bully and bullies tend not to take on madmen.

It was eight o'clock that evening when the office phone rang again. The two women knew it was the kidnapper; no one else would ring the office at this time. Rocky had told them what had happened with Pascoe and that he didn't think it was him after all. Flo had advised him to make himself scarce.

'If he tells the police you'll be back inside before you know it,' she warned him.

'I don't think he's the type to tell the police,' muttered Rocky, uncertainly.

'Let's hope not,' Flo said. It was she who picked up the phone.

'Yes?'

'Yer know who this is?' said the caller.

'I know *what* you are.'

The caller hesitated, then asked, 'Have yer got the money?'

'You know very well we haven't got the money,' Flo said. 'If you've got Cleo she must have told you we haven't got that kind of money. We'd have to sell the business to raise twenty-five thousand pounds, and how long do you think that would take?'

'Yer've got forty-eight hours, that's how long it'll take.'

Flo sensed the caller was about to put the phone down. 'Hold it!' she shouted.

'What?'

'How do we know Cleo's still alive? We need to know that before we do anything.'

There was a pause before the caller said, 'Yer'll just have ter take my word for it.'

'Your word's not worth twenty-five bob never mind twenty-five thousand pounds!' snapped Flo. 'I'll get you your money but you don't get a penny before I get proof she's still alive.'

'What sort of proof?'

'*You're* the bloody kidnapper!' Flo was shouting now. 'Do you want me to tell you your job? Just give me a ring when you've got your bloody act together.'

With that, she put the phone down. She looked at Jenny, seeking her approval.

'Did I do the right thing?' she asked.

'I don't know what the right thing is under these circumstances,' Jenny said. 'I don't know how we're going to lay our hands on twenty-five thousand either.'

'I was playing for time,' Flo admitted. 'And for proof that Cleo's still alive.'

'Oh God! I hope she is,' said Jenny. 'Maybe we should ring the police.'

'I think maybe you're right,' Flo said. 'This thing's too much for us. Hopefully they'll listen to us now.'

The next morning Rocky spoke to Ant on the phone. The girl on the prison switchboard knew him and had arranged for him to talk to his old pal. Rocky had already spoken to Flo who had brought him up to date with events, including the kidnapper's phone call.

'Are you sure it isn't Pascoe?' Ant said.

'Pretty sure.'

'Jesus, Rocky! I wish I wasn't in here. We can't lay our hands on twenty-five grand, not at short notice anyway. I'd probably have to sell the firm and that'd take time.'

'I thought Cleo owned part of it, won't you need her–?'

Ant cut him short. 'No. She'll just be entitled to her share of the proceeds. I retained the right to dispose of the shares as I saw fit. Good job, as it happens.'

'I see,' said Rocky, who didn't see at all.

'Whoever's got her,' Ant said, 'is trying to get back at me for something or other. It's all my fault is this.'

'Who else do you think it might be?'

'I don't know. I've been a bit unorthodox at times but I didn't think I'd offended anyone *that* much.'

'Could it be anyone connected with your step-father?' Rocky asked.

'No,' Ant decided, after some thought. 'Womack was a complete shit. No one would go out of their way to avenge him.'

'Flo says we should leave it to the police,' said Rocky.

'Collins!' said Ant.

'What?'

'My old solicitor. Cuthbert Collins. He tried to screw the firm when I got locked up but we had something on him.'

'I heard about that.'

'Ah, but did you hear that Cleo wasn't content just to get our money back?' Ant went on. 'She shopped Collins to a building society he was scamming. Cost him a fortune, nearly got him struck off.'

'But, would he do something like this?' asked Rocky, doubtfully.

'*He* wouldn't – not personally. But I wouldn't put it past him to hire someone. He knows plenty of villains does cunning Cuthbert.'

'I'll pay him a visit.'

'No you won't,' said Ant, sharply. 'Just tell the police you think it could be him. Let them handle it.'

'But...'

'No "buts", Rocky. If you rough Collins up, you'll end up in here before your feet touch the floor.'

'Right, I'll tell the police.'

'You'd better check that Pascoe hasn't reported you to the police.'

'He hasn't, I checked this morning – I know the bloke on the quarry weighbridge.'

'That's all right then,' Ant said. 'Just don't do anything daft with Collins.' He paused. Rocky sensed he was thinking about something.

'What is it?'

'You like Cleo, don't you?'

Rocky shrugged as though Ant could actually see him. 'Course I like Cleo. She's very nice – and she's been good to me. You both have.'

'Hmm. I don't think you like me in the same way you like Cleo. You've got a thing about her, haven't you?'

Rocky seemed confused. 'I like her very much,' he admitted.

'As much as you like Jasmine?'

'Now, that's different. Not having met Jasmine you wouldn't understand,' Rocky said. 'But I like

Cleo. Very much indeed, as a matter of fact.'

'That's good,' Ant said. 'I need you to like her very much indeed. I need you to settle this thing in my place. Promise me you won't rest until you settle it.'

'You've got my word on that.'

'And don't do anything daft.'

'I'll do what I think's necessary,' Rocky promised.

Collins howled with delight at the news. 'This is the best thing I've heard this year. I hope they send her back in pieces, the treacherous little bitch!'

It wasn't his intention to rough Collins up, but the solicitor's reaction upon being told that Cleo had been kidnapped made something inside Rocky snap. Seeing this oily little man gloating over her plight was just too much. An hour after speaking to Ant, Rocky was in Collins's office, reaching over the desk and dragging the solicitor across it by his shirt collar. Collins tried to cry out but Rocky simply twisted his grip, cutting off Collins's air supply and sending his face purple. Then Rocky pulled the choking man closer to him so that their faces were almost touching. Rage had turned Rocky's handsome face ugly and venomous.

'When I let go you'll tell me where she is – or next time I won't let go. Then we'll see who's laughing.'

He left it a few more seconds before he allowed Collins to breathe again. By this time the solicitor was in some distress.

'For heaven's sake,' he pleaded, between gasps. 'I don't know anything ... anything about Cleo ... I'm a solicitor for God's sake!... I might bend the rules a bit, but I'm hardly a... a bloody kidnapper.'

Rocky had him by the scruff of the neck again but not before Collins managed a scream of terror that brought his secretary rushing in. She stood there, white-faced at the violent scene in front of her, then backed out slowly and ran to her phone. Rocky could hear her ringing the police and he knew he'd done it this time. He threw the solicitor to the floor and ran out of the office.

Detective Inspector Turton, sitting opposite Jenny, sipped the coffee Flo had made him. They were in Kelly Construction's office waiting for the phone to ring. Up until now there had been a couple of dozen business calls, each one dealt with in a very cursory manner by Jenny, whose eyes were red-rimmed, having been up all night awaiting the call from the kidnapper.

'It's a bit stupid when you come to think of it,' said the inspector. 'A kidnapper using a business line. Whoever it is hasn't thought this thing through, which might be to our advantage.'

'Stupid people can also be unpredictable,' commented Flo.

The phone rang again. Jenny answered, then handed it to the policeman. 'It's for you,' she said.

Inspector Turton listened for a few seconds, then his eyes turned to Jenny, as though the conversation he was having concerned her.

'I see,' was all he said, then he put the phone down.

Both Jenny's and Flo's eyes were on him as they waited for the inspector to tell them what he had just heard.

'It appears that someone has been making his own enquiries regarding Miss Kelly's kidnap,' he said.

Both of the women knew exactly who that someone was. Jenny grimaced. 'What's happened?' she said, assuming Pascoe had reported Rocky to the police.

'A local solicitor had just complained of being assaulted by a man accusing him of the kidnap. If the complaint has any substance the man in question is in serious trouble.'

'And this man is?' asked Flo. The question was almost rhetorical, so obvious was the answer.

'The man is apparently Rocky Diggle. There's a warrant out for his arrest. When he's picked up he'll go straight back inside until this latest case is heard. And if he's found guilty he'll be made to serve out the rest of a previous sentence as well as whatever he's given for the assault.'

'I assume this solicitor is Cuthbert Collins,' said Jenny.

'Yes,' confirmed the inspector.

'Collins has got to be suspect,' Flo said. 'He's got reason to hate Cleo. He's a crook and she told everyone about him.'

'She cost him a lot of money,' added Jenny. 'Surely you can't arrest Rocky on the word of a crook like Collins.'

'I'm aware of Mr Collins's reputation and we

will regard him as a suspect. But I'm afraid there's a witness to the assault, which was quite serious by all accounts. Mr Collins is in hospital.'

'Oh Rocky, you bloody idiot!' Jenny voiced her thoughts out loud. The phone rang again. It was the kidnapper. Jenny signalled to the inspector who picked up a second phone the police had installed for the purpose.

'I've taken a photo of her wi' today's *Daily Express,* but you'll have ter develop it yerself,' said the gruff voice. 'I've posted it ter yer. Yer'll have it termorrer. That's when I want me money.'

'It'll take us at least a day to get it developed,' Jenny said. 'Maybe more.'

'Day after termorrer then. That's when I want me dues. Twenty-five thousand. Have it ready or yer'll hear no more from me. Nor her neither.' The caller rang off.

Inspector Turton, who was dressed in workman's clothes to allay any suspicious watching eyes, rubbed his chin. 'I'm a bit puzzled about the word "dues". What do you suppose he meant? It sounds as though he thinks he's owed this money.'

'Come to think of it, he said something like that last time,' Jenny remembered. 'But it doesn't make any sense to me.'

'Nor me,' said Flo. 'And I've known Cleo since she was a girl. She keeps no secrets from me. I still wouldn't rule Collins out. Maybe he thinks she owes him that much money for the trouble she caused him.'

'Mr Collins is in hospital,' Turton pointed out.

'Hospitals have telephones,' countered Flo.

'I'll ring the Infirmary,' said the inspector. 'Find

out if he's up and about.'

Flo motioned to Jenny to come outside. 'I'll leave you to make the call, then,' Jenny said to Inspector Turton. With that she and Flo left the office.

Flo led her by the arm until they stood outside. 'We can't let Rocky get locked up,' she said. 'He's an idiot but Cleo thinks the world of him.'

'Don't we all,' said Jenny.

Flo gave her a disapproving look which Jenny countered with, 'Don't tell me you haven't had the old fantasy about the luscious Rocky. I've seen the way you look at him.'

'All right,' Flo conceded. 'He's a nice-looking feller – but that's not why we've got to look out for him. Rocky might be a bit of an idiot but he's kept your firm going since he came on the scene. I don't think you could manage without him.'

'I *know* we couldn't,' Jenny admitted. 'But what can we do?'

'We can persuade Collins to drop the charges.'

'How do we do that?'

'If necessary, we bribe him.'

Jenny gave this some thought. 'What if he takes the bribe then tells the police what we've done?' she said. 'He's a devious character is Collins.'

Flo's head was spinning. This on top of Cleo's kidnapping was becoming a nightmare.

'We need to see Ant,' Jenny decided. 'He's never been short of an idea in his life.'

'Agreed,' said Flo. 'I wonder if Inspector Turton can swing us a visit today – call it compassionate grounds.'

They walked back into Jenny's office just as the

policeman was putting the phone down. He leaned back in his chair and rubbed his chin.

'Collins had discharged himself,' he said. 'In and out in an hour.'

'What were his injuries?' Flo asked.

'Don't know, can't have been much; but I'm afraid it doesn't lessen the gravity of the offence.'

'Collins could have made the call,' Jenny reminded him. 'This could all be a set-up to throw you off the scent.'

'We'll be interviewing Mr Collins later today,' said the inspector. 'But first I'm calling in to see Cleo's brother. See if he can throw any light on the matter.'

'Can we come?' Jenny asked, quickly. 'I mean, separately from you. It's going to come as a shock to Ant – maybe we should break it to him first. He and Cleo are very close.'

'You might get more sense out of him if you let us go in first,' Flo said, adding weight to Jenny's request. 'He's not the vicious criminal the court made him out to be.'

'Is he not? You could have fooled me. Killing his father with a spade. Not exactly the dutiful son.'

'It was his *stepfather*,' Flo told him, heatedly. 'And he sexually abused Ant as a child.' She bit her lip, realising she'd betrayed a confidence. 'Look, I'd er ... I'd be grateful if you didn't repeat that to anyone,' she added. 'Ant still can't bear the thought of anyone knowing. I'm not supposed to know myself.'

'Oh,' said the inspector, catching the sincerity in Flo's eyes.

Jenny looked at Flo with an expression of hurt

on her face. Why hadn't she been told? Both Flo and Cleo knew of her strong feelings for Ant. Why hadn't they mentioned it? Flo read her thoughts.

'Sorry, Jen,' she said. 'Even Cleo didn't know about it until after the trial. She knew Horace Womack was a brute but he didn't hurt her in that way – apparently he wasn't interested in girls.'

'But...' said a shocked Jenny, 'why didn't it come out at the trial? Ant would have got off ... wouldn't he?' She addressed the question to the inspector, who held up his hands.

'Don't ask me, miss,' he said. 'I wasn't involved in it.' He suddenly felt an affinity with these two women and he wanted to help them – above and beyond the call of duty if necessary. 'I'll arrange for you to see Mr Kelly for a few minutes before I talk to him,' he said.

'Thank you, Inspector,' said Jenny.

Chapter Twenty-Two

Cleo worked out that it was now twenty-four hours since she'd had a drink – a cup of tea with her lunchtime sandwich that she'd shared with Jenny, who was on a no-lunch diet. A regime she'd rarely stuck to, especially when Cleo was having beef and pickle. Maybe she wouldn't have felt quite so hungry if Jenny hadn't looked so longingly at her sandwich. She used to look longingly at Ant when he wasn't looking. Pity Ant was too dumb to realise it. Men.

Then she thought of Rocky and wondered what he was doing right now. He must have realised she was missing. Was he worried or did he think she'd just gone off to be on her own without telling anyone? What would Jenny and Flo be thinking? Flo would have rung the police by now. How would the police find her, though? Cleo licked her cracked lips and longed for a drink. Even in the bogey hole Horace had given her water twice a day. Twice a day – maybe he wasn't so bad after all. Food and water twice a day. That would be luxury compared to how she was being treated now. Her head still ached and her body was racked with constant cramp from being so closely chained to the radiator. Blood was clotted over her head wound and she had spared a few licks of precious spit to wipe away the blood dried on the side of her face. Hours went by and still no one came. Why was this? Was this the plan? To leave her here to die? The way she was feeling it wouldn't take long. She kept nodding off to sleep and each time she woke up her thirst was worse. Night fell again with no sign of her abductor. Cleo's tongue felt like a dessicated Cumberland sausage. She tried to talk, just to see if she could, and the words came out in a strangled croak. She began to hallucinate about Horace placing a cup of water beside her; but when she reached out there was no water. If only Horace would come with a cup of water for her. Water, please. She would forgive him everything. Even being the cause of Ant's imprisonment.

All through her second night she drifted in and out of consciousness, unable to know the difference between dreams and hallucinations. Her world was one of misery, pain, confusion and desperate thirst. Her hunger was forgotten. It had been daylight for several hours when she was shaken awake. Her captor wore a mask, and somewhere in her mind Cleo knew this was good. Why was it good? Because it meant her captor intended letting her go at some stage and didn't want to be identified.

'Water.' Her voice was barely audible.

'What?'

'Please,' she pleaded. 'Can I have some water?'

'Oh I can't be bothered running around after the likes of you. Just sit up and look bloody interested while I take yer photo – and hold on ter this paper.'

A newspaper was thrust into Cleo's free hand. Her captor positioned it so it would face her camera. Headline to the fore.

Choirboy Stabs Music Teacher

And at the bottom of the page another article headed,

BBC2 Starts Today

Cleo blinked as the camera flashed. 'Keep yer bloody eyes open an' look lively,' growled the gruff voice behind the mask. 'Or they'll think yer've croaked. I took a big risk nickin' this camera. Yer should be grateful I gorra good un.'

'Please can I have some water ... please.'

'No, yer bloody can't.'

'Please ... Dobbs.'

There was a long silence. It took Cleo a second or two to realise what she'd said, but her concern took second place to a drink of water. All she wanted was water. Dobbs ripped her mask off and flung it to the floor, angrily. Then she punched Cleo at the side of her face.

'All right, clever cow. How did yer know?'

Dobbs was speaking in her normal voice now. The cruel voice that Cleo remembered and hated. She didn't answer. She was too weakened to think clearly. Dobbs hit her again. This time Cleo's head jerked back against the radiator, cutting it open once again. She wept, tearlessly.

'It's your breath,' she mumbled.

'Eh?'

'I smelled your breath ... remembered it.'

'Smelly breath, me?' Dobbs cupped her hand under her mouth, breathed into it and shook her head. 'Nowt wrong wi' my breath,' she concluded, then she laughed. 'At least I've got some breath, smelly or not. Which is more than you'll have before much longer. Yer see the trouble is, with you knowing who I am, I can't let yer go now. Yer'll have ter stop here, even if they do pay yer ransom. I've asked fer twenty-five grand. I'm told yer worth a few bob now. Must have fallen on yer feet eh?'

'Please ... water.'

'Please ... water,' mimicked Dobbs. 'Why should I? Give me one good reason why I should lift a bloody finger to help you? I spent three bloody years in Peterlee because of you. Do you know what that were like? It were a shit'ole, that's what it were like. An' I've been in an' out of nick ever since – all because o' you an' your big gob. Well, yer big gob's dried up good an' proper now. So don't ask me fer any favours.'

'Please, Dobbs.'

'Smile for the birdie.'

Dobbs took another photo of Cleo with her eyes open, begging for water, then she left, knowing full well that her captive wouldn't be alive much longer – so that was one less thing to worry about. Kidnapping was complicated enough without having to keep the victim alive.

Chapter Twenty-Three

'I gather you heard about your sister,' Inspector Turton said to Ant.

'I did. I heard this morning.'

'This morning? I was under the impression the two ladies who came with me had come to tell you – break the news gently as it were. At least that's what they told me.'

'We mainly talked about Cleo,' Ant said, 'but I already knew and I've put wheels in motion to raise the ransom money. But they also came to tell me you were after Rocky and they needed my advice. It was Rocky who told me about Cleo being kidnapped.'

'Well, we're definitely after him, lad – and when we catch him he'll most likely be keeping you company in here. But never mind Mr Diggle, have you any thoughts on who's kidnapped your sister?'

Ant looked at the barred window above Turton's head. 'My only thought is that I need to be out of here. The hot favourite's Cuthbert Collins.'

'Mr Collins is known to us for various reasons, and for what it's worth, I think you're wrong.'

'Possibly. But it's my fault Rocky did what he did to him. I told him I thought it was Collins.'

'That's as maybe, lad. But it alters nothing.'

'It would if Collins withdraws his complaint,'

Ant said.

'If Mr Collins withdraws his complaint he'll get a bollocking from me for wasting police time.' Turton took out a packet of Craven A and offered Ant one. He refused. The policeman eyed Ant with some curiosity. 'So, you think you can get him to withdraw his complaint, do you?' he said.

'I think he could be persuaded, Inspector.'

'What have you got on him?'

'Just something I heard in here. Nothing you'd be interested in – but his wife might be.'

'I see. He seems a very vulnerable man does Mr Collins. I understand you dropped him in it once before.'

'It was more my sister than me. That's why I suspect him. My new solicitor's coming in later. I'm signing my business over to one of his other clients for twenty-five grand. It's worth twice that but I can't risk losing Cleo.'

'How soon can you get the money?'

'All things being equal, tomorrow. Once the deal's agreed in principle my bank will give me short-term bridging finance. My solicitor has explained what the problem is to them. Don't worry, they're treating it in confidence.'

'I'll say one thing for you, Mr Kelly. You don't waste time getting things done.' He looked around the stark prison room and added, 'Even in here.'

'I haven't got much else to think about, Inspector.'

'No, lad. I don't suppose you have.' Turton got to his feet. 'Right,' he said. 'I'll pay Mr Collins a visit, to eliminate him from our enquiries as it were.' He turned to go, then looked back. 'Will er ... will you have rung him by the time I get there?'

'If I get permission,' Ant said. 'You need permission to fart in here.'

'I'll see you get permission.'

'Thank you ... and, Inspector.'

'What?'

'You're on my side, aren't you?'

'I'm on the side of the law, lad.'

'I know, but you're on my side as well. Thanks for that ... and Inspector.'

Turton was almost out of the room, he turned once again, with his hand on the door. 'What, lad?'

'Please bring Cleo back alive. I'll arrange to have the money brought to you tomorrow.'

'It might not come to that, lad.'

'Don't gamble with my sister's life, Inspector. The money's meaningless to me.'

'It might help when you get out of here.'

'Not without Cleo it won't.'

'I'll do what I can, lad.'

Collins was working late in his office to catch up on time lost at the hospital. He crumbled as soon as he heard the name Daisy Tring. Ant didn't need to mention any of the other prostitutes he could have added to his blackmail list.

'That's way below the bloody belt!' cursed the solicitor when Ant rang him. 'There's some things men just don't do to each other. It's coming to something when a man can't have a sly shag without another feller blowing the whistle on him.'

'I won't blow the whistle on you if you withdraw your complaint against Rocky.'

'The bugger nearly choked me to death,' Collins grumbled. 'He's not fit to be let loose on the streets.'

'He's a better man than you are by a long chalk,' snapped Ant. 'Now do we have a deal or would you prefer to have Daisy Tring or one of your other tarts to come knocking on your door to tell your wife what you've been up to? Because I can arrange that with one phone call.'

Daisy Tring turning up on her doorstep would be enough for Mrs Collins to walk out on her promiscuous husband; and as it was her money that was keeping him afloat during his current problems, Collins couldn't take that risk. When a despondent Rocky turned himself in to the police a couple of hours later, Inspector Turton came to the front desk.

'As luck would have it, we're no longer looking for you, Mr Diggle,' he said. 'The complaint against you has been miraculously dropped. But I thought I'd take the trouble to advise you personally to stop and think next time you beat someone up. Your stupidity isn't helping anyone – least of all Miss Kelly.'

Rocky almost collapsed with relief. It had taken so much out of him to turn himself in after weighing up the pros and cons. Distracting the police from their main aim of finding Cleo wasn't helping her.

'Thank you,' he said, then added. 'If you knew Cleo, you'd know why I did it.'

'I hope to have the pleasure of meeting her

before much longer,' said Turton. 'She sounds a very special lady.'

The following morning the photo negative arrived at Kelly Construction's offices, delivered by a rain-saturated postman. Jenny and Flo had been taking it in shifts to man the phone all around the clock, just in case. With them was a detective constable. Turton was off duty. The constable rang him at home.

'The film's arrived, sir.'

'Is Jenny there?'

'Yes, sir.'

'Put her on ... Jenny,' said Turton, 'I'll have the film developed straight away. If the kidnapper rings up remember to tell him you can't get it developed before tomorrow at the soonest. If you tell him you're having it developed today he might think we're involved.'

'If he sent us the film it means Cleo's still alive, doesn't it, Inspector? This is his proof.'

'It would seem so,' Turton said, non-committally. 'Cleo's brother's arranging for the ransom money to be brought to me today. It looks like you'll be working for a new boss very shortly. I think he's selling the company at a bit of a knock-down price.'

'That's okay by me, if it helps.' Jenny paused before asking, 'Do you think we should pay the money?'

'I'd prefer not to, but we've got to keep all our options open. I'll send someone round to pick up the film.'

The sound of dripping water roused Cleo into a state of semi-consciousness. Through the gaps in the roof she could see dark clouds. Rain hammered against what was left of the glass windows and gusts of wind sent the dust swirling across the floor, disturbing a large, brown rat that had been nosing around for food, sniffing at Cleo's leg at one stage. Her body was racked with cramp and pain. Had she a tear to spare, or a clear mind to think with, she would have wept with despair. But dehydration was affecting her mind so much that she scarcely knew where, or even who, she was. A steady trickle of water dropped through the roof and landed right by her head. A natural instinct for survival made her stretch as far as the chain would allow, and then further still until the handcuff cut into her wrist, but her mouth was now under the stream of water so the pain didn't count. Each drop awakened her numbed tastebuds like French champagne. It almost choked her as she tried to swallow it down her parched and swollen throat. Then the stream of water, diverted by a gust of wind, moved away a few inches and she strained her torn wrist on the chain to try and reach it and cried for it to come back to her. After a couple of minutes the stream returned, then went away again, teasing her, not allowing her too much too soon. A miracle such as this had been uppermost in her thoughts for what seemed a lifetime, but had in fact been less than three days. She drank all she could for an hour until the rain eased off and with it her life-saving water supply. But it had slaked her thirst and irrigated her senses and brought her back to more than just semi-consciousness; and she realised how hungry she was, only there was no chance of any food dropping from the skies. Manna didn't fall from heaven in this god-forsaken neck of the woods.

Jenny burst into tears when she saw the photographs. The first one, where Cleo's eyes were closed, was ghastly. Had Dobbs not taken a second snap, both Jenny and Turton would have thought her to be dead. A pencil-written note was enclosed, probably written by the kidnapper's non-writing hand, guessed Turton, so bad was the printed scrawl:

Your frend is on her last legs and I will not be going back to her so you have no time to waist. This Friday morning at eleven o clock bring the money in a good bag to the phone box outside the Roscoe in Sheepscar. Wait for a messige. You need a car. If I think you are up to any tricks you will not here from me again and she will be left to die. When I get the money I will ring you and tell you were she is.

Inspector Turton read it and handed it to Flo who had her arm around the distraught Jenny.

'He's got us over a barrel,' he said. 'He knows we'll try and play for time. This is his way of stopping us.'

'I just hope she lasts until tomorrow morning,' said Flo. 'God, she looks dreadful! How the hell has she got into that state in the space of three days?'

'Well, we've got the money,' said the inspector. 'All we can do is go along with him and hope he keeps his end of the bargain. Our first priority is to get Cleo back, then we'll try and track him down.'

Jenny parked her car by the phone box with Flo sitting in the passenger seat guarding the money. Inside the pub was Turton and a detective sergeant. Jenny was waiting for the phone to ring when she noticed the broken lead trailing on the floor.

'Bloody hell!' she cursed, picking up the phone. It was dead. Sticking out from the telephone directory was a sheet of paper, on which was written, in the same scrawl as before:

You are being watched by my accomplise. Do not leave any messiges. Go to the Merrion Center car park. Kellys car is parked on the first levell. Next instrucions under drivers matt. If anyone follows Kelly is dead.

Jenny knew Turton would be watching through the pub window. She shook her head as she left the call box and the policeman recognised this as the signal that he must leave the women to it. This kidnapper knew his business which, paradoxically, boded well for Cleo. A criminal who knew his business wouldn't risk a murder charge if he didn't have to. Or would he?

Jenny drove up the car park ramp and turned right along the first level. Cleo's Cortina was the last car on the left, parked just before the door leading into the recently built shopping centre. She stopped in front of it. Flo got out, and waited for a car following her to pass before she tried the Cortina door. It was unlocked. Under the driver's mat was a note written in the now familiar scrawl:

Put money in rubbish bin by door. Then drive up to top levell and wait there half an hour. If everything is okay I will ring you at 1 o'clock.

Flo spotted the rubbish bin a few feet away just by the exit door leading down to the shopping centre.

'It's to go in that bin,' she told Jenny. 'Then we have to drive to the top and wait half an hour. He'll ring us at one o'clock to tell us where Cleo is.'

Jenny nodded, silently. Flo took a zip-up shopping bag from the back seat and waited for another car to pass before she hurriedly stuffed it in the rubbish bin and got back in the car. Then, as instructed, Jenny headed for the top level where she and Flo would wait the stipulated half an hour. Neither of them noticed the young woman carrying a suitcase who passed them on foot, walking down the ramp from level two.

Dobbs grinned to herself as she saw the handle of the bag sticking out of the bin. In a flash she pulled it out, stuffed it into the suitcase and was disappearing through the door into the shopping centre as Jenny and Flo were still driving along level three, and as Cleo was staring at the hole in the roof, hoping for more rain – or for Dobbs to come back.

Over the past twenty-four hours Cleo's thoughts had flickered between Ant, Flo and Jenny – and most of all Rocky. She knew without a shadow of a doubt that she loved that man and all his maddening ways.

Chapter Twenty-Four

Rocky was in the office, staring at the phone, willing it to ring with news of Cleo. It had rung many times that morning and Rocky was wondering how much business he'd lost the firm with his abruptness to the callers, telling them to ring off and not ring back today under any circumstances. It was a poor way to run a business but it scarcely mattered; in a couple of days there'd be a new owner and he'd be out of a job. A small price to pay for getting Cleo back. The phone rang again; this time it was Jenny.

'We've dropped the money off and he's taken it. He's ringing the office at one o'clock to tell us where Cleo is. Turton's keeping out of it until we get her back, but me and Flo are coming in.'

Rocky gave a sigh. It wasn't over but the signs were good. He looked at his watch. Five to twelve. Just over an hour to wait. Please God let her be all right. Flo had told him about the photo of Cleo and how ill she looked. A confusion of rage and frustration boiled inside him as he realised how useless he'd been while this was being done to her.

One o'clock came and went with no call from the kidnapper. Dobbs was on a train to London with her suitcase clutched firmly in her hand and a grin of triumph etched on to her face. Twenty-five grand. Twenty-five years wages for a well-paid man. Kelly would be near enough dead by now and with her would go any chance of Dobbs being identified. They'd be looking for a man anyway. Dobbs couldn't believe how clever she'd been. All her life she'd been told how stupid she was and how she had no future. Now she had a fortune in her bag and a high time ahead of her. The grin didn't leave her face all the way to London.

At half past one Jenny picked up the phone and rang Turton.

'He hasn't rung.'

'I see...'

Turton's end of the line went quiet.

'Inspector?' said Jenny.

'Sorry, love. I'm just wondering what my next move is. I must say I did expect him to ring.'

'We're still hoping he will,' said Jenny. 'I'm just ringing to see what you thought. Do *you* think he'll ring?'

'I honestly don't know, love. Look, I'd better come over. Work out a plan of action if we don't hear from him – as it were.'

For the next four hours the sporadic ringing of the phone and subsequent disappointment when it wasn't the kidnapper was even getting the inspector down. At five-thirty, the end of the working day, the phone went quiet. Turton looked at his watch for the umpteenth time, then at the despondent faces around him.

'Look,' he said. 'The best thing you can do is get some rest. I doubt if any of you have had more than a few hours' sleep since this thing kicked off. I'll leave someone to man the phone.'

'I'll do it,' Rocky said.

Turton looked at him and was about to protest until he saw the look of determination on Rocky's face. 'Okay ... any news ring the station first.'

It was turned seven the following morning when the phone rang. Rocky, slumped over the desk, snapped awake and knocked the phone from its cradle on to the floor. He scrambled around for it, still half asleep, and shouted into the mouthpiece as he picked it up. 'You were supposed to ring yesterday, you bastard!'

There was a long silence at the other end, then a young voice said, 'Hello?'

Rocky was taken aback. 'Who is this?' he said.

'It's Queenie.'

'Queenie... Who the hell? Oh, Queenie, right. I remember you from the other day.'

'Are you that good-lookin' bloke what were in t' car?'

'Er, yes, I suppose so,' answered Rocky, awkwardly.

'That woman yer were with told me ter ring her if I saw that car again. Is she there?'

Rocky sat bolt upright in his chair. 'Er, no, but you can tell me. You've seen Cleo's car?'

'I saw t' car that other woman were in,' said Queenie, who didn't know who Cleo was. 'Is there a reward?'

'What?'

'A reward. I thought there might be a reward.'

'Yes, yes ... where did you see it?'

'If yer bring me reward I'll tell yer.'

'Okay, okay. I'll bring a reward. Where shall I meet you?'

'Same place as before. I'm s'posed ter go ter

school but sod that – specially if there's a reward. How much will it be?'

'I don't know – a pound.'

'A pound! Great. How long will yer be?'

'I'll be there in three-quarters of an hour.'

Rocky's mind was filled only with thoughts of getting Cleo back. He was halfway there when it occurred to him to ring Turton, but finding a phone box and ringing up might waste precious time. He'd do it after he'd spoken to the girl. Besides, the girl wasn't exactly the reliable type. This could be a wild goose chase.

The morning was bright and sunny. It would have been just the day for him and Cleo to go on a picnic or something. Maybe a trip to the seaside. He'd never been to the seaside with a girl. All Jasmine ever wanted to do was go shopping. Queenie was sitting on a fence when he got there, wearing her flat cap and eating an apple.

'Hiya, mister!'

She jumped down and came over to Rocky's van. 'Have yer got me pound?'

Rocky took out his wallet and gave her a pound note. Probably the first she'd ever owned. Queenie held it to the light as though checking it wasn't a forgery.

'Tell me about the car,' Rocky said. 'When did you see it?'

Queenie folded the money up and put it carefully in one of her cardigan pockets. 'Two days ago,' she said. 'No, three days now. It were Wednesday mornin'.'

'Three days,' Rocky groaned. 'How do you

mean, three days? Why the hell didn't you ring us then?'

'I couldn't,' explained Queenie, stoutly. 'Me dad copped me knockin' off school an' I've not been allowed out. Anyroad, what's the rush?'

'Look, love,' Rocky explained. 'The woman in the car was kidnapped just after you saw her. Her life's in danger. It's really important you tell me everything you know.'

Queenie's eyes widened with excitement. 'Kidnapped, honest?'

'Well it's hardly something I'd joke about, is it?' said Rocky, impatiently. 'Now, where did you see that car?'

'I'll 'ave ter show yer, mister,' she said. 'Only I'm norrallowed ter get into cars wi' fellers. That's worse than knockin' off school.'

'Okay, I understand,' conceded Rocky, wondering how to get around this.

'But if someone's been kidnapped it's different, innit?'

'I think so,' he agreed.

Queenie jumped in beside him and instructed him to turn round and go back the way he came. They travelled for about quarter of a mile, then turned left.

'There's a right bad bend down here,' she told him. 'I sometimes go there ter see if anyone's had a bump or owt. Someone once gave me five bob for ringin' a breakdown truck. Better than a smack in t' mouth wi' a wet kipper.'

'You're a proper little businesswoman,' Rocky said. He was halfway round the looping bend and almost in the ditch when Queenie announced that this was the place. 'Jesus!' he shouted. 'Thanks for telling me. Are you always this late passing on information?'

'Nay, you were drivin' not me!' Queenie retorted. She pointed to a junction about a hundred yards away. 'That's where I saw t' car,' she said. 'Just comin' out o' there.'

Rocky drove on and turned at the junction. 'Where does it lead to, this road?'

Queenie shrugged. 'I suppose it comes out at Burton Kyme eventually.'

'What's at Burton Kyme?'

'Nowt much. Me uncle used ter work there.'

Rocky wasn't much interested in her uncle, but out of politeness asked, 'What did your uncle do?'

'Worked in Flatley's flour mill. Flatley's Flour for better bread,' she quoted the well-known advert. 'Me uncle were as sick as a Cleethorpes donkey when he were laid off. Least that's what me dad says.'

'Laid off?'

'Aye,' Queenie went on, speaking with the manner of someone three times her age. 'He's been on t' dole ever since. Me dad says he's an idle bugger.' She pointed to a group of large buildings set well back from the road. 'That's it, over there.'

Rocky's eyes followed her pointing finger. 'Is it still going?' he asked, conversationally. 'This flour mill?'

'Nah. Been shut three or four years now... Hey! Are you thinking what I'm thinking?'

Rocky skidded the van to a halt as they passed the mill entrance, then reversed at speed and turned in through the broken gate.

He drove around the factory buildings and although his thoughts were on Cleo he couldn't help but spare a glimmer of approval at the craftsmanship of the bricklayers and tradesmen in general who had built this place at the turn of the century. The roofs had been stripped of lead and much of the timber removed, possibly plundered by disgruntled former employees who perhaps thought themselves entitled to pick the factory's bones. A place which had once ground the flour for the best bread in the county, had been reduced, by the stroke of a businessman's pen, to just another industrial cadaver. On one wall was a piece of poignant graffiti:

Give us this day our daily bread, you greedy bastards.

'They're gonna pull it all down,' Queenie said. 'Me dad says it's a sin an' a shame.'

At any other time Rocky would have wholeheartedly agreed with her. Destroying a man's hard work was a crime to him as well. But right now there was a worse crime to worry about. He drew the van to a halt and got out.

'We'll start here,' he said, shielding his eyes from the warm sun and pointing to a three-storey building. 'You work your way around the back and I'll go the other way. We'll meet by that big grain silo we just passed. Her name's Cleo, keep shouting it.'

'Cleo? Never hear that one before.'

'It's short for Cleopatra.'

'Cleopatra?' Queenie suppressed an inappropriate grin. 'What's your name, mister?'

'Rocky,' he said. 'Rocky Diggle.'

Queenie's self-control didn't run to this amount of suppression, but she had the grace to cover her beaming mouth. Being called Queenie didn't seem so bad after all.

'I think I'll just call you "mister",' she said. 'What shall I do if I find her?'

'Yell as loud as you can. I'll come running. If I find her I'll do the same.'

Cleo thought she was hearing Rocky's voice in her head. There had been a lot of that in the last twenty-four hours. The world around her was becoming distorted with strange perspectives and the sky through the hole in the roof was deadly blue and it was roasting in this foul, dusty prison. She kicked out at the rat which had become adventurous and had attempted a couple of nips at her leg. It scurried away then stopped and stared at her, aware now that she had little to offer by way of retaliation. The determination in its dark eyes far outweighed the despair in hers. She looked at her fingernails, normally her pride and joy, beautifully manicured and polished. As a kid she had always admired women with nice fingernails, it seemed to reflect their general well-being. All of hers were broken down to the quick, apart from the little fingernail on her left hand which had somehow avoided harm. For no reason she could think of she tore it off, drawing blood but causing no pain. She was beyond that.

Then she heard his voice again, only she couldn't make her presence known because she hadn't the strength; in any case she knew it wasn't really him. The world was playing one last trick on her. She had accepted her fate. Death when it came would come as a friend.

'Cleo!'

That rat heard it as well and thought maybe attacking her wasn't such a good idea after all. Not just yet. There was always another time, she didn't look to be going anywhere. It scuttled off into a dark corner.

Cleo had heard another voice as well. A lighter, younger voice. She opened and closed her parched lips and tried to make herself heard but nothing came out. The voices kept on shouting but they didn't come near her. They were fading now. Just as her life was.

'Anything?' asked Rocky as they met up at the grain silo.

'Nah ... I saw a rat as big as a cat,' reported Queenie.

'I felt sure she'd be here,' said Rocky, wiping the sweat off his forehead with his sleeve. His hopes were sinking by the second. 'I expected to see her in every room I went in.'

To Queenie, who was by now in love with him, Rocky seemed on the verge of tears. She put a skinny arm around him.

'We'll find her, mister – just you wait an' see.'

He felt useless, dejected and empty as Queenie walked him back to the van. Surely he wasn't so useless that he needed to be comforted by a twelve-year-old girl. He removed her arm from around his waist as politely as he could.

'It's okay, Queenie,' he said. 'I'll take you back now.'

The girl was in no hurry to take her leave of him and was about to say she didn't mind stopping a while longer when her thoughts were curtailed by a flutter of wings as a bird flew out of a window. They got in the van and he started up the engine.

Cleo's hopes had soared when she heard them come back and stop right under the window. But why hadn't he come in? Why had he come all the way here and not rescued her? What the hell was going on out there? Maybe it wasn't Rocky, just someone who sounded like him. From the dark corner she could see the rat's eyes glinting at her, awaiting its opportunity. She stared at her feet, then at the window close to her head. Most of the glass had gone and she could hear them talking quite clearly. It was definitely Rocky. He was saying something about taking someone back, only it wasn't her he was taking back. It was someone else. Why was that? Rocky, please don't leave me here. Cleo knew she needed to make her presence known.

'Rocky.'

Her voice was just loud enough to scare away a scruffy pigeon that had been perching on the window ledge just above her head. She looked back at her feet and a plan formed; very much a last-ditch plan – like the time she kicked out the stairs to escape the burning bogey hole.

With her free hand she took off one of her shoes and threw it at the window; then she groaned in despair as it hit the frame and bounced back, out of her reach. The effort had exhausted her. A car door slammed and she knew she only had one chance left. Just one chance of escaping a lonely and painful death in this awful place. She took off her other shoe and took as careful an aim as she could. Her eyes were creased in concentration and her tongue stuck out from the side of her mouth. She threw the shoe with all her strength and let out a small cry of triumph as it flew through the window. Then she lay back, exhausted, and allowed fate to deal with her future as it saw fit. She could do no more. The rat darted towards her and nipped at her leg. Cleo kicked at it and sent it scurrying away, but not very far. It was obvious, even to its tiny rodent brain, that she was helpless and was growing weaker by the minute. It wouldn't be long before many other rats arrived and this one wanted to have first go at her.

'What was that?' said Rocky.

Queenie shrugged. 'What was what?'

'I thought I heard a bang on the van roof.'

'This owd jalopy meks all sorts o' noises,' Queenie said. 'I can't tell one from t' other.'

'How d'you mean, old jalopy? It's only a couple of years old.'

'It must have had a hard life,' commented Queenie. 'Anyroad I didn't hear nowt.'

Rocky sat there for a few seconds. 'Well I definitely heard something,' he said.

'Well, get out an' look. I'm not stoppin' yer.'

Maybe I'm clutching at straws, he thought. Even if there had been a noise it would hardly be Cleo banging on the roof. He put the van into gear and made a threepoint turn to go back the way they'd come. Lying on the road in front of him was a woman's shoe. Rocky stopped the van.

'Was that shoe there before?' he asked Queenie. 'I didn't see it there before.'

'That's 'cos yer'll have been parked over t' top of it before,' she pointed out.

'I don't remember parking over it.'

'Mebbe yer were too busy lookin' round ter notice.' She had a point, Rocky thought. He leaned forward and looked up at the building to his right.

'You did look in there, didn't you?' he said.

'Yer said *you'd* start in there.'

'No, I didn't,' said Rocky. His voice a mixture of exasperation and hope. 'You mean you definitely didn't look in there?'

'No, yer said *you*'d–'

'Never mind,' he interrupted. 'So, no one's looked in there?'

'Not if you haven't.'

He stared at the shoe. 'So, that could be her shoe,' he said. 'She could have thrown it out of a window. She could be up there, right now, wondering why we haven't come to get her.'

'There's only one way to find out,' said Queenie, getting out of the van.

'Right,' said Rocky, getting out himself. His heart was pounding. Please let her be in there. The two of them looked up at the array of broken windows above them.

'Cleo?' he called out. 'Are you there, Cleo?'

No answer.

They raced into the building and clattered up the stairs shouting Cleo's name. She could hear them coming and knew she was saved. The rat turned tail and ran through a hole in the wall just as other rats were arriving.

The sight of Cleo, crouching next to the radiator, delighted and horrified and angered Rocky. She was a pitiful shell of the woman he knew, respected – and loved if only he dared admit it to himself. There was blood on her calf where the rat had bitten her. He knelt beside her.

'Cleo ... are you okay?'

'That's a bit of a daft question if yer don't mind me sayin' so, mister,' observed Queenie. 'She's handcuffed to a bloody radiator, she looks like death warmed up, and she smells like an owd goat. I don't call that okay.'

'Queenie,' he said. 'Could you go to the van, please. There's a tool box in the back. I need to get this chain off.'

'Okay, mister.'

As the girl was running down the stairs Cleo mouthed to him that she needed water.

'Okay, right.' He went to the window and shouted down at Queenie when she appeared in sight. 'Where do I get water from?'

'I noticed half a bottle of Tizer in your van,' the girl called back.

'I can't give her that, it's been there a week, it'll be flat.'

'It wouldn't bother me if it were as flat as a fart – not if I were thirsty.'

'You're right. Good girl. Would you get it for me?'

When she got back it took Rocky less than a minute to batter the chain free from the radiator. He then took the bottle from Queenie and allowed Cleo a couple of sips at a time.

'Don't gulp it, take it steady.'

Cleo allowed it to drip down her throat like the elixir of life that it was. Never had Tizer tasted so good. She remembered the Tizer in Battye's Bakery just after the fire; that had tasted good, but not as good as this. After five minutes she had emptied the bottle and enough of her voice had returned for her to say, 'Thanks.'

Queenie looked at Rocky and said, almost accusingly, 'Is she your bird, mister?'

'I wish she was,' he muttered, looking away in embarrassment. 'I don't even know where my bird is.'

Cleo's eyes said she'd love to be his bird, but Rocky didn't notice. He lifted her up in his arms as though she were weightless and carried her out of the building, with Queenie following.

'I could help yer find yer bird, mister,' she said. 'Is there a reward?'

Chapter Twenty-Five

Cleo looked at the packet of Rothman's being offered to her by Flo and waved it away. 'I think I've given up,' she said, as though surprised at this herself. 'All the time I was chained up I never once fancied a cig. I fancied a drink of water and a bite to eat, but cigs never crossed my mind. Just goes to show, eh?'

'Priorities,' said Flo. 'That's what life's all about – priorities. Get them right and you get your life right. Never managed it myself.' She took out a cigarette and stuck it in a holder. 'Didn't you want to carry on working there?' she asked. 'I mean, it's not as though I don't want you back here, it's just that–'

Cleo cut her friend short. 'Too many bad memories, Flo. It was Horace going for a job there that ended up with Ant in jail. Plus, I only worked there because Ant persuaded me – and you know how persuasive he can be.'

'Not much good at persuading juries, more's the pity.'

'True,' said Cleo. 'Rocky and Jen are staying on. Apparently the new owner's a decent boss. Jen says he even feels a bit guilty about the circumstances under which he got the firm for a knock-down price.'

'Would Ant have felt guilty under the same circumstances?' Flo asked.

'Not a bit,' Cleo said. 'Nor does he feel badly done to. When I spoke to him on the phone he scarcely mentioned losing the business, apart from being glad that Rocky and Jen are staying on – which I think was his doing anyway.'

'It would have destroyed him had anything happened to you,' Flo remarked as she pulled the first pint of a new barrel through a hand pump. She then pulled a half pint, lifted it to the light then took a drink. 'Nectar,' she said, and passed it to Cleo.

Cleo took a drink and nodded her agreement. Then she looked around the empty bar that would soon be buzzing with the sound of customers' voices; laughter, earnest discussions, crude jokes – this was a friendly place with no bad memories. She gave a shudder as a very recent bad memory tried to make its way into her thoughts.

'So, if it's okay by you I'd like to come back and work here until I get my mind clear. I'm all over the place at the moment. Jumping at my own shadow.'

'As soon as you feel fit enough. There's no hurry.'

'I want to start now. The sooner I start, the sooner I'll feel normal again.'

It had been over a week since the end of her ordeal; six days of which had been spent in hospital being rehydrated and fed. The phone rang, Flo answered.

'Hello, Inspector. Yes, she's here, I'll put her on... It's Inspector Turton,' she said to Cleo. 'Fingers crossed, eh?'

Cleo took the phone. 'Hello, Inspector.'

'How are you, Cleo?'

'Better than I was this time last week, thanks to a certain young lady I haven't had the opportunity to thank properly yet ... of course. Rocky as well. That goes without saying.'

'Yes, he *seems* to be a good man,' said the Inspector. 'I mean, considering–'

'How do you mean, *considering?*' asked Cleo, sharply.

'Actually, I didn't mean anything.'

Flo glanced at her, concerned, as Cleo's voice rose. 'You meant considering he's a murderer,' she said. 'He's no more a murderer than my brother is. Most of the real murderers are still running around free.'

'I rang to say there's no news of Dobbs yet,' he said. 'Or your money for that matter.'

Cleo was still annoyed. 'It's my brother's money, Inspector.'

'Right. We think Dobbs might be in London. A woman answering her description bought a one-way ticket to King's Cross just after the money was paid over. Apparently she was a bit rude to the ticket clerk and stuck out like a sore thumb – which could be to our advantage. A woman like her, with that amount of money burning a hole in her pocket is bound to come unstuck before much longer.'

'Let's hope she hasn't spent it all, then,' Cleo said.

'Er, yes.'

'Presumably you'll ring me when you've got something useful to tell me.'

'I er, yes, of course.'

'Thank you, goodbye, Inspector.' She put the phone down and caught Flo staring at her. 'What?' she said.

Flo shrugged. 'You seemed a little sharp with him, that's all.'

'Was I really? Well, he was a bit patronising about Rocky – said he's a good man *considering.* Considering what Rocky's been through at the hands of the law I'd say Inspector Turton's got a bloody cheek! I suppose he think's Ant's a good man, *considering.*'

'He won't have meant anything by it, Cleo.'

'Maybe not. But the law hasn't done me too many favours in the past.'

'I used to be part of the law,' Flo pointed out. 'Does that include me?'

Cleo burst into tears and hurried out of the bar. Flo left her to it. In a minute she'd go through and give her young friend a shoulder to cry on. An ordeal such as Cleo had been through wasn't something you got over in a hurry. A good old weep would do no harm at all.

Detective Inspector Turton put down the phone and sighed. There was something about that young woman that made him want to help her. She certainly hadn't been at the back of the queue when looks were handed out, maybe that was it. He shook his head. No, there was more to it than that. He had unconsciously doodled the name Nelly Kelly on a note pad as he'd been talking to her. Her name had cropped up in conversation while they'd all been waiting for the kidnapper to ring. Flo had asked if he'd ever heard of her and told of how she could be invaluable in any appeal for a reduction in Ant's sentence. He'd later checked with records; they identified Cleo's mother as a somewhat pathetic prostitute who had last appeared before Leeds magistrates over four years ago. This wasn't the sort of information he wanted to share with Cleo – not in her present state of mind. Besides, he needed to find out something a little more concrete – like whether or not Nelly Kelly was still alive.

'Check with Bradford,' the sergeant in the criminal records section had suggested. 'It's a booming business over there. Even Nelly might be able to pick up trade in Bradford.'

Turton was still a little upset by Cleo's sharp tongue when he dialled Bradford Police and asked for the extension he'd been given.

'WPC Elliot,' said a voice.

'Are you the Criminal Records section?' he asked, wishing people would be a bit more informative when they answered the phone.

'Yes.'

'Then why didn't you say so when you answered the phone? That's the way things are done in Leeds.'

'Who am I speaking to?' enquired the WPC.

'You are speaking to Detective Inspector Turton of Leeds CID. I'm enquiring about a–'

'Could you tell me how you spell that, please?'

'Which bit do you want me to spell?'

'Turton, there's various ways of spelling it.'

'Is there really? Well you learn something every day. My name's spelt T for Tommy, U for euphonium...'

'We don't spell euphonium with a U in Bradford, Inspector – in Bradford we spell it with an E.'

'And you're beginning to get right up my nose, Constable. Can you forgo the bloody spelling Bee and deal with my enquiry?'

There was a long silence, then, 'Could you tell me the nature of your enquiry, Inspector?'

'I want you to check through your records to see if you have anything recent for a prostitute called Nelly Kelly. Would you like me to spell it for you?'

'That won't be necessary, Inspector. Would Nelly be her proper name or is it a diminutive?'

Turton took a deep breath, which was something the WPC wouldn't have been able to do if her throat had been within reach of his hands. 'I'm ashamed to say I don't bloody know, Constable. We know her in Leeds as Nelly.'

'She could be Ellen, Helen or Eleanor, Inspector. Unlike Leeds, our records in Bradford are very precise.'

'Well bully for bloody Bradford, Constable. Could you start with Nelly, then go through your own list of alternatives?'

'Can I ring you back, Inspector? It'll take a few minutes.'

Half an hour later the inspector learned that Ellen Womack, alias Nelly Kelly, had last been arrested three months ago for soliciting and fined fifteen pounds. He was also given chapter and verse of every incident involving Nelly over the past three years. She'd been a regular visitor at court and had fine arrears of over a £100, but was too pathetic a character to send to jail. She had no fixed abode but the WPC assured Inspector Turton that they'd soon be able to track her down if he needed any help in that direction from Bradford Police.

He grudgingly thanked her and put the phone down, wondering just how much weight Nelly's evidence would carry in a Court of Appeal. It wasn't part of his job to pursue the matter, but as an officer of the law he had a duty to see justice served. At least that's what he told himself.

Cleo was drying her eyes when Flo went through to the living room.

'Do you think I should ring Inspector Turton and apologise? I *was* a bit rude to him.'

'No,' said Flo. 'He's a copper. You're allowed to be rude to coppers, if you can get away with it.'

Cleo wiped away a belated tear. 'I burst into tears at the drop of a hat. Never used to be like that.'

'You've been through a lot.'

'I've been through a lot before, but it never had this effect on me. I hope I'm not going bonkers.'

'Cleo, seven days ago you'd resigned yourself to dying. Most people would take months to recover from that. All you seem to need is a good cry to get it out of your system. As a matter of fact you're very much like me in that respect.'

'Why, has something like this happened to you?'

'Oh, many things have happened to me, Cleo. Mostly stuff I'd like to forget.'

'Is that why you don't talk about your past much?'

'You know more about my past than anybody.'

'One day I'll drag it all out of you,' Cleo said. 'All your dark secrets.'

There was a tap on the door and Rocky poked his head round, bringing an immediate smile to Cleo's face.

'I've bought her a bike,' he said.

'Bought who a bike?'

'Queenie.'

'It's me who should be buying her a bike,' Cleo said. 'It's my life she saved.'

'I think Rocky had a bit of a hand in it as well,' Flo pointed out. 'If it hadn't been for Rocky...'

'I know,' Cleo interrupted.

Rocky grinned. 'You could buy me a bike,' he said.

Cleo wanted to fling her arms around him and hug him to her but it wouldn't be fair on him. He was still engaged to the lovely but long-lost Jasmine.

'Any sign of Jasmine?' she asked, watching for his reaction. She had reminded him of his lost love, so his expression should, presumably, now change to one of sadness and longing. It didn't.

'Haven't looked to be honest,' he said. 'I've been too busy.'

'Too busy getting your priorities right,' said Flo.

'That's right,' agreed Rocky. 'I hope she's okay though.'

'I'm sure she will be,' Cleo assured him. Her

eyes searched his face to gauge the sense of loss he should be feeling – which was not much, as far as she could tell.

'Now that *you're* all right,' he said, 'I'll take up where I left off. What do you think about me hiring a private detective?'

Flo felt like shaking some sense into him. Cleo just smiled and said, 'Not a lot – the one I got to look for my mother wasn't much cop. He knew how to charge, but not much else.'

'In the meantime,' suggested Flo. 'I think you should both take that bike to young Queenie. Make a day of it. Make a night of it, if you like. The girl deserves a treat.'

She pointedly didn't say which girl.

Queenie was sitting on the fence and Agnes was in the ford, blocking the road, when Cleo and Rocky drove up. The girl jumped down as soon as she recognised them and shooed the ancient animal clear of the stream.

'Oh, we qualify for free passes now do we?' called out Cleo.

Queenie gave a grin that contained very little embarrassment. 'I've had a right bad morning,' she said. 'I should charge yer by rights, but seein' as it's you...'

Without further ado Cleo got out, walked across to the girl and gave her a bear hug that had her gasping for breath. No one had ever hugged her with such a passion before. Queenie looked across at Rocky and wished he would hug her.

'I never thanked you for saving my life,' Cleo said.

'Did I do that?'
'You most certainly did, young lady. You and my friend Rocky here.'
'Flippin' 'eck! I never saved no one's life before. Is there a reward?'
'Well, I wouldn't call it a reward,' smiled Cleo, watching Rocky struggle to get the bike out of the back of the car. 'It's more a token of gratitude.'
Queenie's eyes widened as Rocky wheeled the bicycle towards her. He'd suggested a boy's bike on the grounds that he didn't think Queenie spent enough time in a skirt to warrant a girl's crossbarless machine – and anyway she wasn't the girly type.
'Is that mine, mister?'
'All yours, Queenie. Best in the shop. Fifteen gears, racing saddle, alloy wheels, the lot.'
'How much did it cost, mister?'
'Enough.'
Queenie sat astride it and clicked the lever through the gears; then she looked up at Rocky. 'I'll never be allowed ter keep nowt as nice as this,' she said. 'Me dad'll mek me sell it. He gave me a right bollockin' when t' bobby came round ter find out what 'ad 'appened. I told me dad I'd been ter school.'
'Maybe we should have a word with your dad.'
'He's not in, missis. He's doin' his rounds. He's a rag and bone man.'
'Didn't the policeman tell him how you'd saved my life?' Cleo asked.
'Not really, missis. I've been in bother wi' that bobby before. He's a right miserable owd trout. Me dad gave me a good 'idin' an' sent me ter

bed early.'

Memories of Horace came to Cleo's mind and, just for a second, she hated the girl's dad. Rocky saw it in her eyes. 'He'll be worried about you not going to school,' he said to Queenie. 'I know I would be, if I were your dad.'

Queenie's face split into a broad grin. 'Give over – yer not old enough ter be me dad. Me dad's as old as the flippin' hills. He's goin' bald is me dad.'

'We'll make sure he knows what you did,' said Rocky. 'I bet he'll be dead proud when he finds out what really happened. You might even get an award.'

The girl thought he'd said 'reward' and her eyes lit up. Rocky spotted this. 'I er, I said a-ward not re-ward,' he said, quickly.

'Award? What's an award?'

'It's a sort of a certificate,' explained Rocky. 'A Good Citizen Award.' He had no idea if there was such a thing, nor did Cleo, who gave him a funny look. 'Anyway,' this bike's yours to keep – but tell your dad we've only lent it to you so you can ride to school and back. If it's only lent he can't make you sell it.'

Queenie laughed out loud. 'You don't know me dad, mister. When me mam died he sold our house to a bloke in t' pub. When t' council found out they went mad.'

'Tell him to give us a ring about the bike, we'll make it okay,' said Rocky.

This seemed to satisfy Queenie. 'I've never had a cerstificate. Neither has me dad come ter think of it. He'll have ter let me keep me bike if I've gorra cerstificate – and he'll not be allowed ter clatter me so much.'

'I don't suppose he will,' said Cleo. 'Does your dad clatter you a lot?'

Queenie grinned and shook her head. 'Give him his dues he tries his best, but to be honest he's not much cop. It's like bein' hit wi' a powder puff. Me mam used ter be good at clatterin' – till she died last year.'

'Oh,' said Cleo. 'I'm sorry.'

'So am I,' said Queenie.

The girl didn't elaborate on her mother's death but her eyes were moist as she wheeled the bicycle away. After a few yards she stopped and looked back at them. 'Hey, mister, did yer find yer bird?'

'Er ... no, not yet.'

She looked at Cleo, then back at Rocky. 'Well, I'd help yer, but I don't think yer can see t' wood for t' trees, mister.'

They watched her mount the bike and wobble off, with Agnes demonstrating surprising agility, trotting along in her wake.

'What do you think she meant by that?' Rocky said.

Cleo chose not to enlighten him. That was something he'd have to work out for himself. But it would do no harm to push things along a bit.

'Flo suggested we make a night of it,' she said. 'How about stopping off at a pub for a drink and a bite to eat?'

'Suits me.'

As he ordered the drinks she slipped into the

Ladies to freshen up and add a dash of Chanel Number Five to her armoury. She looked at herself in the mirror and smiled as she remembered Flo's advice. 'There isn't man alive who doesn't fall prey to a dash of decent scent now and again.'

She gave her reflection a reproving frown. Was she actually trying to seduce Rocky? Or was she just trying to make him aware that she was a woman, and not just a friend or a former boss or Ant's sister or whatever? Her mind went back to John Dunderdale and the way she had felt about him that night. How, during that car ride under the stars, she had so desperately wanted him to take from her what she'd refused to surrender to Seamus Jaques. Was her virginity up for grabs again – this time with Rocky? There was an artlessness about him that she found so endearing. Artless to the point of plain daft at times, especially where the lovely Jasmine was concerned. But that was Rocky. Loyal even where it wasn't deserved. He'd been loyal to her. Jeopardised his own liberty for her – according to Flo.

'He thinks a lot about you, Cleo,' she'd said. 'Put his neck right on the line. Would've got locked up had it not been for Ant having a word in Collins's shell-like.'

She owed Rocky her life. Queenie had played her part but it was Rocky who had come for her. Not for the first time either. Memories of Pascoe attacking her and Flo came to mind – and the story she'd heard of Rocky holding Pascoe out over the quarry edge when he thought he was the kidnapper – and Pascoe peeing his pants.

He was sitting at a table when she went through to the lounge bar, smiling his genuine smile and getting to his feet to hold her chair for her. Ever the gentleman.

'Apart from being as daft as a brush do you have any faults?' she asked him, playfully.

He thought for a few seconds then said, 'I'm still a virgin.'

Cleo cringed with embarrassment, and hoped no one else had heard. 'That's not exactly what I meant.' She spoke in a low voice. 'But I must say, you do surprise me. A good-looking man like you.'

The news did in fact please her no end.

'Louis Gardner told me not to,' Rocky explained. 'He said it would affect my performance in the ring. Then I got locked up.'

'Didn't, er ... didn't Jasmine mind?'

'She said she could manage without, if it helped my career.'

'How considerate of her. One in a million, that Jasmine.'

Rocky looked at her with sad eyes. 'Looking back, I don't suppose she *did* go without, though,' he said, 'and to be honest it doesn't bother me.'

'Oh?'

'Cleo, I've been doing a lot of thinking.'

'What about?'

'Well, about me I suppose. What I need and what I don't need. And I'm not going to look for her any more. I've realised it's all been a waste of time – I don't need her.' His eyes were anywhere but on Cleo.

'Good,' she said. 'Any particular reason?'

'Well, there is actually. But I'm not sure you're going to like it. In fact I'm not sure how to tell you. It's very embarrassing but I can't keep it to myself forever.'

'Oh dear. I don't like the sound of this,' Cleo said. 'What is it?'

He looked away, unable to find the right words. Words to fit so important an announcement – an announcement he wasn't sure she'd like. *Oh no!* she suddenly thought. *Too right I won't like it – if it's what I think it is.* The contents of her stomach turned to lead. Just like John Dunderdale, he was too good to be true. Rocky had discovered he was homosexual. She knew this to be an absolute certainty even before he opened his mouth to tell her. Perhaps she should save him any embarrassment and tell him she already knew and that she understood and was happy for him.

Would she be honour-bound to introduce him to the gorgeous John? It would be a fitting reward for him saving her life. Cleo conjured up a mental image of the two of them together, hand in hand – and her heart sank. She placed her hand on top of his.

'Rocky,' she said. 'There's nothing in the world you can tell me that will upset me.' Her other hand was behind her back, fingers firmly crossed. 'I owe you my life.'

He took her hand and held it in his. There was such strength in that hand, strength she needed. Then he looked at her as though he needed to tell her his news with his eyes, his mouth and his heart. Cleo closed her own eyes – her heart was already in her mouth. *Oh God! Here it comes.*

'I'm not going to look for Jasmine,' he said, in a low controlled voice, '...because I love you.'

Her eyes were still closed as the words penetrated her senses. She opened them and said, 'What?'

'I love you,' he repeated. 'There's no point me pretending I don't, because I do.'

The heavy weight in her stomach evaporated. 'So, you're not homosexual?' She blurted it out without thinking.

'Eh?'

'Sorry – you took me by surprise. You've got me talking gibberish.'

'Right,' he said, not understanding. 'Anyway I've got it off my chest, so er ... so now you know ... how I feel about you, that is ... as opposed to Jasmine, who I don't feel anything for. Never have, now I come to think of it. When you were kidnapped it really shook me. I was scared that I'd never see you again. I never felt that way about Jasmine, just a bit concerned, that's all. You know, hoping she's–'

Cleo was glad he was waffling, it gave her time to think. She had never dared admit to herself that she actually loved him; that would have been just another painful burden for her to bear. One-sided love, the worst kind. But now he'd opened his heart to her – and she knew it was right. He had already proved he loved her *enough.* It took her just a few seconds to examine her own feelings and come up with a result. She interrupted him.

'I love you as well, Rocky.'

His eyes lit up. 'Honestly?'

'Honestly and truly,' she assured him. 'And not just because you saved my life. I love you because you're a big, daft, lovely lump of a man. Come over here and kiss me.'

He leaned across the table and did as she ordered, then whispered in her ear. 'What do we do now, boss?'

'I'm not your boss any more. What would you like to do?'

'I'd like to get to know you a lot better.'

'Sounds like a good idea. Your place or mine?'

'Mine,' said Rocky.

'I was hoping you'd say that. I don't want Flo listening at the wall with a glass to her ear. Shall we go now?'

'Maybe we should finish our drinks first,' suggested Rocky.

'Yes,' she said. 'We'll take things steady. One step at a time.'

'But I'd really like to make love to you tonight.'

'Right ... we'll make that our first step then, shall we?'

Any watching voyeur would never have taken them for a pair of novices. Each step was a little more exciting than the last. Starting with Cleo's nervous giggling as Rocky carried her up his narrow staircase; then the holding of hands and kissing; then the gentle, almost polite touching and unbuttoning, which grew feverish as each glimpse of naked flesh aroused more passion, until neither could contain themselves any longer. Cleo was first to get naked and Rocky had never seen such beauty. He pushed her away, stripped off what was left of his clothes, then threw her on to the bed, where she lay, marvelling at his boxer's body as it arched over her, before becoming part of her. Soon he had her screaming with the ecstasy and the agony of her first time and Rocky was expressing concern for her pain, but not enough concern for him to stop.

'I'm okay,' she gasped. 'Just don't stop.'

Rocky did stop, but not before they had both exploded with intense pleasure that had them dripping with sweat and gasping for breath.

They lay side by side, looking upwards and saying nothing for several minutes. Then, as Rocky watched a fly making its way across the ceiling, he said, 'Cleo ... I got the impression it was your first time as well.'

'Correct.'

'You should have said. I'd have been ... more gentle.'

'I didn't want you to be more gentle.'

He turned towards her and propped himself up on one elbow. 'I thought we did very well for a couple of virgins,' he said.

'It was everything I hoped it would be,' murmured Cleo, who had just regained control of her breathing. 'And more. What's that?'

She touched a scar that ran across from his left shoulder down towards his chest.

'I got it in prison. That, and one or two other bumps and bruises. Somebody wanted me to be his girlfriend and I turned him down.'

'It must have been awful – did you get a lot of it?'

'Not once he got the message that I was prepared to look after myself. Besides, I threatened to tell his wife.'

'He was married? But why would–?'

'It's not a sex thing with blokes like that,' Rocky explained. 'It's more to do with humiliation and domination.'

An awful thought struck Cleo. 'What about Ant? Was he ever...?'

Rocky smiled. 'Someone tried it on, but I helped him out. Then he made friends with some very ... what you might call influential characters. They see he comes to no harm.'

'I do hope so.'

'I'm glad my first time was with you and not with Jasmine,' he said. 'I don't think she'd have appreciated my efforts as much as you did.'

Cleo remembered Jasmine's carnal occupation and silently agreed with him but she said nothing because she didn't want Jasmine to interfere with the moment. So why was she suddenly thinking of Nelly?

'The next thing on the agenda is to track down my mother,' she said.

'What?'

Rocky was amazed by this sudden change of tack.

'We need to find Nelly,' she said. 'It's all right us having fun, but we should be getting Ant out of that awful place and we won't unless we find my mother.' Then she looked into his eyes and her thoughts switched back to her more immediate needs. Hooking her arm around his neck, she pulled him to her.

'But in the meantime,' she said, 'I'd like to get on with loving you. You're the one good thing that's come out of Ant going to jail. I must remember to tell him that the next time I see him, which will be the day after tomorrow, now I come to think of–'

'Cleo.'

He stopped her talking with a finger to her lips. While her capricious thoughts were momentarily on him, Rocky had decided to seize the moment. With Cleo, such moments came and went like horses on a whirling carousel. You had to get your timing right then jump on board.

'Will you marry me?'

Her neck jerked back as though he'd delivered a right hook. Her eyes widened for a split second, then she kissed him with even more passion than she had at the height of their lovemaking.

'Yes, Rocky,' she said, when they both came up for air. 'I'd love to marry you.'

Chapter Twenty-Six

A car slowed down. The driver took one look at Nelly and drove on. Situation normal. Nelly looked at her watch to compare the time with St Matthew's church clock which was striking eleven. She took another swig of gin from the bottle in her pocket, lit a cigarette and cursed her luck. It began to drizzle so she sheltered in a shop doorway. There was only her and Lorna Bullock left on the street and Lorna had had at least three punters already that night, which was three more than Nelly. All the other girls in the street had done good business. Most of them were half her age or less. Nelly only appealed to men with poor eyesight and even poorer taste. There had been a time when she was considered attractive but that was before she'd had babies. Rarely a day went by when she didn't curse her children. They had been the root of all her problems. The only decent thing her son had ever done was to top that bastard Horace Womack. She wasn't in the least bit surprised when she heard, after all the stuff Horace had done to him when he was a lad. Womack didn't know she knew, although Ant did. He'd once asked her to get Womack to stop it, but what could she have done? Nothing, that's what she could have done.

So her lad had grown up and done for Horace himself. What goes around comes around. As soon as she heard she'd gone out and got blind drunk – again. If anyone deserved to die it was Horace Womack.

When he found out she was pregnant with his child Womack had gone berserk and accused her of sleeping with other men. He had punched her to the floor and kicked her in her stomach, leaving her squirming in agony as he went off to the pub. It was left to a neighbour to call an ambulance. Nelly would have died if she hadn't made it to the door and collapsed in the street – ending up losing both her womb, her unborn child and her lousy husband in the one evening. She didn't complain to the police; at least he'd done her one last favour before he left, removing any chance of her becoming pregnant again. Thank God.

She read about Cleo in the papers – getting herself kidnapped and losing all her money. Silly little bitch. If Nelly had known her daughter had a bob or two it might have been worth getting in touch. It had even crossed her mind that her putting a bad word in about Womack might not do the lad any harm. Something like that might be worth a few bob. Not now though. Nothing was worth anything now. Another car stopped, another shake of the head from the driver who drove on a few yards and stopped beside Lorna who leaned through the car window with her skirt hitched up so high Nelly that could see she was wearing no pants.

'Get yer arse covered up,' she shouted. 'Have some bleedin' standards.'

'I'm just savin' time,' Lorna retorted, before

climbing into the car.

Nelly's depression took another downward lurch. A train whistled in the distance; soon it would be passing under Gulstead Bridge, enveloping the whole area in steam for a few seconds. She'd once picked up a punter under cover of the steam. He'd paid as well, although the look on his face when he got a clear look at her was a sight to behold. She was forty-five but she hadn't aged well. Her skin had the texture of dried orange peel, and nicotine had yellowed what teeth she had left. People used to say of her legs that she'd 'spun up with a sparrow and lost' so she wore trousers – and a headscarf to disguise her thinning hair. All in all she was in the wrong job. But what else was there? The train whistled once more and steam appeared over the tops of distant houses. In twenty minutes there'd be a train coming the other way. There was a story on the street of how one of the girls had given up on life and had laid her head across the railway line to wait for the London to Leeds express to come and solve all her problems for her. Sadly, the Leeds to London express arrived first and chopped her legs off, which everyone agreed was typical of the luck of the street girls.

Three miles away Gordon Tattersall said 'See you later' to his mother and climbed into his Austin A35 van. The previous night he'd been belittled by a prostitute who had laughed at his pathetic attempts at having sex with her. And she wasn't the first.

He was clumsy and unco-ordinated, but that

didn't stop him having all the needs that other men had. From time to time he'd exposed himself to ladies; once in Woolworths, which had resulted in him being arrested and fined thirty-five pounds for indecent exposure. At work he was the object of fun. Even fifteen-year-old lads, fresh out of school took the piss out of him. Flash Gordon, they called him, among other things. He was thirty-seven and had never had a sexual relationship with anything other than his right hand. Saying 'see you later' to his mother had been a bit optimistic, unless he meant in the after-life. He'd left her lying on the kitchen floor in a pool of blood. It had taken just one blow from the hammer he'd been using to bang a nail into the wall. In his usual clumsy way he'd bent the nail double and made a mess of the plaster when pulling it out. After the day he'd had at work it was the last straw when his mother said, 'Yer big fat-arsed useless pillock, look what yer've done ter me wall!'

Gordon had sat and looked at her corpse as he drank the bottle of sherry she kept in the kitchen cupboard. It was the first drink he'd ever had of his mam's sherry; even at Christmas she kept it for herself. He wasn't used to drink and three-quarters of a bottle of QC Cream took away any remorse he might have felt. If anything he felt an enormous sense of release – as though he'd been freed from a lifetime of coming off second best.

Nelly was sitting on the parapet wall of the Gulstead Bridge finishing off the gin when Gordon drove up. The drizzle had soaked into her clothes but she didn't care, it wouldn't matter where she was headed. She threw the empty bottle down on the railway line and didn't respond when he called out to her:

'Escuse me, missis, are you a prossitute?'

His speech wasn't clear at the best of times but the sherry made it worse. Gordon got out of his van and walked up to her, but she was miles away, in a world of suicide and all the problems it would solve. He awoke her from her drunken reverie by laying a heavy hand on her shoulder. She jumped and almost lost her balance. He helped her off the wall and said, 'Sorry.'

'I should bloody think so.' Her speech was slurred as well. 'I were nearly over then.'

'Yer shouldn't be sittin' on 'ere.'

'Who says so?'

'Well, iss dangerous. A train might come an' then where would yer be?'

'Underneath it, with any luck. At least that were me plan till you showed up. What yer after – a shag or summat?' She peered at him through the gloom. 'It's you, innit – that flasher bloke what couldn't gerrit up wi' Lorna last night.'

Gordon reddened in the darkness and he made up his mind to kill Nelly – and Lorna as well if he could find her. His muscles were tensing as the adrenaline rushed into them to provide the strength for him to commit the crime.

'Do yer still do it?' she asked, curiously.

'Do what?' The adrenaline subsided a little as her question took him by surprise.

'Yer know, flash it about?'

'Now and again,' he admitted.

'Why do yer do it?'

He shrugged. 'Why's anybody do owt? I jus' like showin' me dick ter women. Would you like ter see it?'

'No thanks.'

'I was gonna give it up at Christmas,' he said. 'Then I thought I'd stick it out for a bit longer.'

Nelly screeched with laughter but Gordon didn't see the funny side. He grabbed her by the throat but she grabbed a handful of his reproductive organs and squeezed until he let her go.

'Let me do it my way, please!' she said, when she saw that the pain had gone from his groin.

'How d'yer mean, your way?'

She looked down at the train track. 'I'm waitin' for a train,' she said. 'Then I'm gonna jump off.'

'Oh,' said Gordon. 'I see, sorry. It's jus' that I killed me mam earlier on and I'm in that sort of mood.'

'Summat like that would get you in the mood,' Nelly agreed. 'What did she do?'

'She took t' piss outa me, so I clattered her wi' an 'ammer. Everyone teks t' piss outa me.'

'I get a lot of that,' she sympathised.

'We mus' be a couple o' pisspots, then,' said Gordon.

'Mus' be,' said Nelly. 'Tell yer what, why don't yer join me? We'll go together. I fancy a bit o' company.'

Gordon looked down at the track and then at Nelly. 'Will it hurt?' he asked.

'I don't s'pose we'll know much about it. I s'pect it's better than bein' hanged.'

'I thought they didn't hang people any more.'

'They do if yer kill yer mam,' Nelly assured him.

Gordon's body slumped and he began to cry copious tears. 'I don't want 'em to 'ang me.'

Nelly climbed back on to the wall and patted a coping stone beside her. 'Come on. It'll all be over before yer know it.'

Sobbing, he climbed up and sat next to her. An approaching train sounded its whistle like a death knell and she took his hand.

'What's yer name?' she asked him.

'Gordon,' he blubbed.

'My name's Nelly.'

'Hello Nelly.'

The train came into sight and thundered towards them.

'It'll not be long now,' said Nelly.

'No, I don't s'pose it will.'

'Tara, Gordon.'

'Tara, Nelly.'

At the very last second Nelly lost her nerve. Luckily for her, Gordon held his and pushed her off the bridge. When the steam cleared he was sitting on his own, still sobbing, with a police car pulling up beside him.

WPC Elliot rang Inspector Turton with the news as soon as she heard.

'Ellen Womack, or Nelly Kelly as she's more commonly known, has just been found dead, Inspector.'

'Oh heck!'

'She was found on a railway line late last night, Inspector. We have a man in custody who insists she committed suicide.'

'Really, why is he in custody?'

'He killed his mother earlier in the evening.'

'You lead very full lives, you Bradford lot.'

'We do our best. Is there anything else you need to know, Inspector?'

'No, I think you've told me enough to get my day off to a bad start. But thank you for letting me know so promptly – you're obviously a very efficient officer.'

'Thank you, Inspector.'

He left it until the afternoon before he broke the news to Cleo. She took it badly, as he might have expected.

'She was our only hope of getting Ant's sentence reduced – now he's going to be locked up for life for killing a monster who molested him when he was a child. Where the hell's the justice in that, Inspector?'

'There isn't any justice in it, Cleo.' His sympathy was genuine. 'To be honest I'd more or less tracked your mother down. I'd planned on going over to Bradford to have a word with her. But events have overtaken me, I'm afraid.'

'Was it your job to do all this?' Flo asked him, worried that Cleo might demolish him with one of her outbursts.

'Not really. I just get a bee in my bonnet sometimes.'

'So, we should be thanking you, really.'

'I didn't come here for that,' he said, quickly, noting the resentment in Cleo's eyes. 'And if there's anything at all I can do to help, I will.'

'Thank you, Inspector,' said Flo.

He left, not having fulfilled the second reason for his visit, which had been to tell Cleo that Dobbs had been picked up in London – minus the money. She was being brought back to Leeds for questioning and if anyone could persuade her to give up the ransom money it was Walter Turton; so maybe he might have better news when he went back to see Cleo. Twenty-five thousand quid should get him in her good books, surely.

Ant's smile was genuine for a change when he saw Cleo waiting for him in the visitors' room. Mostly he put on a brave face for visitors, but he never fooled Cleo. She knew all there was to know about putting on faces. He embraced her for longer than was respectable for a brother and sister.

'Put me down,' she whispered. 'You'll set tongues wagging.'

'Oops! Sorry. Just glad to see you, that's all.' Without letting the smile drop from his face he added, 'By the way, I know about Nelly. The governor told me yesterday.'

She searched his face. 'What do you think?'

'I think good riddance to bad rubbish.'

'Ant, she was the best hope you had of getting your sentence reduced.'

They sat down as he considered his answer. 'Cleo,' he said. 'Even if she *had* come forward, who'd have taken any notice of her?'

'Maybe you're right, but it would have been worth a try.' She studied the ends of her fingers, and for a fleeting second, wondered how long it would take for her broken nails to grow back to normal; for her to regain her sense of well-being – whatever that was. 'Ant, did you feel anything when you heard she was dead? Any sense of loss?'

He looked straight at her and slowly shook his head. 'None at all.'

'Neither did I,' said Cleo. 'Isn't that awful? Our own mother.'

'Mother? She was never a mother to us, Cleo.'

She nodded, then her face brightened. 'Hey! Rocky asked me to marry him ... and I said yes.'

Ant roared with delight and leaned over to kiss her. People at adjoining tables smiled at his raucous laughter, although they had no idea what he was laughing at.

'Cleo, that's bloody marvellous news!'

'I think so,' she smiled. 'He's such a lovely bloke. It was him who saved my life.'

'Well, I'd say he's been well rewarded.' Ant's face was full of joy for his sister. 'And I'll tell you what – if I hadn't been in here, you'd never have met him. So maybe there's a reason for me being here after all.'

Cleo didn't agree but it seemed curmudgeonly to spoil his moment, so she just smiled at him. 'But we're not getting married until you're out of here.'

Ant's face dropped and Cleo wondered why she'd just said it. She and Rocky had made no such arrangement. It just seemed the right thing to say. To delay her time of great happiness until she could share it with Ant.

'Cleo, don't talk so soft. I'll be in here for another ten years at least. *I've* accepted it. Why can't you?'

'Because it's not right and you know it. Jen's waiting for you, you know. It's not fair on her.'

'I didn't know, actually. There's nothing official between me and Jen.'

'There is as far as she's concerned.'

'Really?'

His expression told her this was good news. She'd convey this to Jen, who devoured all tit-bits of hope.

'Inspector Turton thinks it's not right you being in here and he's doing all he can to help.'

'He's a good bloke,' Ant said. 'What does Rocky say about waiting till I get out?'

'Rocky will agree with me.'

'You mean he doesn't know yet.'

'Maybe not, but he'll agree with me. It'll give us something to work towards.'

'Well, I think you're being daft, Cleo. Grab your happiness while you can. You never know what's around the corner.'

His sister pulled a face, one he hadn't seen for a long time. It made him smile.

'I'll tell you what's around the corner, Ant Kelly,' she said. 'Your freedom – that's what's just around the corner. You shouldn't be in here and the sooner more people know that the better.'

'Cleo, don't go round telling everyone what Womack did to me. I tried for years to put it right out of my mind.'

'Fat lot of good it did you.'

'I'd prefer it if you didn't make a big thing of it.'

'Ant, I'd read it out on the nine o'clock news if I thought it'd do any good. People knowing can't be worse than you being in here – or can it?'

'I just think it's a waste of time that's all – but I'm really pleased about you and Rocky.' His mouth twitched into a smile, which broadened until it split his whole face in one big, amused beam.

'What?' said Cleo, suspiciously.

'Cleopatra Diggle!' He was laughing now. 'That's a name to conjure with.'

Cleo winced. 'I know – do you think I dare ask him to change it?'

Chapter Twenty-Seven

Ant lay on his bunk, crying. His cellmate was off playing ping-pong but Ant had decided to dedicate the whole of the recreation hour to self-pity. Flush it out of his system – something he did periodically. Weeping was good for the soul. Today was Monday. No use ticking it off a calendar, there were just too many Mondays ahead of him – hundreds of the buggers. All there, one behind the other, taunting him, never ending, disappearing into the distance like in a hall of mirrors. And he could see his reflection in each one, in his cell, lost and miserable. Of course where there was a Monday there was a Tuesday, but Tuesdays were no better, nor were Wednesdays or any other days. He knew, now that his mother was dead, that he had no hope of getting out on appeal. Despite his protests to the contrary, he'd always held out some hope in the back of his mind that Cleo would come through for him. But if freedom was just around the corner as Cleo said, then that corner was a long, long way away.

He thought of Jen and how she'd soon tire of waiting for him. And why should she wait? He hadn't given her much encouragement when he was on the outside so it was a bit much for him to suddenly declare his undying love for her now that he was banged up, and expect her to be faithful to him. But the very thought of her with another man tore his insides apart. *Doing it with another man.* More tears, more pain, more self-pity.

A coloured kid on the top landing had hanged himself the day before yesterday. He was in for assaulting his fiancée's lover with a pickaxe handle, only she wasn't his fiancée any more, she had married the lover – and the coloured kid had tried to spoil their wedding day by topping himself. But rumour had it that the newlyweds would have been on a plane to Majorca as he kicked away the slop bucket and choked himself to death on a noose made up of socks he'd nicked from the laundry. The happy couple wouldn't know about his death till they got back – so it was all a bit of a waste of the grand gesture really. Bad timing. He'd have been better off doing it the day before the wedding. That's what life's all about, timing. Death as well for that matter.

Would Jen care if he topped himself? Ant thought. Don't be so stupid, Ant Kelly – something like that would destroy Cleo. He remembered how he'd felt when that cow of a woman had kidnapped her. How helpless and useless he'd felt ... and desolate.

With a bit of luck he'd only be thirty-four when he got out – still a relatively young man. That's the way to look at it. Next time Cleo came he'd tell her he wasn't interested in Jen, not in *that* way – and for her to pass the message on and tell Jen not to visit him any more and to find herself another feller. Or was he being just too noble for his own good? Maybe.

Jen's frequent visits were the ones he enjoyed most, with no disrespect to Cleo or to Rocky. So he'd leave it a while before he gave Jen the hard word. Leave it until he was good and ready. God, he wouldn't mind her being here with him right now; lying beside him, kissing him, both of them stark nak–

Ant dried his tears on the bed sheet, felt guilty about the lump in his trousers and went downstairs for a game of table tennis. One way of releasing his frustrations.

Monday night was darts and dominoes night at the Bird in the Hand and the tap room was full. Through in the lounge bar Flo had installed a juke box which was blasting out Beatles music and, in the process, attracting a whole new clientele. All in all the place was doing well. It was three weeks since the end of Cleo's ordeal; the smile had returned to her face but she still flared up occasionally and had difficulty gathering her thoughts at times. Rocky had gone along with her suggestion to leave getting married until after Ant had been released. To him, and perhaps to him alone, it didn't seem such an unfeasible idea. His faith in Cleo was matched only by his love for her.

'Nineteen, double sixteen,' called out Flo, the team captain, as Rocky struggled with his mental arithmetic. He was by no means the star player in the team but he had his moments, and he hoped this might be one of them. His first dart hit the wire and bounced on to the floor to accompanying moans from the rest of the Bird team.

'Quiet,' shouted Flo to the rowdy members of

the Angel team. 'Let's have a bit of hush.'

The room went quiet, such was Flo's authority. Rocky's second dart flopped into the nineteen just below the treble ring and clung there, tenuously.

'If it falls out it dunt count,' warned one of the Angels.

'Just shut up,' growled Flo. 'I'll say what counts and what doesn't, it's my pub.'

Rocky picked up his pint and took a sip. Cleo gave him an encouraging wink. One dart to win the match, which would put the Bird through to the finals in Wakefield – a big night.

'Double sixteen,' Flo reminded him.

'No coachin' from the touchline,' called out an Angel wag.

'He'll never hit double sixteen while he's got an 'ole in 'is arse,' observed another.

'Will you shut your bloody cakeholes!' roared Flo. 'Now, come on Rocky. Double sixteen to shut this lot up.'

Rocky knew that if he missed, the Angel's captain and star player was following him to the board with just a double twenty to get – and he hadn't missed double top all night.

Rocky threw his remaining dart with some force, it glanced against the wire and lodged in double sixteen to the delight of the Bird team, but in the process it dislodged his previous dart which fell to the floor, only to be snatched from the air by Flo. She then pulled out his other dart, declared the Bird in the Hand winners, to grumbles of discontent from the Angels.

'If you catch a dart before it hits the floor it

counts as in,' she explained.

'I've never heard that one before,' complained a muttering voice.

'If you don't know the rules, you shouldn't play the game.'

'She meks up her own bloody rules as she goes along.'

This and other such grumbles were dispelled when Flo called out, 'Free drinks for the gallant losers.'

'What about the gallant winners?'

'The gallant winners get free drinks if they win the final.'

'I've never actually heard that rule about catching a dart,' said Rocky from the corner of his mouth.

'Neither have I,' replied Flo, from the corner of hers. 'And what's more important, neither have they.'

Inspector Turton had been watching the darts from the bar. He turned to Cleo who was serving drinks. 'I wouldn't mind a word, Cleo,' he said. 'In private.'

'Is it official?' she asked. He still wasn't her favourite person.

'Not really. It's just a bit of advice.'

Cleo was about to say she was too busy but Flo had overheard. 'The two of you go upstairs,' she said. 'I'll bring a couple of drinks through.'

Cleo led the policeman up a narrow staircase to the spacious living room, sat at the table and indicated him to do the same.

'What advice?' she asked. 'Is it advice as to how to get the money back from Dobbs or is she still keeping quiet about it?'

'She says it was stolen from her,' Turton said.

'Do you believe her?'

The inspector shook his head. 'No,' he said. 'Not for a minute. She knows it'll add time to her sentence if she doesn't give it back but she'll think it's worth it.'

'To Dobbs it probably *is* worth it. Prison won't bother her too much.'

Flo came through with the drinks and placed them on the table. 'Is it about the money?' she asked.

'I think we can forget about the money, Flo,' said Cleo. 'Dobbs won't part with it.'

Turton looked at them both as though making a decision, then he asked Flo to sit down. 'She might be persuaded,' he said.

'How?' asked Flo.

'Mind if I smoke?' he asked.

'No,' said Flo.

'Don't mind me,' said Cleo, who had been deprived of a choice in the matter. Sometimes the smoky atmosphere of the pub got too much for her and she would retreat to the upstairs room for a breather. The inspector took out a packet of Craven A and handed them round, Flo took one and pushed a heavy glass ashtray between the two of them.

'Now, this is strictly off the record,' Turton told them both. 'I'm not trying to persuade you one way or the other.'

'I wish you'd get on with it,' said Cleo.

Inspector Turton lit both his and Flo's cigarettes, blew a cloud of smoke and coughed vigorously.

'Dobbs has been charged with attempted murder,' he addressed himself to Cleo, 'but whether we make it stick depends very largely on what you say in your statement.'

'But I've already made my statement.'

'You can amend it if you like. The defence won't object if it's to their advantage.'

'I can't think of a single reason why I should want to amend it in Dobbs's favour.'

'I can think of twenty-five thousand reasons,' said Flo, who knew what he was getting at.

'If,' continued Turton, 'it came to light that Dobbs had fed and watered you during your captivity.'

'You make me sound like a pet donkey.'

'I'm speaking hypothetically,' he said, patiently. 'And if she had left enough food and water to keep you alive until you were found, we'd have to drop the attempted murder charge and swap it for a lesser one. One that could well be worth twenty-five thousand quid to Dobbs.'

'What would the difference in sentence be?' Cleo asked.

'In actual time spent inside ... with remission, the difference between ten years and five years. In fact three years if she expresses remorse, pleads mitigating circumstance, gives the money back and you speak up for her.'

'Sod that, she left me for dead!'

'I wouldn't be quite so hasty,' Flo said. 'Just think how you'll feel in ten years when she gets out with all that loot stashed away. *Your* loot.'

'Ant's loot, actually,' Cleo pointed out.

'Exactly,' said Flo. 'So, in ten years time they

both come out of jail, she's got all his money and he's got nothing.'

Cleo gave this some thought, then nodded, reluctantly. 'I'd want the money back first,' she said. 'Would she trust me on that?'

'I'm sure the lawyers could sort that one out,' said Flo, looking at the inspector for his confirmation. He just sipped his drink and remained non-committal. 'In fact, I know they could,' Flo added. 'They can have all this case cut and dried behind closed doors, providing everyone agrees what they're going to say.' Her eyes were on the policeman, as though challenging him to argue with her. Turton had said all he intended on the subject and his face now contained as much information as a stopped clock.

'Inspector?' Cleo pressed.

'Cleo,' he sighed. 'If my boss found out what I'd just told you, I'd be in deep trouble. So, if anyone asks, this advice came from Flo, not me. I'll wait to hear from you – there's no rush.' He got to his feet and made for the door, then turned as a last thought struck him. 'I found out an odd thing when I was interviewing Dobbs – just a coincidence, no more.'

'Go on, Inspector,' Cleo said.

'Your stepfather, the one that your brother–'

'I know who you're talking about, Inspector.'

'Well, he was jailed for assaulting Dobbs's brother. Did you know that?'

'I knew he'd been jailed for assaulting a boy, but I didn't know it was Dobbs's brother.'

'Well, apparently it was. Womack was working

as an odd-job man at a children's home the boy was at. I don't think it had any bearing on what Dobbs did to you, in fact I'm fairly sure she hasn't made the connection between you and Womack.'

'But you did?' Cleo said.

'Yes. Well, she's apparently the product of abusive parents and she was waffling on about how she'd been treated at various institutions and how her brother had fared no better and how a man had been jailed for assaulting him at one of these homes – and it just rang a bell. So I checked it out and sure enough it was Horace Womack.'

'It wasn't a sexual assault though, was it, Inspector?' said Flo.

'Apparently not. At least he wasn't charged with that – which is a pity. You might have been able to use it in an appeal against Ant's sentence. Food for thought, eh?'

'Thank you, Inspector,' said Flo.

'Yes, thank you,' said Cleo, 'you're obviously trying to help us. If I sound offhand at times it's because the law has never done me any favours.'

Turton gave her remark some thought, then said, 'We take great pride in pursuing justice with a passion. Unfortunately, passion and common sense don't always go hand in hand.'

'You can say that again,' said Flo, remembering her moments of passion with Sid Millichip.

'All the law can do is its best,' Turton went on. 'But many a time its best just isn't good enough. There are some people who would like to er ... to tweak the rules to suit their own purposes. But of course that would never do.'

He left and closed the door behind him, leaving Cleo staring at it, deep in thought. She then looked at Flo and asked, 'What was he trying to say to us?'

'He was saying there's more than one way to skin a cat, but some of those ways could get him the sack.'

'Hmm.' Cleo sat back and pondered the policeman's final words. 'That thing about Dobbs's brother and Womack,' she said. 'I'm sure that was more than just a parting afterthought. He said it's a pity that Dobbs's brother wasn't sexually assaulted, that's a funny thing for a policeman to say ... and what was all that about *food for thought?* What's there to think about? I'm going to see Dobbs.'

'That's a very bad idea,' Flo said.

'It's the only idea I've got at the moment.'

'In fact I doubt you'll be allowed in.'

'You go then,' Cleo insisted.

'What? To talk about the money? Best to let the lawyers do that, love.'

'I'm not talking just about the money. I want to know about her brother.'

'Then you're better off speaking to him and not to Dobbs.'

'I will speak to him,' said Cleo. 'But I need to know if Dobbs still has the money.'

'Why?'

'I just want to know all I can about things – so I can make my plans.'

'What plans?'

'Flo, how am I supposed to know what plans? I

haven't made them yet. But somewhere, among all this stuff, there's a plan.'

Flo, defeated by Cleo's scattered logic, opened the door and listened to the raucous noise from below. When it got like this it was all hands to the pumps. 'Look, I'm going back down,' she said, 'I'll leave you to your planning.'

Dobbs glared at Flo over the table in the visitors' room. 'If I'd known who yer was, I wouldn't have agreed ter this. They just said it were a woman prison visitor.'

'Which is exactly what I am,' said Flo.

'Yer a mate o' Kelly's.'

'She's got lots of friends,' said Flo. 'Unlike you, who could use a friend right now.'

'I don't need no one, never 'ave, never will.'

'You need Cleo Kelly.'

Dobbs gave a nervous laugh. 'Bloody Kelly! Why do I need 'er?' Then she spoke to Flo under her breath. 'I should've finished 'er off while I 'ad the bloody chance. No one would ever o' known it were me.'

'You're right there,' Flo agreed. 'It was stupid not finishing her off. I would have, if I'd been in your shoes.'

'Hey up, what yer bloody after?'

Flo gave an innocent shrug. 'I just thought I'd pop in and see for myself.'

'See what?'

'See if you're as daft as they say you are. They tell me you're refusing to tell the police where the money is.'

'It were stolen off me.'

Flo laughed out loud, then leaned forward. 'Stolen my arse,' she said, coldly. 'If Cleo goes to town on you in that witness box you'll be all piss and breadcrumbs when you get out of here. Your hair will be dropping out, you'll be humpbacked through sleeping on prison beds, and that boil you've got on your face won't be the last – it's lack of fresh air and the prison diet that does that to you. If and when you come out of here you'll have skin like a ploughed field.'

'Give over,' Dobbs said, uncertainly, 'with remission I'll still be young when I get out.'

'Remission – you?' sneered Flo. 'Don't make me laugh. I know your type. You'll get into more trouble inside – you won't be able to help yourself. Once they capture someone like you they've got you for good. There'll be whiskers growing out of your nose on the day you get out, and you'll keep your teeth in a jam jar on the cell window ledge. That's what this place does to you. It takes away your youth – and in your case most of your middle age as well. And of course by that time the bank notes will be long out of date.'

A worried look appeared on Dobbs's face. 'Out o' date, how d'yer mean, out o' date?'

'I mean,' Flo explained. 'Every so many years the Bank of England bring out new notes and all the old ones become obsolete if you don't change them within a certain time. They're due to change all the fives and tens next year, so if you haven't put the money in a bank you're up the creek without a paddle – your money's no good to man nor beast.'

'Yer a liar.'

'I'm not, actually,' Flo said, evenly. 'Ask anyone. There'll be plenty of people in here who can tell you.' She sat back, satisfied that her ploy had worked. 'You *are* as stupid as they say you are. You've just hidden it, haven't you? What did you do, dig a hole and bury it? It's not *Treasure Island*, this, you know. This is the real world. It's ten-pound notes you've buried, not pieces of eight.'

'You know nowt, you.'

'I know you'll be serving life when you could be serving three years,' Flo said. 'And all for a bag of useless paper. Hey, don't take my word for it, check it out.' She looked around the crowded room to check no one was eavesdropping, then leaned forward again. Dobbs automatically moved in to catch her words. 'If you insist on toughing it out in jail,' Flo advised her, 'the best thing you can do is tell someone where it is and get them to put it in a bank for you.' Then she snapped her fingers and shook her head, sadly. 'I've just remembered, you've got no one you can trust, have you?'

'I've got me brother,' Dobbs blurted.

'That's who the police will be watching,' Flo warned. 'Try and think of someone else.'

A look of realisation suddenly dawned on Dobbs's face. 'Oh, I get it,' she said. 'Yer want me ter trust *you*. That's what all this is about, innit?'

Flo held out her hands, innocently. 'I've only told you a few facts of prison life.'

'I know all I need ter know. I've been inside before.'

'Not in a place like this, you haven't. In fact you might end up somewhere not as nice as this.'

'How can anywhere be worse than this shit'ole?'

'Trust me,' Flo assured her, 'it can get much worse. You'll have to trust someone sooner or later.'

'Yer must think I'm bloody barmy,' muttered Dobbs, getting to her feet and walking from the room. 'I wouldn't trust yer as far as I could throw yer.'

Flo watched her go and allowed herself a nod of self-congratulation. This had been a very productive prison visit.

'Well, she's definitely got the money,' Flo said to Cleo, who was waiting outside the prison in her car. 'She's got it hidden somewhere. But I've put it into her head that the notes will be out of date when she comes out.'

'And will they?'

'In ten years? It's possible. I told her they were changing them next year, which put the wind up her. I told her a few other things that put the wind up her as well.'

'So, she'd go for a deal would she?' asked Cleo.

'Not sure. If she doesn't she's going to have to tell someone on the outside where the money is.'

'Her brother?'

'He seems a likely candidate,' Flo said. 'I can't see someone like Dobbs having too many close friends.'

'She won't have *any* close friends,' confirmed Cleo. 'That's for certain.'

The idea had been germinating in Cleo's mind ever since Turton had said the words, 'Food for thought, eh?' He was the one who had given her Dobbs's brother's address in West Ardsley. Terry Dobbs occupied two rooms in the bottom floor of an end-terrace adjoining a small town of rhubarb sheds. Rocky had refused to allow her to go on her own.

'If he's anything like his sister...' he'd said.

She was being looked after and she liked that. Maybe it compromised her independence, but on balance it was worth it. Being potty about him helped and Cleo couldn't see a time when she wouldn't want him by her side.

The house was as derelict as the one Ant and Cleo had lived in with Nelly and Womack. There were newspapers at the windows and an emaciated-looking dog with a flat face and docked tail was chained to a drainpipe, surrounded by piles of its own mess and various bowls of unappetising dog food. The door opened directly on to a street full of similar houses, most of which looked to be unoccupied, although out-of-tune piano music floated through the open window of the house next door, on which was a sign saying 'Piano Tuition 12/6 per hour. No blacks, or Irish.'

Terry Dobbs came to the door wearing a grubby vest and grey flannels. He was very tall and angular, with a narrow face surmounted by a prematurely balding head. His skin was pale and he had deep-set eyes that had a shifty squint. There were amateur tattoos on his left hand and arm which betrayed him as a right-handed, do-it-yourself tattooist who was bad at spelling. All in all, Cleo concluded, he wasn't God's gift to women.

'Are you Terry Dobbs?' she asked.

No one as pretty as her had ever knocked on his door, which made him suspicious.

'Who wants ter know?' He had his sister's haddock mouth.

'My name's Cleo Kelly and this is my friend Rocky.'

'Well, I've heard o' you,' he said, looking at Cleo. 'You're that tart what our lass kidnapped. So don't go blamin' me for owt she did. She's nowt ter do wi' me, never has been, never will be.'

With that he closed the door in their faces. Rocky knocked again, then shouted through the letter box. 'We haven't come about your sister.'

Terry's face appeared at the other side of the letter box. 'Oh aye. What have yer come about, then?' His teeth were all over the place and his fishy breath made Rocky wince and stand away. Cleo took his place.

'Can we come in?' she asked, with a polite smile.

'Is it owt ter do wi' that dog?'

'No, it's nothing to do with the dog.'

'Good, 'cos it's not my dog. All it does is crap an' howl it's bloody head off. It belongs ter that mad pianna woman next door.'

As if to prove him right the dog commenced its howling. Rocky stepped gingerly towards it and unclipped its lead, allowing the animal to go bounding off down the street.

Terry's voice came through the letter box. 'What's he done?'

'He's let the dog go.'

'Bloody 'ell! She'll go bloody mad. She's a right nutter.'

'Well,' said Cleo, 'you'd better let us in then.'

'It's a bit of a tip in here.'

'It doesn't matter.'

Terry unlocked the door and stood back to let them past. Before he could close it an ancient woman hurled herself at him, pounding him on his chest, screeching about her dog. Cleo pushed her way passed him and confronted the irate neighbour.

'Are you the owner of that dog, madam?' she asked.

The old woman stared at her, uncertainly, breathing heavily. Piano music came from next door, prompting her to walk back to her window and shout through it in a voice that was both cultured and coarse. 'I said pianissimo, you useless little shit!' Then she came back and glared at Cleo. 'Who the bloody hell are you?' she roared.

'My name is Kelly, I'm from the RSPCA and we've had complaints about a neglected dog. Could I have your name please?'

'My name? What's my name got to do with you? I don't go round giving my name to all and bloody sundry.'

'Never mind,' said Cleo. 'I'll get the police to sort it out. They'll probably arrest you for cruelty to animals and lock you up until you go to court.'

'What? Lock me up? You can't lock me up. I teach music and my father was a chiropodist of some standing in this community.'

'I think you'll find we can.'

The startled woman retreated back into her house. The piano music stopped and Terry closed the door.

'Are yer really from t' RSPCA?' he asked.

'No,' said Cleo. 'I just don't like cruel people.'

'I'll put some clothes on,' said an impressed Terry.

'That'd be nice,' said Rocky. 'As many as you can manage. Clean your teeth if you like.'

Cleo nudged him into silence and sat down in a lumpy armchair as Terry Dobbs went into the next room. Rocky chose to remain standing and viewed their surroundings with some distaste. The tenant blended in well with his room. It was sparse and grubby with a balding carpet and unwholesome smell.

'We have something else in common, you and me,' Cleo called out.

'Oh?' Terry popped his head round the door as he buttoned up a shirt that didn't look to have been washed for weeks. 'What's that, then?'

'Horace Womack.'

The name registered immediately. 'That bastard! What's he got ter do wi' owt?'

'Well, he's dead for a start,' Cleo told him.

'Tell me summat I don't know. Some bloke topped him. He had it comin' if yer ask me.'

'The bloke who topped him was my brother. Womack was my stepfather.'

'Bugger me – I never knew that. An' our lass goes an' kidnaps yer. Bugger me, that's bloody offside that is.' He attempted an ingratiating smile. Cleo smiled back.

'I've never been locked up or nowt, me, yer

know,' he said, proudly. 'I've been in a few 'omes, but I never got locked up or nowt. Straight as a bloody die, me, yer know. Not like our lass. She gorrit from us dad. He used ter bray 'ell out of us. That's why I'm so bloody ugly.'

Cleo sensed that Rocky might be about to pass some sarcastic comment about this and she stopped him with a warning glare. 'Womack did the same to me,' she said to Terry. 'My brother got life for killing him.'

'Did he? That's a bastard, that is. Dunt deserve that. Not for killin' Womack. Shoulda gorra medal.'

'Why, what did Womack do to you?' Cleo asked her question quickly while he was still fired up and ready to go.

'He hurt me, that's what he did–'

'Did he rape you?'

She shot the question out right on top of his answer so as not to give him time to think – or to be embarrassed as Ant had been.

'What?'

This wasn't the reply she wanted. She paused then repeated her question. 'I asked if he raped you?'

Terry sat on one of two dining chairs and rolled himself a thin cigarette as he collected his thoughts.

'I knew he were a mucky owd pig but I never lerrim do nowt like that ter me.' He bit the excess tobacco from one end and spat it on to the floor, then lit the other end. It flared then settled down as he sucked at it with hollow cheeks.

'You mean you're too embarrassed to admit it?'

prompted Cleo.

'I mean nowt o' the sort. He'd tried it on wi' some of t' other kids. He used ter pay 'em ter do ... mucky stuff with him.'

'What about you? Did he pay you?'

Terry met her gaze, then lowered his eyes. 'He tried it on, but I didn't want ter know. He had this cupboard in his workshop an' he tried ter lock me in it as punishment.'

'Did you tell anyone?' Rocky asked.

Terry scoffed at such a question. 'Oh aye! An' who'd have believed a scruffy little kid like me?'

Memories of the bogey hole came to Cleo's mind. She shuddered the thoughts away. 'He liked locking kids in cupboards,' she told him. 'He used to lock us in one.'

'I know,' remembered Terry, 'he told me ... about your kid. I dint know about you. He never said nowt about you.'

'Told you!' Cleo exclaimed. 'Told you what?'

'How d'yer mean?'

'What did he tell you about my brother?'

There was excitement in Cleo's voice which Terry couldn't understand. He shrugged as if what he had to say was of no importance.

'He jus' told me used ter lock his own lad up when he wunt play ball, so why shunt he lock me up?' There was sudden dread in Terry's eyes as a memory flooded back to him. 'He said if I dint do what he wanted I'd spend a night in his bogey hole.'

'Bogey hole?' Cleo yelled the word out, almost triumphantly. 'That's what he called the cupboard under our stairs. I nearly died in there. Did he tell you what he used to do to my brother?'

Terry looked embarrassed at the question. 'I don't think he needed ter spell it out, love,' he said. 'I reckon he did to his own lad what he tried ter do ter me. He told me his lad used ter cry like a baby and beg ter be let out. The bastard gorra kick outa tellin' me. I know how your kid felt.'

Cleo felt tears welling. Her brother's tough façade was simply that – a façade. He'd never let her see him cry, probably his way of helping her survive the horror of their childhood.

'Only I wunt lerrim do it ter me,' Terry went on. 'Then he tried ter stick me in his bogey hole, only I'm claustrio ...wotsit?'

'Claustrophobic?' prompted Rocky.

'That's right. I panicked an' lashed out at him. I were only a little skinny kid an' he lost his bloody rag. Christ! I thought he were gonna kill me. If someone hadn't've turned up I think he would have. He broke me jaw, yer know. As a matter o' fact I nearly did die. I were in 'ospital three months. He were drunk as a skunk when it happened – that were 'is excuse in court. He reckoned his missis had left him an' he'd took ter drink – lying' twat!'

Terry got to his feet, wiped a layer of dust from a mirror with his shirt sleeve and examined his jaw, working it to and fro. 'Never been right since,' he said.

'Didn't any of the other boys tell the police what he'd been doing with them?' Cleo asked.

Terry shook his head and gave his reflection a frightening grin. 'Give over. That'd mek 'em as bad as 'im.'

'He raped my brother,' Cleo said, wiping the grin off his face. 'Time and time again – when he was a small boy.' She got to her feet and looked at Terry's face in the mirror. 'You could help us get my brother out of jail. Especially if you gave us the names of some of the other boys he abused.'

Terry went on the defensive. 'Look love, it were a long time ago. I don't think I want ter get involved.'

'It could be worth a lot of money to you,' Cleo said. 'I'm sure my brother would be very grateful if you helped get him out of jail. All you'd have to do is tell the truth in court.'

A greedy light went on in Terry's reflected eyes. 'How much?'

'Ten thousand pounds.'

Rocky made to protest about the excessive amount, but Cleo stayed him with a gesture of her hand.

'That's a lot o' money,' Terry said, with a disbelieving sneer. 'Where's your kid gonna get that sort o' brass from?'

'Do you get on okay with your sister?' she asked him.

'Well, I'm all she's got, put it that way,' he said, wondering where the conversation was now leading. 'What's that got ter do with owt?'

'Does she trust you?'

'She knows I'm a lot more honest than she is, which isn't sayin' much I have to admit.'

'It's good that you're honest,' Cleo said. 'The courts like honest people.'

'Yer mean like tellin' that mad cow next door

yer from t' RSPCA?' grinned Terry.

Cleo smiled. 'Sometimes you need to bend the truth to get the right result,' she said. 'You might have to bend the truth with your sister if you want that ten grand.'

Terry looked at Rocky. 'Do you know what she's talking about?'

'She's a puzzle at times,' Rocky conceded, 'but I think I'm following her on this one.'

Chapter Twenty-Eight

Cleo and Rocky greeted Ant with broad smiles as he weaved his way through the tables towards them. The regime was beginning to get to him and his own smile was very forced.

'Don't tell me,' he guessed. 'You won the darts. Oh, by the way, Rocky, congratulations on getting engaged to buggerlugs. I hope you know what you're letting yourself in for.'

'It's a chance I'll have to take.'

Cleo brought the West Riding Brewery's darts trophy out of her bag and plonked it on the table. 'We beat the Malt Shovel five-one,' she said.

'Before you ask,' said Rocky, 'I was the one who lost. They put me up against their star man in the first game to lull them into a false sense of security. It was Flo's idea.'

'Jen sends her love.'

'Right.' Ant smiled, thinly, at his sister and decided now was the time to tell her that he didn't want to see Jenny again. 'Actually, there's something I want you to tell Jen...'

Rocky interrupted him. 'She's got the money back. Well, most of it, anyway.'

'What!'

'We got the money back,' confirmed Cleo.

'The money, you mean the ransom money?'

'Yes.'

'When ... I mean, how?'

'Last night. Dobbs's brother rang the police to tell them where it was.'

'How did he know where it was?'

'Dobbs told him,' said Cleo. She then explained about Flo's visit to Dobbs and how she been tricked into telling her brother where the money was.

'Good old Flo. But why would Dobbs's brother tell the police were the money was?'

Cleo looked around the room and decided it was better not to discuss the details. 'He told them a lot more than that,' she said.

'What?'

'Did you know he was the one Womack went to jail for assaulting?'

'What?'

'You keep saying "What",' said Cleo. 'Terry Dobbs was the lad Womack got locked up for assaulting.'

Ant looked at Rocky. 'Is this right?'

'If buggerlugs says it is, then it must be right,' said Rocky.

'If either of you calls me buggerlugs again I'll flatten the both of you.' Then to Ant, Cleo said, 'Do you want to hear this or not?'

'Course I want to hear it. I just don't understand what it's got to do with anything, that's all.'

'Well, if you listen, you will. Terry Dobbs told Inspector Turton that Womack had told him all about what he did to you.'

Ant's first reaction was one of dismay. 'He did what?'

'Apparently,' Cleo continued, 'Womack told Terry Dobbs how he'd abused his own stepson.

He was trying to rape Terry but the lad put up a fight and Womack ended up knocking him about. Which is why he got locked up.'

'Is this true?' said Ant, looking from one to the other.

'It's what Terry Dobbs told Turton,' Rocky confirmed, 'and it's what he'll tell the court.'

Ant leaned towards his sister and asked in a low voice. 'But is it true that Womack told him about all this?'

'Yes, it is,' she said, 'and it verifies what you said in your affidavit. He tried to lock Terry in a place he called the bogey hole and Terry got scared, so Womack beat him up.'

'Jesus! I should have stabbed him through his black bloody heart, not just in his arm. I'd have been out by now.'

'He messed about with some of the other kids at this same children's home,' added Rocky. 'Turton's trying to track them down for them to give evidence.'

'And I've been to the papers,' said Cleo. 'There'll be a story in the *Daily Mail* on Thursday.'

Ant's head was spinning. 'Cleo, you told the bloody papers that Womack used to do ... stuff to me?'

'Yes, I did,' she said. 'It needed doing, so I did it. Ant, the more people who know about it the more pressure we can put on the Court of Appeal to give you a hearing. Apparently, if we can get the crime reduced to manslaughter and throw in mitigating circumstances, you could be out before you know it.'

Ant smiled at the excitement building up in his

sister and laid a calming hand on hers. 'Let's not get too excited, Cleo. What I can't understand,' he said, 'is why Dobb's brother would go to all this trouble to help–' He noticed the look in his sister's eyes and suddenly he understood everything. He lowered his voice. 'How much?' he asked her.

'Ten thousand,' she whispered. 'Worth every penny. Payable when you get out. He wanted half now, but I pointed out that him suddenly becoming wealthy might raise a few eyebrows.'

'He could have picked up the whole lot himself and cleared off abroad,' Ant said.

'I told him the police were watching for him to pick the money up and as soon as he did he'd be arrested as an accessory to kidnapping and attempted murder. I think that did the trick.'

'Do you know what the penalty for bribing a witness is?'

'It's not really a bribe,' said Cleo. 'It's more of a reward from you. We're tweaking the rules a bit that's all. Terry knows not to tell anyone about it.'

This brought a grin to Ant's face. 'Tweaking the rules – I like that.'

'If Turton tracks down some of the other kids Womack messed with, we're home and dry. Any kind of evidence that he sexually abused you as a child puts a whole different complexion on the case; it was never mentioned in your trial. Our solicitor reckons you could get an Appeal heard as early as November – and they might even let you out on bail straight away.'

'Has Turton had a hand in all this?' Ant asked.

'I think it was his idea,' Cleo said. 'Only he didn't tell us in so many words.'

'I like Turton.'

'I've invited him to the wedding,' Cleo said. 'If you get out on bail, we're getting married in October.'

'What chest size are you?' Rocky asked.

'Eh?'

'For the suit.'

'What suit?'

'Cleo wants us to wear morning suits and with you being best man, you'll need one as well.'

'What was it you wanted me to tell Jenny?' Cleo asked him.

Ant's head was swimming now. 'What?' he said. 'Oh ... erm, tell her, tell her there's something I want to ask her ... and er, just tell her that.'

'And this question, is it the one I think it is?' Cleo asked him.

Ant tapped the side of his nose. 'Never you mind,' he said.

'Jen, where is everybody?'

The Appeal Court judge had just told Ant that after taking into consideration the time he had already served he was free to go, which was music to Ant's ears. He stood in the doorway of the Law Courts in the Strand expecting a rapturous reception from Cleo and his friends. But only Jenny was there.

'Blame me,' she said. 'I told them I'd like you to myself for a while – in fact I insisted.'

'Insisted?'

'Yes... No one's more delighted than me that you're free at last. Flo's laid on a bit of a do at The Bird tomorrow night, but until then I want you to myself.'

'You do?'

'Unless you don't want me.'

'No...'

Ant was unsure what to do, what to say to this woman he'd dreamt about for the past few months. She took his hand and led him out into the street.

'It was actually Cleo's idea,' she said. 'That I should get you to myself. We all made a bit of a racket in court when the judge gave his verdict.'

'Yes, I heard. I thought he was going to lock you lot up instead. Where are they all?'

'If you want them, I can go and get them.'

'Well...'

'You see,' explained Jenny. 'I need to know where I stand and if I let you loose in London with everyone else I wouldn't be able to...'

'Have me to yourself?'

'Not till we got back to Leeds I wouldn't – and I want you now. Ant, it's important to me. I think I've waited long enough.'

'It's important to me as well.' He looked into the grey sky, breathed in the late autumn air and gave a sigh. 'Can you smell it?' he said.

'Smell what?'

'Freedom ... freedom to do what I like.'

'What would you like to do?'

'Right now?... I'd like to give you a kiss,' he said.

'What? Out here where everyone can see us?'

'That's just it,' said Ant. 'I want to do it because I can – and no one can stop me.'

He took her in his arms and looked down at

her. 'You know, Jenny,' he said. 'I've done some stupid things in my time and I might not know much, but I do know one thing.'

'What's that?'

'I know ... I love you.'

He said it guardedly, as if ready for it to be thrown back in his face. Jenny knew that 'love' wasn't a word that Ant would bandy about cheaply. Just to hear the word on his lips sent a shiver down her spine. He had been out on bail since leave to appeal had first been granted him; and despite his solicitor's assurance that bail was only granted in cases where success is almost certain, he wasn't going to tell Jenny he loved her until he heard the judge actually pronounce him a free man. He needed to be absolutely sure he would be there for her – if she wanted him.

'I suppose you know I love you as well – always have,' she said. 'You big lump.'

'I hoped you would.'

They kissed. Clumsily at first, with cars hooting and a group of youths catcalling from across the road. The problems Womack had caused him were dead and gone, along with their creator. But he did lack experience in such matters.

'I'm not very good at thi–'

'Shhh.' She silenced him with a finger on his lips. 'I know, and I understand. It's nothing that can't be put right. I thought when we got back to Leeds we might go somewhere a bit more private. My er, my parents are away for a few days.'

'I'd like that,' Ant said. 'In fact I think I've been dreaming about that for quite some time.'

'What sort of dreams?'

Ant grinned. 'I'm too embarrassed to tell you.'

'Ah, naughty dreams.'

'Very naughty.'

'In that case,' said Jenny. 'I'll just have to do my best to make these very naughty dreams come true.'

As they strolled down the Strand, hand in hand, Cleo, Flo, Rocky, Inspector Turton and Stanislaus Pacholski watched with approval through the window of a nearby pub.

Epilogue

'Could the gentlemen please put their top hats on,' called the photographer, 'preferably the right way round.'

Ant grumbled to his best man once again for suggesting they wear such a thing. 'Rocky, this is cheap revenge,' he said. 'Just because you had to wear one at your wedding.'

'There's nothing cheap about it,' grinned Rocky. 'Why should I be the only one to suffer?'

'Ant's moaning again,' Cleo said to Jenny. 'Why is it that my brother will wear the most dreadful clothes and think he looks smart – and yet put him in a nice top hat and tails and he moans?'

'Stop moaning, Ant,' said Jenny. 'You look very handsome.' She glanced at Rocky and mentally made an uncharitable comparison. Ant was a nice-looking chap but his best man was in a different league. Still, Ant Kelly was the man she loved, and had just promised herself to, for better or for worse. *For better or for worse.* It was a phrase which seemed to have an ominous significance when attached to Anthony Kelly.

They were standing on the steps of Saint Joseph's church and the bride was radiant as brides should be; even outshining her chief bridesmaid, which took some doing as her chief bridesmaid was Cleo. The sun was shining and making a valiant attempt to thaw out winter goosepimples on naked arms. All in all things were going well, which was a pleasant surprise to Jenny, considering whom she'd just married. But a suspect cloud appeared on the Kelly horizon in the shape of Vincent Pascoe.

'What's *he* doing here?' asked the maid-of-honour, who was giving her own middle-aged goosepimples a warming rub with her white-gloved hands.

'Who?' said Cleo.

'Him.'

Flo nodded her head towards the quarry owner, whose face was blacker than the marble headstone he was standing beside.

'Ah, now that might be my fault,' Ant said, smiling as the photographer asked them all to say 'silly sausages'.

'Your fault?' said Jenny. 'In what way, your fault?'

'Oh, it's just business. Nothing for you to worry about, Jen.'

Jenny gave the camera a plastic smile as she nudged her new husband. 'I *do* worry where Pascoe's concerned. I'd like to think we'll be able to celebrate our first anniversary with you still in one piece.'

'Rocky'll look after me,' Ant reassured her.

'I'm supposed to be your business partner,' protested Rocky, 'not your minder.'

'Why's he looking so upset?' asked Cleo. She was watching Pascoe through the fixed smile that was meant for the clicking camera. 'I don't like the look of him at all.'

'Could you all move in a little closer, please? I

can't quite get you all in the picture.'

'Well,' explained Ant, moving close to his sister. 'You know that contract you signed for the land leading to his quarry?'

'What about it?'

'Well, as luck would have it it turns out it's invalid ... not worth the paper it's written on. It needed my signature.'

'Could we have the bride and groom's parents in the group, please?' called out the photographer.

'I don't have any parents,' said Ant, cheerfully. 'Jenny has though, one of each.'

'Hang on,' said Cleo to her brother. 'If I remember rightly, you gave me the authority to sign on your behalf.'

'Perhaps we could have one parent on each side of the bride and groom,' suggested the photographer, trying to make up for his lack of tact.

'Apparently they've got no proof of that,' said Ant, shuffling to one side to allow Mr and Mrs Smith into the group. 'It was a mistake on Pascoe's solicitor's part. Then he fell out with Pascoe and er ... he just happened to mention it to me. Our solicitor's just sent Pascoe an injunction preventing him from using the land until the problem's sorted out.'

'Blimey! No wonder he looks cross,' said Rocky. 'It must be costing him thousands. Last I heard his wagons were flat out running stone to the motorway.'

'Ten thousand, actually,' Ant said. 'Which is exactly what it cost me to pay off Terry Dobbs.'

'Mum, Dad, you didn't hear that,' said Jenny.

Her fascinated parents nodded, but hung on to

every word that was being said around them.

'I wouldn't like to be in Terry's shoes when his sister gets hold of him,' said Rocky.

'It'll be a few years before she gets out,' Flo said. 'Six, if she behaves herself.'

'Trouble was,' said Ant. 'I needed that money to pay for the hotel we've just bought. So it was fate in a way that Pascoe's solicitor should turn up like that.'

'Hotel, what hotel?' asked Jenny.

'Excuse me, Mrs Kelly,' said Ant. 'But it's our wedding day and you've got me talking about business.'

'Do you two know about this hotel–?'

Before Cleo or Rocky could answer, Ant explained: 'It belonged to a bloke I met in prison. He needed some quick money, this thing with Pascoe came up, so I bought it cheap – very cheap as a matter of fact.'

'I wish Pascoe wasn't here,' muttered Cleo, who was used to her brother's unusual dealings. 'Can't we get rid of him?'

'Give him a threatening look, Rocky,' suggested Ant. 'He thinks you're a lunatic.'

'Not right now,' said Rocky. 'We're having our photos taken.'

'I really think we ought to smile for the camera,' said Jenny's father, 'while the sun's out.'

They all smiled and the camera clicked rapidly as the photographer grasped this rare opportunity to catch them all being co-operative, then Jenny said to Ant, 'So, it's not a dodgy deal, then?'

'Jen, I'm not a dodgy person.' Ant earned himself three disbelieving and two relieved looks for this.

The photographer was becoming tetchy. '*Please* look at the camera, ladies and gentlemen. If you can't see the camera, the camera can't see you.'

They all turned to the front and Ant spoke through the side of his mouth, 'I just tweak the rules now and again. That's how things get done in this world – isn't it, Cleo?'

'Can you have a word with your brother, Cleo?' implored Jenny. 'I'm not going to have a minute's peace married to this lunatic.'

'Ladies and gentlemen, you're really not trying you know!' The photographer all but stamped his foot in frustration, and decided to prune the unruly group to a manageable size. 'Could I just have the bride and groom on their own please?'

Cleo took Rocky's arm and led him away as she called back to Jenny over her shoulder, 'Sorry Jen, he's all yours now. I've got enough on my hands looking after my own lunatic.'

'Are you calling me names, Cleopatra Diggle?' said Rocky, wrapping his arm around her. 'I thought you loved me.'

'You know I love you, Rocky,' said Cleo. 'But talking of names – I think I'd rather be called Floribunda Dunderdale.'

The publishers hope that this book has given you enjoyable reading. Large Print Books are especially designed to be as easy to see and hold as possible. If you wish a complete list of our books please ask at your local library or write directly to:

Magna Large Print Books
Magna House, Long Preston,
Skipton, North Yorkshire.
BD23 4ND

This Large Print Book for the partially sighted, who cannot read normal print, is published under the auspices of

THE ULVERSCROFT FOUNDATION

THE ULVERSCROFT FOUNDATION

... we hope that you have enjoyed this Large Print Book. Please think for a moment about those people who have worse eyesight problems than you ... and are unable to even read or enjoy Large Print, without great difficulty.

You can help them by sending a donation, large or small to:

The Ulverscroft Foundation,
1, The Green, Bradgate Road,
Anstey, Leicestershire, LE7 7FU,
England.
or request a copy of our brochure for more details.

The Foundation will use all your help to assist those people who are handicapped by various sight problems and need special attention.

Thank you very much for your help.